NATHAN'S RUN

"Gilstrap pushes every thriller button . . . A nail-biting denouement and strong characters."
—*San Francisco Chronicle*

"Gilstrap has a shot at being the next John Grisham . . . One of the best books of the year."
—*Rocky Mountain News*

"Emotionally charged . . . one of the year's best."
—*Chicago Tribune*

"Fast, intriguing . . . a clever plot with enough menace to keep readers on the edge of their seats."
—*Boston Herald*

"A heart-pounding tale of suspense."
—*People*

"See Nathan run. Better, read *Nathan's Run*. It's serious fun."
—*New York Daily News*

"Brilliantly calculated . . . With the skill of a veteran, Gilstrap weaves a yarn that demands to be read in one sitting."
—*Publishers Weekly* (starred review)

"Like a roller coaster, the story races along on well-oiled wheels to an undeniably pulse-pounding conclusion."
—*Kirkus Reviews* (starred review)

"A top-notch thriller."
—**Jeffery Deaver**

"A tense tale of courage . . . an impressive debut."
——**Marcia Muller**

"A fine thriller debut . . . Gilstrap is a writer with a great future ahead of him."
—**Stephen Hunter**

SCORPION STRIKE

"Relentlessly paced as well as brilliantly told and constructed, this is as good as thrillers get."
—*The Providence Journal*

ALSO BY JOHN GILSTRAP

JOHN GILSTRAP

NATHAN'S RUN

PINNACLE BOOKS
Kensington Publishing Corp.
www.kensingtonbooks.com

PINNACLE BOOKS are published by

Kensington Publishing Corp.
119 West 40th Street
New York, NY 10018

All Kensington titles, imprints, and distributed lines are available at special quantity discounts for bulk purchases for sales promotions, premiums, fund-raising, educational, or institutional use. Special book excerpts or customized printings can also be created to fit specific needs. For details, write or phone the office of the Kensington sales manager: Kensington Publishing Corp., 119 West 40th Street, New York, NY 10018, attn: Sales Department; phone 1-800-221-2647.

PINNACLE BOOKS and the Pinnacle logo are Reg. U.S. Pat. & TM Off.

First Pinnacle mass market printing: January 2020

10 9 8 7 6 5 4 3 2 1

ISBN-13: 978-0-7860-4551-8
ISBN-10: 0-7860-4551-5

Printed in the United States of America

Electronic edition:

ISBN-13: 978-0-7860-2827-6 (e-book)
ISBN-10: 0-7860-2827-0 (e-book)

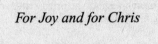
For Joy and for Chris

ACKNOWLEDGMENTS

There are so many people to thank . . .

. . . My wife and best friend, Joy, who did all the things I neglected, yet continues to love me in spite of my obsessions . . .

. . . Brie Combs, who believed in my writing when no one else did, and who ruthlessly kept pushing till I got it right . . .

. . . My son, Chris, who always laughed at the funny parts and whose interest in my imaginary characters was always pure and genuine . . .

. . . My dad, who read the early draft—and liked it . . .

. . . Stephen Hunter, who tolerated countless unsolicited phone calls, and in the process helped to keep my head screwed on . . .

. . . And Avram Davidson, God rest his soul, who gave me something to prove . . .

. . . Sheri Holman, who saw past the title and gave me my first break . . .

CHAPTER ONE

THE MUFFLED *WHUMP* of a distant mortar marked the beginning of the main event. Thousands of eyes tracked the skyrocket as it corkscrewed hundreds of feet into the air and disappeared into the night before erupting into a shower of red and gold glitter. An instant later, the concussion bursts detonated. People seated up front felt the noise in their chests and screamed their approval.

Warren Michaels smiled in the glare of the display. Today marked the thirty-seventh year in a row that he'd done the same thing on the same day of summer. Traditions were important in raising a happy family, he thought. Stretched out on the hood of his cruiser with his wife tucked next to him and his daughters perched above on the light bar, he felt true contentment for the first time in a long while.

"So, ladies, have you all had fun today?" Warren asked.

"Yep!"

"Absolutely."

Monique only groaned, making Warren laugh. His

wife hated heat, bugs, and loud noises. That she endured this ritual year after year only proved that she loved him.

"I think Brian would've really had fun today," Kathleen announced out of nowhere.

Monique squeezed Warren's hand and agreed. "I think so, too, sweetheart."

Warren drew his wife closer, and without a word, she responded with a gentle pat on his thigh.

The Michaels family had been on the go since nine that morning, when the celebration had begun with a reenactment of the signing of the Declaration of Independence on the steps of the town hall, followed at ten by a huge parade.

Spanning three hours, and stretching nearly as many miles, the parade sponsored by Warren's hometown of Brookfield, Virginia, had grown dramatically over the years, robbing spectators from the nearby Washington, D.C. counterpart. People didn't mind sacrificing a little glitz, it seemed, in favor of down-home patriotism. The spectacle featured fire departments from three states, along with no fewer than eight high school bands.

On the heels of the parade came Old-Fashioned Fireman's Day. The competition among the fire companies was fierce, testing their skills in driving, hose handling, strength, and even aim. Younger spectators lived for the water target competition. The goal of the event was to knock down three targets with a water stream, a task that looked easier than it really was. Each team's aim was a little wild at first, drenching gleeful kids (and their parents) with hundreds of gallons of high-pressure water.

The carnival was next, running concurrently with

the City-Wide Cook-Out. Even as the Tilt-a-Whirl set undigested lunches in motion, hundreds of barbecue grills were fired up in the baseball field. Families, friends, and strangers all mingled together in a patriotic cooking frenzy. At any given moment, parents had no idea where their children were, but it didn't matter. Bad things just didn't happen in Brookfield.

Only a dozen or so rockets into the display, Warren's pager vibrated in the pocket of his tennis shorts. Annoyed by the interruption, he brought the two-inch box—his leash, he called it—in front of his face where he could see it. The green luminescent display showed his office number, followed by "9-1-1," indicating that it was urgent.

"Nuts," he grumbled, pulling his arm from around his wife.

"What's the matter?"

"I don't know yet. I just got paged."

"Oh, no," Monique moaned, mostly out of sympathy for him. "Not *tonight.*"

Warren swung his legs over the fender and slid to the ground, pausing to nod his approval of the latest starburst. "For Jed to call me during the fireworks, it can't be good."

Warren scooted quickly into the front seat, conscious of nearby spectators and the glare of the interior light. He removed his cell phone from its charger on the cruiser's center console, flipped it open, and punched a speed-dial button.

A harsh female voice answered on the third ring, "Braddock County Police. Is this an emergency?"

"Hi, Janice, it's Michaels. What's up?"

"Oh, Lieutenant," the call-taker gasped, "thank God

you called. There's been a murder down at the JDC. Sergeant Hackner said to get you down there right away."

Warren swiveled his body and craned his neck to get a look at the latest skyrocket. "Look, I'm not on duty tonight. Isn't there someone else who can handle this?"

"I don't know, sir. Sergeant Hackner was very specific. He said he wanted you."

Warren sighed. What the hell, he thought, the mood had been broken anyway. With his curiosity piqued, he wouldn't be able to enjoy the rest of the fireworks, even if he stayed.

"All right, Janice, but if Jed calls back in, you tell him that his lieutenant is not pleased. Also, you're going to have to send somebody to pick me up. My cruiser is completely blocked into Brookfield Park for the fireworks."

Using a county vehicle—even a take-home—for personal outings was a clear violation of procedure, for which there would be no repercussions. As it was, Warren grumped that he had to drive a cruiser at all. In neighboring jurisdictions, his position as the number-one guy in the detective division and number three in the department would have qualified him for an unmarked take-home without restriction. Braddock County's bean-counters had their own priorities, though, and ultimately, Warren had decided not to push the issue.

"Yes, sir," Janice acknowledged. "Where do you want to get picked up?"

Warren sighed again. Too many decisions on a night when he wanted to relax. "Get me at the corner of Braddock and Horner. It'll be a few minutes, though. I'm going to have to walk through this crowd to get there."

"Okay, sir, I'll tell them to wait on you," she said, as if there were really an option. "Do you want me to mark your cruiser out of service?" Obviously, Janice understood that Monique was going to have to drive the vehicle home; another blatant violation of procedure.

"Yeah," Warren grunted, "that's a good idea."

He clapped the phone closed and slid out of the car to break the news to the family.

CHAPTER TWO

IT HAD BEEN YEARS since Warren had last entered the Juvenile Detention Center. Such a depressing place.

From the outside, the JDC—Warren still thought of it as a reform school—bore the earth tones that were the architectural signature of the early eighties. Trees and flowers adorned manicured gardens; there were no fences or barbed wire. The place easily could have been a medical building, or even a small elementary school. The last thing it looked like was a warehouse for violent children.

The interior, however, screamed *institution*. Clearly, there had been a time when the cinder block had been freshly painted and modern, but now the once-white walls were yellowed from cigarette smoke, age, and abuse. A bold navy-blue racing stripe eighteen inches wide ran around the interior perimeter, jutting up and down at odd angles. Intended to inject architectural excitement, the stripe now served as a continuous picture frame for all manner of graffiti. The tile floors were clean enough, waxed and buffed on a regular basis by some of the more trustworthy residents, but in the corners where the walls joined the floors, years' worth of dirt had accumulated, unnoticed.

As he passed through the lobby, Michaels clipped his gold badge to the waistband of his shorts. But for his rank, he would have felt self-conscious abut his casual dress. As it was, his Izod shirt with tennis shorts and shoes (no socks) communicated to his subordinates a certain full-time dedication to the job. He was escorted by two uniformed officers through the inner security door under the watchful eyes of Spencer Tracy's Father Flanagan. The caption along the bottom of the poster read, "There's no such thing as a bad boy."

Down a short hallway and to the right, Michaels encountered a knot of uniformed men and women, all busily moving about, but few with any apparent purpose. Especially useless, it seemed, were the personnel bearing the uniform of the Juvenile Detention Center. Prison guards, like mall security personnel, liked to think of themselves as part of the law enforcement community, and prized their association with real police officers. Warren thought of them as groupies. Though he could see no role for them in a criminal investigation, he recognized that they had to stick around to look after the remaining residents, who he assumed were locked behind the rows of closed wooden doors visible beyond the thick windows of the security station.

Everyone's attention was focused around a small doorway bearing the label Crisis Unit. He couldn't see inside the room itself, but the flash of camera strobes gave it away as the crime scene.

"Excuse me," Michaels said, gently touching the shoulder of a uniformed officer from behind.

The initial annoyance in the young officer's eyes disappeared as he recognized the man making the request. "Lieutenant Michaels coming through!" the officer announced to the others, causing the crowd to part.

Michaels smiled to the officer, noting the name emblazoned on his silver name tag. "Thanks, Officer Borsuch."

"You're welcome, sir." Michaels was the only white-shirt in the department who treated patrolmen as real people.

The scene was gruesome. A white male, maybe thirty and dressed in the uniform of a JDC guard, lay sprawled on the floor of the tiny room, surrounded by a pool of coagulating blood that encircled his body like a crimson aura. An upended cot had been tossed into the corner, its mattress, such as it was, still in place relative to the frame. Every surface had been splashed with gore—drips, smears and spatters extending high onto the walls. A child-size bloody footprint pointed out the door—just a partial, actually, a ball and five toes. Michaels's mind worked to re-create the enormous struggle that had gone on in here.

As Warren surveyed the scene, a cheerful and familiar voice boomed out of the din.

"Nice outfit there, Lieutenant," Jed Hackner said from behind, clapping his boss on the shoulder. Hackner and Michaels had been classmates through the academy, and back as far as junior high school. That one outranked the other spoke only of the limited availability of lieutenant slots, not of any lack of ability. Each man thought of the other as his closest friend.

"Yeah, well, imagine me thinking that just because I

had the day off, I wouldn't have to work. You certainly are your usual dapper self this evening." Hackner had a reputation as the department's clotheshorse, preferring the latest styles from *GQ* over the clichéd rumpled look of most detectives.

"Pretty disgusting scene, huh?" Hackner said, noting Michaels's body language.

"What happened in here?"

Hackner pulled a notebook from his inside jacket pocket. Always a notebook, Michaels thought with amusement. Not a single note more than one hour old, yet Jed still needed to read his findings.

"From what we've put together so far, this is Richard W. Harris, age twenty-eight. He's been employed here for the past four and a half years as a child care supervisor."

"Is that the same as a guard?" Michaels interrupted.

"Yes," Hackner acknowledged with a smile. "But only to politically incorrect old people." At thirty-seven, Michaels was eight months Hackner's senior. Jed continued from his notes: "At seven o'clock, Mr. Harris had some kind of an altercation with one of the residents, a Nathan Bailey, and assigned the kid here to the Crisis Unit."

"And is a Crisis Unit something like solitary confinement?" Michaels interrupted again.

Hackner smiled broadly. "Yes, it is. Very similar indeed. From that point on, all we have is conjecture. But the bottom line is, we believe that Nathan Bailey killed Ricky Harris and then escaped. Bailey is on the loose as we speak. The coroner hasn't been here yet, but my examination of the body shows at least five stab wounds to the abdomen and chest."

"Care to conjecture a motive?"

Hackner shrugged. "My guess is he wanted to get out of this place. Wouldn't you?"

Michaels frowned. "I don't know that I'd kill for it. Do we have a murder weapon?"

"Sure do. It's still stuck in the body. Good eye, Lieutenant."

The brown wooden handle of a Buck knife protruded from the decedent's chest, just below his embroidered name. From Warren's angle to the body, the weapon was partially concealed. "Bite me," he growled.

Warren pointed to the security camera in the upper left rear corner of the room. "Have you checked the tape?" he asked. "Maybe we have a movie of this whole thing."

"Checked it, and no, we don't. The video system is down."

"Of course it is. Where did the knife come from?"

"Don't know."

"How long has he been dead?"

"Can't tell for sure. My guess is about two hours."

Michaels's eyes bored into Hackner. "Two *hours*! How long did they sit on the body before they called us?"

"Apparently they called right away. Seems they only work one person at night. Harris was found by his relief when he came in at nine. It's nine-forty now."

"Where did all these people come from, if they only work one to a shift?" Michaels couldn't see across the room through all the spectators.

"I guess word travels fast. Everybody wants to be where the action is."

Michaels planted his fists on his hips and shook his

head in disbelief. "So that means the kid has a two-hour head start on us, right?"

Hackner shrugged. "Not really. We've had people out looking for him for about fifteen minutes now."

Michaels glared again.

"Okay, okay," Hackner conceded. "He's got two hours on us. But we've got a call in to Old Man Peters for him to get his dogs up here, and we're in the process of setting up roadblocks at strategic points. You know, the whole drill."

Michaels sighed deeply. "Well, I guess it'll have to do, won't it? Hell, if we can't track down a kid, I guess we've got a problem. How old is he, anyway?"

CHAPTER THREE

TWELVE-YEAR-OLD NATHAN BAILEY tried to press his thin frame below the surface of the damp mulch and wedge in closer to the brick wall. Try as he might, he couldn't disappear entirely.

Despite the night's oppressive heat and stifling humidity, he couldn't stop shaking. Like the time two years ago—a whole lifetime ago—when he had an ear infection and a high fever; except this time, he didn't think he was sick. Just scared.

His efforts to blend in with the surroundings only made him more aware of how much he stood out. Everyone from the outside world wore shorts and T-shirts in the summer night, while he swam inside his ill-fitting orange coveralls, emblazoned across the back with the letters "JDC." The letters were supposed to arc across his shoulder blades, but in his case, they drooped above the small of his back. Ricky had told him on his first day that Medium was the smallest size available. It was a lie, of course. Ricky was such a jerk.

Nathan had no idea where he was. Once he was free of the JDC building, he'd just started running as fast as his bare feet would allow. At first the sticks and rocks had hurt as he ran over them, but once the fireworks started with all the explosions and lights, Nathan stopped feeling anything but his fear. He just kept running, with no idea where he was going. The only thing he knew for sure was that he was not going back *there* again.

Sharp explosions popped to his right.

Someone was *shooting* at him. Nathan jerked violently at the sound and reflexively clapped a hand over his mouth to keep from screaming out. His instinct was to bolt out of his hiding place, but a voice deep inside told him to stay put.

If they were shooting at you, you'd be dead now, he reasoned. His heart pounded in his temples.

By pressing the left side of his face further into the mulch and closing his right eye, Nathan could see through the bottom of the boxwood that served as his shield against the world. There were no gunmen. Just a bunch of kids, five of them about his age, setting off firecrackers in the street. Ladyfingers, it looked like. As Nathan watched, the tallest of the kids lit another pack and dropped it casually onto the curb, moving back a couple of steps for safety. Another extended ripple of explosions followed, sending sparks and paper dancing randomly along the pavement in the dark.

Nathan's mind played back a scene of his father and him lighting off their own ladyfingers out in front of their own house. The scene in his head had all the clarity and detail of a Panavision movie. He remembered his dad assuring him, "They won't put you in jail for playing with firecrackers, son."

No, just for getting beat up.

A thousand thoughts and pictures suddenly flooded

Nathan's mind. Life sucked. It wasn't fair. It wasn't right how his dad went off to heaven and left him in hell, alone with Uncle Mark; how people treated you like crap when there wasn't a grown-up around to help you; how everything you said was a lie just because you're a kid, and every lie a grown-up told was the truth just because they're a grown-up; how sometimes you had to kill . . .

For the first time, the enormity of what he had done came crashing down on him, with all the force of a rupturing dam. He'd been in trouble before, but never like this. They'd be looking for him. He had to get away, but he had no place to go.

He started to tremble again, his breathing becoming rapid and noisy. Even as he realized that he was making too much noise, he also realized that he couldn't stop it.

Nathan took a giant breath and let it out slowly.

Calm down, he commanded himself silently, but his breath shook just like the rest of him, making a steam-engine sound as he exhaled. *You've got to calm down.* He tried another breath, and it was a little better. The third time did the trick. He knew that if he panicked, he'd do something stupid, and that his only chance of survival depended on his being smart. Panic was right there, though, always a single thought, or a single noise, or a single encounter away.

He needed a plan. More than that, he needed sleep. He couldn't remember ever being this tired. He found himself drifting off where he lay, and he shook himself back to alertness. *No,* he told himself, *not here.*

He also needed better shelter and proper clothes. He

needed food. Every house within his sight could offer him exactly what he needed, yet he was locked out of those houses just as tightly as he was locked out of every kindness and every bit of normalcy he had ever known.

Wait a minute. Just because the doors and windows were locked didn't mean they couldn't be entered. An idea began to take shape.

Soaked from sweat and dew, Nathan pressed his belly against the mulch and elbow-crawled along the narrow tunnel between the hedge and the side of the house to get a better view of the street. A branch snagged his ear and broke off, carving a gouge out of his flesh. Sharp, bright pain brought tears to his eyes. He brushed them away with a filthy hand. Stopping long enough to blink his vision clear, he inched forward a little more.

By pivoting his head, he could see the length of the block. It was a nice neighborhood, not unlike his own. Well-kept houses, all brightly lit, with well-kept lawns. The neighborhood was crawling with people. They talked in their yards. They played badminton—in the dark, for crying out loud. Kids down the block a little ways had punks in their hands, using the glowing tips to pretend they were smoking cigarettes. And cars. Jeez, there were a lot of cars moving up and down the street. Nathan guessed they were filled with people coming home from the fireworks.

One house, though, stood out from the others. The place directly across the street was neither well-lit nor well-kept. The grass was too long, the flowerbeds un-manicured. Only a porch light was on. A dozen or so newspapers, all rolled up and unread, lay scattered on the driveway. Nathan figured that the occupants must be on vacation.

That meant that the house was empty, and that he could safely stay there, at least for tonight.

He'd have to cross in the open, though, and if he tried that now, they'd catch him for sure. He told himself that he could be patient if he had to.

He settled back into his tunnel to begin his wait, forcing his mind to think about anything but sleep.

CHAPTER FOUR

IT WAS TEN-FORTY NOW, and the media people who'd stationed themselves in front of the JDC were clamoring for information. A knot of reporters had already blocked the front entrance, and more were arriving by the minute. The television people were particularly aggressive, shouting questions at anyone wearing a uniform. Of all journalistic deadlines, none were less forgiving than the eleven o'clock news. Immediacy was television's single trump card over their print counterparts, and they would do whatever it took to lead their newscasts with the big story. Michaels knew from experience that this meant fabricating details from rumor and assumption if the available facts didn't seem juicy enough. When they became desperate, news agencies would merely report on the rumors reported by the other agencies. It was a crazy way to make a living, but Michaels respected the fact that reporters had a job to do. He was committed to getting them the information they needed in time for them to do a live report at eleven, if not before.

The nameplate on the desk where Michaels sat read

HAROLD P. JOHNSTONE, SUPERINTENDENT. The superintendent—warden, to Michaels—had cordially invited the police to use his office as a base of operations.

Jed Hackner sat on the other side of the desk, briefing his boss on the latest details. At best, things still looked pretty sketchy.

Michaels scanned through the two pages of handwritten briefing notes a third time, committing times and names to memory.

"So, the kid's a car thief, right?"

"Right."

"Nothing like a murder charge to up the ante," Warren thought aloud. He turned the page. "Ricky Harris got a family?"

"Not in the area. He's from Missouri. We've notified their state PD to make the notifications."

"Uh-huh." Warren flipped the sheaf of papers over by their staple and started over. "There's no mention of the dogs," he commented without looking up. "What's their status?"

Jed's uncomfortable silence drew Michaels's eyes from the papers. "Jed?"

Hackner recrossed his legs and cleared his throat. "There's a problem with the dogs, Warren. It'll be another couple of hours before Peters can be here with the hounds. Seems he went downtown for the Fourth. I talked to him on his cell about twenty minutes ago. He's hopelessly stuck in traffic. On a good day, he says he could be here in an hour and a half. With the traffic, he just doesn't know."

The muscles in Michaels's jaw twitched. "When were you going to share that little tidbit with me? That's not the kind of thing to spring on me in front of the cameras."

"I wasn't hiding it from you," Jed said sheepishly. "It just didn't make it onto the briefing sheets."

Michaels rubbed his eyes with the heels of his hands, then rested his forearms on the desk. He gave a wry chuckle and shook his head. "I hate talking to those vultures. Won't we look like a bunch of hayseeds? Yessirree," he mocked, affecting a hillbilly accent, "we got the best gol-durned K-9 team in th' state. Jest when we need 'em, they're on vacation in the Nation's Capital!" The accent was gone. His volume increased. "God almighty, Jed, the kid's trail will only be fresh for so long! And they're predicting rain for tonight. If it rains, we might as well shoot the dogs, for all the help they'll be. Right now I'm inclined to shoot 'em anyway."

When Michaels finished his tirade, he stared at Hackner.

"What do you want me to do, Warren? They're not my dogs. We've been pushing for years for the Board to fund a K-9 team, but they won't do it. This is what happens when you try to pinch pennies."

Michaels smiled, the anger gone. "Wonderful civics lesson, Sergeant Hackner. Can I quote you on camera?"

Hackner smiled back. "Sure, why not? It's only a career."

Michaels checked his watch. Ten forty-eight. Through the drawn venetian blinds the night glowed like noon in the glare of the television lights. Michaels stood. "Come on, Jed," he said. "Time to go feed the birdies."

CHAPTER FIVE

TWELVE MILES FROM BROOKFIELD, in the farthest southwest corner of Braddock County, Mark Bailey sat Indian-style on his torn Naugahyde sofa, nursing the last three inches of his bottle of generic bourbon. The only light in the house emanated from the stove and the television. It seemed important that he remain in the dark, out of sight. He avoided windows. He didn't want to be seen, not tonight. He just wanted this dirty business with Nathan to be over and done with so he could get on with the rest of his life.

Until forty-five minutes ago, the bottle in his hands had served as his monument to conquering alcoholism. He had bought it four years before, on his twelve-month anniversary of sobriety. He had long since fallen off the wagon, of course, but until tonight, he could never bring himself to open that bottle. That would mean admitting failure, and Mark Bailey was nobody's failure.

But Mark Bailey had done a terrible thing this night. Maybe he wasn't a failure, but he was certainly no one he could respect. For three weeks now, he had known that after tonight, self-respect would forever be pushed into his past.

And what the hell, it was only a bottle of booze. Nothing more, nothing less. All that symbolism crap really didn't mean a thing.

Events of the night notwithstanding, Mark had felt well under control, until the face of Harry Caruthers appeared on television for the teaser to the-eleven o'clock news. "Murder at the Juvenile Detention Center. Details at eleven." Those nine words, delivered in just under five seconds, confirmed for Mark that it was all over; that he had been granted a new lease on life, albeit at the expense of his immortal soul.

He was surprised at just how much that religion crap had been weighing on him recently. The word pictures painted by the nuns and priests of his past lived on in his mind, pictures of fire and torture and misery. Unspeakable pain for all eternity.

That was the thought that sent him searching for his monument to sobriety.

His first toast was to his dear departed brother, Steve. Old Steve-o. Mr. Perfect Life, Perfect Kid, Holier-Than-Thou, Pain-in-the-Ass Steve-o. "Sorry it had to end this way, bro, but you didn't leave me much to work with."

For Mark, the first priority had always been survival. Even as a child, adults and peers alike had pronounced him street smart. That meant he was a survivor. He'd dealt with every bit of adversity life had handed him, and moved on to conquer another day. That's what life was all about: getting knocked down, and pulling your-self back up again. When Social Services dumped

Steve-o's hatchling on his doorstep, he'd first seen it as just one more turd on the shit pile that was his life. But then, eventually, he even turned that into opportunity. Like turning straw into gold.

The longer Mark lived, the better he got at beating the odds. It was just that the price kept getting harder to pay.

Now that this Nathan thing was done, though, and his blood was warmed by alcohol, Mark felt damned philosophical about it all. One day he'd go to hell, he supposed, but so what?

There's nothing you can do about it now, old sport. No sense dwelling on the past.

As the opening credits for *Action News at Eleven* flashed across the screen, Mark finished the last of the bottle. If his timing was right, he'd pass out just after the report on Nathan was over.

As always, Harry Caruthers was first with the lead story: "Law-enforcement officials are stunned this evening by the brutal murder of a staff member at the Brookfield Juvenile Detention Center. Twenty-eight-year old Child Care Supervisor Richard W. Harris was found slain at around nine o'clock this evening by a fellow staff member. The suspected killer: a twelve-year-old boy who subsequently escaped from the facility, and is currently at large. John Ogilsvy is live in Brookfield with a report. John, what do we know about the details?"

Mark Bailey's first thought was that the bourbon had mushed his brain. What he thought he had heard was simply unthinkable. Trying to blink his head clear, he slid onto the floor and scooted closer to the television, forcing himself to concentrate on every word.

The screen changed to young John Ogilsvy, dressed in a crisp button-down shirt and tie. The lighted façade of the Juvenile Detention Center served as his backdrop.

"Well, Harry, the details at this moment are still rather sketchy, but as you can imagine, police and detention center personnel are scurrying like crazy to pull this case together. Sometime between seven and eight-thirty this evening, staff member Ricky Harris was stabbed repeatedly while making his rounds in the facility.

"Mr. Harris's body was found by another staff member in a cell occupied by a twelve-year-old car thief named Nathan Bailey, of Braddock County." An institutional photo of Nathan, full-face and profile, dominated the left-hand side of the screen, while the other side displayed a smiling Ricky Harris.

"All we know for sure is that Nathan Bailey has escaped, though it's safe to assume, I believe, that he is the primary suspect in the murder as well. Residents of the area are advised to double-check their locks this evening . . ."

This was unbelievable. "You son of a bitch," Mark hissed through clenched teeth. "SON OF A BITCH!" He heaved the empty monument through the picture tube, instantly drenching the living room in darkness.

How could this happen? Mark reeled, wishing distantly that he could drain the numbing alcohol from his veins. It was so simple, like shooting birds in a cage. How could Ricky have screwed it up so badly?

Mark tried to stand, rising to all fours, but tumbled to his side like a fallen buffalo. There he lay, panting, cursing unintelligibly under his breath.

"You shoulda let him do it, Nathan," he moaned.

"Harder on both of us . . ." His brain clouded. "The guy they send next won't be as quick."

His last coherent thought before slipping off into a stupor was that the street-smart Mark Bailey might not survive this one after all.

CHAPTER SIX

HIGH BEAMS WASHED over Nathan's face, startling him awake. For a long moment, he was disoriented, unable to piece together the bright lights, the wetness, the smell of dirt, the sense of fear. The headlights blinded him as they came closer, only to pause in the driveway in front of him. The characteristic rumbling sound of a garage door opener followed next, with the headlights disappearing from view a moment later into the garage.

A scant four feet to his left, separated only by single layers of plywood and vinyl siding, car doors opened and closed. Conversations continued uninterrupted. A woman's voice said, "Chris, can you carry Suzie in while I unlock the door?" A male voice responded with a single syllable. More sounds of movement; another car door opening and closing. The male voice softly sang, "Shh, sweetheart, go back to sleep. Daddy's going to take you right to bed. Shhh." The garage door rumbled shut again.

Through it all, Nathan lay perfectly still, half expecting to be yanked from his hiding place by his collar. As seconds passed, and then minutes, he allowed himself to relax. If they'd seen him, they'd have done something by now. He cursed himself for having drifted off.

Three minutes later, the light on the garage door opener cycled off, once again flooding his hiding place with darkness. The street looked completely different now. Most of the houses were dark. No one moved about. The neighborhood was asleep. It was time for him to make his move.

Using only his elbows for propulsion, Nathan snaked from behind the boxwood onto the grass. Free of the leafy tunnel, he drew his feet under him and was instantly reminded of the beating they'd taken through the woods. Though his soles stung badly, the cool wetness of the grass was soothing.

Nathan now had a full and unobstructed view of the street. Crouched like a cat, he looked around and calculated what needed to be done. The space that separated him from the shadows of the house across the street looked like the same distance as the fifty-yard dash he'd had to run in school. Fifty yards. Last time he tested out, he had covered the distance in 7.8 seconds, fastest in his class. That was no time at all.

From his crouched position, he counted down in his head. *On your mark . . . get set . . . GO!*

He covered the front yard in five quick strides, hit the street on his sixth step, and a well-camouflaged rock on his eighth. The rock hobbled him and made him stumble face-first onto the grass across the street.

Beyond his aching right foot and a little road rash, he was unhurt. But holy crap, he had made a lot of noise!

At that instant, an explosion of light blasted from

the house he'd just left as the garage door once again rumbled upwards. Even as the door cleared the first two inches from the ground, Nathan could see the feet, legs, and ultimately the entire body of the man who lived there.

Nathan nearly panicked. He was completely out in the open, easily twenty feet from the nearest shadow. With no real alternative, he resumed his crouch and froze in place. Sometimes the best place to hide is out in the open, his father had once told him.

Nathan's eyes never moved from the man as he rolled a trash can out to the curb, followed by a container full of newspapers. Never once did the man even glance across the street. No sign of recognition at all. Once the man disappeared inside and the garage door started down again, Nathan dashed into the shadow cast by the house he hoped would be his home for the night.

Thanks to the lessons of MacGyver, it took Nathan about ten seconds to break into the house. He chose as his point of entry the French doors on the main level in the rear. Using his elbow to break out a single pane of glass near the lock, he winced in anticipation of pain that never came. It wasn't even noisy, thanks to the lush carpeting on the other side. Nathan reached through the opening he had created and turned both the dead bolt and the knob.

The door swung open into a darkened rec room, dominated by a floor-to-ceiling stone fireplace on his right, and by a huge entertainment center on his left. In between skulked the shadowy outlines of various pieces of

furniture. Nathan gently closed the French doors again.
And locked them.

Though his eyes were well-accustomed to the darkness, he moved cautiously, paranoid of jamming a bare toe into some unseen obstacle.

This place is huge.

The kitchen, with an eat-in breakfast area, sprawled to his left beyond the entertainment center. Beyond that, and out of sight, were a living room, formal dining room, and library, all on the first floor.

A place like this ought to have an alarm system. The thought nudged his panic button just a little before he realized that he'd already been inside long enough that it would be too late to react. One way or another, it was a done deal, not worth worrying about tonight. Still, it was a good thought to keep in mind for the future.

Nathan's first destination was the refrigerator. He was starving. He had to yank hard to get the door to open, but it was a wasted effort. The shelves were barren; no pizza, no leftovers, not even a carton of milk. From a compartment in the door, he pulled out a jar of sweet pickles.

Then he froze. In the dim light of the refrigerator, he got his first good look at his hands. They were filthy, caked with dirt and grass stains. And blood. Lots and lots of blood. Ricky's blood.

In an instant, his hunger disappeared, replaced with an urgent need to go to the bathroom. He found one in the main hall, across from the stairs, with exactly no time to spare. In the darkness, he purged his bowels with a single liquid blast.

Finished, Nathan closed the door and flipped on the

wall switch. With no windows in the bathroom, he could safely turn on a light. The image of the boy in the mirror frightened him. That boy looked sixty years old. His eyes were dark hollows, one of them severely swollen. His blond hair was brown with grime and matted to his head, pushed in every direction. He looked frail in the drooping coveralls, the shoulders of the garment hanging nearly halfway to his elbows. And the blood. He was soaked in it. When he moved, little chips of coagulated blood flaked off like powder and drifted to the floor.

Using both hands, Nathan pulled the lapels of the coveralls apart and ripped the zipper from its stitching. More than anything else in the world, he wanted out of those clothes. He moved quickly and clumsily, as though the prison uniform were covered with spiders. With his shoulders clear, he dropped the collar to the floor and quick-marched free of the pant legs.

There was blood on his underpants, too, which he ripped off and tossed onto the pile. Staring at the mess on the floor as though it were some kind of beast, he retreated into the corner near the bathtub. He crouched in a ball near the floor, wondering how he was going to get past the pile of clothes without touching it.

It still was not off him! Ricky's blood had soaked all the way through his clothes and stained his skin. His *skin*.

Nathan jumped to his feet. With one hand he tore open the shower curtain, while the other turned the shower knob all the way to hot. He didn't even wait for the water to run warm before he stepped inside and closed the curtain.

At first the frigid water took his breath away, cleared his mind. Nathan stood unmoving as the water pelted his face, moving past warm and into hot. Not until he felt that he would be scalded did he reach out to normalize the temperature. He found a bar of soap in the dish and slowly, deliberately began to wash away the nightmare. Behind closed eyes, he tried to revel in the simple pleasure of the hot water, a privilege he had been so long denied. But the darkness brought demons instead.

The image of Ricky Harris lurked behind Nathan's eyelids. He watched the man die all over again. Nathan saw his own hands covering the hole in Ricky's belly, trying desperately to slow down the bright red spurts, only to have them leak through his fingers. Nathan replayed the horrible sounds that Ricky made; the horrid gurgling, choking sound as he sought a breath that wouldn't come. Then he saw Ricky's eyes, angry and frightened. He felt Ricky's bloody hand around his throat. . . .

The pictures stopped when Nathan opened his eyes. As the water and grime ran down his body and swirled into the drain, he wiggled his toes in the soapy froth and tried to smile. A smile makes the saddest man a little happier, his father used to say, but had he ever felt this much sadness?

"God, I miss you," Nathan said aloud, his voice a whisper. He turned his face toward the ceiling. "I'm in so much trouble, Dad. Please help me. You've got to help me."

The emotions Nathan had fought so long to control broke free all at once. He started to cry, silently at first, and then, dropping his chin to his chest and covering his eyes with his palms, he gave in to long, miserable sobs.

Outside, a hard summer rain pounded heavily, providing nourishment for the ground, swelling creeks to their banks, and forever washing away the trail of a frightened twelve-year-old boy.

CHAPTER SEVEN

"TELL ME WHAT WE KNOW, JED," Michaels invited, leaning back in his squeaky vinyl desk chair. It was morning again, the day after the Fourth of July, and Michaels wore a lightweight khaki suit with a crisply starched shirt and a yellow tie with tiny red polka dots. While he would never admit it aloud, there was no question that Hackner's attention to style had impacted the dress code of the entire division.

Thumbing through his ever-present notebook, Hackner ticked off the failures of the past twelve hours. "The searches and roadblocks didn't turn up a thing last night, and created a nightmare during rush hour this morning. The rain last night obliterated any trail we might have had for the dogs. Dr. Cooper's on vacation, so the medical examiner's office told me this morning that they probably won't get to Ricky Harris's autopsy until tomorrow afternoon at the earliest.

"By the way," Hackner noted parenthetically, looking up from his notebook, "the stab wound count went up this morning to at least six. Apparently I missed one when I was counting last night."

Having missed the presence of the murder weapon himself, Michaels knew better than to make a smartass comment.

Hackner continued: "Our esteemed county prosecutor, the Honorable J. Daniel Petrelli, has caused a run on the pancake makeup market this morning, getting himself interviewed on all the local morning talk shows. Word has it that *Good Morning America* has a call in to him for tomorrow morning."

"Oh, Christ," Michaels moaned. Having gotten into bed at a little after three, he'd opted to sleep through the morning news. "And what does Mr. Hollywood have to say to the residents of our fine community?"

"Same old, same old. He's going to prosecute the Bailey kid as an adult and throw his ass in jail for the rest of his life. When pressed by the reporter, he said he would not rule out the death penalty."

Michaels laughed. "Oh, right. He's gonna find a judge that'll fry a twelve-year-old."

"He didn't say he was going to," Hackner corrected dutifully. "He said that he couldn't rule it out."

"Well, of course he couldn't. He hasn't had a chance to do a poll yet." Michaels made no attempt to hide his disdain for Petrelli. While ambitious prosecutors normally made some pretense of denying their political ambitions, Petrelli had for the past five years made it known to the electorate that he wanted to be the next U.S. Senator representing the Commonwealth of Virginia.

The only cases he prosecuted personally were the ones that met the two-part standard of being both highly publicized and sure to win. Only when there were three eyewitnesses and a videotape of the crime would the public see J. Daniel Petrelli in the court-room. Unless, of course, it was to claim credit for the hard work of one of his assistants in winning a more difficult case. Michaels could only imagine what Petrelli had had to say this morning. A central theme of his campaign rhetoric had been the loss of morality among young people. With elections only four months away, Petrelli could not have asked for a better platform from which to pontificate.

"I presume that he has been true to his form and set us incompetent flatfoots up to take the fall if something goes wrong?"

"Of course."

"Of course. I swear to God, Jed, if one of my kids grows up to be an idiot, I'm gonna make her become a politician."

Hackner smiled. "I guess *your* father had a different strategy."

Even Michaels's signature glare looked tired. "You're getting pretty quick there, Patrolman—er, excuse me, *Sergeant* Hackner. Anything else?"

"Nothing good. Patrols are all looking for the kid; we got a better picture to work with by lifting it out of his fifth-grade yearbook." He handed a copy to Michaels.

"Doesn't look much like a murderer, does he?" Michaels commented.

"The good ones never do."

The boy in the picture could have stepped off the front of a cereal box. This boy smiled easily, flashing blue eyes and sparkling teeth at the camera. Tow-headed and athletic, the boy in the picture appeared not to have a care in the world. Such a contrast to the official photo attached to his Juvey file jacket.

Michaels sighed. "No, I suppose they don't. By the way, who released the kid's picture to the media?"

"Guess."

"Petrelli?"

"I can't prove it, but who else? I talked to one of his minions about it this morning and he got real defensive, babbling that the law allows the release of a juvenile escapee's picture so long as certain criteria are met. Frankly, I lost interest halfway through the answer. One thing he never said, though, was 'no.'"

Warren shook his head and handed the photo back to Jed. "Well, screw it. Are the troops assembled?"

"Yep. All ready and waiting to be inspired."

Together, Michaels and Hackner rose from their chairs and headed across the squad room to the small conference room, where three other division heads had gathered. Michaels marched to the front of the room and went straight to the point.

"Thanks for coming on such short notice. You all know by now that there was a murder at the JDC last night, and that the suspected killer is out there on the streets. The killer is a twelve-year-old boy." As Michaels spoke, Hackner passed out copies of the yearbook picture.

"The press is already beginning to have some fun with this story," Michaels continued, "reporting along your basic David and Goliath theme—SMALL BOY OUT-WITS POLICE FORCE, you know the deal. I want to stress to each and every one of you that I want this case closed, and Nathan Bailey reincarcerated, today. Thus far, our searches and roadblocks haven't turned up a thing. Sergeant Hackner will be getting the state boys involved in this after our meeting, but I personally would like this to be resolved while it is still a local matter. Frankly, I don't need the crap that's going to come down on us if we get beaten by that kid. Have I made my position clear?"

Heads nodded across the conference table.

"Good, then get your folks on the street motivated to catch him."

With that, the meeting ended.

As Michaels traversed the twenty feet to the door, he overheard one of the division heads comment, "Sure is a cute kid."

Michaels stopped and turned in his tracks to face the source of the comment. The patented glare was retuned and working perfectly. "I'll remind you, Bob, that that cute kid murdered a fellow law-enforcement officer last night. If you do your job, he won't have the chance to do it again."

CHAPTER EIGHT

NATHAN AWOKE NAKED but warm under a downy comforter in the middle of a king-size bed. The sun shone through the open blinds at just the right angle to sting his eyes into wakefulness. The last time he looked at the digital clock next to him on the nightstand, it had read 2:43. Now it was 9:48. Annoyed that his rest had been cut short, he grumbled and rolled to his side, turning away from the invading rays of the sun and burying his head between two pillows.

Moments later, the room was filled with the sound of a disc jockey, blaring from the clock radio. Some chatter followed, which Nathan tried to ignore in an effort to recapture the peace of sleep. The content of the conversation drifted in and out of his consciousness, something to do with a health plan and taxes. Whatever it was, it sure sparked a lot of emotion, with people yelling at each other. Finally, enough was enough, and Nathan blindly slapped at the top of the radio until the noise stopped.

At peace once again, and in a quiet room, Nathan settled his head back between the pillows and waited for sleep to return. But it was too late. The spell had been broken. He was awake, and his mind was already beginning to fill with thoughts of what he needed to do to plan his escape.

Kind of hard when you don't even know where you're going.

Whatever he decided to do, he was going to have to think things through very carefully. The nervous, fluttery feeling returned to the pit of his stomach. The images of Ricky were lurking just behind a closed door in his mind. If he wasn't careful, he'd have to look at them again.

He pushed the thoughts away. There was plenty of time to plan, he told himself, and God knew there was plenty of time to worry. He'd get to all of that later. It was ten o'clock now; there had to be some good cartoons on cable. Last night—or really this morning, he supposed—as he wandered into the master bedroom in the dark, the first feature he noticed was the enormous big-screen TV in the corner opposite the enormous bed.

Nathan found the remote on the nightstand and thumbed the ON button. The huge screen jumped to life with startling speed.

The channel was set on a news station, with the volume turned all the way down. Nathan looked down at the remote to figure out how to make the proper adjustments, and when he looked up again, he was greeted with a table-sized picture of himself glaring sullenly out of the screen. It was the picture they took of him when he was first arrested. He mashed the UP arrow on the volume control and left it there until the voice-over was plainly audible.

". . . at large. Police refuse to speculate on a motive

behind the murder, but sources close to the Braddock County Prosecutor's Office advise that the age of the fugitive will have little effect on the manner in which the case is prosecuted."

The screen cut to a videotape of an older man wearing a suit, standing in front of the JDC building. Nathan didn't like the man's eyes. They had the heartless look of all the creeps he'd had to deal with in the juvenile justice system. The electronic letters superimposed across the man's chest identified him as J. Daniel Petrelli, Commonwealth's Attorney.

"We cannot overstate the seriousness of this crime," Petrelli said, looking directly into the camera. "We believe that Nathan Bailey killed Mr. Harris, and we will pursue him and the charges against him with all the vigor appropriate to the offenses with which he is charged."

"What will happen to him if he's caught?" a voice asked from off-camera. "Will you return him to the Juvenile Detention Center?"

Petrelli didn't even pause to consider the options available to him before answering, *"When* he is caught, which we have every reason to believe will happen today, it is my intent at this time to prosecute the young man as an adult. If he can commit a grown-up crime, he can pay the grown-up price."

"Surely you're not suggesting the death penalty," the off-camera voice asked.

Petrelli chuckled coolly and raised his hands next to his face. "Let's not get ahead of ourselves. First, let's get Mr. Bailey back behind bars. We'll worry about his ultimate disposition as we prepare for trial."

"The death penalty," Nathan gasped aloud. "Geez,

that means the electric chair." He was completely mesmerized by what he was watching. He'd never heard his name on television before, and he'd certainly never seen his picture there. (He wished they could have found one that made him look less evil.) Filling out a morning of firsts, he had never been called a murderer before, either. "You've really pooped in the punch bowl this time, buddy," he scolded himself, swiping a phrase often used by his father.

The screen cut back to the anchorman behind a desk. "John Ogilsvy has been tracking the police investigation for us since this story first broke. John, are the police even close to finding Nathan Bailey?"

"Well, Peter," John Ogilsvy said, "all morning long, the Braddock County Police have been long on details about the effort to locate the boy, but short on information about the results of their efforts." The picture changed again to show a tired-looking man in a red-and-blue Izod shirt standing behind a bank of microphones. The electronic caption identified this man as Lt. Warren Michaels, Braddock County Police Department.

The only sound associated with the pictures continued to come from John Ogilsvy. "Detective Lieutenant Warren Michaels addressed reporters late last night and in the very early hours of this morning with what has to be very embarrassing news for the police. According to Michaels, there may have been as much as a two-hour delay in beginning the search for the escapee, and once that search finally got under way, a number of factors conspired to foul up the operation. These factors included everything from traffic delays to last night's torrential rainstorm, which rendered useless the bloodhounds normally used to track down fugitives.

"Before the book is finally closed on this case, somebody may have to answer some very tough questions on the handling of it. With elections just around the corner, it seems likely that J. Daniel Petrelli may be that person, and that the people asking the questions may be the electorate. Reporting live from the Brookfield Juvenile Detention Center, this is John Ogilsvy, *Action News*."

The anchorman shifted gears to Cuban refugees coming to Florida, so Nathan punched the MUTE button on the remote, rendering the newscaster voiceless. Nathan knew that the news report should have frightened him, and it did a little, but mostly he felt proud. He'd been gone over twelve hours now, and they still didn't know where he was.

That meant he had some time to think.

Cartoons were suddenly unimportant in the extreme. He still had to find clothes and food and a way to stay ahead of the cops. For the first time, Nathan began to believe that he might actually outwit them. The problem with grown-ups was that they always thought like grown-ups. It was funny, really. Kids had never been grown up, yet they knew exactly what older people were thinking, while adults had spent years being kids, but they could never figure out how to think like kids. Nathan had heard countless adults complaining over the years how they didn't understand what was going on in their own kids' heads. It was simple. They were trying to piss off their parents.

Nathan wondered if, normally, any kids lived in this

house; specifically, a kid his size. Thoughts of prosecutions and death penalties were foreign to him, and easily pushed aside. But the prospect of being captured naked was too awful to even think about.

The upstairs hallway was arranged in a sweeping semicircle that spanned out to Nathan's left. The bedroom doors, all constructed of heavy lumber and stained mahogany, were closed. The center area leading to the bedrooms was big enough to be the site of a good-sized party. To Nathan's right was a curved stairwell, dominated by a four-tiered gold chandelier with a million glass ornaments dangling from every surface. He'd seen a similar fixture in the lobby of a hotel once, but never in a house.

The carpet in the hallway was every bit as lush as it was in the master bedroom, and it showed very little sign of wear. *These people must never wear shoes.* As Nathan stepped out into the hall, he felt suddenly self-conscious and covered his privates with his hand. *Wouldn't this make an interesting picture for TV?*

The first door to the left of the master suite opened into a little girl's room, adorned in pink and lined with shelf after shelf of Barbie paraphernalia.

Okay, he conceded silently, there was at least one thing worse than being captured naked, and that would be getting captured in girl's clothes. He pressed on.

Nathan found what he was looking for behind the third door. The interior was smaller than the first two, denoting the occupant's rank within the family. Decorations on the wall included posters of Michael Jordan—back where he belonged, in a Bulls uniform—the Navy Blue Angels flying in tight formation and spewing red, white, and blue smoke; and two versions of the Teenage

Mutant Ninja Turtles: cartoon and live-action. Before he went to live with Uncle Mark, Nathan had had the cartoon poster on the wall of his own bedroom. Sad memories again tried to sneak into his mind as he stood there, but he shoved them out of the way. He laughed aloud at the stuffed Garfield that was hung by a perfectly tied noose from the cord to the venetian blinds.

Relieved that the regular occupant of the room was clearly a boy about his age, Nathan rummaged through the heavy pine dresser, selecting underwear, socks, a Chicago Bulls T-shirt, and a pair of denim shorts. Everything was two sizes too big, but they all fit better than the monkey suit from the JDC, and they would certainly cover what needed to be covered. The only real problem was the shorts, which were size Nathan-and-a-half. "This kid needs to go on a diet," he mumbled.

"Let's see if Tubbo owns a belt." The first belt was still too loose, even on the tightest setting. *Little Nathan No-bottom. My razor-butted son.* Finally, in the very back of the top drawer, he found a green Boy Scout belt that was infinitely adjustable. By cinching the waistband tight, the pants felt like they almost fit, even though the material scalloped up in several places. Keep the shirttail out, and no one would notice.

For shoes, Nathan went to the closet, a huge walk-in with cubbyholes built in all along one wall. They were stacked full of shirts, pants, sweaters, linens. And shoes; all manner and sizes of shoes. Bedroom slippers, soccer shoes, baseball shoes, dress shoes, and tennis shoes. Nathan concentrated on the tennis shoe collection. Judging from the number and condition, this kid must

have kept every pair he ever owned. The newer ones
were clearly too big for Nathan.

Tubbo has fat feet, too.

Before long, Nathan had his hands on a pair of ancient Reeboks that were the right size, but looked like
they had been hiked from coast to coast. The laces on
one shoe had been broken and retied, the tread was almost gone, and the leather was severely scuffed. But
by God, they looked comfortable, and that was his primary concern.

When he was completely dressed, Nathan ventured a
look in the full-length bathroom mirror. A little scrawny
and pale, maybe, but the boy he knew to be himself had
returned. No blood this time. His hair was blond again,
with a wispy, freshly shampooed look that needed some
assistance from a comb. The bruise on his eye had gone
down considerably, and was already beginning to turn
shades of orange-yellow around the edges. All in all,
he approved of what he saw.

Nathan could feel his confidence growing, born of a
hope for himself and his future that he hadn't felt in
nearly a year; not since Uncle Mark had him thrown in
jail.

There he went thinking about that stuff again! He had
to stop doing that. Dark thoughts and painful memories
only made him feel frightened and confused, neither of
which could he afford.

There was a spring in his step as he reentered the
master suite. It lasted just long enough for him to realize
that the clock radio had cycled back on, blaring a new
talk show. It took Nathan five seconds to realize that the
people on the radio were talking about him, which was
pretty cool at first. Then he heard what they were saying.

CHAPTER NINE

DENISE CARPENTER, SINGLE MOTHER of twin girls, had been "The Bitch" on NewsTalk 990 for nearly five years, a transformation that was so accidental it somehow seemed ordained that the show would become a success.

In October, four and three-quarter years before, she had been a traffic reporter, granted thirty seconds of airtime every half hour. The regular late-morning talent, Boss Johnny, called in that morning from the D.C. jail, where he'd been offered a guest room in return for seven outstanding warrants for offenses ranging from failure to pay child support to assault with intent to murder, the latter being the result of too much Jack Daniel's and too little temper. With only twenty minutes' advance notice, Denise was told that she would get her big chance in major-market radio. The news should have thrilled her, but at the time she was not looking for work in front as a deejay. She was perfectly content to monitor the police scanners for accidents and devise alternative routes for frustrated commuters.

But she was smart enough to realize an opportunity

when she saw it. At the time, her daughters, Laura and Erin, were only five, and between day care and rent, there was barely enough cash left in any given week for food. A social worker friend of hers had told her that she qualified for food stamps, but Denise refused. She wasn't about to give Bernie the satisfaction of seeing her take charity. *She* had wanted the divorce, and *she* had wanted sole custody, and she had let him off the hook for even the tiniest amount of child support, against the vehement objections of the judge. The last thing "Bernie the Bastard" said to her as they left the courthouse was, "You're gonna starve without me." Over the ensuing six years, she'd come to think of those words as her good luck charm.

With no notice, and facing a once-in-a-lifetime chance to make an impression, Denise had walked into the booth briskly and confidently. Years later, her then-engineer and current producer Enrique Zamora confided to her that he'd lost twenty dollars that day by betting that Denise would leave in tears before the end of the first commercial.

Far from tearful, Denise came out of the theme song swinging.

"I'm not the voice you were expecting to hear this morning," she'd said, her first words ever as a disc jockey. "That voice is learning to sing the song of the jailbird. It seems that Boss Johnny had more mouth than he had heart. Right now, he's in jail downtown on a number of charges, one of which is failure to pay child support. If he's innocent, I can't wait to see his smiling face back in the booth. If he's guilty, I hope he rots in a cell with Bubba the Love Muffin teaching him things he never knew about sex."

For the next four hours, Denise railed on about what was wrong with the social fabric of America, not hesitating to traipse on territory normally considered forbidden. She established her position in favor of a woman's right to choose abortion when the circumstances warranted it, but suggested that murder charges be brought against anyone and everyone who participated in an abortion—including fathers and doctors—when the procedure was used solely as a means of birth control. When she was asked how she could justify such a self-contradictory position, she answered, "I don't have to justify anything to you. I'm just telling you how I feel. If it upsets you, turn that little knob on your radio till I go away."

Through her entire first show, the telephone lines remained jammed with callers trying to assail her positions. Denise's defining moment came when Barbara from Arlington, Virginia, called in to tell her, "No offense, Denise, but you're really coming across as a bitch on the radio."

Denise responded, "Why, thank you very much Barbara, because you're right. But I'm not just a bitch; I'm *the* bitch of Washington, D.C." In an industry where a marketable identity means everything, Denise had stumbled upon a winner.

By the time Boss Johnny was able to scrape together bail money, two days after his arrest, his job had been given away to an upstart bitch from the news staff.

Within a week after she'd started her new career, Denise's salary had been quintupled, in return for her signature on an unheard-of three-year exclusive contract. The Bitch represented everything that is supposed to fail in radio: a black female who speaks openly and evenly about everything from racism to child-rearing. Politically, she was more conservative than liberal, but she didn't hesitate to torpedo anyone who stepped out of line.

Three weeks after her first show, NewsTalk 990 had picked up a full six percentage points in the ratings during the coveted morning slot. Denise the Bitch had been featured in both Washington, D.C., newspapers, and thoroughly dominated the trade press. According to her fans, The Bitch offered a real person's view on life. Like most Americans, Denise had no political ax to grind, and she certainly had no political ambitions, so when she said what she thought, it had the ring of truth with which her audience could identify.

One month after her first anniversary as a talk-show host, Enrique Zamora sat her down in his office, looking like a little kid who was going to burst if he didn't reveal a secret. "I overheard the station manager talking with some guy on the phone today. They're going to syndicate us!"

Even as Denise heard the words, she didn't understand his enthusiasm. "So?"

"So! Don't you get it? Syndication means we'll be on the radio in every major market in the country. A *nationwide* audience."

For a long moment, Denise had just stared in disbelief, her hand frozen over her gaping mouth. "Oh, my God, Rick. Are you serious?"

"Yes, I'm serious! Think of it. Millions of people listening to you from coast to coast. Millions of dollars in your pocket."

Enrique's last comment took Denise's breath away,

making her feel light-headed. "No," she commanded, mostly to herself. "We're not going to get all excited over something you think you heard other people talking about. This kind of thing just doesn't happen to me."

"I don't *think* I overheard it," Enrique protested. "I know what I heard, and they were talking about you."

"And they said we were going into syndication?"

"Yes."

"You're a liar."

Enrique laughed. "I am not a liar. I'm a busybody and an eavesdropper, but I am not a liar."

Sure enough, later that day, the station manager approached Denise with the official news. Their initial syndication would be in twelve markets, from Tampa to Bloomington, Illinois. Her already comfortable salary would double once again. Within a year, there were thirty-four stations on the network, prompting another doubling of her salary.

By the time Nathan listened to her for the first time in the bedroom of a strange house, Denise was being heard on 327 stations across the country, and was earning well into seven figures.

During her monologue at the beginning of the show that morning, The Bitch had railed against the state of the youth of America, citing as an example of the decaying moral fabric the local Washington story of a twelve-year-old boy who'd escaped from prison after killing a guard.

"The prosecutor on this case says he's going to try this kid as an adult, and I think that's great. How many times do you hear stories of gang killings, and drive-by killings and robbery killings, only to find out that the killing is being done by pint-sized monsters? Twelve-, thirteen-, fourteen-year-olds who have so little to live for that they take the most precious possession from others—their very lives.

"I for one am tired of hearing it. I for one am prepared to stand up and say, man or woman, underage or not, if you intentionally take the life of another human being, I don't want you as a part of my society. I want you in prison for the rest of your life, or certainly until you're old enough to be strapped down in one of those electric chairs they have collecting dust across the country, where you can be zapped straight to hell, and spend all eternity considering just how cool and courageous murder really is."

The phones went nuts, every light blinking by the time she was done with her tirade. Promising to talk to the listeners on hold as soon as she came back, The Bitch went into commercials.

"Half the calls want to hang the kid, and the other half want to hang you," Enrique said into Denise's headset. She smiled stunningly. To Enrique, everything that Denise did was stunning. Always well dressed and always wearing makeup, Denise was a sharp contrast to the rest of the on-air talent, whose sense of fashion focused mainly on using a napkin rather than their sleeves to wipe their mouths during lunch. Fans who knew Denise only from her voice invariably commented, when they met her, on how beautiful she was, and, privately, how surprised they were.

Denise raised her onyx eyes from her notes to stare through the glass at Enrique. "Listen, Rick," she said. "Screen out the callers who want to tell me that the kid is innocent, okay?" Enrique nodded and gave a thumbs-up. "And I don't want to talk to anyone who's going to tell me that I'm a bad mother. I just want to discuss the pros and cons of trying kids as adults, and proposed solutions to the juvenile crime problem."

"You got it, Denise," Enrique told her. "We're coming out of commercial in twenty seconds. Your first call is Robert on line four. I think he wants to agree with you."

Denise nodded with mock enthusiasm. "That sounds like a perfect place to start."

Enrique used his fingers to count down from five, and then gave Denise her cue.

"And you're back in the room with The Bitch. Not much trouble collecting phone calls this morning." She stabbed the blinking line four. "Hello, Robert, this is The Bitch. What's on your mind?"

"Hello, Bitch." Robert's voice had the gravelly sound of a smoker, maybe forty-five years old. "I'm calling to agree with you, believe it or not."

"Why wouldn't I believe that? Since I'm always right, I always expect people to agree with me."

Robert laughed, initiating a juicy cough. "But this is the first time I've *ever* agreed with you."

Denise laughed, too. "Well, tell me, Robert, what have I said to deserve such an honor?"

"I say the youth of America are going down the toilet. I get sick and tired of hearing that abusive families and racial strife are responsible for kids' actions. It's the kids themselves. They don't respect anybody or anything; they just look at everybody as their next potential victim."

"You keep referring to 'they,' Robert. Who exactly are 'they'?"

"The juvenile delinquents out on the street. The courts are afraid to do anything about them. If they throw them in prison, the ACLU screams that they're not being treated fairly, and the media paints this picture of an innocent who's been victimized by his surroundings. On the other hand, if the judges don't put them in jail, that means they just come back out onto the street."

Denise tried to interrupt, but Robert was on a roll.

"I read a story in the paper just a few months ago about some kid in Chicago, eleven years old, who killed a girl in a drive-by shooting. I was in Chicago at the time, and all we heard was how they were looking for this kid, who had an arrest record as long as my arm. Two days later, the kid showed up dead in some drainage ditch, shot in the head. Then the local media cried all over themselves, showing the kid's smiling face on the news and interviewing his relatives about what a wonderful kid he was!"

"And you don't believe he was a wonderful kid?"

"He was scum. Let's call it as it is. He might have been young scum, but he was scum. We've got no place for people like that on the streets."

Denise made the "okay" signal to Enrique through the window. Robert was a live one.

"So where does that leave us with this kid, Nathan Bailey? What should we do with him?"

"Honestly?"

"Of course. Nothing but the truth on my show. That's the first rule."

"Honestly, I don't have a problem executing him. He killed a prison guard, for crying out loud. If he's tried as a juvenile, he'll be out in nine years, if not before, but that guard'll still be dead. That doesn't seem fair to me."

Enrique's voice in Denise's headphones told her it was time to move on to Barb on line six.

"Thank you, Robert, I have to say I agree with you. Now it's on to Barb, who's live on the air with The Bitch. What's on your mind, Barb?"

The voice was timid, maybe twenty-two. "Hello?"

"Hello, Barb, you're on the air with The Bitch."

"Oh, hi. This is Barb. Thanks for taking my call, B——" Her hesitation in saying the word was not uncommon among young women.

"It's The Bitch, honey. Come on, you can say it. If I can be it, you can say it."

Barb giggled on the other end. "Anyway, thanks for taking my call . . ."

Denise interrupted again. "No, you've got to say it, or I'll hang up on you. Say, Hello, Bitch."

Barb giggled nervously. "I . . . I don't want to."

"Sure you do. It should be easy, the way I'm treating you right now in front of millions of listeners. Just say bitch."

"I can't."

"Sure you can. I'll give you a running start at it. You just complete the sentence: Jeeze, you're a . . ."

"Bitch." Barb said it so softly, it was barely audible.

"Okay, that was a good start. Now, try it again with feeling. Son of a . . ."

"Bitch."

"Okay, that was much better. Now let's go for the gold. Say, Hello, Bitch."

"Hello, Bitch." Barb was laughing.

"Howya doin', Bitch."

"Howya doin', Bitch."

"Son of a bitch. You're a real bitch, Bitch."

Barb was laughing hard now. "Son of a bitch. You're a real bitch, Bitch."

Denise slapped the table triumphantly. "By George, we did it. Don't you feel better now?"

"Absolutely."

"And aren't you glad that my radio name isn't Vagina?"

Hard laughter from the other end of the phone.

"Or better yet, maybe I'll change my name to Scrotum. Think of it: 'Hello, America, don't forget to listen to your scrotum every morning.'" Denise started to laugh herself. "Like men need any more encouragement to do that. Anyway, Barb, you've been a good sport. What's on your mind?"

Barb composed herself more quickly than Denise expected. "Well, Bitch, I'm just not comfortable treating children the same way as adults. A child who's a criminal can still be turned around. It's not like an adult, where they know better and decide to commit crimes anyway."

"So you don't think that Nathan Bailey, at age twelve, knew that it was wrong to kill?"

"I think he knew it was wrong, sure. I just don't think that children can put an act like that into perspective."

"Come on, Barb, what does perspective have to do with anything? A public servant is still dead. That's the only perspective he and his family will ever have."

"I just don't think it's that simple. To try a child as a criminal requires more than just determining what the kid did. You have to look at what they *thought* they were doing."

"What makes you think that little Nathan thought he was doing something other than killing?"

"What makes you think he didn't?" Barb's tone had a real "gotcha" edge to it.

"That's just it, Barb. I don't care. It really doesn't matter, and that's my point. The act of killing speaks for itself, as far as I'm concerned."

The Bitch took two more calls before the break. Neither thought that Nathan should be treated differently from any other criminal. The time had come, the callers agreed, when people had to take responsibility for their actions, whether good or bad. The courts had gone way too far in protecting the rights of the bad guys at the expense of the good guys.

Denise could not have agreed more.

Nathan sat on the edge of the big bed for twenty minutes, listening to a long string of grown-up strangers passing judgment on him.

How can they say those things? They weren't there. They didn't hear Ricky's threats, or feel his hands around their throats. They didn't know—they probably didn't even care—that if he hadn't killed Ricky, then Ricky would have killed him. They hadn't seen the crazy look in his eyes, or have their brains rattled by a punch in the eye. They didn't see the blood.

Oh, God. The blood.

The more he heard, the more he realized that the truth was becoming irrelevant. People were telling lies about him again, and he knew from experience h̶ quickly lies can become reality in people's m̶ how once that happens, they can do anything they want to you. No one had even heard his side of the story. All they had heard was what the police and the JDC assholes were saying about him. All they had heard were lies.

But he could change that, couldn't he? All he had to do was pick up the telephone and call. He had the number memorized already; God knows they said it enough on the air. He could just pick up the phone and tell his side of the story, and set the record straight. Except it wouldn't be that simple. They wouldn't believe him. She'd make fun of him, and say terrible things to him, and he'd get upset, and the thoughts would come back to him and he'd get caught doing something stupid. He couldn't afford to get caught.

But he couldn't afford to let people think those things about him, either. There was no harm in just a phone call, was there? If things got bad, he could always just hang up.

The phone was a cordless one, resting on the night-stand next to the radio. Nathan picked it up, pushed the ON button, and just sat there silently for a long while, staring at the handset. Finally, the dial tone changed to a horrid screeching sound that caused him to hang up quickly. Taking a deep breath, he pushed the button again and dialed The Bitch's 800 number. He noted the odd sound of the touch tones, which were all the same pitch. At home, he used to be able to play tunes with the tones. When he was done dialing, he brought the phone to his ear to hear an immediate busy signal.

Nathan felt relieved; the pressure was off. He had tried. Even though he had failed, trying was enough, vasn't it?

He listened to two minutes more of the radio and decided that no, it wasn't enough at all.

He dialed the number again. And again. And again. Each time, he got a fresh busy signal. On his ninth try, he heard some odd sounds in the handset, and had to stop himself from automatically pushing the flash and redial buttons. He had a rhythm going. Finally, the phone on the other end began to ring.

After what seemed to be a hundred rings, someone picked up on the other end. "You've reached the Bitch Line," the voice said. "What do you want to talk about?"

"I want to talk about this Nathan Bailey thing."

"Are you a kid? The Bitch doesn't talk to kids."

"I think she'll want to talk to me. I'm Nathan Bailey."

Denise was ready to shift gears again. They had been on the Nathan Bailey topic for the better part of forty-five minutes, and they had stopped receiving original input. Once the callers currently on lines one and four were taken care of, there would be a commercial break, and then they'd move on to some tidbits on the way the president was handling foreign affairs.

Gordon, a psychiatrist from Stockdale, Arizona, was on the line, babbling psychological double-talk about how children under fifteen don't have a strong enough system of values to make adult-level decisions regarding right and wrong. Denise smiled contentedly. When the good doctor paused to take a breath, she was going to eat him alive.

She had just opened her mouth to begin her meal when Enrique's excited voice popped in her earphones. "You've got to take the caller on line six," he said.

The look Denise fired to her producer should have melted the glass that separated them. One of the most basic, cardinal rules of talk radio was, never interrupt the host when she is talking—or about to talk.

Recognizing the look for what it was—a threat to his career—Enrique explained, "It's a kid claiming to be Nathan Bailey. *The* Nathan Bailey. I think he's telling the truth."

Denise completely lost her train of thought for a moment. If it was true, they could be on the verge of some terrific radio. After a pause that was long enough to make some of the audience wonder if their radios were broken, Denise regained her composure and dumped the doctor from the phone line. "Thanks, Doc, but that's about as much of that as I can handle. My kids are a hell of a lot younger than fifteen, and they have an excellent feel for what is right and what is wrong.

"Well, now, it would appear that we have a celebrity on the line, assuming that my producer is telling the truth." She made quite a show of pushing the button numbered six. "Nathan Bailey, are you there?"

"Yes, ma'am," said a small but strong voice from the other end. There was determination in the boy's husky voice. For years, Denise had prided herself in her ability to recognize personality traits just from listening to people's voices. This was the voice of a Boy Scout and Little League baseball player; the voice of someone who was honest. Denise instantly began to second-guess her conclusions about Nathan.

* * *

Michaels was already feeling the result of too little sleep, and the coffee he had consumed to compensate had formed an acid bath in his stomach that could etch glass. Without consciously realizing that it had made any noise, he picked up his phone after the first ring.

"Lieutenant Michaels."

"Michaels, this is Petrelli," the other voice said.

Oh, crap. "Good morning, J. Daniel. I see you were up early for the cameras."

Clearly agitated, Petrelli ignored the barb, which was uncharacteristic of him. "Turn on The Bitch," Petrelli barked.

"I beg your pardon?"

"The radio, dammit. Turn on The Bitch. The Bailey kid is on there talking to her right now!"

"Really?" Michaels was in no hurry. He knew he'd be able to catch whatever he missed by listening to one of the many tapes of the program that were being made by any number of police officers who would soon march them into their supervisors, making a show of how conscientious they'd been.

"Yeah, really," Petrelli growled. "Turn it on and listen. I'll call you when they're done."

CHAPTER TEN

NATHAN'S NERVOUSNESS DISAPPEARED as soon as he started talking. As he spoke on the phone, he paced a repeating course around the bedroom and the master bath. It seemed that when his feet were moving, so was his mind.

"Whatever happened to being innocent until proven guilty?" he demanded.

"Whatever happened to the sanctity of human life?" Although her voice was smooth and soothing, her manner was very abrupt, putting Nathan on edge.

"What does that mean?"

"That means that killing is wrong. Don't you think that killing is wrong?"

"Of course I do. But it's no wronger than getting killed. I don't remember you being there last night. You don't have any idea what went on in there."

"Did you kill the guard?"

Nathan's voice rose in volume and pitch with his frustration. "Yes, but . . ."

Denise cut him off. "No buts, Nathan. Stop right there. You killed the guard. What more is there to know?

You're on the run, boy. You're a fugitive, a hazard to our society. I don't want you on our streets. I want you under control, behind bars."

"There aren't any bars," Nathan corrected.

"What?"

"There aren't any bars. Just heavy doors. In Juvey, I mean."

"Don't change the subject, Nathan," Denise scolded. "Why don't you hang up the phone right now and call the police? Turn yourself in, before you or somebody else gets hurt."

Nathan sat back down on the corner of the bed. "I can't go back," he said matter-of-factly. "If I go back they'll just hurt me again. Or kill me. That's what Ricky was trying to do! I can't go back and just let them finish the job."

The line was silent again while Denise put it together. "Let me get this straight," she said. "You say that the guard was trying to kill *you*?"

"Yes, ma'am."

"And why would that be?"

"How the hell should I know?"

"Kids shouldn't cuss on the radio."

"Oh, sure, you're a fine one to talk. You can't even say your name without cussing."

Denise laughed. This was a pretty sharp kid she was dealing with. "Maybe that explains why we don't get too many kids calling in here."

Or maybe it's because what's-his-name said you don't talk to kids, Nathan didn't say.

"All right, Nathan," Denise said, "let's start over again. You say, in essence, that you killed the guard in self-defense."

"Yes. Right. Except they're not called guards. They're supervisors. You get in trouble if you call them guards."

"Well, the last thing I want to do is get in trouble with the supervisors." Denise was surprised to hear her own voice become warmer. There was something about this kid that was truly disarming. "Why don't I just shut up and listen. You tell us what actually happened last night."

Nathan propped himself on three pillows against the headboard of the big bed and stretched his feet out in front of him. "It's kind of hard to know where to start," he began. "I learned the hard way that I'd never get along with the other residents. Their idea of a good time was to beat the crap out of me and steal my stuff and, well, do really bad things to me. They'd steal my food and stuff like that. I tried to ignore them, you know? Like my dad used to tell me? But jeez, you gotta eat sometime. It got to the point where I had to snarf everything off my plate while I was still in the food line. For the first month I was there, they wouldn't let me alone. I tried fighting back, but I just got smeared."

"Why didn't you tell someone?" Denise interrupted.

Nathan snorted bitterly. "Yeah, right. I tried that once on my first day there. Big mistake. It was Ricky that I told, as a matter of fact. He's the guy that, well, you know . . . that I . . ." He just gathered up his strength and he said it. "I'm sorry, ma'am, I know I shouldn't have done what I did, but Ricky was a real dickhead. Um, sorry.

"Anyway, there's this area in the JDC where everybody gets together for school or basketball or just talking, or whatever. I was in there, trying to read, when Ricky came up to me and told me I had to come with him. I knew I was in trouble, but I didn't know why . . ."

For the next eighteen minutes, Nathan unraveled his side of the story for millions of radio listeners from coast to coast. He spoke articulately and with the kind of animation that only a child can generate. Denise interrupted only three times to clarify what he was saying, but otherwise sat silently, staring at her control board, envisioning in her own mind the events described by Nathan. By the time the boy was done, The Bitch was twelve commercials behind, but even the sponsors wouldn't complain. This was great radio.

Nathan had long since finished the books in the JDC library that were worth reading, preferring novels to the comic books favored by the other residents. That day being the Fourth of July, it seemed appropriate to reread April Morning *by Howard Fast, a story about a boy whose life is changed by the Battle of Lexington.*

The recreation hall was literally and figuratively the center of activity at the Juvenile Detention Center. Roughly hexagonal in shape and fabricated out of concrete block painted yellow-orange, the rec hall served all nonsleeping activities. Three glass-partitioned rooms served as makeshift classrooms during the day, with the largest of the rooms doubling as a dining hall. The detention cells extended down two hallways on opposite ends of the hexagon. From seven in the morning until eight at night, the doors to those hallways remained locked. By eight-thirty they were locked again, with their residents inside.

The sixth side of the hexagon was the control room, half-Lexan and half-concrete. When residents were in the rec hall, the control room was occupied. Reinforced doors on either side led to the administrative areas and to the Crisis Unit.

At around seven o'clock that night, Ricky entered the rec hall from the administrative section, walked directly over to Nathan, and lifted him out of the chair by his ear. "Come with me," he said.

Nathan yelped, "Ow! What'd I do?"

"You know what you did," Ricky hissed, his breath smelling of booze and cigarettes. He yanked Nathan across the rec hall toward the door on the other side of the control station. "Maybe a night in the Unit will teach you to draw on the walls."

Nathan hung onto Ricky's forearm with both hands and danced along on tiptoes to keep his ear from being ripped from his head. "Let go, Ricky, please," he pleaded. "I didn't do anything. Honest to God, Ricky, I didn't do anything!"

Ricky didn't reply, except to lift a little higher on the ear. All activity in the rec hall stopped as dozens of eyes watched the smallest resident of the JDC being dragged across the room by the man they all feared most. Each of them looked away as Nathan made eye contact with them, silently pleading for help that he knew they couldn't offer, even if they'd wanted to.

Ricky paused at the door to the Crisis Unit long enough to snap his key ring from his belt. As the lock turned, Nathan began to panic. The Crisis Unit was little more than a single cell, set apart from all the rest as a place where a resident in crisis could regain his composure and set his head straight. In reality, it was a place of punishment, where food or clothes or even light could be denied until such time as the resident was prepared to change his ways. Although it was rarely used, the Crisis Unit had a reputation among the residents. Nathan was terrified.

The lock turned, and the door opened. Nathan yelled louder still, crying like a baby, and promising not to be bad anymore. He started to grab the door-jamb, but had to return his hands to Ricky's wrist. "Ricky, you're hurting me!"

"If you yell one more time, you'll find out what hurt really means."

Once they were through the door, they were in an area of the JDC where Nathan had never been. The hallway was narrow, barely enough room for the door to swing open. Ricky changed his grip to Nathan's biceps and shoved the boy against the opposite wall, holding him in place with a stiff arm while he once again locked the door to the rec hall. Down to the left, maybe eight feet, the hallway opened up again slightly. Around an angled corner was the door marked with the dreaded words, "CRISIS UNIT."

Nathan renewed his struggle, pulling his arm from Ricky's grasp, only to be taken to the floor by his hair. Ricky followed him down to the ground and placed his mouth an inch from Nathan's ear. "Listen to me," he growled, droplets of spittle splashing against Nathan's cheek. "You're going in that room over there, one way or another, if I have to break bones to make it happen. Do you understand me?"

Nathan nodded, his face pressed against the tile floor. He tried to look at Ricky but couldn't focus through the tears in his eyes.

"And stop crying." He stood once again, keeping a tight hold on a fistful of Nathan's hair and dragging him down the short hallway. He one-handed the lock and half-shoved, half-tossed Nathan into the tiny cell.

The cell was surprisingly like Nathan's own quarters, though about half the size, with a metal cot and thin mattress on one side of the room, and a combination toilet and sink on the other. There was no source of outside light, the only illumination coming from a glaring bank of fluorescent lights set above the ceiling behind reinforced glass. The floor was bare concrete, without the tile he had in his own cell. And it was cold, much colder than the always-chilly residential wing.

"Take off your shoes and hand them to me," Ricky commanded.

"Why?"

"Do what I tell you, boy."

Nathan knew better than to argue. Nathan did as he was told, kicking off the standard-issue black sneakers without untying them. He handed the shoes over to Ricky with one hand while rubbing his sore ear with the other.

"And the socks."

"But it's cold in here."

Ricky just glared and held out his hand expectantly. Nathan slumped to the edge of the cot and started to cry again. He hated himself for giving in to the tears. No matter how hard he tried, he always ended up crying in front of these people, and the tears always inspired more cruelty.

One foot at a time, Nathan scooped off his socks and handed them to Ricky, who abruptly left, locking the door behind him. Nathan listened to the footsteps disappear down the hall.

"What did I do wrong?!" he shrieked, loudly enough that his ears rang from the echo off the concrete walls.

Cold, confused and miserable, Nathan drew his legs up and rested his forehead on his knees, forcing himself to regain his composure. A single swipe of his sleeve cleaned his eyes and nose. *Only ten more months,* he told himself. *Only ten more months, and I'm out of here. It's been eight months already. In half that time, it'll be a year, and after half of that, I get out. I can do this. Easy as pie.*

The trick, he had found, was to make the time go as quickly as possible; and no time passed more quickly than sleep. Keeping his knees up, Nathan lay on his side and tried to make his feet disappear into his coveralls for warmth.

"These people are such assholes," he said aloud.

The sound of a key in the lock awoke Nathan with a start. Though the light was on within his cell, he could tell through the three-by-five-inch observation window in the door that the hallway beyond it was dark. For a long while after the lock turned, nothing happened. Nathan sat up and brought his knees to his chest again. He remembered seeing a scene like this in a movie once, where the door creaked open and at first there was nothing there. But then, all of a sudden, a vampire appeared and made everybody scream in their seats.

It was a stupid thing to think about, he scolded himself. There were no such things as vampires, and that stuff in the movies was all made up anyway. They called it special effects, things that some brainiac engineers thought up just to scare people.

His dad had always chided him for imagining creatures and burglars in the dark. Though he told himself in those seconds when he sat on the bunk waiting for the door to open that there was nothing to be afraid of, the fear he felt was quite real. His heart pounded in his chest like a hammer on steel. His breathing started to get noisy. Should he get up and go to the door? Was somebody coming in? Maybe he had a friend in the JDC after all, and this was a signal that it was okay for him to walk out.

Nathan jumped again when the door finally started to move inward, revealing Ricky standing alone in the doorway. He was drunk. Or stoned. Nathan could tell by the empty look in his eyes. It was the look that always preceded the beatings from Uncle Mark. Ricky was hiding something in his right hand, keeping it just out of sight behind his back. The look in his eyes got even emptier.

Nathan knew something was going to happen. For the first time in his life, he felt that his life was threatened. Without thinking, and without changing his position on the bed, he rolled his weight to the balls of his feet. He had an idea there was going to be a fight, and while he wasn't much of a fighter, something in Ricky's face told him that this would be the fight of his life—for his life.

Ricky entered the room slowly and smiled oddly. "You never really belonged here, you know. Sooner or later the others would have killed you anyway."

Anyway? Nathan's mind raced now. Did he say anyway? That meant . . .

Ricky halved the distance between them in a single step.

Nathan reacted by pressing himself against the block wall. He was cornered.

"I'll try not to make it hurt too bad," Ricky said, his weird smile getting broader. "You ever cleaned a fish?"

Nathan stared at Ricky's hidden right hand. Sure, he had cleaned a lot of fish. You start with a sharp knife low in their bellies, and then split them open up to the head. You let their guts slide out onto the table. Then . . .

Nathan looked desperately for a way to dash around Ricky. It was easy to outmaneuver a drunk; he had proven that a hundred times with Uncle Mark, though there was always hell to pay later. But the cell was so small and Ricky was so big that there was nowhere to duck and dash to get around him.

He saw the knife. If Ricky had acted quickly and just lashed out, it would have ended right there. He was certainly close enough. But Ricky had chosen drama over efficiency, waving the knife around in front of Nathan's face. "What do you think it's gonna feel like . . ."

Nathan didn't hesitate. Bracing his back against the wall, he shot his leg straight out, driving his heel squarely into Ricky's testicles. Ricky staggered a half-step, then slumped to his knees. Nathan attempted to vault over Ricky's stooped shoulders, but the cot moved as he pushed off and he only made it halfway, his knees contacting Ricky's head and making them both tumble to the ground. Before he could get fully to his feet, Nathan felt a strong hand around his wrist, pulling him back down to the floor.

"*Let go!*" *Nathan yelled, launching another kick, this one impacting Ricky's nose and making a loud crunch.*

Ricky's hold on the boy's wrist weakened, but it didn't break. Nathan tried another kick, but this time missed completely, losing his balance and falling back down to the floor. Ricky was bleeding profusely from both nostrils, and as he struggled to catch his breath, he blew a bloody mist into the air. "I'm gonna cut your head off," Ricky hissed.

The knife came down at Nathan in a wide, powerful arc from above. Using his free hand, Nathan was able to deflect the trajectory just enough to make it miss, absorbing most of the energy in his elbow. The knife hand recoiled for another strike, but Nathan held onto the wrist, causing Ricky to let go of Nathan's own wrist. Using both hands now, Nathan concentrated his whole struggle on the hand with the knife, slowing down his assailant's motion and limiting his ability to get a good stroke.

When the knife was back to the top of its arc, Nathan pulled himself up on his knees and lunged at Ricky's knife hand with his teeth. He bit down as hard as he could on Ricky's clenched fist, and he could feel the skin break and little bones give way to his incisors. The taste of blood filled his mouth, but he ignored it.

Ricky howled like a dog when the pain registered. He waved his arm wildly, trying to break Nathan's grip, but the teeth only sank deeper, until he finally let go of the knife, allowing it to drop to the floor. "Goddammit!" In one smooth motion, Ricky swung Nathan close, then drove a pistonlike punch into the boy's right eye.

Nathan felt an explosion in his brain. He had never been hit that hard, and the impact of the punch sent him reeling against the cot, knocking it on its side. For a full five seconds, Nathan and Ricky stared at each other, allowing some of the agony to drain from their bodies. Then, together, they eyed the knife on the floor, and together they lunged for it.

Nathan had told himself a million times: a sober kid can outmaneuver a drunk adult any day of the week. And the Fourth of July was no exception. He snatched the knife from the concrete and whirled around in a backhanded slashing motion designed to make Ricky jump back.

But just as offensive moves are slowed by alcohol, so are defensive ones. Unable to react quickly enough to protect himself, Ricky seemed to watch dumbly as the blade came around in a horizontal arc and buried itself to the hilt in his abdomen.

Nathan felt as shocked as Ricky looked as the knife drove itself home. Ricky fell straight back, like a tree, his lower legs folding under his butt, and his head impacting loudly against the concrete.

"I'm sorry!" Nathan shouted. "Oh, God, Ricky, I'm sorry!"

Ricky didn't respond; he just stared at the ceiling. His hands gently massaged the handle of the knife, as though he was thinking of pulling it out, but couldn't muster the courage.

Nathan didn't know what to do. But he knew that if he didn't do something, the man would die. Ricky seemed obsessed with the knife; maybe he should pull it out for him. That would make him feel better. Nathan looked over his shoulder toward the door, in hopes that someone might have miraculously arrived with the answers. No, he was going to have to do this on his own. He moved hesitantly closer to the knife, closed his eyes, and pulled it free of the wound.

As the knife pulled clear of the wound, Nathan was splashed with a torrent of blood from the gaping wound. The sound from Ricky's throat was inhuman, half moan and half howl. His breath gurgled in his throat, like the sound of blowing bubbles through a straw.

Nathan knew right away that removing the knife was a mistake. Instinctively, he put his hands over the wound to try to stop the blood from spurting out, but it was useless; the gore pumped relentlessly from Ricky's belly, and now from his mouth as well.

"Oh, God, I'm sorry, Ricky," Nathan said over and over again, mantralike. In his heart, he knew he had killed him.

Out of nowhere, Ricky's hand shot up to Nathan's throat and shut off his air supply. For what felt like the hundredth time that night, Nathan locked his hands around Ricky's wrist, trying to make him let go. But, like a mouse caught in an eagle's talon, Nathan was trapped, feeling that his head was going to explode from the pressure. Ricky's eyes showed murder. He was going to die, and he was going to take Nathan with him.

The knife! It was still on the floor! Nathan ventured a hand away from Ricky's wrist, and found the blade an inch from his knee. This time, it would be no accident. Nathan mustered all the strength he had left to straight-arm the knife into Ricky's chest. He struck over and over again, each impact making a grotesque slurping sound. After the second thrust, Ricky's grip relaxed a little, once again allowing air and blood to flow to Nathan's brain. After the fifth, Ricky let go completely, and with a last rattling breath, he died.

Nathan panicked. The Crisis Unit looked like a house of horrors. A supervisor was dead, and they were going to blame him. Sure as hell, there would be nothing that he'd be able to say to anyone to make them believe that Ricky had started it.

Say good-bye to a ten-month release. No sirree, baby, killing a supervisor was about the worst crime there was. They'd throw his young butt in jail until he was twenty-one, if he could get out even then.

No, staying there and facing the music was not an option. Nathan had to get the hell out of the Juvenile Detention Center. He had to run fast, run hard, and run now. But he'd need keys to get out. Tiptoeing through the river of gore on the floor, Nathan pulled the key ring off Ricky's belt and darted out of the room, locking the door behind him.

From there it was easy. Every key he needed was right there on the ring. The door at the end of the hallway to the left led him into the area he recognized from his first night as the in-processing area. Nathan briefly considered rummaging through the storage closet for the clothes they had stolen from him eight months before, but he decided that every second spent inside the building was a second closer to getting caught. Moving swiftly and silently, he glided past the one-armed chair with the built-in handcuff, next to the desk where that fat fart Gonzalez asked new arrivals endless questions to which he already knew the answers.

The final door was the easiest; Nathan picked the right key the first time. He opened it only a crack at first, praying there wouldn't be a cop or a supervisor on the other side. Again, luck was with him. He slipped through the opening, locked the door from the outside, and tossed the keys into the bushes. Ahead of him lay fifty feet of open grass, leading up a tall hill, and beyond that, freedom. He covered the distance in nothing flat.

Pausing for just a moment at the top of the hill, Nathan looked back at the JDC. Though the elevation changed his perspective, the view was exactly the same as when he had first arrived so long ago. It looked like such a friendly place, constructed of ornamental brick and stone and adorned with pretty flowers and shrubs. Yet, on the inside, the Brookfield Juvenile Detention Center was a garden for hatred. The seeds planted within its walls grew well, nurtured and cultivated by the likes of Ricky and Gonzalez.

From atop this hill, overlooking the entire compound, Nathan swore to himself that he would never allow himself to be confined within those walls again.

". . . and so I started running," Nathan finished. He was lying on his stomach now, resting on his elbows and tracing the wood grain of the headboard with his finger.

"So, are you all right?" Denise asked, genuine concern evident in her voice.

"I guess so. My eye hurts some and my ear is sore as hell, but other than that I think I'm okay."

"Do you have any idea at all why the supervisor would want to kill you?" As unbelievable as the kid's story was, Denise believed him.

"Yeah, I think he was crazy. He was drunk. He was stoned. Grown-ups always get like that when they drink."

"Grown-ups like whom?" Denise prodded, sensing a new wrinkle to this extraordinary saga. "Like your father?"

"No." Nathan's reply was startlingly emphatic. "My dad was a good man. He'd never drink or hit anyone. He was terrific."

"What about your mother?"

His voice softened. "I never met my mom. She died when I was just a baby."

There was another avenue to pursue. Denise jotted a note on a legal pad. "So, did anyone in your life beat you?"

"I don't want to talk about that."

"Why not? It might help if people understood some of what you've gone through."

"Bull. People want to think that everybody lives like those perfect families on TV. If I tell them different, they'll just think I'm lying. They can yell and scream and hit their kids, and that's okay, so long as the kid keeps it quiet. But if he hits back, or tries to leave, they call you incorrigible and throw your butt in jail."

"Is that how you ended up in jail? Did you hit back?"

Nathan thought back to all the fights at Uncle Mark's house. He pictured the comical lumbering stride Uncle Mark had when he was drunk, and the numbers of books and utensils and appliances that had been flung across the room, only to miss hitting Nathan not by inches but by feet. He nearly laughed at his memory of the stupid, gaping look on the drunk's face. But then he remembered the leather cowboy belt, and the sound it made when it contacted the bare flesh of his backside, and the traces of humor were gone, snatched out of his soul just as Uncle Mark had snatched all the humor out of his life. Through it all, though, Nathan had known better than to hit back. That would have been his last act in life if he had ever tried it.

Maybe I should tell her everything, Nathan thought. Maybe he should tell her how he once did live a normal life; how his dad had raised him in a nice house in a nice neighborhood, just the two of them. Maybe he should tell millions of people that only three days after Dad's funeral, Uncle Mark locked him in the crawl space under the living room just for grins, and how he only got out by making such a racket that the asshole saw the neighbors looking out their windows.

Surely the audience would enjoy hearing that his screams for help had earned him his first belt licking. Maybe he should tell all those people listening in their cozy houses and offices and cars how Uncle Mark used to like parties with all his druggie friends, and how some of those friends, men and women alike, used to come into his bedroom and touch him in places where kids weren't supposed to be touched.

There were so many things that he could tell, but he wouldn't. There was nothing there that he hadn't already told judges and lawyers and police officers. And all that confiding had certainly cut him a great big fat break, hadn't it?

"No," Nathan answered at length, "I didn't hit any-body back. I stole a car."

Denise was flabbergasted. "You're twelve years old, and you stole a car?"

"Actually, I was eleven when I stole the car." There was a trace of pride in his answer.

"And why did you do that?"

"I don't want to talk about that, either."

"Why not?"

"Because it's nobody's business."

"But that's why you got sent to the detention cen-ter?"

"Yeah, except call it what it is—a jail."

Was it possible that she was admiring this kid? This killer? There was something in the directness of his an-swers that struck a chord with her. It was within his power to lie about things he didn't want to discuss, but he chose instead to not answer the question. He was sharp, all right. And he was apparently facing some-thing that had more layers than she had first thought.

"So, what's the end of the story?" Denise asked. "Where did you run to? Where are you now?"

Nathan sighed. "I don't think it would be real smart to tell you that, do you?" Grown-ups just couldn't help trying to trick you. He gasped as a terrifying thought jumped into his mind. "Oh my God, can they trace this call?" He suddenly sounded panicky.

"No, no," Denise assured him. "This is a radio sta-tion. As long as there's a First Amendment, no one can trace our calls."

"You sure?"

Denise looked to Enrique, who was no help. "Sure

I'm sure," she guessed with a shrug. At least it sounded like the reasonable answer. She shifted back to the subject at hand. "So, what are you going to do next? You can't just keep running."

"Why not?"

Denise started to answer, but stopped. She really didn't know why not. "Because you'll get caught."

"Well, my only other choice is to turn myself in. How is that any different than getting caught?"

"Nathan, I'm just afraid you'll get hurt."

"Yeah, me too. That's why I'm gonna keep running."

This kid was good. "You're making a fool of me out here, Nathan," she said.

"No, you're doing fine," Nathan comforted. "But you see my side now, don't you? When I was in Juvey, I did everything I was supposed to do and got the crap beat out of me. I turned the other cheek, just like I was supposed to, and they just beat me up some more. I tell the supervisor, and he tries to kill me. I defend myself, and the people who listen to your show call me a murderer and want to put me in the electric chair. Nobody really . . ." His voice caught in his throat. He fell silent. The silence lasted a long time.

"Cares?" Denise helped.

Nathan's lower lip was trembling now, and he hated himself for losing control on national radio. He'd felt so together at the beginning, but suddenly a terrible sadness poured over him, like a bucket of lukewarm water. "Yes," he whispered.

Denise's eyes welled up unexpectedly at the sound of the tiny voice. "You're frightened, aren't you, honey?"

"I've got to go," he croaked. He hung up.

In the dead air that followed, Denise looked to Enrique for guidance, but he just stared back.

"Well," Denise said at length, "that was something. Nathan, if you're still listening, we wish you all the luck in the world, however this turns out. Sounds to me like maybe you're due for some. I think everybody needs a minute or two to regain their composure. We'll be back after these messages."

CHAPTER ELEVEN

PETRELLI WAS ON THE LINE five seconds after the radio conversation ended. He must have had the number programmed into his speed-dial.

"That lying son of a bitch is pandering for public sympathy," he railed at Michaels. "The issue of whether or not he was treated well in Juvey has no bearing on this case whatsoever. What matters is that he escaped from a detention facility, and he killed a supervisor to do it! His act's good enough to take on the road."

This tantrum, like so many others Petrelli had unleashed against Michaels over the years, was bullshit. Warren knew that Petrelli couldn't have cared less about an escapee on the street, or about the deaths of a hundred supervisors. The issue here was the fact that J. Daniel had taken to the airwaves with partial information, convicting a minor of a capital crime even before the evidence was collected. In this oh-so-important election year, the county prosecutor suddenly stood a very good chance of looking less like a tough-on-crime law enforcer than a child abuser. Warren knew that these rantings on the phone were just the first act in a long drama of posturings and spin controls that would attempt to explain to the press how he never really said what they had all heard him say just a few hours earlier.

For reasons that Michaels could never understand, it was important to Petrelli that all bad guys be portrayed as sociopaths whose actions were irrational. He had no tolerance for extenuating circumstances that might have driven the criminals to behave the way they did. His obsession with dehumanizing lawbreakers pushed him to be the first to the microphones with a hard-line prosecution strategy. His approach had certainly served his career well, but Michaels, as cynical as he himself had become, couldn't help feeling sorry once in a while for the poor bad guy.

In the case of Nathan Bailey, Michaels didn't know what to believe. Prisons of all sorts, whether built for adults or for children, were inherently violent places, occupied by criminals with violent pasts and staffed by personnel whose primary function was to quell violence. It didn't stretch his imagination at all to envision a staff member becoming homicidal. As unlikely as Nathan's story was, the boy's presentation of the facts was too detailed, too articulate, to be written off as a complete lie. Indeed, if it weren't for the fact that Ricky Harris was dead, Michaels might have been inclined to launch a second felony investigation.

Yet, even if he accepted Nathan's claim that he had killed in self-defense, it was still true that the boy had broken the law when he escaped from the Juvenile Detention Center, and he remained a fugitive from justice. As a law enforcement officer, Michaels's obligation to apprehend the escapee had not changed one whit. While he agreed with The Bitch that the kid was due a little luck in his life, Michaels would continue to turn the area inside out until Nathan was caught. He'd also continue reminding his patrol officers and detectives that a prisoner capable of killing once was capable of killing a second time.

For Michaels, the most telling and convincing words the boy spoke on the radio were his vow never to return to the JDC. They were the words of desperation; and desperate people were known to do foolish things, even in the face of outrageous odds. Nathan still was a very dangerous young man indeed.

On the other end of the phone line, J. Daniel Petrelli had built a much more complicated world for himself than the one in which Warren Michaels lived. In addition to considerations of mere guilt and innocence, Petrelli had to consider how each prosecution would play in the press, constantly weighing the political impact of every win and every loss. There were times when pollsters in his employ could barely keep up with the changing tides of investigations. The perceived guilt of any defendant was a key element in determining how public and how aggressive the pursuit of a guilty verdict would be.

This morning, it had seemed so clear in the Bailey case. People were sick and tired of being frightened of out-of-control kids, and the blatant and willful murder of a corrections official by an escaping convict had been more than the public could bear. Rarely had there been such an opportunity to show strong leadership in the Commonwealth's Attorney's office.

True, the initial stages of the investigation *had* begun to unearth some dirt on Ricky Harris, but Petrelli and his staff had already devised a strategy whereby any leaks about violence in the detention facility would be made a secondary issue. It would be stressed that no child had the right to take the life of a corrections officer just because he claimed to be frightened.

Who in the world would have thought that the kid would take his case directly to the people on a nationally syndicated radio show? The kid's performance was perfect. It was still way too early to have any hard polling numbers, but there was no doubt what they would show. Americans loved the underdog, even underdogs who killed. In twenty short minutes, Nathan Bailey had placed the police and the prosecutors on the defensive.

Petrelli saw it all so clearly. The Bailey kid had been incarcerated by a judge for stealing his uncle's car, and for being declared incorrigible. He was to have remained in detention for eighteen months. He had taken it upon himself to unlawfully leave the Juvenile Detention Center, and in the process killed a supervisor. He was a thief, a jailbreaker and a murderer, and he deserved to be punished to the fullest extent of the law.

But Petrelli knew, even before the first polling question was asked, that all the public would see was a small, beaten boy being pursued and outnumbered by big bad cops. Petrelli was reminded of *The Fugitive*. Everyone knew from the outset that Richard Kimble was a fugitive from the law, and that Lieutenant Gerard was just doing his job, but who did everyone see as the villain?

The senator-to-be was sitting on the edge of a public

relations nightmare, and he held Michaels responsible. If the police hadn't botched the response, the kid would have been reincarcerated before dawn. Now he'd been on the run all night, and he had done incalculable damage to a political career in its infancy.

"Listen to this carefully, Lieutenant Michaels, because I will only say it once. I expect you to apprehend Nathan Bailey by this afternoon at the latest. And I don't want to hear any excuses!"

That was it. Michaels had been able to tolerate Petrelli's rantings to this point, busying himself with other trivial tasks on his desk. But the prosecutor had crossed the line.

"All right, J. Daniel, I've listened carefully," Warren said in measured tones, "and I guarantee you'll only say it once. Here's how I see it: You just couldn't wait to open your big mouth this morning and make wholly unjustified comments to the press. I'm the cop, J., you're the mouthpiece. If you'd have waited for us to collect evidence before you rested your case, you wouldn't be looking like such an asshole now. My heart bleeds for you.

"Personally, I don't give a rat's ass who's elected senator this year. I probably won't even vote. All I care about is doing my job. Save your speeches for the press, J. And stay off my phone!"

He slammed the receiver onto the cradle. *Damn, that felt good.*

"Feel better?"

The familiar voice startled him. When Michaels

looked up, he saw Jed Hackner's form filling the doorway. "Jesus, Jed, I don't need a heart attack today."

Hackner smiled, helping himself to one of the straight-backed chairs in front of Michaels's desk. "Talking to your buddy Petrelli?"

"You got it. He's beginning to panic after Nathan Bailey's radio debut. Did you hear it?"

Hackner nodded. "Yeah. Well, most of it. I missed the first couple of minutes. He sounded pretty convincing to me. Overall, I think Petrelli's got reason to panic. He made the kid sound like young John Dillinger, when Oliver Twist might have been a better choice."

Michaels smiled wryly. "Yeah, well, I don't remember little Oliver killing any law enforcement personnel." He changed the subject. "I don't suppose you have any good news for me."

"Well, I don't know if it's good or not, but it certainly is interesting."

Michaels's thick eyebrows raised in anticipation.

"First of all, we haven't been able to contact the kid's uncle and ex-guardian, Mark Bailey. We tried on the phone; even sent a unit around, but if he was home, he wasn't answering the door."

"You think he helped in the escape?"

"Not likely. There's not a lot of love lost between the two of them." Hackner removed the notebook from his pocket and started reading. "This all comes from the Juvey files. Judge Potter unsealed them for us this morning. Kind of a sad story, really. For the first ten years of his life, Nathan Bailey was raised by his father. His mother died when he was just a baby. Daddy was a lawyer with lots of bucks, but not much in the way of estate planning. Two years ago, Daddy's car got whacked by a train, killing him. With no provisions for who was gonna take care of Nathan, custody went to Uncle Mark, way down in the Jackson's Corner area. Apparently Mark thought that the kid would be supported by a trust fund, but Daddy had just sunk two-plus million into his practice, secured against every asset he owned. By the time his estate cleared probate, there was nothing left.

"Needless to say, Uncle Mark was not a happy camper. Not only did he have custody, but he had no way of paying for Nathan's upkeep. So, he didn't. Social Services was out to the house a half-dozen times over the year Nathan was there, responding mostly to neighbor complaints, but nothing ever came of it. Finally, about a year ago, Nathan stole his uncle's car, claiming that it was the only way he could get far enough away from the son of a bitch. Of course, Uncle Mark pressed charges. Record shows that Judge Potter offered a sweetheart of a probation deal, but Uncle Mark didn't want to hear it. He told the court, and I quote, 'A little time in prison never hurt anyone.'"

"Nice guy," Michaels snorted.

"No, he's not," Jed corrected, very serious. "Mark Bailey knows whereof he speaks, having logged seven years at Leavenworth for burning down an officers' club in Texas. In the eight years he's been in the county, he's had three DWIs, two disorderly conducts, and an assault and battery charge that was dropped when the victim had a change of heart about testifying. He's also logged about a million bar fights, almost all of them on the losing end."

Michaels was incredulous. "Did Social Services know about all this when they assigned custody to him?"

Hackner shrugged. "I guess so. To be honest, there really wasn't much of a choice. It was either Uncle Mark or foster care."

Michaels shook his head slowly, briefly pushing aside his cynical cop's perspective and seeing it as a father would. "Tough breaks for a little kid."

Jed flipped a page in his notebook. "Yeah, well, it gets worse. Two different psychiatrists, paid for by Daddy's lawyer friends, submitted petitions to the court for the kid to be kept out of the Juvey system, claiming that the emotional stress would be too much for him." Hacker held up a yellow sheet of paper. "Report here says the two docs claimed the kid 'lags behind his peers physically and emotionally.' But you know Judge Potter. He feels for the kids whose cases he hears, but if you've broken the law, you're gonna pay. So he shipped Nathan, who'd just turned twelve, up to Brookfield and put him in the general population. He arrived on a Wednesday afternoon. Wednesday night, he's gang-raped with a broom handle and has to spend a week in the infirmary."

Michaels winced and held up his hand. "That's enough. I don't want to hear any more. Is the rest just gossip, or does it have any real bearing on the case?"

Jed shrugged, his feelings hurt. He was a cop, not a columnist. He didn't deal in gossip; every detail had a bearing on a case. But he had known Warren long enough to know his meaning. He flipped his notebook closed. "No, I suppose that's about it. But there is more news."

"And what might that be?"

"Turns out we've got a videotape after all."

"I thought the camera was broken."

"The camera in the Crisis Unit was. But we were able to catch Master Bailey on his way out through the in-processing area."

"Were other cameras working, too?"

"Not all of them. The rec hall camera was off-line as well. All the others seem to be in good shape. But the Bailey kid only passed through that one zone. Plus, we've got another couple of seconds of him exiting the back door. You want to see the tape? I've got it set up in the conference room."

Both men rose together, Michaels following Hackner out of the office. The squad room beyond the glass partitions of Warren's office was crammed with twice the number of desks it was designed to contain, providing space not only for Michaels's eight subordinate detectives and the clerical staff, but also for three building inspectors, a probation officer, and a displaced Welfare staffer who never seemed to move up on the priority list for space at her own agency. Wedged into a third-floor corner of the forty-year-old Civil Defense Building, the view from the windows was dominated by the Adult Detention Center on one side and a sprawling magnolia tree on the other.

"So how come the only cameras that weren't working were the ones we needed to see?" Michaels asked, navigating a serpentine route through the maze of desks.

Hackner shrugged. "Pretty convenient, isn't it?"

"I want you to look into that angle, okay, Jed? I

want to know if somebody helped him. Start with the uncle."

Hackner agreed. "I've already got Thompkins trolling that line."

They entered the conference room opposite Warren's office and closed the door. The television was on, the tape cued. With the press of a button, the image on the TV screen wiggled and danced while the heads in the VCR took up the slack. In the fuzzy black-and-white shadows typical of security cameras, Michaels watched an empty room he recognized from the night before as the in-processing area. From the upper right-hand corner of the screen, a boy appeared, looking ridiculous in a hugely oversized pair of coveralls. He looked frightened; his movements were simultaneously quick and hesitant. He was barefoot. His clothes were smeared with what could have been ink, or even chocolate syrup in the colorless image, but what everyone knew was his victim's blood.

"Stop the tape," Michaels commanded. An instant later, the boy on the screen stopped, his legs slightly skewed from his torso, a fuzzy electronic line bisecting the two halves. "Bailey said on the radio that the guard—the supervisor—took away his shoes. Why did he do that? Is that standard practice?"

Hackner shook his head. "Don't know for sure yet, but I don't think so. If we believe Bailey's story on the radio, could be that Harris was just trying to be nasty. I'm meeting with Johnstone this afternoon to find out what I can."

Michaels motioned with a nod. "Go ahead. Start the tape again."

The boy's body became whole again, and he darted straight for the camera, looking over alternating shoulders with every step. He moved like a dog encountering a shadow in the night, not sure whether to stand and fight or to run away. The boy on the screen was visibly startled when he noticed the camera. He turned completely around, presumably checking to see who would be following him.

When Nathan turned back to the camera, Michaels's heart stopped beating for just the briefest of moments. The expression in Nathan's eyes was one he had seen before.

"Stop the tape!"

The command was louder this time. The body was cut in half again, more severely this time, but the face and eyes were untouched by the interference. Nathan's eyes spoke of fear and uncertainty, the wrinkled brow showing greater age than the smooth features should allow. Beyond the blood and the fear was the face of a young boy begging for help.

Michaels had seen that very expression dozens of times from the face of another insecure, introverted twelve-year-old who'd once depended upon him for so much, but now was silent forever. An image flashed though his mind of that other boy's face—now expressionless—reclining against a satin pillow, looking so uncomfortable in an ill-fitting suit, a ridiculous gap around the shirt collar. So confined in a narrow box.

Michaels felt suddenly light-headed and lowered himself clumsily into a chair at the conference table. His face was drained of color.

Hackner reached out to help his friend into the chair. "My God, Warren, are you all right?"

Michaels thought he shook his head, but in reality didn't move. "I don't know, Jed." His eyes never left the screen. His throat was thick. "Look at his face, Jed. Look. He's got Brian's eyes."

Jed saw it, too. The likeness was remarkable, though not so much in the eyes as in the expression. He felt awful for not catching it during his previous viewings of the tape. He could have warned Warren up front, or even avoided that portion of the tape. Jed felt genuine pain for him.

"I'm so sorry, Warren," Hackner said. "I'll turn it off."

"No, don't," Michaels said firmly, having regained his composure before ever really losing it. "Jeez, Jed, I thought I was past it. I can't keep reacting like that. I'm okay. Let's watch the rest of it."

Jed kept a careful eye on his boss as he restarted the tape. Once again, the electronic image melded together, just long enough for the boy to slip quickly out of the frame. There was a quick editing blip on the screen, and then they were looking at the exterior of the exit. In the foreground were a portion of the driveway and a short sidewalk. In the background was a door, which opened slowly to reveal the hero of this little television drama as he slipped out of the door, relocked it, and then sprinted out of the picture. One more blip, and the screen was blank.

Neither man said anything for a long moment while Hackner thumbed the power button and killed the television. "Well, boss, what do you think?"

Michaels sighed loudly, rubbing his face with both hands. "I think I wish I hadn't watched it. That tape's going to make my job a lot harder. Does the press have it yet?"

"What, are you kidding? Petrelli's hounds were all over that tape like flies on dog crap. He's got a movie of a blood-soaked murderer. My guess is they had it to the news stations even before we had copies made."

Michaels chuckled softly. "I don't know about you, Jed, but what I saw looked less like a murderer than a frightened puppy." He could just imagine the look on Petrelli's face the first time he viewed the tape and realized that his minions had already turned it over to the press. It wasn't going to be pretty, but Warren would have paid a hundred dollars just to be there.

"J. Daniel's going to shit pickles."

With the briefest movement of his head, Michaels returned to the business at hand: catching the whipped puppy who was making Petrelli sweat so much. Rising abruptly out of his chair, he led the two-person parade back toward his office. "One thing I want you to check up on, Jed, is the telephone records to that radio show. Every time a call is made to an 800 number it's got to be logged into a computer somewhere. I want you to tap into that computer and find out the number where that call originated. We'll trace it and get the kid back home."

Hackner moaned. He had done similar searches before, most recently for a fraud case, only to be inundated with hundreds of telephone numbers, each of which had to be checked. The case he recalled was an investigation of a small consulting business, and that investigation had taken a week to complete. The Bitch had a nationwide audience, attracting probably a thousand calls an hour. There weren't enough police officers in the world to complete that kind of investigation in anything close to a reasonable time.

"We'll need a court order," Jed stalled. "We won't stand a chance against a radio station."

"Get them to volunteer the information," Warren suggested without breaking his stride. "Be persuasive. You know, invaluable service to their community, that sort of thing."

"They'll never buy it, Warren."

Michaels stopped abruptly. Jed missed a collision by inches. "Look, Jed, we've got a job to do, and so far we haven't been doing it. We don't have a clue where this kid went, so don't tell me what we can't do until we've at least tried, okay? You were at the meeting this morning, and I think I was pretty clear. I want Nathan Bailey in custody tonight. Understand?"

Jed sensed that the others in the squad room were desperately trying not to hear. He turned and left without saying a word.

Five minutes later, Michaels left as well, telling his secretary that he could be reached on his cell phone.

CHAPTER TWELVE

OVER THE LAST FIVE YEARS, Denise Carpenter had interviewed hundreds of guests, ranging from the famous to the infamous, but never had she received such a response as the one generated by her conversation with Nathan. Her plans to discuss the president's foreign policy would have to wait for another day. The lines were so jammed that other 800 numbers with the same three-digit exchange were unable to receive calls, creating a nightmare of enormous proportions for the phone company.

On the other side of the glass, Enrique was struggling to manage the tidal wave of calls, coaxing those who'd been on hold for over an hour to hang in there while screening the few additional callers who'd been able to get through. For Enrique, the universe of callers fell neatly into only two categories: sincere and crackpot. His job was to make sure that the only people who got to talk on the air with Denise were stating their legitimate beliefs, and were able to remain topical. This was not the time to discuss the moral aspects of capital punishment, as Maureen from Seattle had wanted; nor was it the time to discuss the weaknesses of the foster care system in Des Moines, as Charlie had wanted to do. In practice, it was impossible to keep callers on the topic once they started talking, but that was okay, so long as they started out on the right track.

Then there were the sickos. Like William from Bakersfield, who wanted to point out the most efficient ways to kill with a knife, or Paula from Bangor, Maine, who wanted to see Nathan hoisted slowly by a noose so that he could suffer the way he had made Ricky suffer.

Enrique's job was to find a trace of sanity among a group of listeners who seemed to exhibit that trait only rarely. Once found, he then had to convince them to hang on the line while Denise spoke to each of them in turn. What most callers didn't realize was that the talk radio business was not first come, first served. Once they made it past Enrique, he entered their names, cities of origin, and a brief description of what they wanted to talk about into a computer terminal on his side of the window, which simultaneously displayed the information on a screen on Denise's side. She then made the decision, sometimes arbitrarily, as to which callers would be spoken to first. He'd make suggestions, but she'd listen to him only about half the time. It was not unusual for a caller to remain on hold for the entire four hours of the show, only to be told thanks but no thanks. That job, of course, also fell on Enrique.

Enrique had met The Bitch when she was still a program assistant, and even thought for a brief while that he was in love with her. She'd just broken up with her husband, and Enrique had had exceptionally strong shoulders to cry on. As Denise's career blossomed and she healed emotionally, he tried dozens of times to summon the courage to ask her out, but he could never make the words form in his throat. They were "just friends"—intensely dear friends. Like brother and sister.

As Denise rose to stardom, Enrique followed closely behind in producerdom, each day engineering the opportunities for his boss to sound great on the air. The Bitch was a hit in syndication for two reasons: First, because Denise was the most talented on-air personality that he had ever seen, and second, because he was the best producer in the business. It wasn't bragging if it was true.

But even the best in the business couldn't keep up with this volume of calls. On his side of the window, there was total bedlam; on hers, total silence, pierced only by the sound of her own voice. People often asked Enrique if he got jealous, him doing all the work and Denise getting all the credit. His answer was always the same, and completely honest. There was no room for jealousy on a team. And in a business measured by individual achievement, theirs was the only real team around.

A tap on his shoulder startled Enrique. He turned to see one of the summer interns standing next to him, holding a pink telephone message slip. Annoyed at the interruption, Enrique pulled one earphone away from his head. "What is it, Tim? We're in the middle of a show here."

"Uh, it's, uh, *Tom,* sir."

Enrique's reply was a silent look that eloquently stated how little he cared what the hell Tom's name was. NewsTalk 990 worked their summer interns like slaves, allowing them to hang around the station for no pay, in return for the privilege of working twelve to eighteen hours per day. The station did it because it was free labor. The students did it because they knew there was a line a hundred deep just waiting to take the places of people who were stupid enough to put sleep or a social life ahead of their dreams of broadcast stardom.

"It's, uh, the police, sir," Tom stammered. "They want to talk to you on the hotline. They say it's very important."

"Quit calling me sir, you moron. This isn't a ship. Tell them we're in the middle of a show. I'll call them back when we're done." He moved to replace the earphone, but Tom's body language told him there was more. "What's wrong?"

Tom shifted his feet uneasily. "Well, I already tried that, and they said something about obstruction of justice charges."

Enrique looked as though he'd just been slapped. "Obstruction of—*Shit!* That's exactly what I need right now," he said through clenched jaws. "Okay, fine. I'll take it in here." Dismissing Tom by turning his back on him, Enrique angrily snatched the phone from its hook.

"This is Enrique Zamora, can I help you?" His tone sounded anything but helpful.

Patrolman II Harold Thompkins of the Braddock County Police Department was determined to be noticed. After five years of rotating shifts, traffic stops, and every conceivable piece of grunt work, he was ready to try some real police work. Even as a little kid, watching *Columbo* and *McMillan & Wife,* Harry knew that he'd be a detective one day. He was willing to pay his dues, work his way through the ranks. So far, he'd punched all the right tickets, getting his Associate's degree in Criminology before applying to the Academy, and busting his balls to graduate at the top of his class. He took the detective's exam at his first opportunity, just two weeks after his fifth anniversary with the department, and, true to form, finished in the top three percentiles. Problem was, he was a healthy white Christian of European ancestry who was too young to have gone to Vietnam, and at this particular time in his department's history, that put him at a significant disadvantage.

What he needed was an opportunity to shine on the job, not just in the classroom. He needed the big success. He needed to find just the right piece of evidence or uncover just the right lead to break a big case. He'd studied the rise of other officers in his situation, and it was clear as crystal that the most reliable road to a gold badge was to get a tenured member of the club to carry your flag. For the last six months, Harry had volunteered for all the right cases, attended all the right meetings, and engineered the right introductions to get himself known in the network. But he was still missing the big kill.

When Sergeant Hackner came to him that morning with the task of tracking down Nathan Bailey's location through the telephone records, he knew this was the opportunity he'd been waiting for. Hackner was a good guy and a known flag carrier. The fact that he was best buddies with Lieutenant Michaels made it all the better. For Harry, the mission was clear. He'd do his job quickly and efficiently, making Hackner look good to his boss, and at the same time have a pivotal role in what was turning out to be a high-profile case.

Utilizing what he'd learned at the Academy, he'd started his quest with the obvious—a call to the phone company. After being handed off a half-dozen times from one bureaucrat to another, Harry was finally connected with the Vice President of Customer Service, who broke the news that absent a court order, he could not authorize the dissemination of telephone records without the customer's permission. Invasion of privacy and all that, don't you know. Harry asked if he understood that this could be the key to corralling a murderer, in response to which the vice president said something about a call waiting on another line.

Court orders took forever, and they were well outside Harry's power to obtain. Legal briefs would have to be filed, and arguments would have to be heard. Even on an expedited basis, obtaining a court order could easily take more time than the Bailey kid figured to take holing up somewhere. If they waited, they could lose their prisoner. And even if they caught him, it would be the Commonwealth's Attorney who would get the credit, not him.

No, Harry needed to go to the source. He needed to talk the owners of those telephone records—The Bitch and her production staff—into releasing the records to his custody. He just had to be persuasive. He briefly considered a soft-pedaled, altruistic approach, but rejected it as too wimpy. Instead, he settled on the forceful approach. Those radio people didn't know squat about the real world. If he leaned on them hard enough and played the obstruction of justice card just right, they'd cave in. After all, what did The Bitch have to lose? Helping to solve a murder case was the kind of publicity anyone would welcome.

By the time Harry was done with Enrique Zamora, the producer could hardly speak, he was so befuddled. Now, as he sat on hold, Harry found himself regretting some of the things he'd said. In the spirit of the moment, Harry had led Enrique to believe that there was imminent danger of jail if he didn't cooperate. Harry had no such power, of course, but he supposed that really didn't matter. What the American public didn't know about their rights was amazing. Even more amazing was how willing people were to surrender those rights if you just gave them half a chance.

As he sat on hold, listening to some inane car commercial, Harry decided that if challenged on his representation of fact, he would simply tell whomever that the producer must have been mistaken.

On her side of the glass, The Bitch sipped at her Diet Coke and took another caller. The message on her screen said that Joanne from New York City didn't believe that Nathan did anything wrong.

"This is The Bitch. Joanne from New York, what's your problem?"

The Brooklyn accent from the other end of the phone was as thick as syrup. "My problem is that I don't think that sweet voice could do any of the things that the police are claiming he did. He sounds like he could have been my son when he was that age."

"What's not to believe, Joanne? The kid says he stole a car to get into jail, and that he killed the guard—supervisor—to get out. Granted, he claims it was an accident rooted in self-defense, but you have to believe the basic facts."

Joanne explained her position, but Denise was distracted by Enrique's voice in her headphones telling her to go to a commercial. She shook her head and scowled, pointing to her watch. They had another six minutes before the next set of spots. Enrique scowled back and mouthed something unintelligible through the glass. Then he held up the telephone.

When Joanne from New York paused to take a breath, Denise dumped her call. "Well, I guess everyone's entitled to their opinion," she said. "Some folks just want to make them up on the fly. We've got to do a couple more spots, and we'll be right back."

As soon as the commercial started, she wheeled back around to Enrique. "What the hell's the matter with you? I don't take hotline calls during the show. You know that."

"Lighten up, Denise," Enrique shot back. "I've got a cop on the phone who wants to use our telephone records to trace down Nathan's call."

Denise evaluated the options in an instant. If word got out that the police could trace calls through a radio talk show—*her* radio talk show—that would spell the end of controversial discussion. Government and military officials would stop calling to complain about their bosses for fear of being fired. Citizens would stop calling to complain about the president for fear of being audited. Every well-placed source she'd established over the years would instantly evaporate. Without controversy, and without callers, The Bitch would be just another disc jockey.

"Hell no," she responded quickly. "You tell him that

our telephone records are off limits. We're talking a serious First Amendment issue here."

"Well, I already told him that—at least the 'hell no' part—and he says he's going to bring us up on obstruction of justice charges if we don't cooperate."

Denise recoiled at the thought. "Oh really? Well, patch him through to my board. We'll put him on the air when we come out of commercials. What's his name?"

"Thompkins."

The current commercial ended fifteen seconds later, with Crazy Somebody-or-other screaming about thousands of dollars in savings at a local car dealership. At her cue from Enrique, Denise opened her microphone.

"Welcome back, America, to this most unusual show this morning. The interest spawned by my conversation with Nathan Bailey just continues to grow. On the line with us now is a police officer from Braddock County, Virginia, who's threatening to send my staff and me to prison over all of this. Officer Thompkins, this is The Bitch, and you are on the air." She stabbed his blinking light with her forefinger.

For a long moment, there was no sound from the other end. Finally, a tentative voice said, "Hello?"

"Officer Thompkins?"

"Yes, ma'am."

Denise cackled into the microphone. "Ma'am? Did you just call me ma'am? You must not listen to this show very often, or you'd know better than to call me ma'am. That word's got the same letters as mama, and honey, I ain't your mama. Now, I understand you want to throw me in jail. What gives?"

The voice stammered badly on the other end. Denise loved it. "Am . . . am I on the radio?"

"You called a radio station, mister. That generally gets you on the radio. So, why do you want to toss me in the hoosegow?"

"I'm sorry, but I think we need to discuss this in private. I didn't call to get put on the air."

Denise's voice was suddenly devoid of all playfulness. "I'm sure you didn't. According to my producer, you want to use this program's telephone records to find out where Nathan Bailey was calling from this morning. Is this correct?"

"Look, ma'am, I don't want . . ."

"Yes or no, Officer Thompkins. Is that why you called?"

"Well . . . uh . . . I suppose so." He sounded deliciously evasive.

"You suppose so. I'll interpret that as a yes. And now I'll give you an answer that needs no interpretation. You can have those records when hell freezes over. Or when you have a court order. If I were to allow you access to our records, the effect would be to inhibit free speech. And free speech is protected by our Constitution. You've heard of the Constitution, right?"

Annoyance was beginning to show in Thompkins's voice. "There's really no need to be so—"

"Angry?" Denise interrupted again. She had no intention of letting Thompkins complete a thought. "Do you also suppose that you told my producer that if we didn't let you rummage through our records you'd charge us with obstruction of justice?"

Thompkins sounded suddenly dejected, like he'd been caught in the act of doing something wrong. "I think I might have mentioned—"

"Oops, sorry to interrupt again, but that sounded

like another yes. Let me get this straight, Officer
Thompkins. You're going to charge me with a crime
for exercising my First Amendment rights. Does that
seem reasonable to you? Or maybe you were just
bluffing, using scare tactics to get what you want, so
you don't have to go through the proper channels mandated by law."

Boy, they didn't call her The Bitch for nothing.
Without even completing a sentence, Thompkins had
made a fool not only of himself, but of his entire department. In front of millions of people. A minute ago,
this had seemed like a good plan. Now he wished he
could just dissolve. He thought of two or three different angles to extricate himself, but none of them would
work. He could see his career unraveling before his
eyes. With no options remaining, he abruptly hung up.

Denise heard the click and smiled slyly to Enrique.
"He hung up." She laughed into the mike. "Well, hanging up's not really an answer, I guess. But I certainly
think there's a message there, don't you?"

CHAPTER THIRTEEN

LYLE POINTER LIKED TO THINK OF HIMSELF as the Hit Man. At five-eleven, 180 pounds, his appearance was anything but intimidating; not the brutish lout that Hollywood had cast as the stereotypical thumb-breaker. Good-looking, smart, and possessed of a sense of humor uncommon among people in his business, he had to struggle for the respect that his work deserved.

No one was more loyal to Mr. Slater, no one more efficient in carrying out his orders, yet people still assumed because of his size that he could be pushed around. Few made the assumption more than once. Boldly decisive and seemingly fearless, Pointer had slowly but surely earned the respect of the one person who mattered. And he had done that through sheer brutality.

His first job for Mr. Slater had been to deliver a message to a punk drug dealer who'd opened up shop on the wrong turf. It was the kind of message that couldn't be written on paper. It was Pointer's job to make sure that the young man would leave Washington forever. It was also important for other would-be intruders to know that gangs could have as much of the city as they wanted, so long as they never, *ever* set foot on Slater ground.

Pointer's solution sent shock waves through the Washington underworld. Abducting the young man at gunpoint, Pointer handcuffed him to a Dumpster, beat him unconscious, and cut off his upper lip with a razor blade. When the dealer came to his senses, Pointer doused the teenager's genitals with gasoline and struck a match.

The notoriety that followed this job served Pointer well, and set a precedent for what was expected from him in the future. He was earning the kind of reputation he'd always sought. Proud of his ability to strike terror in some of the toughest people on earth, he was also acutely aware that with fear came jealousy. Each day was a new chance to prove himself, and each job was a new test of his resourcefulness. A single misstep could easily cost him everything he'd struggled so long to build. Including his life.

As appreciative as Mr. Slater was of a job well done, he wouldn't tolerate a fuckup. Pointer often heard his boss say that every man deserved a second chance, but that no one deserved a third.

On this day, Pointer was grateful for the second chance. He needed it.

As he sped through the Virginia countryside en route to his meeting, Pointer could barely control his rage, which he expressed with a heavy foot on the Porsche's throttle. Having driven out of civilization twenty miles ago, he was confident that no police would be around to annoy him. And even if they were, those heavy metal Chevys and Fords were no match for his own piece of German engineering. Despite the searing heat and drenching humidity, he drove with the top down, calfskin jacket and gloves in place. It was a look. And for this meeting, it was exactly the right look.

This whole business with Mark Bailey and his nephew was so out of control that Pointer was ready to kill. He never should have listened to Bailey's plan in the first place, let alone agree to it. But it was so simple! The elements were all there. An inside job, big man, little boy, small room. How could they screw it up? Well, he'd know in about fifteen minutes. By the clock on the dash, Bailey had already been waiting for a half-hour. Shitheads like Bailey were so much easier to communicate with after they'd been kept waiting for a while. He'd probably already wet his pants. If not, he would by the end of the meeting.

Only three hours before, Pointer had come perilously close to wetting his own trousers. He'd never seen Slater like that, his face beet red and trembling with rage. Humiliated was the word he used. Pointer had humiliated Slater's entire organization. You could live with the news that a hit on a politician or a dealer went sour. But Pointer had screwed up a hit on a boy in a cage! Once word leaked out, it would take years for the street punks to stop laughing. Laughter meant disrespect, and disrespect meant challenges to Slater's turf. Challenges, in turn, meant violence, and violence was bad for business.

Since when, Pointer had wondered as he endured Slater's wrath, did the old man hate violence? Then he realized that Slater had been listening to the cluckings of that old hen Sammy Bell, who no doubt talked the old man into turning weak. Not that you could tell from the way he disciplined his employees.

It was only because of Pointer's loyalty and history of good work that Mr. Slater had granted him his second chance.

"By the time this is over," Mr. Slater had said with grave seriousness, "one of you will be dead, Lyle." Mr. Slater was not a man given to hyperbole.

So Pointer took control of this thing personally, effective this morning. His meeting with Mark Bailey was to extract his pound of flesh and gallon of blood. Mark needed to learn not to make promises he couldn't keep. The good news for Bailey was that he would live to see morning. The way the whole plan was put together required that much. Maybe he wasn't such an idiot after all.

Thirty minutes earlier, Mark Bailey had carefully eased his Bronco into a remote parking space at the Hillbilly Tavern. His was the only car in the lot, though three hard-ridden Harleys were parked along the front of the place, like so many horses at the hitching post. At just after noon, he was still too hung over to be moving, let alone driving. What Mark really needed was a wheelbarrow for his head. One day he was going to go on the wagon and stay there.

He paused for a long time after slipping the truck into Park, certain that at any second his window and his head would be shattered by a rifle bullet. He carefully scanned the area with his eyes. If there was a sniper, he was well hidden.

Come on, Mark, he told himself, *they can't kill you. At least not yet. Without you, they've got nothing.*

Ever since Pointer's call this morning, he'd been repeating this sentence over and over again, sometimes aloud, sometimes in his head. On the trip out to this godforsaken hole in the wall, he'd even come to believe it. Now, though, at the end of the road, the logic seemed tragically flawed.

For an instant, he considered throwing the Bronco into reverse and just getting the hell out of Virginia—out of the country if he had to. But he knew that wasn't a solution. Pointer was not the kind of guy you said no to. With his connections, escape in the longer view was simply not possible. In his heart, Mark knew that he'd likely not survive this chapter in his life, but he took comfort in the hope that once the money was delivered and he'd kept his end of the bargain, Slater and his goons would make the end quick. He'd heard stories through the grapevine of horrendous tortures at the hands of Slater's men. He'd even heard of them burning off a guy's balls. Mark himself had never had the stones to ask who in the organization would do such a thing. He was pretty sure he knew, but there was solace to be found in shadows of doubt.

The Hillbilly Tavern was the kind of place that could only exist in the rural Virginia countryside. Home to thousands of unspeakable secrets and schemes, it was the kind of place where a person with the guts to enter could discuss anything with anyone, with the full knowledge that nothing said would ever be repeated. Unlike some of the more fashionable rattraps in the suburbs, this one was never frequented by passing sheriff's deputies or by lost motorists in search of a bathroom. Sane tourists would piss all over their leather interiors before they would willingly cross the threshold of the Hillbilly Tavern.

The place didn't even have a telephone anymore. After it was busted up once in a brawl, the phone company sent a repair team out to fix the damage, but after they were relieved of their wallets and phone company equipment, no one ever tried to repair it again. One of the repairmen actually tried to put up a struggle, thus creating one of the longest and strangest workers' compensation claims in the company's history.

As he approached the door to the bar, Mark noticed the absence of windows. The panes had been boarded over and overlaid with a collage of neon signs, still burning in the bright sunshine. The wood siding bore countless coats of dark brown paint, which seemed to serve as the only support for the ancient structure. He was intrigued by a colorful bit of artwork painted on the stoop, but looked away when he saw it was a vomit splash, left uncleaned since God knew when.

Mark paused for a long moment before entering, once again checking over his shoulders for hidden snipers. It still wasn't too late for him to leave, he told himself, knowing even as the words formed in his brain that they were a lie. It had become too late for him the instant he'd turned to Pointer for help. But what the hell, he had taken a shot at the big leagues and he lost. In any other business, he could have taken pride in having the guts to try. On the other hand, in any other business, the financing arrangements would not have involved so much blood.

Taking a deep breath, Mark turned the knob on the door and entered the Hillbilly Tavern. The transition from searing sunshine to near darkness left him momentarily blind. He stood still in the doorway, waiting for his eyes to adjust.

"Who the hell are you?" a gravelly voice barked from behind the shadows.

"My name's Bailey," Mark replied, invoking a tone of voice he hadn't used since prison. "Who the hell is asking?"

"I think you're in the wrong place," another voice said, this one from his right.

"I'm here to meet a man named Pointer. You heard of him?" The silence told him that they had.

"Dammit," the first voice growled again, "either come in or get out. I don't like people standing in my doorway."

Mark shut the door behind him and edged his way toward a table in the corner. He ordered a beer, hoping that the hair of the dog would take the edge off his hangover. The tavern stank of cigarettes, sweat, and countless spilled drinks. That rodents and insects roamed wild inside went without question.

Seated now, with his back against the corner, Mark allowed his vision to adjust to the darkness, and he scanned the room. Gravel Voice lumbered awkwardly behind the bar fulfilling his beer order, having difficulty maneuvering his three-hundred-plus pounds in the confined galley lined with off-brand liquor bottles. A huge, tangled beard sprouted from his cheeks and neck, resting like a furry bib on his Harley-Davidson T-shirt. His hair had last been trimmed during the same decade that the beard was last checked for mice and squirrels. He at least showed the courtesy to wear his mane in a tight ponytail that swung just below his shoulder blades. That way, it didn't dangle into the drinks as he prepared them. Mark assumed Gravel Voice was the owner, though for all he knew, that poor soul was just as likely dead in some meat freezer in the back.

Mark's beer was served in the bottle. By his count, in addition to himself and the bartender, there were three other people in the tavern, all of whom looked as though they had been there for a very long time. Conversations among the men varied from quiet to loud, sad to animated, but always punctuated with the slurred drawl of hill folk. Mark's mission now was simply to wait, and to avoid being caught in the act of staring at this collection of people fresh from Darwin's waiting room.

When Lyle Pointer finally entered the Hillbilly Tavern, the eyes of the regulars looked up just long enough to look away. No one said anything. The seam of sunlight created by Pointer's entrance disappeared as he closed the door behind him. In the quick wash of light, Mark clearly saw the leather jacket, the open collar, and the gold baubles draped around his neck and his wrist. *I'm in bed with a damn gangster,* Mark thought.

Either Pointer knew in advance where Mark was sitting, or his eyes adjusted awfully quickly to the change in lighting. Either way, he walked without hesitating directly over to Mark's table in the corner and took the seat immediately next to his host, not across from him as Mark had expected. It was the seating arrangement typical of a date, not a business meeting. But then, Mark had no way of knowing just how intimate an act of true intimidation could be. In Pointer's presence, the fat bartender moved almost gracefully, bringing his new guest a drink—could it be *water*?—without even being asked.

For a long moment, Pointer stared at Mark, twice making him break eye contact. At length, he said, "You broke your promise to me." His voice had an odd quality to it, simultaneously quiet and angry. The effect was thoroughly frightening. "You promised me that you could handle this thing, and then you screwed it up."

Sweat beaded on Mark's forehead. He could feel perspiration soak his armpits and his back. He'd come to the meeting armed with excuses and explanations for Ricky's failure to perform, but he had suddenly lost the nerve to say anything. Instead, he just stared at his second empty beer bottle, spinning it slowly with his fingers in its own puddle of sweat.

"Look at me, Bailey," Pointer commanded softly.

Mark raised his eyes.

"I talked to Mr. Slater this morning, and he wasn't pleased. And do you know who he wasn't pleased with?"

Mark shook his head silently.

Pointer slammed the table with his fist, making the empty beer bottle jump almost as high as Mark. "Answer me!"

For an instant, Mark forgot the question, then his mind cleared and he stammered, "N-no, I d-don't. Me, I suppose. I guess he's not pleased with me."

Pointer leaned forward, close enough for Mark to smell his chewing gum. Juicy Fruit. "No, Bailey, you're wrong again," he said measuredly, his voice once again menacingly smooth. "He wasn't mad at you. He was mad at me. Because I was stupid enough to believe that you could pull off a foolproof plan to kill a kid inside a concrete *room*." His voice boomed at the end, prompting Mark to glance nervously at the others seated in the tavern. None of them moved, though certainly all of them were listening. Clearly, that didn't matter to Pointer.

"Look, Pointer, I can explain," Mark attempted to say.

Pointer cut him off. "I don't want an explanation from you. Obviously, you weren't there. Let me guess. You poured yourself inside a bottle last night, didn't you?"

Mark looked away again.

"Didn't you?"

He nodded.

Pointer took a deep breath and let it out noisily. "So that's the thanks I get, huh? I go to bat for you, keep you from getting your throat cut, and the best you can do is subcontract your work to some incompetent prison guard so you can drown yourself in booze. Does that seem fair to you, Mark?"

Mark said, "No." What he didn't say, they both knew already. The only reason that Pointer had gone to bat for him was to protect the two hundred thousand dollars he stood to make in the deal, unbeknownst to the angry Mr. Slater.

"Well, Mark, we finally agree on something. It doesn't seem fair to me, either. But you know what? I did it for you again. Mr. Slater's first solution to this little problem was for me to cut out your liver and stuff it down your throat."

Mark felt his heart rate double, knowing without question that Pointer was reporting fact. He sweated like a marathon runner now. His hands trembled.

"But I talked him out of that for the time being. I told him that there was too much money in play just to kill you without at least another try. And you know what he said to me?"

Mark was looking away again. Pointer grabbed his face in the vise of his left hand and pulled him around so they were face-to-face, only inches separating them.

"He told me that he didn't care about the money. Imagine that. Imagine getting to that point in life where five hundred thousand dollars just doesn't mean anything anymore. He told me that the honor and dignity of his name were at stake now, and that the only thing that mattered was killing you."

Mark's hangover flooded back into his brain. His stomach churned. It was entirely possible that he would barf on Pointer's shiny leather jacket.

Pointer let go of Mark's face and leaned back into his chair. "But I talked him out of it. I talked him into one more try. So here's where it stands. If your nephew dies and we get our money, you live. Otherwise, you're dead."

Mark saw a distant light on his horizon, the faintest glimmer of hope. "That's good, Pointer. Give me one more chance—"

Pointer cut him off again. "What, do I look crazy? You're not getting a second chance at anything but living. I'll take care of whacking the kid. Your job is to wait for the papers from your lawyer."

In the long pause that followed, Mark knew there

was something else coming, but he chose to wait rather than ask.

"There's one more matter we need to discuss—two, actually. First, you're a minority shareholder in your inheritance now. Mr. Slater's share went up to two million. That's the price of a screwup these days. Plus, I'm gonna add another three hundred thousand to let you live. Add to that another two hundred thou that you already owe me personally, and that makes your total bill about two million five. What's left is yours."

An objection formed in Mark's throat, but he swallowed it quickly, before it could do any damage. The price of staying alive had suddenly become awfully steep. "I can live with that," he said, wincing at the unintentional pun.

Pointer laughed. "I bet you can. Now, that leaves us with one more bit of business."

Sensing, incorrectly, that the worst was over for now, Mark sighed deeply and leaned forward to listen.

"You see, Mark," Pointer explained, "I have a reputation to consider, too. And the simple fact of the matter is that I can't afford to let you go without hurting you." He smoothly and slowly withdrew a pistol from a holster somewhere beneath the slick leather jacket, thumbed the hammer back, and placed the muzzle an inch from Mark's right eye. He stood and pushed his chair back with his foot, giving himself some room to move around. Once standing, he shifted the gun from his right hand to his left, never moving the barrel from its perfect line to Mark's brain. "Are you right-handed or left-handed?" he asked.

"L-left," Mark stammered, in a whimpering tone that made Pointer feel sick to his stomach.

Pointer pulled a pen and a scrap of paper from an inside pocket and handed them over to Mark. "Here," he said. "Let me see your signature."

Mark's shoulders sagged visibly as he realized that his lie was transparent. There were real tears in his eyes now, to go along with the very real fear. "I'm sorry, Pointer," he pleaded. "I made a mistake. Actually, I-I'm right-handed."

"Put your right hand on the table," Pointer commanded. As he spoke, something changed behind his eyes. Even in the darkness of the tavern Mark could see it. It was a chilling, calculating coldness. They were the eyes of evil.

Mark was vaguely aware that he had just pissed all over himself, adding yet another odor to the offensive bouquet that greeted him when he entered. He shook his head pitifully, not in defiance, but as a plea for leniency.

"Don't make me ask more than once," Pointer advised. "You need to remember that Mr. Slater and I don't need your money. The money's only important because it hurts you. And we owe you a lot of pain. Now, you make the choice. I can put a bullet in your eye right now, or you can put your hand on the table like I asked."

Mark's hand shook violently, out of control, as he complied with the orders and placed his hand on the table. His entire world consisted only of the huge circular void that was the muzzle of the cannon pointed at his face. He wondered morbidly if he'd actually be able to see the nose of the bullet as it cleared the opening on its way to kill him.

"These are the rules," Pointer explained. "If you

make a sound, I'll pull the trigger. No matter how bad it hurts, you just sit there quietly for once in your life and be a man. You understand?"

Mark was openly sobbing now, his facial features contorted like a small child's as tears cascaded down his cheeks. But there was no sound.

A look of amusement settled into Pointer's face as he wrapped his fist around the forefinger on Mark's right hand and pressed his thumb firmly at the digit's base, halfway between the second and third knuckle. Amusement turned to a wide grin as he steadily added more pressure with his thumb and leveraged upwards with the fingertip. His other hand remained firmly wrapped around the grip of his pistol.

After about five seconds, Mark's second knuckle dislocated with a soft *pop,* like the sound you'd get pinching bubble wrap. Lights danced before his eyes, and he felt his gorge rise in his throat, but he swallowed it back down. And he didn't make a sound. Ten seconds later, the finger broke midshaft, under Pointer's thumb. Mark's whole body jumped as pain shot like a spike all the way to his shoulder, causing him to bite through his lower lip.

When Pointer let go, Mark's finger stuck straight up at the break, like a fleshy flagpole. Proud that he had made no noise, and that he was still alive as a result, he recovered his mangled hand and cradled it like a baby in the crook of his left elbow. Then he noticed that the gun hadn't moved.

"I'm sorry, Mark," Pointer said, the grin still there, "but we're not done yet. The first finger was for screwing up. Now we've got to break one for telling me you were left-handed. We have to discover a basis for trust in our relationship. Now, put your hand back on the table."

Mark's hand had already swollen to twice its normal size as blood poured internally from ruptured vessels. Movement of any sort was excruciating, but the mental agony of going through this one more time was almost more than he could bear. Without the gentle support of his other hand, the broken finger wobbled back and forth at the break line, grinding bone ends against each other. He hoped he would pass out, giving Pointer the option of ending this while he was unconscious. But of course, no such thing happened.

This time, Pointer made it easy, grabbing Mark's pinky even as he rested it on the table and wrenching it quickly backwards and sideways, nearly severing the finger at its root. This time Mark howled in agony, unable to control his voice, and he slipped from his chair down onto the filthy floor. Pointer considered shooting him on principle, but decided to ignore it. The son of a bitch had held out longer than he would have thought, anyway. He eased the hammer down and reholstered the Magnum. "It's been a pleasure doing business with you, Bailey. Write when you can. I'll call you when we need you."

As deliberately as he'd entered, Pointer strolled to the exit, telling the bartender as he passed, "My friend over there will pick up the tab. Be patient with him, though. Might take a few minutes for him to get the money out of his pocket."

In reply, the bartender nodded politely and studiously avoided making eye contact. No one in the Hillbilly Tavern had seen a thing.

CHAPTER FOURTEEN

NATHAN LICKED THE LAST OF THE PIZZA SAUCE off his thumb and forefinger and slumped backwards into the soft leather cushions of the sofa, thoroughly satisfied. Where a family-size frozen pizza had once resided on a cardboard tray, there were now only crumbs and a single orphaned pepperoni, which he quickly dispatched with one bite. He launched an enormous belch, and laughed as the sound reverberated off the walls of the family room.

After hanging up with The Bitch, he'd listened for another hour or so in the bedroom as callers branded him either innocent and cute—*Jeeze!*—or guilty and vicious. There seemed to be no middle ground. He thought it was pretty cool that The Bitch was supportive. The more he listened, the more he became convinced that she was on his side.

A guy could only ignore his stomach for so long, though. He was getting bored with the radio anyway, so he switched it off with an hour still left in The Bitch's time slot and headed downstairs, where he launched a search-and-destroy mission looking for something to eat. The pantry proved to be as empty as the refrigerator had been the night before, but a quick look in the mudroom revealed a freezer full of his favorite foods. Once he realized that the pizza was too big for the microwave, he followed the directions on the back of the box and cooked it in the oven. While he waited the required twelve to sixteen minutes, he mixed a vat of orange juice from frozen concentrate. He couldn't find a pitcher, so he used a stew pot.

Once lunch was ready, Nathan camped out on the floor of the family room, in front of a round coffee table. The remote control he found for the entertainment center looked like something invented by NASA, with blue, green, red and yellow buttons. He pushed buttons at random until the big screen popped to life. None of the cable cartoons he liked were on, so he settled for a *Star Trek* rerun. Those guys were so lame. By the time the twenty-third century came around, you'd think people would wear something more hip than high-heeled boots and skin-tight polyester. Captain Kirk was in the process of being beaten up—with his shirt off, of course, while everyone else was fully clothed. Nathan wondered with mild amusement why anyone would agree to be the guest star. Sure as hell, when you got beamed down with the regulars, you were doomed.

At the bottom-of-the-hour break, Nathan saw his face again on the screen—from a fuzzy video picture he hadn't seen before—with a teaser voiceover for the *News at Noon.* Being famous was getting to be pretty cool. He wasn't afraid anymore; at least not the same way he had been. He wasn't sure where that shot of emotion on the telephone had come from, but he still hated himself for nearly breaking down. He still had friends, after all—somewhere. There was Jacob Protsky, his best friend and soccer teammate, and David Harrellson, who'd shared every classroom with Nathan since first grade. They'd undoubtedly be paying attention to all of this, and a guy had to be careful about his reputation.

Nathan thought about Huck Finn—not the one in the book, which was too boring for him to finish, but the one in the movies. When Huck was about his age, he outsmarted everybody and got away from the law. Even helped people along the way. That's what Nathan was going to do. He was going to live an adventure, moving from house to house, maybe sometimes camping out in the woods. Problem was, Huck had Jim to talk to and help him figure out his problems. Much as Nathan hated to admit it, grown-ups just knew more about certain things that he really needed help with. Like coming up with a plan. Huck and Jim had a plan. They used the cover of night to raft upstream to the free states, where Jim could find his family and Huck could start a new life.

What am I going to do?

He knew that his first priority should be putting distance between himself and the JDC, and though he had no real concept of where he was, he figured he couldn't be more than a mile or two from where he started. That put him in the hottest part of the search area. The morning news shows had shown pictures of search parties and roadblocks, all looking for him. The reporter had even gone so far as to say that there were no leads as to his whereabouts. He figured, then, that he'd made a "clean getaway," as they said in the movies. Now he just had to work out the next step.

Huck was little help to him here. Nathan had no raft; hell, there wasn't even a river. And Huck didn't have to worry about everybody in the country seeing his picture on TV and knowing what he looked like. He also didn't have to worry about police cars and radios and faxes and radar and all the other stuff the cops had today just to make your life miserable.

On the other hand, Huck didn't have *access* to those things either, did he? In one morning, Nathan had heard people change their minds about him, just because he talked on the radio. If he could change minds with a single call, what could he do with more calls? He was already the lead story on all the news shows, but television was still portraying him as the bad guy. He had to figure out a way to switch that around. He was a decent guy who'd gotten into trouble. He'd killed only to protect himself. If he could get the opportunity to tell the truth often enough, then people might start believing him. Television commercials did the same thing all the time, didn't they? If people could accept what a make-believe psychic said, they had to believe *his* story, didn't they? It was the truth, after all. All he had to do was call every radio station in the state and tell them his story.

Shit! Cops can trace phone calls!

Sure, The Bitch said they couldn't trace the calls to her show, but what about the others?

Maybe The Bitch was wrong and the cops were outside waiting for him right now. Maybe there were rules about breaking down the doors to houses this nice. A quick and cautious check of the street from behind the small seam in the living room drapes out front revealed just a normal, empty summer street. Not even any kids running around. He figured that in a neighborhood like this everybody went away to day camp in the summer. That's what he used to do.

So The Bitch was right after all—at least so far. And if she *was* wrong and cops were still on the way, well, that wasn't something he could worry about. But he decided to cancel his planned telephone blitz. No sense taking unnecessary chances.

So now there was the matter of distance. Walking wouldn't do. Not only was it too slow, but the news had said something about dogs trying to sniff him down. There had to be another solution.

If I could only drive.

Wait a minute! Why couldn't he drive? Driving Uncle Mark's pickup truck was what had gotten him into this mess in the first place. And it wasn't so long ago that Nathan had driven Granddad's ancient pickup truck around the fun farm in Gainesville. Purchased for a song in 1979, the eighteen-acre spread with its squalid little ranch house and collapsing barn had served as a place for Granddad to play farmer during his retirement years. Nathan loved going out there, mostly for the well-stocked ponds, but also for the old standard-shift '68 Ford, which he was allowed to drive anywhere on the property so long as he stayed away from the water and the buildings. Granddad had even fashioned some detachable wooden blocks so he could reach the pedals.

After Granddad died, Nathan found out that the fun

farm would be his one day, but that he couldn't visit the place anymore because some lawyer in New York had rented it to somebody who turned it into a bowling alley. Nathan didn't even like bowling.

A year ago, Nathan had made it nearly twenty-five miles in Uncle Mark's truck before the cop pulled him over, and that was in the middle of the day when everybody noticed a kid driving a car. He smiled as he remembered dragging Uncle Mark's prized vehicle along fifty feet of guardrail and into a maple tree before surrendering to the police. He realized that it was this final act of defiance that likely got him thrown into Juvey, but he still thought it was funny.

If he could do his traveling at night and avoid the major roads with their roadblocks, and if he could keep the car on the road, he might just be able to drive himself right out of the country!

Like everything else in this palace, the garage was huge. Closest to the door from the kitchen was a blank space, the home for the vehicle currently in use by the family. Dry stains on the concrete floor told the story of a once-leaky transmission. In the middle slot, there stood a gleaming fiberglass speedboat with twin Evinrude motors, mounted securely on a trailer.

Huck Finn's book would have been a lot shorter if they had one of those babies, he thought as he ran his fingers wistfully over the slick, sparkle-flecked surface of the hull. Waterskiing was one of the skills his father had promised him, way back when promises were still kept.

The item he'd hoped to find was in the third and

final stall, covered by a light-olive tarp. Only the very bottom radius of the wheels showed beneath the cover. Without hesitating a beat, Nathan grabbed the front corner of the tarp and pulled it off the car.

"Wa-hoa!" he exclaimed aloud, showing the purest possible admiration. Before him rested a brand-new cherry-red BMW convertible, the coolest-looking car on the street. The keys, bearing the handwritten tag, BMW, were on a hook labeled KEYS that was mounted on the wall just to the left of the driver's door. The other keys on the peg were labeled BOAT and RANGE ROVER. He figured they took the Rover on vacation.

The driver's door was unlocked, so he opened it and slid into the front seat. The leather was softer even than his dad's old lounge chair, and a hell of a lot more comfortable than the vinyl in Uncle Mark's old pickup. His jaw was slack with wonder as he stroked the seats and gripped the steering wheel, navigating the vehicle in his mind through the turns in the highways he'd soon travel. Almost as an afterthought, he put the key in the ignition and turned it just enough to arm the electrical systems. By process of elimination, he found the buttons controlling the seat position and adjusted it all the way forward, till his feet could touch the pedals. It would be a stretch, but at least they reached.

A grin crossed Nathan's face. This could work. It had to work. As he played the scenario in his mind, he felt his confidence grow geometrically by the second. All the ifs and maybes were of no consequence to him. He'd beaten the odds to this point, and he'd beat them the rest of the way. Whether it would work or not was irrelevant. What mattered was that he had a plan.

* * *

Denise felt like dancing. In the hours since she'd signed off the air, she'd received countless phone calls and faxes from people expressing interest one way or another in the day's show. Each of the three network morning talk shows had asked for live interviews the next day, but only *Good Morning America* offered to bring her to their Washington studios via limousine, so that was the one she accepted. The rest wanted to interview her from her home, and as someone who obsessed about cleaning up for relatives, she wasn't equipped to entertain 40 million Americans before dawn.

If Denise looked ecstatic, Enrique looked like he'd taken a beating. The show had been over for hours, yet calls kept pouring in. Denise had only spoken to the people who got past Enrique, and *he* had personally spoken with over three hundred people. Even his hair was disheveled, and his hair was *never* anything short of perfect. Per the secret pact he had made with himself at the conclusion of the show, at exactly four o'clock, he laid the receiver on its cradle, with a caller still running her mouth, and turned off his telephone, routing all calls electronically to The Bitch Phone, a glorified answering machine that was billed as a way for people to sound off during hours when the usual lines were jammed.

Relieved at last to be in a quiet room, Enrique rocked lazily back into his leather chair and crossed his feet atop the corner of his desk. He knew about Denise's agreement to go on the tube tomorrow morning, which meant that she wouldn't sleep. Instead, she'd spend the night preparing for her two and a half minutes in the spotlight.

As her producer, sounding board, and designated hand-holder, he knew that, like it or not, sleep was not in the cards for him, either.

If any rest lay in his immediate future, it would be during the next couple of hours, while Denise was basking in her recent glory. It wouldn't be till 2:00 A.M. that her serious self-doubt would materialize, and that's when his real work would begin. He'd never understand why she kept doing this to herself. Before drifting off for his power nap, he checked his watch. It was 5:03.

Enrique nearly fell backwards when his sleep was shattered by a ringing phone. His watch now read 5:08, and he prayed that it had stopped working.

"I thought I turned you off," he grumped at the phone, but by the second ring, he realized that it wasn't the 800 line. It was Denise's private line. By the third ring, it was clear that she wasn't going to answer it herself, so he snatched it to his ear. "Bitch," he answered. It was the usual one-word salutation to callers, but this time it seemed to ring with emotion.

The female voice on the other end of the line was at once cordial and efficient. "Mr. Dorfman calling for Ms. Carpenter."

Enrique's feet shot to the floor, and he was instantly wide awake. "One moment, please," he said. Ronald Dorfman was president of Omega Broadcasting. Head-quartered in New York, Omega was the company that syndicated Denise's show and wrote their paychecks. In all the five years that The Bitch had been on the air, Mr. Dorfman had never called the show personally. Whether his presence on the phone was good news or bad, Enrique had no way of telling. But one thing was certain: he needed to find his boss right now.

As he'd expected, Enrique found Denise at the coffeepot, accepting kudos from a group that rarely showed interest in the work she did—the news staff.

A card-carrying pessimist at heart, Denise naturally assumed that she was in trouble. Unlike Enrique, Denise had, in fact, spoken with Mr. Dorfman twice: once on the day she signed her syndication contract, and a second time when a caller pushed her a little too hard and her language exceeded FCC standards by a significant margin. That latest occasion was three years ago, and since then she'd been perfectly content to limit her contact with the Big Guy to the sterile holiday greetings he sent to all on-air personalities at Christmas.

Three minutes after Enrique had pushed the hold button, Denise was on the line. "Hello, this is Denise Carpenter," she said, her voice full of business, and totally devoid of the talk host jive. "I'm sorry to keep you waiting."

"Not at all, Ms. Carpenter," the secretary said. "Please hold for Mr. Dorfman."

So now it was Denise's turn to wait. Enrique sat anxiously on the worn sofa across the tiny office from her desk. There were many perks in radio, and countless ways to stroke the substantial egos of on-air talent, but among these was not plush office space. Hers was little more than a cubicle, ten by ten feet, if you cheated a little with the yardstick. The walls were adorned with pictures, mostly of or painted by her children. There was no degree to post, no brag wall in the traditional sense of lawyers and doctors. Her bragging rights belonged to her single-handed rise through the ranks to command a top-rated show. As she waited for Mr. Dorfman to pick up her line, she sent up a private

prayer that she hadn't inadvertently done something to
risk all of this.

"Good afternoon, Denise, this is Ron Dorfman." His
tone was quite friendly, causing Denise's shoulders to
slump a little, a visible sign of relief that made Enrique
relax as well. "It's been a very long time since we
talked. How have you been?"

"Really quite well, Ron, thanks for asking. The
show seems to be doing great."

The smile stayed in her boss's boss's boss's voice.
"Indeed it is," Dorfman agreed. "In fact, I had the opportunity to listen to you today. Please don't take offense,
but with my job, I really don't get that opportunity very
often." She could tell that he was talking around his ever-
present stogie.

"Oh, I certainly understand." Her shoulders tensed
again, bringing Enrique to the edge of his cushion.
This was going somewhere.

"This business with the boy who killed the prison
guard. Tell me what you think about it."

"I think it's great radio," she said without hesitating.
It was the answer she thought he wanted to hear.

"No, that's not what I mean. What do you think
about the situation?"

Denise's instincts told her to fall into a defensive
mode, justifying her decision to talk with Nathan on
the air. But she opted to hold back instead; to feel out
Dorfman's purpose for calling. "If you're asking me if
I think he's telling the truth, the answer is, yes, I do."

"And why do you think that? There's an awful lot of
people out there who don't agree with you."

"With all due respect, Ron, those people haven't
been calling our station."

"Trust me on this, Denise. There are people, and then there are *people*. The ones who wear badges don't agree with you, and they're making their positions to that effect very well known here in New York." There was nothing at all adversarial in his voice. "Now, please, tell me why you believe the young man's story."

Denise looked to Enrique, who, of course, had no idea what was being said. How do you answer a question like why? How do you sum up a feeling, an intuition, in a way that would make sense to the head of a $700 million corporation? Put in the same situation, a child would respond with the most honest answer of all: "Because." But that wasn't the kind of answer Ron was looking for, was it? She shrugged and stammered a bit as she tried to find the words.

"That's a tough question to answer, Ron," she tried, hoping for a reprieve.

"I understand. Take your time."

He was not going to let her off the hook. "Pardon me for being so unscientific," she said at last, "but the main reason I believe him is because I have kids around the same age, and I just know when they're lying. His telling of the story was just too . . . *real*."

Dorfman was quiet for a moment as he considered the answer. "And if we accept that he is, in fact, telling the truth, what does that mean in the grand scheme of things?"

Denise was ready for this. "It means that there are a whole lot of policemen wandering around northern Virginia scouring the countryside for an 'escapee' who never had any choice but to run away. I'm not sure what the grand scheme of things is, but I know where my sympathies lie. Nobody—not even Nathan—disputes the basic events, that he killed the supervisor and ran away. What's in play here is who really is the murderer and who is the victim. Sometimes you can't tell that merely by counting who's standing and who's lying down."

There was a deep sigh on the other end of the phone, perhaps a drag on the cigar. "Very eloquently put," Ron Dorfman said at length. "And I agree with you. I had the same feeling, but it's been so long since I've been around twelve-year-olds that I needed some affirmation from a second source. It was a sensational interview."

Denise would have thanked him, but she sensed there was another shoe to drop. She didn't have to wait long.

"A New York State Trooper was in my office just a half hour ago to present me with a summons to appear at the Braddock County Courthouse (wherever that is) tomorrow afternoon at two o'clock to argue against an emergency petition filed by one J. Daniel Petrelli, Commonwealth's Attorney for Northern Virginia. Seems they want to have access to our telephone records. What do you think about that?"

Once again, Denise was at a loss as to the right answer, so once again, she opted for honesty. It had been working pretty well so far.

"I think it stinks, Ron." Hearing those words out of context, Enrique nearly fell off the sofa, certain that Denise had finally lost her mind. "You said you listened to the show today. Did you hear my conversation with the policeman?"

Dorfman chuckled. "Yes, I did. And I'd be real careful not to be caught speeding anytime in the next couple of years."

"Well, I think I stated my position pretty clearly then."

"And so you did. But Denise, I want you to understand what the stakes are here. First of all, our attorneys tell me that your First Amendment argument is viable only if the government is put in a position to compel us to hand over the records. If we simply agree to do so, then that whole argument is moot. Follow me so far?"

"Yes, I suppose. But Ron—"

"Hear me out." He sounded like a CEO now, his words delivering a direct order. "The attorneys also tell me that if we refuse to allow access to the records, and we prevail in the court proceedings, we open ourselves up to enormous civil liabilities if the kid turns out truly to be a murderer and he goes forth to do it again. All of this before we even try to calculate the public relations disaster that would result from that turn of events." He paused a long moment to let his words settle in Denise's brain.

"So here's where we stand," Dorfman summarized. "On the one hand, we have an obligation to the greater good, to assist the police in their efforts to protect society, and to bring an admitted killer to justice. On the other hand, we have an ethical obligation to ourselves and to our industry to protect that which is ours, if only on principle. You can probably guess what the legal department wants me to do, but you're the one who talked to the boy. You're the one who got us into this. I want to hear what you think we should do."

This wasn't fair! Denise wasn't an executive, never wanted to be. She was a talk show host, nothing more. She wasn't paid to carry this sort of burden. Where did Dorfman get off unloading this on her shoulders?

As quickly as the protests flashed through her brain, they were followed by the answers. She had forced him into a crack. She had taken such pleasure defending the high ground against attacks from that cop, Thompkins, that she'd left Dorfman with no "wiggle room," no face-saving route of escape or compromise. And she'd done it in front of millions of people. Suddenly she was filled with admiration for her great-grand boss. He wasn't even angry at her for pushing him into a very public corner. He was, however, waiting for her answer.

"Ron, I think you might have missed one important issue here," she said carefully. "I know what the legal department says, and everything you said makes sense, but this is bigger than just our rights versus the rights of the community. There's a scared little kid in the mix here. Maybe my emotions have been sucked deeper into this than they should have, but my heart really goes out to that boy. I want to hold his hand and help him out of this. But I can't do that. I can't do anything to help him at all. I guess . . . Dammit, Ron, the odds are stacked too high against him. He's just one little boy trying to fight a losing battle, and it just doesn't seem fair to give them access to computer records when they already hold all the cards." There, she said it. And she sounded just like an irrational, overly emotional woman.

Ron chuckled. "You'll forgive me if we don't present that argument in court," he said. While the words were patronizing, the message was not. Another deep draw on the cigar, followed by a long, measured exhalation. "Well, Denise, here's what we're going to do tomorrow. I'm going to bet my job, and yours, and a substantial chunk of this company's assets, on the assumption that this boy is telling the truth, and that he will not, in fact, embark on a multistate crime spree. We'll argue to the court that our telephone records are private, and that we won't share them with anyone."

Denise was stunned. It was not what she'd anticipated. Able to think of nothing more profound, she simply said, "Thank you."

"Don't thank me yet. This might be the stupidest decision I've ever made."

"It's certainly one of the most courageous." The words came directly from her heart.

This time, it was Dorfman who was caught off guard. "Why, thank you, Denise," he said. "We chief executives don't get to hear things like that very often." He cleared his throat. "Listen, you did a good job today. I appreciate it. Hope you sleep better tonight than I will." He hung up, leaving Denise staring at her phone.

Enrique couldn't stand it anymore. "Well?" he insisted.

A huge smile blossomed on Denise's face. "He said we did a good job."

CHAPTER FIFTEEN

JDC Superintendent Harold Johnstone went ballistic at the very notion that Sergeant Hackner would believe such slander about one of his most loyal and effective employees. "I heard what Bailey had to say on the radio this morning, and every word of it is a lie. Ricky Harris worked at this facility for five years, and had a spotless record. I will not allow you to defame the—"

Hackner cut him short with a quick gesture of his hand. "We're not defaming anyone, Mr. Johnstone. We're simply asking questions." In the manner of most police officers on official business, Hackner referred to himself in the first person plural.

"Then you should know that your questions are offensive," Johnstone retorted. He was a big man, at least sixty pounds overweight, who apparently bought his clothes hoping that one day he'd fit into them comfortably. His shirt collar was perpetually open, with his tie cinched as tight as the girth of his neck would allow. The buttons on his shirt strained to the point of causing danger to anyone sitting in front of him. A walrus mustache completely concealed his upper lip. Large, flapping jowls completed the image of a bureaucrat who'd been in his position a few years longer than he should have.

Even though he'd repeatedly relearned the evils of judging books by their covers, Hackner found it difficult to muster respect for this man.

"Mr. Johnstone," Jed said measuredly, clearly annoyed at the irrelevance of all of this, "you may take offense if you wish, or you can answer the questions in the spirit in which they're offered. I really don't care. Either way, there are issues that remain unresolved, and it's my job to resolve them. Your job is to cooperate. Unless, of course, you have something to hide." Hackner couldn't resist that last jab. Johnstone was one of those guys who was simply fun to piss off.

The superintendent rose from his chair, using his arms to lift at least half of the load. "How dare you imply that I'm somehow culpable—"

Hackner waved him off again, instantly sorry that he'd goaded him further off the subject. "Sit down, sit down. I'm sorry about that last comment. It's been a long day."

Johnstone studied Hackner's face for a long moment, gauging the other man's sincerity. Hackner was well-practiced at concealing his real thoughts, so Johnstone was appeased.

"Indeed, it has been a very long day," Johnstone said, returning to his seat. "This entire episode has been very unsettling. Nathan Bailey killed a fine supervisor whom I will miss a great deal."

Hackner's eyes narrowed considerably. "You know, that sentiment is a substantial departure from what we've been led to believe."

Johnstone frowned. "After the lies that Nathan told on the radio, I don't wonder that you feel that way."

Hackner shifted in his seat. He sensed that there was a game being played here, the rules of which he was only dimly aware. Johnstone was certainly smart enough to know that Nathan's allegations would make a huge splash in the press, and that his career trajectory would ultimately be determined by the public's perception of how he ran his little domain. He had every reason in the world to equivocate.

"Why was Nathan placed in the Crisis Unit last night?"

Johnstone looked embarrassed. "I'm afraid we can only conjecture. Ricky hadn't had a chance to write any notes before he was murdered." His choice of words demonstrated that he, too, knew how to goad a potential adversary. "My guess is that there was some sort of behavior problem."

"Did the other kids notice any behavior problem?"

Johnstone chuckled and shook his head.

Now the fat fart is patronizing me, Hackner thought.

"Sergeant Hackner," Johnstone explained, "in this facility, we use a lot of euphemisms in an effort to project our mission as something less . . . well, disturbing than it really is. We are, in fact, a prison. Our residents are really inmates, our housing units are really cell blocks, and our supervisors are really guards. We know this, you and I, because we are part of the system. But it makes us feel better somehow to think of this place as a sleepover camp for disadvantaged children. It is no such thing. Even the children are not children, in the sense that people in the world think of them. They are human flotsam, assigned here by the courts because society doesn't want them anymore. In this place, a behavior problem becomes a very relative term. In your world a fight among kids in the hallway in school is a behavior problem. Here, it's an everyday occurrence. I don't ask our *kids* questions about other *kids'* behavior. Not only would I not believe their answers, but I wouldn't put them in a position of having to give information to me. To do so may well involve them in a behavior problem from which they would not be able to walk away."

"So, what's your point?"

"My point is that you can't believe what the residents tell you, and that to solicit their input is an exercise in futility."

Jed couldn't believe what he was hearing. "Right or wrong, then, your staff is always right."

Johnstone considered the statement for a long moment before buying into it. Then, "In a word, yes."

"Good Lord, Johnstone!" Hackner protested. "You're telling me that your staff can do whatever they please, and as long as they hide it well, that's okay with you."

Johnstone slammed his fist on his desk, sending a ripple through the surface of his abundant torso. "Don't lecture me, Sergeant. Open your eyes. This whole system is corrupt already! We pretend there is hope for these kids when there is no such thing. We use words and phrases to soften realities that no one wants to face. These kids are animals, Hackner. *Animals.* And we are the zookeepers. So, do I think the residents here lie? Yes, because they do. And do I accept what my staff tells me as true? Yes, because I have to. In a place like this, it's the only reality there is."

For the longest time, Hackner just stared, his face showing a combination of disbelief and disgust. He'd spent enough years on the force to know what these kids were capable of, but from his perspective, Johnstone, given the position he held, should at least be giving lip service to the goal of rehabilitation. Instead, he'd clearly given up. Every two weeks, he collected a paycheck on false pretenses. On a different case, the hypocrisy might not have registered, but on this one, it really pissed Jed off.

"Is it standard procedure to relieve a resident of his shoes when placing him in the Crisis Unit?" Jed asked, shifting gears.

Johnstone appeared relieved to be once again discussing factual issues instead of theoretical ones. "I wouldn't say it was common, but it certainly isn't unusual."

"What's the purpose?"

Johnstone spoke as though he were prepared for the question. "When residents arrive here, they arrive with nothing of their own. They're made to shower in the stall immediately adjacent to the in-processing area, after which they hand over all of their personal belongings. At that point they become dependent upon the system for everything. We give them their underwear, their clothes, their toiletries, everything. Beginning on that first day, they learn that dignity is a function of respecting the system. If they behave, for example, they can earn points toward the purchase of their own bar of soap, or a bottle of their favorite shampoo. These things then become status symbols. When they misbehave, however, the most basic elements of dignity become vulnerable. Thus, it is not uncommon for a resident to be relieved of something of importance as they're placed into the Unit. In severe cases, they must strip completely for their term in the Unit. It's all part of a behavior modification program with which we've had a great deal of success."

Hackner launched his next question like a weapon. "Your records show that Nathan Bailey was raped with a broom handle during his first night at the JDC. Was that part of your dignity deprivation program?"

Anger burned behind Johnstone's eyes, of a magnitude beyond hatred. "Think what you will of me and my operation here, Sergeant," he hissed through clenched teeth, "but I have never once condoned an act of violence on these premises."

"Yeah, I'm touched," Hackner replied. "But you don't seem to do much to prevent it, either."

"I merely live in the real world, Sergeant. 'God grant me the serenity to accept the things I cannot change.' That's not a bad prayer to live by."

"Yeah, well, I prefer, 'Do unto others as you would have them do unto you.'"

CHAPTER SIXTEEN

NATHAN SAT IMPASSIVELY on the sofa in the family room, using the nuclear-powered remote to thumb endlessly through the channels—all 153 of them. How on earth did these people ever decide on what to watch? Half of what he found was old crap that he'd already seen a dozen times before, and the rest was a collection of infomercials, foreign-language variety shows, news and the "life sucks" shows hosted by Phil, Oprah, Geraldo, Jenny, Sally, and anybody else who could convince a group of weirdos to go on television. Even the news about *him* had gotten boring, with sad-faced anchorpeople saying the same things over and over. He did note, however, much to his relief, that at least one of the stations had found a better picture of him, the one out of his fifth-grade yearbook.

Partly because he had been raised right, as his dad used to say, but mostly out of sheer boredom, he'd laundered the sheets from the master bedroom. It wasn't right to leave a place without making the bed. *Especially if you broke a window to get in while your hosts were on vacation.* He was also careful to clean up during his ongoing eating binge. He was almost sorry he'd found the Pepperidge Farm cookies and the vanilla ice cream in the freezer. Absent anyone telling him he couldn't have another helping, he'd pretty much obliterated the contents of both containers.

Despite his desire to be a good houseguest (breaker?), he couldn't bring himself to do anything with the JDC jumpsuit, which still lay where he had shed it on the floor of the hall bathroom. That would remain behind closed doors at least until he left. He did feel sorry, though, for whoever would have to clean up the mess.

It took enormous self-control to keep from executing his plan early. While he realized the importance of darkness to his chances of success, this was July, and it didn't get dark until almost nine, for crying out loud. But wait he would, because impatience spelled a trip back to the JDC, or maybe even worse. If all it took was a little patience to keep that from happening, he could endure the boredom.

As he flipped mindlessly through the channels, his thoughts turned once again to the trouble he was in. He was developing a new perspective on it all. He was beginning to accept his situation as an unchangeable fact that had to be dealt with, rather than a series of events to be regretted. Okay, so he'd killed a guy and that was bad, but it really was an accident, and it really was in self-defense. In his heart, Nathan was certain that he only intended to make Ricky jump back. It might take a while for him to sleep through the nightmares of the blood and the noise, but there wasn't a lick of remorse in his heart for protecting himself.

He conceded, however, that running away from the JDC might have been a stupid thing to do. It sure made him look guilty, and in retrospect, with Ricky dead, he probably didn't have to worry about anyone else trying to kill him. So, why had he run? The best answer he could think of was the simple truth: because he was scared, and most important of all, because the opportunity presented itself. Given those circumstances, who wouldn't run? And now that he was out, staying out seemed more important than . . . well, *anything*.

What really surprised him was how quickly his list of crimes grew. He had already added burglary—he supposed that's what it was called—to the list, and within the next few hours, he was planning to steal a car. By the time he reached Canada, he figured he'd have to burgle at least two more times, and steal at least two more cars. No doubt about it, if he got caught, he'd be in deep shit.

The only answer, then, was not to get caught.

He stopped his tour of the channels to watch a couple of minutes of *Butch Cassidy and the Sundance Kid,* until he remembered how it ended, and he started flashing through the channels again.

It had been a long time since Michaels had heard Hackner so agitated. "Calm down, Jed. He was just telling you his opinion. You want the guy to lie?" Jed's conversation with Johnstone had put a burr six inches up his butt, and he was taking it out on his lieutenant over the phone.

"Opinion my ass, Warren! This guy is a menace to the very kids he's supposed to be protecting. He couldn't care less about anybody in there!"

If it had been anyone else taking up his time with

such irrelevant bullshit, Michaels would have lost his temper long ago. But it was Jed, and Jed didn't go off the deep end very often. Michaels decided to cut his sergeant some slack.

"Okay, Jed, accepting the fact that he's a menace, what would you have me do about it?"

"Get his fat ass fired!"

"I can't do that. He doesn't work for me."

"Come on, Warren, don't you see . . ."

"Jed . . . Jed . . . ," Michaels tried to interrupt. "Dammit, Jed, shut up!" That did it. "Listen, I understand that Johnstone's a hateful son of a bitch, and I'll stipulate that he's a menace to the people under his control. But the fact of the matter is, we're already up to our ass in alligators over the kid's escape, we've turned up exactly zero worthwhile leads, and I simply don't have the time to worry about the staffing of the Juvenile Detention Center right now. And, I might add, neither do you."

When Hackner didn't respond, Michaels knew that he'd made his point. "Now, then," he continued, "do we have any evidence at all to corroborate the Bailey kid's self-defense story?"

Jed sighed. "I just got finished telling you—"

"Yeah, I know, that Johnstone's a bad guy," Michaels finished for him. "What about Ricky Harris, what did Johnstone say about him?"

Hackner clearly didn't want to answer. "He said he was a model employee." Jed's reply was little more than a mumble.

"And his personnel jacket?"

"Same thing."

"Face it, Jed," Michaels concluded. "We're still looking for a murderer. I want to give the kid the benefit of the doubt just as much as you do, but they taught us both in cop school to let the evidence guide our conclusions, not the other way around. And frankly, right now, the evidence against Nathan Bailey is pretty damning."

Jed wouldn't let it go. "I'm telling you, Warren, there's something else here—something we're missing. We don't have any evidence as to motive. All we've got is a dead body and a very plausible story from the boy. You believe him as much as I do. You said so yourself this morning."

This really wasn't going anywhere. "Tell you what, Jed, let's split this case into two parts. The first part: we've got to bring the kid into custody. His motivation for killing Harris doesn't affect that. Once we've got him back, we'll have all the time in the world to prepare the case against him. That's the time to hang Johnstone out in the breeze—and Harris, too—if that's what's appropriate. Fair enough?"

Hackner was quiet again, as though he wasn't sure whether he had won or lost. "I guess it'll have to do. But I'm going to dig deeper into this guy Ricky."

Warren smiled. Jed was too hardheaded to answer with a simple *okay*. "Now that that's out of the way, we've had the uncle's place under surveillance, I trust?"

Jed was all business again. "Yep. Not a sign of either one of them."

"Think maybe they skipped town together?"

"I guess that's possible, but considering their history, I don't think it's likely. The uncle's the whole reason he ran away, remember?"

Michaels thought it was a long shot as well, but he

had to pursue it as an option. One of the most basic principles of investigative police work was to eliminate the obvious before searching for the obscure. And as unlikely as it might have been for Nathan to return to the uncle he purported to hate, it *was* a place that he knew, and where he had roots. It would have been irresponsible not to surveil the house. "So, where else might he have gone?"

Jed answered succinctly, "I can't think of a single place where he *might* not have gone."

Michaels conceded that the question *was* ridiculous. If the uncle were deleted from the equation, Nathan had no one left in his life. And sad as that was, it left him with limitless options. Owing allegiance to no one, without so much as an obligation to phone anyone to say he was all right, the entire world belonged to this fugitive from justice; his options were limited only by the breadth of his imagination and his cunning. If he were an adult, these conditions would add up to the most difficult type of search. Since he was just a kid—hell, Michaels didn't know what that meant. Certainly there were options available to adults that were not available to children, but on the other hand, children sort of blended into a crowd, and to a large degree, they all looked alike. Not feature for feature, of course, but human nature was such that people didn't notice children's features. Police were fortunate if people even remembered the presence of children in a crowd, let alone any specifics. Consequently, a child on the run could have options that would never be available to an adult.

The bottom line was this: They had no way of quickly focusing their search.

* * *

Dr. Baker's day had begun nearly eight hours ago with a SIDS baby who had arrived by ambulance, unnecessarily, as it turned out. The baby had likely been dead for hours, already showing signs of lividity and rigor mortis when he was transferred from the ambulance cot onto the gurney in the ER. Even the medics had known that there was no hope, but they weren't paid to deliver that kind of news to frightened, desperate young parents. As medical director, that was Baker's job.

Life and death were his business, and this was neither the first nor the last time that he would hold the hands of sobbing adults, as he sewed his own emotions together with a thin suture of professional aloofness. Still, it was a shitty way to start a day.

As of twenty minutes ago, however, the world had been brought back into balance as he delivered a very fortunate young man into this world via emergency cesarean section. Not one to show emotion on the job, he was self-conscious of the tears in his eyes as he handed the wailing infant over to his grateful mother. Somehow, it was easier to let the emotions go on the good news than on the bad. For Tad Baker, it was what had kept him coming to work every day for the past eight years.

Between the day's two momentous events was an endless stream of broken bones and sliced flesh, all of which had to be handled in due course, prioritized in order of the injuries' threat to the long-term health of their owners. As he slipped a set of X-rays into the clips on the viewer, he frowned, instantly regretting the decision of the triage nurse to put this case at the end of the line. Ordinarily, broken fingers were, on the ER's scale, a low-priority injury, but this guy was the exception. The ghostly white hand on the screen before him was more than just broken; it had been mangled. The pain must have been excruciating, Tad thought. How odd that he would have sat so patiently in the waiting room for—he referred to the admissions chart—*four hours!* Cringing at the potential liability an event like this posed to his hospital, he made a mental note to follow through on it later. It was, after all, not the sort of note one would want to have in writing, in case Mr.— he referred to the chart again—Bailey turned out to be the litigious sort.

Putting on his best clinician's face, Dr. Tad (as he was called by his staff) slid back the curtain and addressed for the first time the occupant of Bed Four. "Good afternoon, Mr. Bailey," Tad greeted his patient. "I'm Dr. Baker. I see by your chart that you've had an accident. Hand injury, huh?" Mr. Bailey looked awful. He was drawn and pale, like someone who was fast approaching the limit of his pain tolerance.

Mark jumped at the suddenness of the doctor's entrance, mustering only a wan smile in response to Baker's clinically cheerful greeting. The intense throbbing in his hand had transported itself all the way back to his shoulder blades now, and lighthearted conversation was no longer in his repertoire.

Tad reached gently out toward his patient. "May I see it, please?" he asked, nodding toward the hand. The look he received as his reply told him that Mark Bailey had no plans to let anyone within five feet of his injury. Tad softened his voice nearly to a whisper. "I promise I won't move anything around, okay? I'll be very, very gentle."

Mark studied the doctor's face for a few seconds, then gently passed his right hand over, carefully supported by his left. "It really hurts, Doc," he said.

"I bet it does," Tad agreed. "I've seen your X-rays. It's really quite a significant injury you've sustained. How did it happen?"

The first time that question had been asked, by the triage nurse, Mark had been caught off guard, and he had stammered clumsily through the poorly formulated lie. In the ensuing hours of his wait, he had worked through most of the details, actually practicing the answer out loud once, albeit at a whisper. "I was changing out the brakes on my car when the jack slipped," he explained. *Smooth as silk,* he commended himself.

Tad winced at the thought. "Didn't have it up on blocks, huh?"

"Nah, I was too stupid to do that," Mark said. "You know. I was in a hurry; took shortcuts. Same old story I guess you guys hear every day."

Tad smiled noncommittally, knowing right away that the story was a lie. First of all, the fingers were still on the hand; a highly unusual outcome for that particular scenario. For another, the angulation of the fractures was all wrong. An impact from a single heavy object should project a uniform force more or less perpendicular to the plane of the body part being injured. In Mark Bailey's case, the displacement of the bone ends was longitudinal in the case of the first digit, and lateral in the case of the fourth.

The fact that patients lied to him—and many of them did—was typically not a source of great concern to Tad. Quite often, he had to admit that if he were in the position of the patient, he, too, would probably try to float a story in hopes of mitigating the embarrassment. Nine times out of ten, he played Mr. Gullible. People had the right, after all, to live their lives any way they wanted to, and it wasn't his place to interfere with their fantasies, so long as they weren't harmful to others.

But harmfulness was the key. In the medical world, as in the legal, the good of the many outweighed the privacy of the one. When a gunshot case or a case of suspected child abuse came to him, he was legally bound to report it to the police, even over the objections of the patient. The same was true for knife wounds and other acts of criminal brutality, but only when there was clear, irrefutable evidence that such acts were the source of the injury. While few doctors argued the spirit of the law, the way it was crafted put them in a very difficult position, because the burden of proof ultimately fell on the physician. Overreacting and reporting a case based merely on one's supposition of foul play would place a doctor in violation of the Hippocratic Oath if his or her suspicions proved groundless. On the other hand, ignoring a bona fide criminal act would place a doctor in violation of the criminal statutes of the Commonwealth of Virginia. In either case, the doctor's license to practice medicine would be at risk.

There was no doubt that Mark Bailey's injuries were the result of something other than the cause described by the patient. In Tad's judgment, these fingers had been broken intentionally, by someone who seemed talented at doing such things. This judgment was not something he could prove, however; nor could he ignore his suspicions. He needed to delve a little further into the details—not because the law required it, but because it was the right thing to do. Finger-breaking was not a talent he preferred among his neighbors.

"So your hand got caught under the wheel itself?" Tad asked as he gently turned the hand over in his own, trying for the sake of argument to match the purported mechanism of injury with the damage done to Bailey's hand.

"Sure did," Mark said, his body tense and ready to take back his hand if the doctor broke his promise not to hurt him.

Tad noticed his patient's uneasiness and smiled kindly, tenderly resting the injury back on Mark's chest. "Relax," he said. "The last thing I want to do is to hurt you."

Now that he was back in sole control of his pain, Mark did, indeed, relax. "You're right, Doc," he said. "You didn't hurt me a bit. Kinda nice, for a change."

Interesting turn of phrase, Tad thought. "Oh, really? How do you mean?"

"How do I mean what?"

"You said it was a nice change that I wasn't trying to hurt you. I was just curious what you meant."

Mark was exhausted, mentally and physically. He didn't even remember saying that, but now he had to come up with something to cover it. "Did I say that?" he stalled.

Tad pretended to be distracted by Mark's chart. "Mm-hmm. Somebody been hurting you, have they?"

Mark laughed at the very thought of it. "Nobody but myself, Doc. I guess I meant doctors. You know, even when they're trying to help you it still hurts."

Tad nodded and smiled. "Really no such thing as a painless shot, is there?" He finished jotting his note on the chart and flipped it closed. "Here's what we're going to do with that hand," he explained. "We're going to put you under a light general anesthetic, and we're going to have to set the bones. Looks like somebody might have already tried to do that, but made a bit of a mess of it." He looked to Mark for a reaction, but none showed.

Tell me about it, Mark thought. His stomach turned all over again at the memory of sitting there on the filthy floor of the Hillbilly Tavern, grinding his own bone ends together as he brought the fingers back into alignment. It was the only way to even begin to walk out of there. Despite the initial agony, his efforts had reduced the sharp, electric pain to the dull throb that currently wracked his entire body.

"Once we've got that taken care of," Tad continued, "we're going to put you in a soft cast for a couple of days just to make sure we've got the swelling under control, and then we'll do a hard cast for probably ten to twelve weeks. How's that sound?"

"Just peachy."

"There's also a chance you'll need surgery," Tad finished. "The X-rays show some possible involvement of the metacarpals—the little bones in the back of your hand that run from your wrist to your fingers—and that can mean tendon or ligament damage that can't be fixed as easily as bone. We won't know for sure, though, for another couple of days. There's been a lot of bleeding in the hand, making damage assessment by X-ray a little more complicated."

"So you're gonna have to knock me out?" Mark asked. There was an edge of hope to his voice.

Tad nodded. "It'd be pretty tough getting bones set any other way." It was time to push. "Why do you suppose only two fingers got broken instead of your whole hand?"

Shit. He suspects something. But suspicions were different from knowledge, and Mark was in too deep to change his story. "I have no idea," he said. "Just lucky, I guess."

"You can do without too much more of that kind of luck," Tad joked, his eyes probing Mark's face for the truth, and getting a "kiss my ass" in response. "It's interesting, too, that the fractures angulate in different directions. If I didn't know better, I'd swear that your hand was deliberately broken." *That was smooth as gravel,* he chided himself.

"Well, you're the doc, Doc. Maybe you can write me up in a medical journal or something."

"You're sure that's how your hand got broken—a jack fell on it?"

Stick with medicine, Doc, Mark thought. *This police work just ain't for you.* "A jack? God, no. The whole damn car fell on it. You don't think I'm lyin' to you, do ya?"

Tad stared just long enough to convey his true thoughts. "Of course not. No sane person would lie to his doctor. To do that would just delay recovery."

Piss on it, Tad thought, *it's your hand and your life. I've done my part.* He clicked the ballpoint back into its casing, and stuffed the pen into the breast pocket of his lab coat.

"Rest quietly for a little longer, Mr. Bailey. The orthopod will be here in a minute to work on you. I'll see you later."

It was just after seven-thirty, and Monique Michaels was surprised to hear the sound of Warren's car in the garage. Most nights he didn't get home until nearly seven, and she'd assumed that his investigation of the Bailey thing would keep him much later than that. After fourteen and a half years of marriage, she could tell just by the way he slammed the door of his patrol car that he'd had something less than a good day. Having heard a good portion of The Bitch that morning, followed by continuing coverage not only of the Bailey boy's escape but of his media appearance as well, she couldn't blame him if he was a little cranky. Plus, it had been a long time since he'd had to play policeman for real, and he probably was exhausted.

The meal of the day had been spaghetti, and the kids had scarfed up all but a thimbleful of what she fixed. Even as the doorknob turned, she was already pulling a frozen Mexican dinner out of the freezer.

Warren's look said it all as he entered the kitchen. Rigidly well-postured by nature, and normally energetic even in the evenings, he looked as though he'd slept fully clothed in a windstorm. Monique nearly laughed at the sight of him. "Boy hunt getting you down, dear?" she teased.

A wry smile brightened his face. "Don't *you* start with me. I'm getting too old for this shit."

"Is my baby tired?" Monique mocked in a little-girl voice as they hugged and kissed. "Not enough sleep last night?"

As part of a well-practiced ritual, Warren went directly to the cabinet over the stove and pulled down a gray lockbox, the kind secretaries normally used to store their petty cash, and thumbed the combination. When it opened, he slid his .38 caliber Police Special, holster and all, off his belt and deposited it in the box. He still preferred the five-shot snub-nose over the bulky cannons selected by most of his subordinates. Next came the speed loader he carried in his suit coat pocket. After locking the box again, he placed it back in its assigned spot over the stove. As a young, newly married police officer many years before, he'd balked at the notion of being separated from his weapon. In the end, Monique had prevailed, of course, and in the succeeding years, he had come to be far more satisfied knowing that the kids couldn't become a statistic than he was paranoid that he wouldn't be able to repel an attack on his family.

There just was no denying it anymore. He had become the old fart he'd always feared.

"It's been a zoo, hon," he explained as he put his weapon away. "Just an absolute zoo. You'd think Al Capone had escaped, instead of some kid."

"Do you think you'll catch him?"

"Oh, we'll catch him, all right," Warren said. "Once we figure out where to start looking for him."

Monique led her husband into the living room and sat him down on a chair, where she moved around behind him and began massaging his shoulders. "I guess that means you don't have many leads."

"Leads," Warren snorted. "It's not that we don't have *many* leads. We don't have *any* leads."

"What about your man Thompkins?" Monique teased. "He seems hard-charging enough to turn up some clues."

Warren dropped his chin to his chest and rubbed his forehead. "You heard that, did you? Could you believe it? He was supposed to get their permission, not beat them into submission. What a bonehead."

"Now, Warren, I'm sure he was just trying to do his job and make a good impression."

Warren snorted again. "Yeah, well, so was Barney Fife. And I can assure you that Patrolman Thompkins made an indelible impression on a lot of people. The county executive even called me today and asked me to send his regards. I have a meeting scheduled tomorrow afternoon for just that purpose."

Monique hugged him from behind and kissed his ear, crossing her forearms under his chin. "Now, you go easy on him. It wasn't so long ago that you were a stupid rookie."

"I was never *that* stupid," Warren grumped.

"Oh yeah? How 'bout that time you shot at yourself in that lady's house?"

Warren's head sagged even further. He laughed. He reached up and rubbed the back of her head as she rested her forehead on his shoulder. "You just don't forget anything, do you?" That incident had occurred fifteen years before, when he was in the process of tracking down a prowler in an old woman's house. As he swung into the bedroom in a full crouch, he saw a man crouched down on the other side of the door, aiming a pistol directly at him. Not until Warren had squeezed off three rounds did he realize that he was facing down his own reflection in a full-length mirror. The woman nearly had a heart attack, and he was suspended for a week while Internal Affairs did an investigation. Worst of all was the merciless ribbing to which he fell victim for years after the incident.

"Tomorrow should be interesting," Warren said, changing the subject. "I understand Petrelli's taking the radio station to court tomorrow with an emergency petition to compel release of the telephone records."

"Do you think it will work?"

"Hell, no, not a chance. I'd pay a thousand dollars, though, just to see Petrelli get trashed one more time in front of the cameras. The only good thing about my day today has been the thought of how really shitty a day he's had."

Monique slapped his arm playfully and stood up straight again. "You're terrible," she scolded. "What happens if the judge says no?"

"Then we're left with plain old police work. I think the kid's holed up somewhere. He can hang loose for a day or two, but sooner or later he'll have to move, and when that happens, he'll start leaving another trail. That's when we'll get our next good shot."

Monique came around the chair and kneeled down in front of her husband, resting her elbows on his knees. "Do you think he killed that guard—or supervisor, or whatever—in self-defense?"

Warren shrugged and closed his eyes. "Doesn't really matter right now. He still has to go back."

"But what do you think?"

"Honestly? In my heart of hearts?"

"Yes."

"I really don't care. I think it's a red herring, something I have no business thinking about. At least not until we get him back in custody and he goes to trial for killing the supervisor. The escape and the murder are separate issues."

From out of nowhere, their conversation was interrupted by the thunder of footsteps coming down the stairs. "Daddeeee!" His seven-year-old, Shannon, turned the corner into the living room at full tilt and vaulted into his lap, followed closely by her sister Kathleen, two years her senior. A round of hugs and kisses followed, along with a couple of tickles.

"You're home early!" Kathleen proclaimed, genuine delight twinkling in her eyes. "Mommy said you wouldn't be home till late."

"Well, if it makes you feel any better, I probably *shouldn't* be home till late, but I just couldn't stand the thought of not tucking you two characters into bed for a second night in a row." He kissed her on the cheek.

"Can I ask you a question, Daddy?"

"Any time at all."

"Are you trying to put Nathan in the electric chair?"

Warren shot a look across to Monique and got a shrug in return. Incredulous that his daughter considered herself on a first-name basis with an accused murderer, Michaels leaned back in his chair and gently repositioned his older daughter on his lap so that she was facing him directly. "What kind of a question is that?"

"I was playing with Benny Parker today, and he said that you were going to kill that boy on television by putting him in the electric chair."

"And what did you say?"

"I told him that he was a liar, and then I popped him in the nose."

Warren laughed in spite of himself. "Kathleen!" he scolded, embarrassed by the pride he felt at his petite little girl punching a kid the size of Benny Parker. "You can't hit people just for saying something you don't like."

"It *is* a lie, isn't it?" From the look in Kathleen's eyes, Warren suddenly was not sure who was scolding whom.

"Honey, they don't put children in electric chairs."

"So what's going to happen to Nathan?"

Warren fought the temptation to lie. It would have been easy to give her a fairy-tale answer, but he had long believed that truth was the only way to maintain credibility with his kids.

"That's really not for me to decide, Kathleen. That's why we have courts. My job is to arrest Nathan and bring him back to the Juvenile Detention Center so that a judge can decide what ultimately happens to him."

"But Nathan says that people tried to kill him in the Juve . . . whatever that place is. Are you going to send him back to that same place?"

Warren looked to his wife for some help. Monique gave it a try. "Kathleen, sweetie, this boy Nathan isn't like boys in your school. He was in jail for stealing, and he killed a man to get out of jail. That makes him a bad guy. And bad guys go to jail."

"The kids don't think he did anything wrong," Kathleen protested.

Warren's patience for all of this suddenly evaporated. "Well, he did do something wrong!" he erupted, far more loudly than he had intended. "He killed a man, and you can't go much more wrong that that! My job, Kathleen, whether you like it or not, is to put murderers away in a place where they can't harm other people. Just because he's a kid doesn't make him any less dangerous!"

Both girls fell silent and slid down off his lap, disappearing back upstairs. Kathleen looked as though she might cry; whether for herself or for Nathan, he couldn't tell. When the children were out of sight, Monique returned to Warren's shoulders and started massaging them.

"Did I overreact?" Michaels asked.

"Mm-hmm," she replied, leaning over to gently bite his ear. "You always overreact when you lose your sense of humor. Remind me in a couple of hours and I bet I can help you find it again."

It was nearly ten now, and it was dark, inside as well as out. Nathan put the finishing touches on his note to the Nicholsons—he'd found his hosts' name on a magazine—and walked from the kitchen into the garage. His stomach was in a knot again, but he knew there was no turning back now. The one thing he needed more than anything else was distance between himself and the JDC. The fulfillment of his need lay just on the other side of the garage. The seat and the steering wheel were already adjusted, and he'd killed an hour or so in the afternoon memorizing the locations of all the important levers, switches, and buttons, so that he could make the BMW do as he commanded, even in the dark.

On the outside chance that he might do something stupid, such as locking the keys in the car, he'd kept them in his pocket all afternoon. He moved cautiously now, in the dark, as though someone might be home, even though he'd been in and out of the garage a dozen times that day. He winced at the *click* the car door made as it opened, and was startled when the inside light came on. He moved quickly, the better to get the door opened and shut without anyone seeing him. Once comfortably in place in his seat, he fastened his seat belt, held his breath, and started the engine. He'd barely turned the key when the motor roared to life. He reached up and pushed the button on the sun visor to raise the garage door, working quickly, because he had seen in a movie once that you can die if you run the car engine indoors.

With the movement of the door came an explosion of sound and light, a stark contrast to the otherwise still evening. Nathan was certain that every neighbor in a two-block radius was on the phone calling to report the theft of the Nicholsons' automobile. As the garage door reached the top of its climb, he slipped the BMW into reverse and turned in his seat to guide himself down the long, steep driveway. When he turned, though, all he could see was leather headrest. He jammed on the brakes and lurched to a halt. The stupid car wasn't built for twelve-year-olds. How was he going to see where he was going?

It took a moment for him to reason that once you've broken into somebody's house and stolen their car, it really didn't matter a whole lot if you drove over a bit of their lawn. He let the brakes slip again, and he slid farther down the driveway, pausing halfway to lower the garage door again. Nervous glances out both sides of the car revealed an empty street—clear passage for him to begin his journey in earnest. When the back wheels bottomed out at the end of the driveway, he cut the wheel hard, slipped the transmission into Drive, and gently stepped on the gas. The Beemer lurched forward to the end of the street, then lurched to a stop at the stop sign, flinging Nathan against his seat belt. He remembered from his previous driving adventures that steering wasn't the hard part, really. The tough part was making the car move smoothly. But he'd gotten the hang of it before, and he was confident that he could do it again.

While he'd plotted his trip carefully on a Rand Mc-Nally map he'd found in the glove compartment, he still didn't know exactly where he was, and now he was faced with his first critical choice. He could go left or right. The lady or the tiger. On the logic that left and lady began with the same letter, he turned left in hopes of finding the road that would lead him out of the neighborhood.

After about ten minutes, and only one real mistake in navigation, he found himself on the Cannonball Parkway, whose name he recognized from his months with Uncle Mark. He knew for sure that the Cannonball Parkway intersected with Prince William Road, not too far from where Uncle Mark lived. From there it was a straight shot out to Route 66, which in turn would take him to Route 81, and from there north toward Canada. The digital compass in the Beemer displayed SE, and he was once again faced with a left-right decision. Knowing that he ultimately needed to head west before he could go north, he turned to the right. Happily, the SE disappeared from the display and was replaced with W. He beamed with pride.

The Beemer handled smoothly, and he felt well in control of the vehicle, except a couple of times when the road turned sharply at the same time the headlights from an oncoming car hit him in the eyes. After another fifteen minutes or so, the scenery along Cannonball Parkway began to look familiar to him. On the left was Oliver Wendell Holmes Middle School, the last one he had attended before becoming a ward of the state. About a mile up the road, he knew, was the intersection with the 7-Eleven and the McDonald's, marking the road that led to Uncle Mark. Just sharing the same air with that place brought back memories he'd hoped he'd never face again.

Drunk son of a bitch, Nathan thought. *I hope you drown in your own puke someday.*

As he neared the intersection, traffic slowed considerably and finally stopped. In the distance, the night was alive with the strobes and light bars of emergency vehicles. Nathan's first instinct was to turn around and head the other way, but there was no way to cross the median without drawing all kinds of suspicion. It was probably just a traffic accident, anyway. Nobody was going to notice him.

It took another quarter-mile of bumper-to-bumper backup to confirm his worst fears. This was no accident. This was a roadblock, just like they had described on the news. Cops in brown uniforms were stopping every fourth or fifth car to shine a flashlight around and talk to the driver.

"Oh, God," he prayed aloud, "please don't let them stop me."

Hoping to stay as invisible as possible, Nathan had chosen the left lane. Without moving his head, he glanced over at the driver to his right. Even in the darkness of night, that driver was fully recognizable. Blond hair and mustache, maybe twenty-three years old, with a mole on his left temple.

If I can see him, they can see me, Nathan thought. He felt his heart gain speed, and he gripped the steering wheel hard enough to make his fingers go numb. "Stay in control," he told himself again, out loud, for perhaps the hundredth time that day. "Sometimes the best place to hide is out in the open."

He felt like he was living out his only recurring nightmare, where he was naked in school and everyone was laughing, but there was nothing he could do to cover up. People were all around him, any one of whom could end his flight with a single word, but none of them were looking yet. Up ahead, the very people he feared most were planning to shine a flashlight in his face and throw him back in jail. All day long, he'd carefully planned this night, but he hadn't allowed for the scenario unfolding in front of him. Like the house alarm and the call tracing, he'd figured that it was useless to worry about such things that he couldn't change. If only he'd known.

In Nathan's lane, twenty-three cars and two motorcycles stood between him and the roadblock. Six cars were let through without being checked, leaving seventeen in front of him. His hands were moist with sweat now, and his legs were shaking so badly that he was concerned whether he was going to be able to control the car.

Please, oh, please God, he prayed, silently now so

as not to attract attention. *Please let me get by them. Please don't stop me now. I'll be good, I swear I will. I'm sorry for every bad thing I've ever done. Please let me get through.*

Tears tried to well up in his eyes, but he willed them away. Whatever happened, it was going to happen quickly, and there would be no time for that kind of emotion. In the next round, the cop let only three cars through before he searched the fourth. After that, he let five through. There seemed to be no pattern; he just stopped cars at random. If it didn't end soon, Nathan thought, his heart would explode right out of his chest. Wouldn't that just startle the living daylights out of the policemen?

There were only eight cars ahead of him now, and the cop let three go unnoticed. Next time, only two.

Oh, shit, I'm the third car now, he thought, feeling himself on the edge of panic. *He's been stopping number threes. Oh, God, please!*

To Nathan's horror, the cop stopped the very next car. Nobody got through on that round. Desperate, he tried to plan his way out if they caught him. None of them were in their cars, he thought. If they made eye contact, he'd just stomp on the gas and take his chances. It was the only choice he had.

Once the cop was done with the car, he waved that driver on with a smile. And stopped the very next car!

"Oh, shit!" This time he said it out loud, a whisper. In the green light of the instrument panel, he could actually see his right leg shaking now as it tried to maintain even pressure on the brake pedal. He tried to swallow, but his mouth felt as if he'd been eating chalk.

The officer seemed particularly interested in the

vehicle in front of Nathan, spending a long time shin-ing the light carefully around the interior of the back-seat, and then talking for a good thirty seconds with the driver. Nathan couldn't hear the words—he couldn't hear anything but the drumbeat of blood in his ears—but the conversation seemed to be heating up. The cop opened the driver's door and motioned for him to step out, motioning for his partner in the other lane to come over and help. Obediently, the driver of the car stepped out and placed his hands on the roof of the car.

As the cop reached for his handcuffs with one hand, he motioned with the other for Nathan to drive around. There was some very brief eye contact, and Nathan thought for an instant that he was busted. But whatever recognition there may have been on the part of the cop quickly evaporated when his prisoner started to struggle, and they both tumbled to the ground. Nathan watched the brawl for a moment in his sideview mirror, and nearly rear-ended the car in front of him in the process.

It took a couple of miles of driving for Nathan to re-alize that he'd made it. After the roadblock, the traffic thinned out, moving at posted speeds or better. Nathan cruised into the right-hand lane. A green-and-white sign announced that Route 66 was just three miles away. He felt nearly dizzy with a sense of pride and ac-complishment. He'd beaten them again. With each passing hash mark on the road, Nathan sped closer to his freedom, and farther away from the nightmare that his life in Brookfield had become. Before him lay his future, where his past didn't have to matter. He could start over and somehow pretend that Uncle Mark and Ricky and judges and death itself had never entered his life and so abruptly shut down his childhood.

The windows were up, the radio was blaring, and the air-conditioning was turned on high. He was free, and he planned to stay that way. As a sense of pure triumph washed over him, he threw his fist into the roof liner and shouted at the top of his voice, "Yes!"

When Monique Michaels rolled over to spoon up with her husband, she noticed he was gone, and she was instantly wide awake. The digital clock on her nightstand read 3:21, while the one on his read 3:28 and the VCR across the room flashed its perpetual 12:00. Leaning up on her elbow, she listened for sounds, but the house was silent. She was worried about Warren. He wasn't himself tonight. Even the sex was a little off. He did his part well enough, but half his mind was somewhere else.

It was happening again, she knew. He was shutting them out. Something was chewing up her husband's insides, and rather than sharing it with her, or leaning on her for support, he was falling back into his macho, suffer-in-silence bravado.

Before she could control it, old anger bubbled up again from deep within. It had been nine months since their son, Brian, had been killed on his newspaper route, but only two since Warren had started to deal with it. In between, Monique and the girls had been stranded alone, left to deal with unspeakable grief in virtual silence.

Monique thought—she prayed—that they'd worked through it all. Through counseling that Warren had fought every step of the way, Monique was finally given the freedom to grieve openly. Freed from the shackles of the make-believe strength she showed to the girls, her emotions had flooded out of her, raw and bitter in their purity. Week after week, the anger and grief and bitterness spilled out to the therapist.

Yet, week after week, Warren just sat stoically, clearly in control and clearly concerned for his bride. He held her hand; he spoke sympathetic words; yet he never shed a single tear where she could see. God, how she'd hated him for that!

In the end, as the counseling diminished from three sessions a week to two sessions a month, her anger subsided just enough to let the love return. And Warren was still there. Still stoic. Still strong. Still kind.

But the pain remained as an open wound.

Slipping on the summer-weight robe with the big flowers—the one Warren hated so much, making it fun to wear—she swung out of bed and left to find him. On the way out, she reflexively checked on the girls, who were sound asleep.

Normally, when Warren couldn't sleep, he simply went downstairs to watch TV until he faded off, but tonight he wasn't there, either. "Warren?" she asked the house softly. "Where are you?" No answer. Now she was really concerned.

Then she saw movement on the front porch, and noticed the door was ajar.

"What's wrong, honey?" she asked as she glided silently out onto the porch to join him.

Warren greeted his bride of nearly fifteen years with a smile. He was sitting in one of the wooden rockers, holding three fingers of Scotch in a glass, wearing a T-shirt and sweatpants, with his bare feet crossed on the porch rail. "Hi, babe," he said. "Kids okay?"

Monique sat down in the rocker next to his. "They're fine," she said. "Out cold. You're the one I'm worried about."

"I'm fine," he assured her. "I've just got a lot on my mind."

He was anything but fine, and Monique could tell. "Like what?" she probed.

"Work stuff."

"What kind of work stuff?"

"Stuff stuff," he insisted, trying to blow her off. "Really. It's nothing for you to be concerned about. Why don't you go on back to bed? I just need to work through some things."

"Warren, look at you." It was the same tone she used to scold the kids. "You never sit on the front porch, and I don't remember the last time you had a drink by yourself."

"If I was by myself, you *couldn't* remember me having a drink. Sort of by definition."

"Don't change the subject. Tell me what's going on in there." She tapped his temple with her forefinger. "You promised you'd never shut me out again."

Warren inhaled deeply and noisily through his nose and let it go as a silent whistle. He started to answer once, but stopped and looked away. "I'm—ah—I guess I'm having some problems keeping this Nathan Bailey thing in perspective." His voice sounded weak, and a little shaky. He told her of the video and of Nathan's transient likeness to Brian.

So that was it. Monique hugged him as best she could from a different chair. "Oh, honey, I'm sorry," she soothed. "I know how much you miss him. But all kids that age look alike sometimes."

He forced a chuckle. "I guess. But it makes it tough to throw him in jail."

"But it's your job. You said yourself . . ."

"I know what I said, Monique," he barked, much more harshly than he would have wanted. "You don't know the whole story. You don't know what his life has been like. In the past two years, he's lost everything." *So have I,* he didn't say.

Monique let the silence that followed linger in the humid night air. Promises aside, this was how Warren worked out his problems. He guarded his pain the way a gambler hides a losing hand. As long as no one could peek at the cards, he could bluff forever.

The moment when Jed Hackner entered the house with the news about Brian, Monique watched her husband die inside. Warren was a man of many talents and many interests, but his son was his life. They breathed the same air and thought the same thoughts. Identical in looks and personalities, they laughed at the same movies and together dreamed up the most ridiculous practical jokes, which only they thought funny. They shared a very special world, those two, one in which girls were simply not allowed.

Brian was Warren's reason to stay young. He told everyone who would listen that the girls were important to him—and they absolutely were—but that it was his son who'd fulfilled the order he placed at the baby store.

On that day in October when Brian was stolen from their lives by a drunk teenager in a crush of twisted steel and aluminum, Warren's personality changed. He went through all the motions of life, but something was gone, like a table lamp, perhaps, with a 25-watt bulb where a 60-watter belonged. At first he withdrew completely, grieving in silence while he made a great show of helping others cope.

Next came the anger. He attended both days of the teenager's trial, arriving early to sit up front where he could stare at the defendant and be clearly visible to the jury.

When the driver was convicted as an adult of voluntary manslaughter and sent to the state prison in Richmond, it was as though the anger had been exorcised from Warren's soul. A spring returned to his walk, and he began to show an interest again in the family. He told Monique one night that justice had been done, and now he could begin to put this all behind him.

But he'd never be the same, and they both knew it.

The look in Warren's eyes and his posture in the chair reminded Monique so much of the bad days following Brian's death. She didn't know how much more of this he could hold in until he just came apart. It would happen one day, she was sure, just as it had happened to her time and again in the therapist's office. She wouldn't force it. But she prayed she'd be there for him the day it happened.

"It's just not fair," he said after a very long time.

Together as a couple, yet alone with their thoughts, they sat in silence on the front porch for more than an hour, listening to the shrill chirping of a million night creatures as they screamed their battle cries and sang their love songs in the darkness. They had been through a lot together, most of it wonderful, some of it horrifying. But on balance, they'd grown closer through it all. In the deflected glow of the stars and the streetlight, Monique held Warren's hand and secretly watched as tears balanced themselves on the edge of his eyelids and rolled down his stubbly cheeks. He said nothing, and he made no move to wipe them away.

As a knot formed in her own throat, Monique realized that she loved her clumsy, intolerant, macho, sexist husband more at that moment than she had on the day he proposed.

CHAPTER SEVENTEEN

BY 4:15, NATHAN WAS SOMEWHERE between Harrisburg and Wilkes-Barre, Pennsylvania, and looking for his next rest stop. In six hours of driving, he hadn't gone nearly as far as he'd hoped. Distances on the map just looked shorter. The Beemer's gas gauge was nudging empty when he pulled off the highway and headed toward what appeared to be a residential area.

This driving stuff had turned out to be less exciting than he'd expected. Once past the roadblock near his ex-home, he'd blasted straight through Virginia and Maryland without incident. His biggest problem turned out to be cramping in his right leg from keeping his toe pointed all the time to reach the gas pedal. Sitting in one spot for so long, without the option of moving his butt more than a half-inch at a time, had begun to take its toll on him as well. He was hungry. And thirsty. And he had to piss so bad he thought he'd explode.

The exit ramp off Route 81 dumped him out onto another four-lane strip, this one crisscrossed with traffic lights all blinking yellow in perfect unison. He was in a low-rent business district, surrounded by darkened grocery and hardware stores, fast food places, and a dollar movie theater showing year-old movies for a third of what you could rent them for at the video store. Directly across the street was a competing marquee advertising triple-X-rated movies twenty-four hours a day. Sure enough, there were a dozen cars in the parking lot.

Though the Beemer's need for gas and Nathan's need for relief were becoming critical at the same time, he decided to press on farther down the road. Maybe he'd become spoiled the night before, but this wasn't the kind of neighborhood he wanted to move into—even as a burglar. A sign on a telephone pole told him that Little Rocky Creek was selling single-family homes from the low $180s just eight miles down the road.

"Little Rocky Creek it is," he announced to the car.

It was a new housing development, still largely under construction. The house designs appeared similar to the neighborhood where he grew up, but they were much smaller, and so close together that from a distance some looked like they were actually touching their next-door neighbor. The main drag through the development, predictably enough, was Little Rocky Trail, which fed ten cul-de-sacs, around which most of the houses were situated. He began his tour of the neighborhood by cruising each of these side streets.

Everyone in the whole damned neighborhood received a morning paper, many of them two. How was he going to pick out the house on vacation if every driveway had newspapers on it? It was just one more thing he hadn't planned for. He was scared to think about how many other things could go wrong that he hadn't even considered. And whoever heard of a paperboy who had his route taken care of before five? When he was a paperboy a hundred years ago, he was lucky to get the *Washington Post* on his customers' doorsteps before six, and even then it was because his father had wrestled him out of bed.

"Stay cool," he told himself. "You'll think of something."

He finished his first complete pass without finding a single driveway buried in papers. But this was still the Fourth of July holiday, and he knew in his heart that at least half of the neighborhood had to be on vacation. All he had to do was figure out which half, and make sure he didn't make a mistake.

Your real mistake was getting yourself into this in the first place, he thought. Not that it mattered.

At the end of the tenth cul-de-sac, he swung the turn and came to a stop against the curb. The Low Fuel light was burning a bright orange now on the dash. He needed to think things through. How would MacGyver handle this, he wondered.

The first thing he'd do is take a leak

He switched off the Beemer's headlights and, moving as quietly as he could, slipped out the driver's-side door, leaving the car running, and darted up the lawn to the shadow cast by a dogwood sapling near the front corner of the house. He turned his back to the road, and began relieving himself onto what appeared to be some sort of spider plant. In the silence of the night, he might as well have opened up with a fire hose, but once he'd started, there was no stopping until it was done. Middle school scuttlebutt had it that if you made yourself stop peeing before you were empty, you'd rupture your balls.

As he finished up and tucked himself away, his attention was drawn to a collection of three spindled handbills that had been stuffed into the handle of the screen door.

I wonder.

By taking four steps out into the yard, he could see the front doors of the neighbors' houses, and none of them had any handbills on their doors.

Nathan, you're a genius, he congratulated himself. To confirm his suspicion, he tiptoed up to the garage door. By standing on the metal handles he could peer through the small-paned windows into the darkness of the garage. Just as he'd hoped, there was an open spot. Better yet, there was a second car still there—a Honda, it appeared. He pumped his fist in the air. *Yes!* he cheered silently.

After making a mental note of the house number—4120—he jogged back to the Beemer and drove away. The first order of business was to ditch the car. He remembered passing a church just before turning into the development that would suit the task perfectly. He paid special attention to street names and the looks of his surroundings as he exited Little Rocky Creek, hoping to simplify the task of finding his way when he returned on foot.

Again, his sense of distance had betrayed him. "Just before the turn" worked out in reality to be about a half mile down the road. By the time Nathan drove the Beemer into the church lot and parked it in the farthest space out, the eastern sky was already beginning to burn red. He had no idea that dawn came so early. It wasn't a time of day that he frequently witnessed firsthand. To his growing list of obstacles, he now had to add time.

Once out of the vehicle for the last time, he hid the keys under the mat on the driver's side, locked the door, and closed it as quietly as he could. He hoped that maybe it really wasn't stealing if you gave back the keys.

Sprawling before him was Saint Sebastian Catholic Church, looking more like a grounded flying saucer than it did a house of worship. For a brief moment, Nathan considered going inside for a brief chat with God—and Saint Sebastian, for that matter, if he was in the mood to listen in—but thought better of it. He was running out of time. Besides, God seemed to be listening so far.

About the time that Nathan was watering the plants, Denise Carpenter was pacing her kitchen, waiting for the limo to arrive. Enrique sat with her, propped up in a hard-backed chair, wishing with all his might that he could trade his boss in for one who was sane. For the past hour and a half he'd issued positive reviews for no less than six different outfits, this on the heels of a previous hour rating hairstyles. If he'd told her once, he had told her a thousand times that she was a beautiful woman, that it didn't matter what she wore because she looked good in everything. It was close enough to the truth that no one could call him a liar.

More by default dictated by the ticking of the clock than by rational decision, Denise had settled on a very professional, understated kelly green suit with a gold bead necklace and matching earrings. She decided to wear her professionally straightened hair pulled back in a tight ponytail, which Enrique didn't particularly like, but he would have cut his tongue off with a pair of scissors before he'd have said anything. Besides, she didn't listen to any of his fashion opinions anyway, which led him to consider the option of just shooting her and moving on to a better job.

"Maybe I shouldn't have pulled my hair back," Denise whined.

Enrique lowered his head onto the kitchen table and closed his eyes. "Jeez, Denise, why don't we just shave you bald and you won't have to worry about it at all anymore?"

Her eyes shot darts, but they never got through the force field of her producer's exhaustion. "Come on, Rick," she begged. "Stay awake with me. Here, have some more coffee." She refilled his mug, emptying their second pot since midnight.

Enrique sat up straight again and gently gripped her elbow. "Den, listen to me," he said lightly. "You look great. You're going to do great. The only thing you have to worry about is staying awake through your radio show. America is just going to love saying good morning to you."

Denise smiled and ran her hand through Enrique's hair. "Thanks, Rick," she said. "You're such a good friend to put up with me."

His reply was a warm, if tired smile.

"The red outfit looked better, didn't it?"

Enrique's head made a loud *thunk* when it fell back onto the table.

* * *

As the darkness lightened and the shadows turned gray, traffic started to pick up, and Nathan was forced farther from the roadside and deeper into the woods. Another planning failure. He had no business being outside in the daylight where people could see him and recognize him. At least he wasn't driving anymore, he consoled himself.

It took him every bit of forty-five minutes to make the trek back to Little Rocky Creek. Deadfalls, creepers and briar bushes all conspired to slow his progress.

It wasn't yet six o'clock, yet the air was thick with humidity and the temperature was approaching ninety already. His clothes were soaked with perspiration, his hair matted to his forehead and the back of his neck. The hike was taking long enough that if he hadn't just driven the route, he would have sworn that he'd made a wrong turn.

Finally, through the underbrush, he could see the turn for Little Rocky Trail. He turned parallel to the new road and soon was crossing behind backyards. It was the time of morning when people let their dogs out. One of them, a German shepherd, spied him through the slats of his fence and barked ferociously, baring its teeth and lunging against the pickets, thus igniting a chorus of barking dogs throughout the neighborhood. Nathan barked back at the dog and flipped him off. Nothing like a six-foot oak barrier to help a guy feel brave.

Backyards seemed to stretch on forever as he traipsed through the woods. Even in the comfort of his borrowed Reeboks, the cuts and bruises on the soles of his feet were reasserting themselves. In time, he reached the end of the existing construction, and could see before him where a new section of townhomes would be built. At that spot, the woods ended, opening up into a huge open swath of dirt, excavated basements, and construction materials.

Forty-one twenty was at the end of the cul-de-sac located on the other side of Little Rocky Trail from where he was right now. His plan had been to make entry from the rear of the house, accessing it by walking in a big circle through the woods until he wound up where he needed to be. Now, he realized, the construction made that impossible.

He faced a new set of choices. If he crossed through the construction zone, he'd be sure to be seen, probably by some security guard, and this game would be over. He rejected that option first. Another possibility would have been to stay in the woods and walk all the way around the periphery of the construction cut until he ended up where he needed to be. Problem was, he couldn't tell how long or how far that would take him. From where he stood, he couldn't see the far edge of the construction.

Nathan decided it was time to be bold. He straightened his shoulders, combed his hair with his fingernails, and just walked out of the woods, looking for all the world like he belonged there.

Todd Briscow tossed the wad of paper towels into the kitchen trash, then stared at his hand as though to figure out where to throw it out next. His wife, Patty, was busy looking for the carpet stain remover while their six-year-old son and one-year-old Labrador cowered together across the room.

"Dammit, Peter," Todd cursed as he washed his hands in the kitchen sink, "how many times have I told you to put away food after you use it?" The dog had just barfed up an entire jar of strawberry preserves that young Peter had left out on the counter after fixing himself some toast. And, of course, because they were finally able to afford the Persian rug they'd been saving to buy, that was the precise location the dog had selected as its vomitorium.

Peter wisely chose to say nothing, staying well out of range and well protected by his only friend in the family right then.

When Patty returned from the basement with the stain remover, she was lockjawed with anger. Todd checked his watch for the hundredth time this morning and said exactly the wrong thing, not because he wanted to, but because he had to.

"Patty, I've really got to go. It's nearly six, the Reischmann proposal begins at eight, and I've still got view graphs to print."

"Why, of course you have to go," Patty replied icily. "There's work to be done around the house, isn't there?"

Her words were a blatant attempt to pick a fight, leveraging the neverending argument centered around the you-never-do-anything-I'm-always-stuck-with-the-rotten-jobs theme. The premise of the argument was as true as it was false. His work as an account executive for the telephone company kept him working most nights and weekends, but he tried his best to factor in family time. It was the major frustration of his life that he no longer controlled his time—the one element he valued most over all the others. What time he had left after doing his job was controlled by Patty and her assigned chores. To be sure, there were hours left at the end of each day, but his body demanded that he dedicate those to sleep.

He declined to take the bait, choosing instead to ignore her comment. She was as stressed as he was, and that damned rug meant a whole lot to her. When he bent down to kiss her good-bye, she turned her face away. He kissed her on the neck anyway.

"I'm really sorry, Patty, but I've got to go," he said. He picked up his briefcase and walked toward the garage, pausing for a moment at the door. "I hope you learned something from this, Peter," he said to his son, who remained silent on the far side of the room. "And Patty?"

She looked up from her task, her eyes still hard.

"Please don't kill the dog." Through the mask of anger, he saw the faintest glimmer of a smile. He blew her a kiss and left.

The garage was like a sauna, the unmoving air instantly bringing beads of sweat to Todd's forehead. Even as the overhead door rumbled open, there was no relief, not the slightest trace of a breeze. It was on days like this that Todd wondered how he ever grew up without air-conditioning.

As he backed down the driveway, he admired his landscaping efforts from the previous weekend. After three months of watching the house rise from its origins as a plot of dirt, and only four weeks after closing on the mortgage, the house was beginning to look like a home, like someone actually lived there. He half hoped that Patty and Peter would appear in the window to wave good-bye, but a glance back caught no evidence of a curtain parting.

Little Rocky Creek was turning out to be a terrific place to live. The neighbors all knew each other, and everyone seemed to be at the same stages of their lives: young professionals struggling to establish themselves and every month barely scraping together the cash necessary for the mortgage payment on these, their starter homes. There were lots of kids in the neighborhood, no crime to speak of, and a strong community spirit that bonded everyone together.

Who's that?

A boy, maybe twelve, thirteen years old, was crossing the street in his direction. The face looked vaguely familiar, though he couldn't place it with any of the families in the neighborhood. But then, Todd didn't know too many of the folks who lived up in the first section that was built. He was a good-looking kid, long and thin with disheveled blond hair, but there was something in the way he carried himself that made Todd think he was up to no good.

By the time Nathan saw the car approach, there was nothing he could do. His first instinct was to run and duck out of sight, but his last opportunity to do that without being seen came and went in the two seconds it took to consider the option. All he could do was try and blend in. He didn't even alter his stride as he crossed the street, though he did change his course to head back toward the front part of the neighborhood. No sense showing this guy where he was going.

The Chevy approached from behind him on the left, slowing ever so slightly as it passed. Nathan smiled politely and waved.

Todd waved back. The kid looked normal enough, and he certainly wasn't trying to run away. Just a tired kid on his way home from whatever a kid that age could be on his way home from at this hour of the morning. One thing was for sure, Todd thought: When Peter got to be that age, he was going to be kept on a tight leash.

As he accelerated toward the end of the street, Todd's thoughts turned to the Reischmann proposal and the details of how he was going to structure his presentation. He never even looked back in the mirror.

As soon as the Chevy was out of sight, Nathan made a right-angle turn and headed back for the woods, suppressing his urge to run. Once back in the comfort of shade and obscurity, he leaned his back against a tree and slumped to the ground, taking a minute or two to collect himself.

"That was *stupid*!" he declared in a whisper, banging the back of his head against the tree bark. "I never should have gone out in the open! What'll I do if that guy recognized me?"

Just one more thing to worry about over which he had no control. He hated himself for making so many mistakes. In the past twenty-four hours, luck alone had pulled him through every challenge. One of these times, luck was going to look the other way, and he was going to have to engineer his own solution. His head told him that it was useless to worry about things he couldn't change, but these were things that could get him thrown back in jail, or even killed. That was why you needed grown-ups, he figured, to help keep it all in perspective. That was why he was so lonely without one around.

He felt like he was stuck in quicksand. Everything he did to get himself out of this mess just got him in deeper and deeper. Killing was wrong, stealing was wrong, breaking and entering was wrong, yet he'd done all of them. These were things you went to hell for, yet he was planning to do most of them again.

And how could he stop? One way or the other, his future was sealed. Either he was going to get out of the country successfully, or he was going to spend a very long time in prison for doing what he'd already done, even though he'd had no real choice. How much worse could it be getting caught doing more of the same?

As these thoughts ricocheted through his brain, energy drained from his body. He needed sleep and the brighter outlook that rest always brought. With an enormous effort, he gathered himself to his feet and embarked on the last two hundred yards of the night's journey.

Ten minutes later, he had gained entry to 4120 through a ground-level basement window, made his way to the master bedroom, stripped down to his borrowed undershorts, and fallen fast asleep.

CHAPTER EIGHTEEN

FOR ENRIQUE, THE BIGGEST SURPRISE of all was his continued surprise at Denise's ability to suck him into her crises. All night long, through the endless hours of rehearsal and hand-holding, the single thought that propelled him through the agony was that of the sleep that would be his reward after the limo finally picked up Denise to take her to the studio.

Then, somehow, he found himself with her in the limousine, and now in the wings just off-camera, waiting for her satellite interview to begin.

He had to hand it to her, though. In the presence of others, she handled herself like a pro. Calm and articulate, she carried herself as though she'd been born in a television studio. The difference between her real self and her stage self was near schizophrenic. She was born for this line of work, just as he seemed born to the task of helping her access the TV star that was hidden deep down inside a paranoid single mother who never came to grips with the depth of her natural talent and who feared unemployment more than anything else in the world.

The ABC staffers in Washington went to great lengths to make Denise comfortable as she was prepped for the interview. Her job, it turned out, was to sit quietly while she was serviced. Makeup was applied by a professional artist in a very comfortable, if Spartan, dressing room equipped with all manner of junk food. It occurred to her that a doctor would have a field day bringing the blood sugar and caffeine levels of television people under control. The issue of her hair had been settled by the hairstylist, who told her that ponytails on black women made them look hard and unattractive. Under different circumstances, Denise might have taken offense, but she found that the prospect of facing millions of people made her extraordinarily receptive to suggestions. With far greater speed and efficiency than she had ever experienced in a hair salon, her "do" was transformed into a much more stylish, professional bob. Enrique seemed relieved when he saw it for the first time.

With seven minutes left before she was to talk with Joan, or maybe Charlie—there was still some problem with the scripting in New York—Denise was seated in a well-worn though surprisingly comfortable chair, in front of some cheesy faux-glass blocks through which the audience was supposed to believe you could see the Capitol building. Up close, the scenery wouldn't fool anyone, but in the monitors, sure enough, it looked convincing. Presently a technician was fitting Denise with an earpiece, the coiled cord for which ran under her hair and was clipped to her collar in the back, and from there joined the tangle of cables and cords that covered the floor. A tiny microphone was clipped to her lapel, and the technicians stepped away, allowing her to see herself for the first time as she would appear on network television. She was not at all displeased with what she saw.

"Ms. Carpenter?"

The voice, from very close by, startled her until she realized it came from her earpiece. "Yes?" she said, as though she were calling across a room.

"Hi, Ms. Carpenter, I'm Allen, the director of this segment. Do you mind if I call you Denise?"

"No, not at all."

"Good," Allen said, even as she gave her permission. For just an instant, Denise wondered what would have happened if she had answered: Yes, I mind. "You look great," Allen continued. "Couple of things to think about before we go on-air. First of all, you don't have to shout. Even if you mumble, that mike will pick up everything. Shouting just gives headaches to us folks in the control room."

"Okay," Denise said. "Sorry about that." It was a common mistake among new radio jocks as well.

"No problem," Allen laughed. "Now we can put our headsets back on and not have to worry about nose-bleeds. This should be really simple stuff. There was some kind of scheduling problem in New York, so they've expanded your segment by ninety seconds to four minutes. That might not sound like much time, but trust me, it's plenty of time to get the whole story out, okay?"

Denise nodded. "Okay," she said.

"Have you ever done a television interview before?"

"No," she said, suddenly embarrassed. "But I do a lot of radio."

"I know," Allen acknowledged. "I listen to you every day. You're great. Just remember, though, that no one can see what you're doing in radio. On TV, you need to be conscious of where your eyes are, okay? Always direct your answers straight into the camera."

"All right." This seemed like pretty basic stuff.

"Start now, Denise, okay? You look like you're trying to figure out where I am. Don't worry about that. Just give your answers to the camera. Talk to it like you would to a friend. And we're going to turn the monitors away from you so you don't get distracted."

"I can do that," Denise said into the camera. It did feel a little awkward.

"Good. Now here are the ground rules, okay? You're going to be sharing this spot with some other guy on the set in New York. Be careful not to answer the questions directed at him, and try to keep your answers short but complete. Okay so far?"

"No problem yet," Denise said with mock confidence. Into the camera.

"And now for the last bit of advice," Allen went on, giving the impression that he was working off a checklist. "And this one's for you, not me. Remember, it's only four minutes, okay? You can do anything for four minutes. I took a CPR class one time, and they told me you can cut off the blood to the brain for four minutes and still be okay. That means that you can endure any itch, stray hair, or urge to sneeze for four minutes. Once the light goes off that camera and you hear the bump into the commercial, you can pick your nose for all I care. But for your own sake, please don't do anything distracting during the interview—even if you're not on-camera at the time."

Instantly Denise sensed dozens of itches all over her body. "Not a big believer in the power of suggestion, are you, Allen?"

The director laughed in her earpiece. "Of course I am. I just like to watch people squirm. One last, final thing. Don't get bothered if I tell you something in your ear while you're talking."

"What kind of thing are you going to say?" Clearly, Denise was bothered and he hadn't even done it yet.

"No speeches, I promise." Allen said. "Just maybe a suggestion like 'speak up' or 'slow down' or 'there's a booger in your nose.' You know, that sort of thing."

Denise's hand jerked to her nose, eliciting a hearty laugh from the director.

"Just kidding, Denise. You look great and you'll do great. We go live in three minutes and twenty seconds. Break a leg."

With that, her earpiece went dead, leaving her alone with her thoughts and the horde of butterflies in her stomach. When she glanced off into the wings toward Enrique, he flashed her a smile and a thumbs-up. She had to laugh. God, he looked miserable. And what a good sport he was for helping her through this.

After a successful career founded on the qualities of her voice, Denise was unexpectedly aware of her hands. They seemed like unnatural appendages. Should they be folded on her lap, placed on the arms of the chair, or maybe just rested on her knees, where they would undoubtedly leave indelible sweat stains on the fabric of her skirt?

"We go live in thirty seconds, Denise." Allen's familiar voice had a sweet smile in it now; carefully practiced, she was sure, to keep nervous guests from bolting at the last minute. "And I vote for keeping the hands crossed on your lap. Looks most natural that way, even though they'll never be in the frame."

When Allen was done, the audio in her ear switched to the familiar theme music for *Good Morning America*. The sound quality wasn't bad, though nothing compared to the stereo 'phones she was accustomed to. Denise took a deep breath and let it out slowly. As she did, a feeling of calm poured over her. She was in control again.

"Okay, Denise," Allen coached in her ear. "Don't say anything until you're asked a question. Your mike is live . . . now."

Denise acknowledged him with a slight nod. And waited for the light on the camera.

"Welcome back," Joan's voice said to America. "Much has been said and written recently about the increase in violence among children. Law enforcement officials have become concerned in many areas of our country about violent crime that not only victimizes children, but which is committed by them as well.

"Over the Fourth of July holiday, in a quiet suburb of Washington, D.C., a guard in a juvenile detention facility was murdered, apparently by one of the residents—a twelve-year-old boy named Nathan Bailey, who subsequently escaped and is still at large. Joining us this morning in our studios here in New York is the Honorable J. Daniel Petrelli, the prosecutor with jurisdiction in this case, and from our affiliate in Washington we have Denise Carpenter, a syndicated radio personality, who talked with Nathan Bailey during her radio talk show yesterday morning. Welcome to both of you, and thank you for joining us."

With the mention of her name, the two lights on the bottom of Denise's camera lit up, and she smiled pleasantly into her fish-eyed reflection. *Nobody said anything about Petrelli being on the show!* "Thank you, Joan," she said. "It's nice to be here."

"Mr. Petrelli," Joan said, "let's start with you. What happened the other night?"

Petrelli had been flown to New York the previous night—first class, of course—where he'd spent the night in a deluxe hotel, and had been shuttled to the ABC studio by limousine. He sat across from Joan on a tan leather sofa, wearing a charcoal-gray suit with the blue shirt and striped tie that had been selected by his media consultant. He was trim, if somewhat soft, with a bald pate that had to be matted with pancake to prevent reflection of the bright lights off his normally shiny crown. When he spoke, his voice masterfully mixed professional disinterest with compassion, his Richmond accent adding a certain air of sophistication.

"Sometime between seven and nine P.M. on July fourth, Nathan Bailey, a very troubled young man with a history of car theft and violence, attacked and killed one of the child care supervisors at the Brookfield Juvenile Detention Center, and subsequently escaped. He remains at large, and our search for him continues to this moment."

"How did he kill the guard—excuse me, child care supervisor?" Joan asked.

Petrelli looked uncomfortable in a professional gee-I'd-like-to-tell-you-but-I-can't sort of way. "I really can't go into detail, because it's part of a continuing investigation . . ."

But we all know you will anyway, Denise thought.

". . . but I can tell you that he was brutally stabbed to death with a knife."

Joan seemed incredulous. "Where would a prisoner get a knife?"

Petrelli resisted the urge to snicker. Like it wasn't common knowledge that prison inmates fashioned shivs from anything they could get their hands on. "I really can't go into specific detail. But we are very concerned at what may be a serious breach of security there at the Juvenile Detention Center."

"I'm sure you must be," Joan said, her voice full of compassion. "Now, Denise," she went on, turning her attention to the television monitor in the studio, "I understand that Nathan called your program yesterday."

"That's right, Joan," Denise confirmed, smooth as could be. Into the camera. "But the story we got was considerably different from the version told by Mr. Petrelli. According to Nathan, he killed the supervisor in self-defense." In just under sixty seconds, Denise gave the short version of the story Nathan had related. In concluding, Denise offered, "Killing is always a terrible thing, and we certainly can't condone escapes from jail, but I have to tell you that after talking with Nathan on the telephone, I'm not sure what kind of choice he really had."

"I'll tell you exactly what choice he had," Petrelli drawled without being prompted by Joan. "He had the choice of reporting these alleged events to the proper authorities and letting us take action accordingly."

"You're thinking like an adult, Mr. Petrelli," Denise reproached. "We're dealing with a child, whose imagination can be many times bigger than reality. I got the impression talking with him that if you hadn't promised to try him as an adult, with veiled threats of execution, he might have turned himself in already."

Petrelli's face reddened through the makeup.

"So you *have* determined that you will try Nathan as an adult?" Joan prodded.

With the exaggerated patience of a schoolmaster repeating a lesson to a dense child, Petrelli repeated the position he'd already stated so many times. "We have determined that Nathan Bailey is the prime suspect in the murder of a law enforcement official, and we will pursue his arrest and ultimate prosecution with all of the commitment and dedication that should be expected under those circumstances. As I said yesterday, if he's adult enough to commit such a crime, we should expect him to pay an adult price."

"So you're assuming that the story told by Nathan on Denise's show was a lie?" Joan goaded.

Petrelli sensed where this was going, and he circled his wagons. "I'll say again that we really cannot go into the details of this case at this point, but I have reason to believe that Nathan Bailey's story is a fabrication."

"Did you hear him on my show yesterday, Mr. Petrelli?" Denise asked, her volume rising.

"I'm afraid not," Petrelli lied. His voice dripped with condescension. "My work schedule rarely allows me a chance to listen to the radio."

"So how is it that your office was so quick in issuing a subpoena to see our private telephone records?" Though it was never her intent to be on the attack, it was part of her nature, and something about Petrelli's sanctimonious attitude really pissed her off.

Clearly, Joan's researchers had missed this development. She turned to Petrelli for comment. "What sort of subpoena did you issue?" she asked.

Petrelli's jaw flexed, making his sideburns move up and down. This was outrageous. The Bitch had turned this into a personal battle, and she was free to say whatever she liked, while he was bound by professional ethics. "Again, I hate to sound like a broken record, but this is another area where I really cannot comment," he said.

"Well, I can comment all I want," Denise attacked. "The police and the prosecutors in Braddock County can't figure out where Nathan has gone, so they're resorting to Gestapo tactics to seize the private records of our production company. Can you imagine, Joan, what would happen if the police or the FBI could gain access to ABC's telephone records? What do you think the effect would be on the news-gathering capabilities of your network?"

"Oh, come now, Ms. Carpenter," Petrelli moaned as the theme music potted up from the background. "I really don't appreciate your characterization of this situation—"

Joan interrupted, "I'm sorry, Mr. Petrelli, Ms. Carpenter. I don't think any of us anticipated the level of controversy here, but we really must break; we're out of time. Thank you both for joining us." To the camera, she added, *"Good Morning America* will be right back."

The lights on Denise's camera went dark, but she continued to sit well-poised until Allen told her, "We're clear. Way to go, champ. You really had him on the ropes."

Enrique joined the technicians who swarmed in to dismantle her electrical connections. "Well?" she asked.

"You looked great," he said, genuinely pleased.

"How'd I sound?"

"Like a bitch."

"Thank you."

Enrique laughed. "You're welcome."

CHAPTER NINETEEN

As HACKNER PULLED IN to the JDC parking lot, Michaels was waiting for him. After their conversation yesterday afternoon, Jed had been shocked by Warren's sunrise call to meet him here at nine. When pressed for a reason, he would say only that he wanted to talk to some of the residents. Jed didn't ask why the change in heart. With Warren, it was always best just to accept the little victories silently.

"Mornin', Boss," Hackner called as the two men converged in the parking lot. Two minutes outside the air conditioning and Jed could already feel his undershirt sticking to his back. "Did you get the sleep you wanted last night?"

The circles under Warren's eyes answered that question without words. "Johnstone came up and chatted with me while I was waiting. He's getting the interview set up for us."

"Does he know I'm coming with you?"

"I mentioned it, but he didn't say anything about your conversation yesterday."

"Imagine that."

Warren extended a reproachful forefinger. "You behave yourself, okay? No fighting."

"Yes, Dad," Jed promised with exaggerated innocence.

As they approached the main entrance, they removed their weapons from their holsters and placed them in the lockers designed for that purpose, just outside the door.

"Mine's bigger than yours," Jed commented as he put his newly issued seventeen-shot 9mm Glock into the locker.

"You're just like the kids," Michaels scolded, adding his Smith & Wesson snub-nose and closing the door. "If I can't hit what I'm shooting at in five tries, I'll be damned if I'm sticking around for twelve more."

At Michaels's request, Johnstone had set up a private meeting with Tyrone Jefferson—street-named Aces—a fifteen-year-old three-time felon whose rap sheet included a drive-by shooting. Fortunately for all concerned, his marksmanship matched his aptitude for evading the police, and no one was hurt. If he served out his whole sentence, he wouldn't see freedom until his twenty-first birthday. Aces occupied the cell next to Nathan's, and it was Michaels's hope that they might get a clue as to where Nathan might have escaped to, and who might have helped him. Several investigating officers had attempted to obtain similar information the day before, with no success, but Warren wanted to give it a shot personally. For a lot of reasons.

Johnstone was waiting for them in his office. After the obligatory pleasantries, they walked together through security.

Aces was already seated at a table when the officers

entered the otherwise empty classroom for their chat. To protect the boy from the prying eyes of his fellow residents, the venetian blinds had been pulled shut.

Johnstone spoke first. "Aces, this is Lieutenant Michaels, and this is Sergeant Hackner, both with the Braddock County PD. They want to ask you a few questions." Warren and Jed both extended their hands, but Aces didn't move. Johnstone sat in a chair in the corner.

"Could you excuse us, please, Mr. Johnstone?" Michaels asked. His tone was friendly, but they all knew it really was not a request.

Johnstone sat frozen for a moment, trying to think of a dignified exit line. When none came to him, he stood and exited the room. The look he shot at Jed showed that he held him responsible for this humiliation. Aces seemed to take pleasure in the superintendent's discomfort. So did Jed.

Michaels took the seat immediately opposite Aces, swinging it around so his chest was leaning against the seat back. The young black man across the table was sullen, impassive, dressed in the orange coveralls worn by all the residents. His face was a mask of practiced indifference, his expression telling them that they were wasting their time. At age fifteen, he was tougher than either one of them would ever be.

"I'm gonna cut to the chase . . . Aces, is it?" The single, subtle movement of his head could have been mistaken for a nod. "You don't like me because I'm a cop, and I don't want you dating my daughters, okay? But we both have a problem. Nathan Bailey ran away from here the other night after killing one of the guards. Your life in here isn't gonna be the same until we find him and bring him back. The evidence points to an accomplice, and until we find that accomplice, or rule it out as a possibility, you're gonna spent a lot more of your day locked up. So I want you to answer some questions for me, okay?"

Aces's eyes shifted to Hackner, and then back again. "Which one o' you dudes is the good cop, an' which one's the bad cop? I want t' get the cast right before the show starts."

Warren smiled, but otherwise ignored him. "Nathan had the house next to yours, right?"

Aces remained expressionless, examining his fingernails.

"Do you know who might have helped him escape?"

Silence.

"Any idea where he might have gone?"

No response.

"Look, Aces, I know you don't want to believe this, but I'm only looking out for Nathan's best interests. If we don't bring him in, he's liable to get killed."

"Why? You gonna kill him?"

"No," Michaels said after dropping a beat. "That's Sergeant Hackner's job. He's the bad cop."

Aces acknowledged the riposte with the slightest movement of an eyebrow.

"Fact is, Aces," Michaels went on, "there's a whole bunch of people with guns out there looking for that kid. They think he murdered Ricky Harris in cold blood. Sergeant Hackner and I are willing to believe there was more to it than that. If we can find him before the others, there's just less chance he'll get hurt."

"But if I stay quiet," Aces reasoned, "there's that

much less chance he'll get caught at all. Seems it was pretty important to him to get outta here. I hope he makes it. If he gets killed, well, 'least he was killed tryin'."

Michaels studied the boy's eyes for a long time, but saw nothing. With Aces, the system had won, even as Aces thought he had beaten it. The look in the boy's eyes was the same one Michaels had seen in the eyes of countless adults in countless interrogation rooms. Aces had trained his entire life to be king of the prison system. He had risen to the top of the juvenile pyramid, where he would remain for another six years. If the model proved correct, he'd last maybe a year on the streets before signing on as a rookie in the big leagues at Richmond. Michaels was about to get up and leave when Hackner spoke up.

"What about Ricky?" Jed asked. "Was he as much of an asshole as I've heard?"

Something flashed behind Aces's eyes as they darted over to Jed. Where there had once been studied indifference—maybe even mild amusement—there now was a raw hatred. Had the setting been different, the transformation would have been frightening. In seconds, the emotion was gone, replaced once again with total neutrality.

"Let's just say I hope he died slow," Aces said, an evil smile just bending the corners of his mouth.

"And why's that?" Jed baited.

Aces didn't even sniff the hook. "If you heard he was an asshole, then you don't have to ask."

"Fair enough."

They all sat in silence for a long, awkward moment until Michaels broke the tension.

"Thank you for your time, Aces," Warren said, rising from his chair. "You've been very . . . tolerant. I hope your time goes smoothly." Jed rose with him and they walked to the door.

"Yo, cops," Aces said as Warren's hand touched the knob. They both turned. "Bailey's a pussy. Harris had it in for him, but I don't know why. It's good Bailey got out o' here. This place was gonna kill 'im."

Warren nodded respectfully toward the prisoner. "Why, thank you, Aces."

"I didn't say nothin'."

CHAPTER TWENTY

KENDRA AND STEVE NICHOLSON hadn't spoken to each other in the last hundred miles. It had been Steve's idea to drive straight through for their return from Disney World, thinking it better to get the driving—and the attendant whining from the kids—out of the way in one endless marathon, rather than prolonging the agony over several days, the way they usually managed their longer trips. Even after thirteen years of parenthood, he was surprised at just how miserable kids could become during an eighteen-hour drive.

Somewhere in South Carolina, Kendra had reached the end of her rope, and had begun lobbying for a stopover for the night. Steve talked her into going just another hundred miles, and once that was done, another hundred didn't seem so unreasonable. But as Norfolk disappeared in the rearview mirror and Richmond remained a distant goal, Kendra reached her breaking point and just stopped talking.

Steve was on a quest now. And even though he knew that the drive home would in all likelihood be the only part of the trip that Kendra would remember five years hence, he had made a commitment to drive straight through, and by God, he was going to do it, even if it killed them all. As morning approached afternoon and the misery of the dark hours faded from memory, Steve sensed that the tension was easing a bit. And now, as they got within a mile of the house, Kendra would start warming up again. He was sure of it. He hoped.

"There it is!" he announced to the family as their house came into sight. "Be it ever so humble, there's no place like home."

The kids—Jamie and Amy—bolted upright in their seats and cheered as they saw their house.

Steve playfully squeezed Kendra's knee. "There. Now aren't you glad we're not still somewhere in South Carolina with five hundred miles left to go?"

Kendra's response was a blistering glare. Okay. So he'd pushed too hard. She'd come around.

Steve piloted the Range Rover into the driveway and pressed the visor-mounted garage door opener. Even as the weather seal parted from the concrete floor, he recognized that something was wrong. Curiously, the first thing he noted was the cover shroud on the floor. *I didn't leave that there,* he thought. It all crystallized for him an instant later, but it was Kendra who spoke his thoughts.

"Where's the car?" she gasped.

Harry Thompkins actually watched the digital display on his wrist count up the last sixty seconds to ten o'clock. Just four more hours of agony until his meeting with Lieutenant Michaels, at which time he was certain that the career at which he had worked so hard to excel would come to a disgraceful end. With only 240 minutes left in his professional life, he had all but given up on the divine assistance that might somehow salvage his job, or at the very least, a tiny shred of his dignity.

His assignment until further notice was to sit in an unmarked car out in front of Mark Bailey's house, waiting for someone to arrive. Harry prayed that that someone might miraculously turn out to be Nathan Bailey, but such things didn't happen outside the movies. He'd be lucky if he could get a glimpse of the elusive Uncle Mark, whom no one had seen since his nephew's disappearance. It certainly was interesting how both Baileys disappeared at the same time, Harry thought. As he sat alone and bored in his car, Harry began to wonder if perhaps they hadn't disappeared together. If he got the chance before he was fired, he'd mention it to Lieutenant Michaels.

Harry closed his eyes and read the description sheet on Mark Bailey without looking at it. White male, 175 pounds, with blond hair, blue eyes and a mustache. Drives a late-model red Bronco, license plate WLD-MAN. Wanted for questioning. Not a suspect at this time. He opened his eyes to check his recall and smiled. He had missed a few words, but the essentials were all there.

And so was Mark. Or at least the red Bronco. Harry watched as it nosed into the driveway and parked. Out of the car came a white male, about 175 pounds with blond hair and a huge bandage on his hand. The man moved as though he were in considerable pain, every movement slow and deliberate.

Harry slipped out of the car and jogged across the street. "Excuse me!" he called. "Mr. Bailey!"

Mark turned at the sound of his name, then quickened his pace toward his front door. Before he could take three steps, Harry was next to him.

"Excuse me, sir," Harry said. His voice was polite, but his eyes were not. "You *are* Mark Bailey, aren't you?"

Mark tried to look bored as his mind raced to figure out what the cop could possibly know. "Yeah. What do you want?"

"I want to ask you a few questions. Why are you trying to run away from me?"

Mark glanced down at his arm, and hefted it up as if making an awkward toast. "Do I look like a man who could do much running, away or otherwise?"

Harry knew right away that he was hiding something. Perhaps it was a boy? "Maybe I was mistaken," he conceded, preferring to discuss the real issues at hand. "It looked like you might be trying to avoid me. Where have you been all night, sir?"

"Have I done something wrong, Officer?"

"Could you answer my question, please?"

"Is that a request or a demand?"

Harry considered another naughty exaggeration, but, remembering the beating he took on the radio, thought better of it. "It's merely a request, sir," he replied, adding the sweetest of insincere smiles.

Mark smiled back. "In that case, Officer, I've been in the hospital all night." He again gestured delicately with his mangled hand. "I had a bit of an accident. A car fell on me while I was working on the brakes."

Harry couldn't have cared less about how Mark had been injured, and his practiced caring nod showed it. "Are you aware that your nephew escaped from the Juvenile Detention Center night before last?"

"I said I was in the hospital, not a cave. Yes, I'm aware." The realization of Harry's suspicions hit Mark suddenly, and felt better than a cool breeze on this blistering day. He smiled broadly. "Are you thinking that I might have Nathan here?"

Harry raised an eyebrow. "Should I be thinking that?" he asked.

Mark tossed back his head and laughed loudly, genuinely amused. "Not if you know anything about Nathan and me. Look, Officer . . . uh . . ."

"Thompkins," Harry offered.

"Thompkins. Yes, of course. I didn't even look at your name tag there. Officer Thompkins, my nephew and I hate each other. I sent him away—*asked* him to be jailed—mainly just to get rid of him. This is the last place Nathan would go." It was refreshing to tell the whole truth for a change, Mark thought. "And rest assured," he added, "if Nathan shows up here, he'll wish he hadn't."

As they conversed, Harry edged toward the door. "Then you wouldn't mind letting me in to look around, would you?"

"Actually, I would," Mark said coolly, the image of the broken TV and God only knows what else he had left behind flashing through his mind. "I would mind that very much."

Harry looked as though no one had ever said that to him before. "But why?" he asked. "You said you have nothing to hide."

Mark studied the policeman's face for a long moment. "No, we all have something to hide, don't we? Even you, I wager. What I said was I have no*body* to hide. And that is the honest to God truth."

"Then why won't you let me in?"

"Because you don't have a warrant, and because I don't have to." Mark's tone was suddenly flat. "I spent some time in prison. When I was in the joint, I had to put up with you assholes searching my asshole, and anything else you wanted to peek into, night or day, whenever it floated your boat. I'm back in the world now, and you have to play by the rules."

Harry smiled the way a poker player smiles when he's caught bluffing. "Fair enough, Mr. Bailey," he said, turning back toward the street. "You're a man who knows his civil rights. Thank you for your time." As he stepped onto the street, he heard the front door to the house open.

"Mr. Bailey!" he called out, wheeling around again.

Mark turned in the open doorway, leaning against the jamb. "Yeah?"

"You said a car fell on your hand. Where did that happen?"

"Right at the end of my arm." Mark disappeared inside the house, and the door closed behind him.

Alone again in his car, Harry considered Mark's last flippant remark in the context of their entire discussion. He looked nervous as hell until he started talking about Nathan. Then he got cocky and talkative. When the subject of his injury came up, he got nervous again.

Harry turned his head to face the house and the Bronco in the driveway. Had to hurt like hell to have a vehicle that size fall on your hand.

Wait a minute! There's only one car here! If it fell off its blocks, who put it back together for him to drive to the hospital?

No doubt about it, Mark Bailey was guilty of something. Whatever it was, it had something to do with his injury.

Harry checked his watch again, and was relieved to see he still had three and a half hours left in his career. He thought he'd spend part of it down at the hospital. Maybe one of the ER docs would know something helpful.

Michaels was the first investigator to arrive at the Nicholsons' house, just behind the satellite van from a local television station.

My, but word travels fast, he thought. Neighbors and assorted onlookers—children and their mothers, mostly—had begun to gather in tight clumps in the street, drawn to the scene either by word of mouth or by the presence of the barricade tape whose sole purpose, ironically, was to keep people away.

According to the dispatcher, officers were originally sent to the house in response to a burglary call, but when they arrived on the scene, they radioed back for a senior presence.

As Warren approached the front door, he recognized a familiar face from the first night at the JDC. "Good afternoon, Officer Borsuch," he said as he approached. "Got you working days now?"

The cop guarding the door looked proud that he'd been recognized. "Nah," he said with a smile. "Workin' double shift. I need the money. Tryin'to buy a boat."

Warren clapped him on the shoulder. "Boat, huh? Haven't you heard that there's only two happy days in a boat owner's life?"

"What's that?"

"The day he buys it and the day he sells it."

Officer Borsuch had heard the saying a hundred times but laughed anyway as he stepped aside to usher Michaels through the front door into the enormous foyer. "Quite a place, huh?"

"I'll say," Warren agreed. "So, what makes you think the Bailey kid was here?"

"Well, I wish I could say it was brilliant detective work, Lieutenant," Borsuch said good-naturedly as he led Michaels down the main hallway. "But it really was pretty easy." He pulled open the door to the bathroom to display the pile of bloody clothes left where Nathan had dropped them.

Warren laughed. "I guess there are different levels of deductive reasoning, aren't there? Did he take anything?"

"Yes, sir. He took some clothes belonging to one of the Nicholson kids, ate a bunch of their food, and drove off with their BMW."

Warren's eyebrows arched high on his forehead. "BMW, huh? Kid's got good taste. Didn't even think about him driving out of town. How do you suppose he got through the roadblocks?" he wondered aloud.

"There's also this," Borsuch said, handing over a piece of lined notebook paper. The writing was done in the studied cursive of a child's hand.

"He left a note?" Warren asked, incredulous. It took him less than fifteen seconds to read it. "I'll be damned," he said when he was finished. "Are we sure this isn't some red herring? Have we checked the facts?"

Borsuch nodded. "From what we can tell so far, he's telling the truth. The most polite burglar in history."

Warren read the note through again and shook his head. "Where's the family?" he asked, looking up.

Borsuch gestured out to the yard, through the front door. "Looks to me like they're getting their fifteen minutes of fame."

Warren's eyes followed Borsuch's arm. The random mingling of people by the curb had metamorphosed into a press conference. Two more TV vans had arrived since Michaels had arrived on the scene, their transmitters elevated high into the air, ready to start beaming signals. Four people, two adults and two children, stood at the curb, their backs to the house. The press faced them, camera lenses glinting in the sun and handheld boom mikes dangling in the air like so many branches of a willow tree.

"The way this case is shaping up in the press," Warren said, "I think the Nicholsons ought to get used to being on television."

As he pulled his patrol car into one of the slots reserved for police officers, Harry Thompkins noted that the hospital parking lot was relatively empty. With luck, that meant he'd be able to talk to somebody right away.

He took the short cut through the ambulance entrance, smiling politely to the triage nurse as he walked past her station and entered the Emergency Department. He was right. Only about half the beds were full, mostly with older people who looked to Harry's untrained eye like they needed a general practitioner more than they needed an emergency room.

He stopped at the trauma desk, where a frighteningly young physician's assistant was filling out some paperwork.

"Excuse me," Harry interrupted.

The youngster held up a finger and finished the paragraph he was writing. Finally, he looked up. "Can I help you?"

"Yes, you can. I need to speak to the doctor who treated a patient named Mark Bailey yesterday."

"Is he in trouble?" The PA's enthusiasm made him look even younger.

"Don't know yet. That's why I need to talk to the doc."

The PA looked to the ceiling as he searched his memory. You could almost see the cartoon lightbulb go on over his head. "Hand injury, right?"

Harry couldn't help but smile at the kid's enthusiasm. "Yeah, right. Hand injury."

"That would be Dr. Baker."

"Tad Baker?"

"You know him?"

Harry shrugged. "Everybody knows Dr. Tad. Us cops bring you a ton of business, you know. Plus Tad and I played each other in a tennis tournament a couple months ago."

"Who won?"

"Don't ask." Harry turned away from the desk.

Tad was in the far corner, putting stitches into the back of a patient's head.

"Afternoon, Dr. Tad," Harry said as he approached.

Tad looked up from his work and smiled. "Well, if it isn't Braddock County's finest." The patient—a teenage boy clad in swim trunks—tried to raise his head to see, but was gently kept in place by Tad's gloved hand. "Jeez, Harry, I'm sorry, all the doughnuts are gone."

Harry flipped him off.

"What brings you to the Band-Aid barn?" Tad inquired, returning his eyes to his work.

"Got some questions to ask you."

"Official business?"

"Yep."

"All right, then, let me just finish up my needlepoint on Tyler here, and I'll be right with you."

"Mind if I watch?" Harry asked. Unlike so many of his colleagues who could not stomach hospital scenes, Harry was fascinated by medical procedures. *Maybe they'll hire me here after Michaels fires me this afternoon,* he thought.

"Not my call," Tad said. "It's really up to my patient here. Tyler, do you mind if my friend Harry watches me put you back together?"

"Who is he?" Tyler asked, not trying a second time to see for himself.

"He's a cop with a big gun."

"If I let him watch, will he promise to give me a warning instead of a ticket?"

Tad laughed. "Harry?"

Harry was laughing too. "Where do you live, Tyler?"

"Fairfield."

"Sure, no problem," Harry promised. Fairfield was on the far end of the county from his patrol area.

"Fine," Tyler said. "Let's throw a party."

Harry wedged in close enough to see. Squarely on the back of the boy's head, an area about the size of an index card had been shaved bald, exposing a smile-shaped laceration about four inches long. By Harry's eye, it was sewn about half shut.

"What happened?" the cop asked.

Tad answered before Tyler had a chance. "Tyler does backflips off the diving board only slightly better than you play tennis."

Ten minutes and as many stitches later, Tad was done. He advised the boy to take Tylenol for the pain, to take all of the antibiotics he had prescribed, and to stay out of the water for at least two weeks while the wound healed. That done, he walked with Harry into the privacy of an empty trauma room.

"What's up?"

"Did you work on a patient named Mark Bailey yesterday?" Harry asked. "He had a broken hand."

"Yes, he certainly did," Tad confirmed, growing visibly uncomfortable. "Harry, you know I can't discuss the details of patient histories."

"I just need a little help, that's all," Harry said hurriedly. "Did he tell you that he was injured when his car slipped a jack?"

This was exactly the sort of legal pinch point that Tad worked so hard to avoid. Bailey was a scumbag, and everyone knew it. He was supposed to stay over for one more night in the hospital, but chose instead to check himself out against his doctor's advice. Those were the actions of a person with something to hide. And he bore the injuries of someone with evil friends.

But the sad fact was that it was *Harry's* job to catch bad guys and throw them in jail, not Tad's. Conscience aside, the doctor wasn't going to put everything at risk just to help a friend.

"I'm sorry, Harry, I can't help you. All of my conversations with patients are privileged."

"I know, I know," Harry said. There was an edge of desperation to his voice. "But bear with me on this. My career might be riding on it. I just want to give you some opinions of mine. If you agree, you don't say anything. But if you don't agree, you can cough. When we're done, we can both swear under oath that you never gave me any information. Okay?"

Tad had known Harry for a long time, seeing him in and out of the ER a thousand times, escorting victims and bad guys alike. He seemed to be an honest, hardworking, ethical guy. What he was proposing, though, beyond being a little childish, pushed the envelope of ethics and honesty to the breaking point.

On the other hand, Harry's plan had taken the downside away from the equation, hadn't it? If he could deny honestly that he had ever given information, then an ethics case could never be brought against him. Plus, was it any less ethical than letting a scumbag wander the streets just so you can protect your own butt? He worded his answer to Harry very carefully.

"I could never agree to do that," he said, but his eyes said something else entirely.

Over the course of five seconds, Harry's face showed dejection, followed by confusion, and, finally, understanding. "Yes, of course you couldn't," he said. He paused for a moment to collect his thoughts. "I think Mark Bailey is lying about how he got injured."

Tad said nothing.

"I think he's afraid that we're going to find out what really happened to his hand."

No response.

"I think he broke his hand while he was committing a crime, and that he's afraid that if we find out about the injury, we'll find out about the crime."

Tad was suddenly overcome with a coughing spasm.

Harry was stunned. His whole theory hinged on the assumption that Mark had somehow broken his fingers while he was helping Nathan escape. Maybe Harry had made the wrong statement. He tried again.

"I think Mark Bailey was injured when he was helping someone escape from a prison."

Bailey. So that's where Harry's coming from, Tad thought. He had heard about the kid Nathan Bailey on the news the previous night, and the staff had been talking about him all morning, but Tad had never put the names together. Nonetheless, he had no way to link the elder Bailey's injuries with any kind of illegal activity committed by him; rather, it was tied to activities committed against him. He coughed again.

Harry looked thoroughly confused now, but Tad would have to let him sort it out alone. "I've got patients piling up in the waiting room, Harry," he said apologetically as he opened the trauma room door. "Your theories are interesting. Feel free to share them with me at any time."

With that, Tad returned to work, leaving Harry alone with his confusion.

CHAPTER TWENTY-ONE

THE HOUSE AT 4120 LITTLE ROCKY TRAIL wasn't half the size of the Nicholsons' place, but it did afford Nathan his first experience with a water bed, and a full pantry more than compensated for the lack of a big-screen television and supersoft carpeting. After awakening around 10:30 and treating himself to another long hot shower, he'd spent what was left of the morning down in the living room, stretched out on the sofa, barefoot, watching cartoons and pigging out on Doritos and root beer.

The good cartoons ended at noon, when his only remaining options were the life sucks shows, soaps, or stomach-wrenching junk like *Barney and Friends* or *Smurfs*. He turned the TV off. Within minutes, he was bored. Whoever lived in the house had no kids, he figured, because there wasn't anything that even resembled a toy anywhere to be found, not even Nintendo. He decided to explore.

Figuring that people kept the good stuff in their bedrooms, he started there, returning upstairs to the master suite. The first order of business, before he forgot, was to strip the bed and wash the sheets. It went a long way toward easing his conscience about all this burglary stuff. One thing 4120 had over the Nicholsons' was a laundry on the second floor. After gathering the sheets into his arms, he walked them out into the hallway and dumped them on the floor in front of the washer. He'd wash them in a minute, but first he wanted to look around.

The master suite was done in a mismatched assortment of light pine and heavy oak. Everything was immaculately clean, evidence of owners who cared about their things. Except for the bed, there were only two major pieces of furniture. The double dresser was chock-full of ladies' things, underwear on the left and sweaters and blouses on the right. Nathan was aware of a curious stirring in his loins as he handled a bra, and he quickly tucked the garment back in the drawer and slid it shut.

On the other side of the room from the oak collection was a tall highboy. The lower drawers had men's clothes: socks and underwear in the bottom two, and T-shirts in the next tier. The tag on one of the shirts said SIZE 44. There'd be no additions to his wardrobe from this house.

He slid the chair from a small makeup table over to the highboy to see into the upper drawers. The topmost full-size drawer held dress shirts, ties, and assorted jewelry—cuff links, tie tacks, that sort of thing. The last two drawers were small ones, arranged side by side at the top. In them, he found the neatest kind of toys. The drawer on the left had a box of bullets. On the right was the revolver itself. It was big, blue-black, and heavy as a brick. Nathan had seen such things on

TV and in the movies hundreds of times, but he had never actually handled one before. It was another one of those things his father had promised they would do when he got older.

He could see the heads of four bullets peeking out through the cylinder openings. There was a way to make the ammunition cylinder flop out of the side of the gun, and he was determined to find out how. Maybe you had to pull the hammer back. He rolled it back to the first click, and nothing happened. The next click took a lot of effort, but as the hammer moved, the cylinder began to turn. As it did, the fifth and sixth bullets peeked their noses out. He got nervous before he had the hammer all the way back, and eased it down slowly.

The hell with it, he thought. He could play with it just the way it was, so long as he didn't pull the trigger for real. For the next twenty minutes, he did room searches the way he saw them done in *Cops,* with the weapon held at arm's length, gripped by both hands. When he played that he was holstering the gun, he stuffed it up to the trigger guard down the back of his pants, the way Mel Gibson did it in *Lethal Weapon.*

With the upstairs cleared of bad guys, of which he'd had to shoot at least half a dozen while catching two bullets himself—one in each shoulder—he paused long enough to put the sheets in the washer and took his battle to the first floor.

He noticed the telephone at about the same time that he was getting bored again. He wondered what The Bitch was talking about today. After hesitating for just a moment, he picked up the phone and dialed. This time he had to keep his pacing to a minimum, because he was tethered by a real phone cord. Like the day before, it took many tries to get through, but when he finally did, he went right to the front of the line.

Denise was talking to Quinn in Milwaukee about the caller's fears for Nathan's safety when she got the note that the real star of today's show was on line fourteen.

"Hey, Quinn?" she interrupted.

"What?"

"I've got a surprise for you on our other line here." She stabbed the button. "Nathan Bailey, are you there?"

"Yes, ma'am," the voice said. This afternoon, he sounded like the boy he was, his tone free of the burdens it carried the day before.

"Try not to call me 'ma'am,' okay, Nathan?" Denise said. "I've got a reputation, you know."

He giggled. "Yes, ma . . . Okay."

"Say hi to Quinn, Nathan. She's from Milwaukee, and she thinks you're pretty cool."

"Hi," he said.

"Hi, Nathan!" Quinn nearly shouted. "I just want to tell you that I believe you, and I hope all of this works out for you. For what it's worth, if I ever have a little boy, I hope he's every bit as polite as you."

"Thanks," he said a little sheepishly. He wasn't sure he knew what she was talking about, and he was certain that he didn't like that "little boy" crap, but it was a nice thing for her to say.

"Listen, Quinn," Denise said, "what do you say I hang up on you and chat with Nathan for a little while?"

"Of course," Quinn said agreeably. "You've got a

great show, Bitch. Keep up the good work. And Nathan, you be careful."

"Yes, ma'am," he said. "I'll do my best."

"So, have you been listening to the show this morning?" Denise asked. "You're quite the celebrity today."

"No, I'm sorry, I haven't," he said, his tone genuinely apologetic. "I've been sleeping."

"Well, I don't wonder," Denise laughed. "I guess doing all that laundry tires a boy out, huh?"

Nathan's bowels turned to ice. "What?" he gasped. His voice was cold as stone. How did she know? How could . . .

"You didn't see the press conference, either?"

Press conference? What the hell is she talking about? His mind raced to put the pieces together, but they weren't there. He said nothing.

"So you don't know!" Denise announced, clearly tickled to be the one breaking the news on the air. Talk about great radio! "Your *hosts* from last night—the Nicholsons—came home this morning and found some things missing. Like a car. They also found your note."

Nathan's heart began to race. His hands were shaking. This wasn't going right. Not the way he had planned it at all. He didn't think they'd get home so soon. And if they got the note, then how come everyone knows? He asked them specifically . . .

"CNN had you tagged this morning as the world's favorite burglar," Denise explained. "It's hard to think bad thoughts about a kid who does laundry."

Nathan still didn't see what was so funny. It was great that people thought nice things about him, but what did that matter? What it really meant was that the cops were still only a few hours behind him. How long could it be before they found the Beemer, especially if they were looking for it? The good news was that people didn't go to church in the middle of the week, and the car wasn't visible from the road.

It'll be okay, he thought, calming himself down. *I only need a few more hours.*

A thousand questions flooded his mind all at once. He needed to get caught up fast on what everyone else knew. So he started asking.

Lyle Pointer watched the press conference live from his living room as he slowly and methodically reassembled his just-cleaned .357 Magnum. The Nicholsons looked like they had stepped out of Little House on the Damn Prairie. Steve looked like the ex–college football star type, probably a quarterback or maybe a kicker. Kendra, no doubt, was the drooling cheerleader, though Pointer was willing to bet that she'd put on a good thirty pounds since they were married.

The kids were like all other kids, nondescript. Both had dark hair and dark eyes. Jamie, the older of the two at maybe thirteen, was clearly thrilled to be on television, though like his mother he could've afforded to drop a few pounds. His sister, Amy, was about nine, Pointer figured, and far too shy to say anything to the reporters.

Considering the work that had to be done, Pointer was none too pleased with the attention the Bailey kid and his antics were getting in the media. The more people watched, the tougher it was going to be to whack the kid and get away. But he had done tough hits before, and within a day or two this business would be done and Mr. Slater would be off his back. And the reporters, God love them, would have plenty to report.

The very fact that CNN had chosen to carry the Nicholsons' comments live spoke volumes about how out-of-control this media frenzy was spinning. The questions were all shouted at once, and each family member would take a shot at giving a rambling, disjointed answer consisting mainly of incomplete sentences. Jamie, in particular, was intent on getting his two cents' worth in at every conceivable opportunity, and nearly beamed with pride that America's criminal *du jour* had chosen to dress himself in his clothes.

Yes, they said, Nathan had broken into their home through the French doors in the back. Except for clothes and the car, nothing appeared to have been stolen, though he had consumed three frozen pizzas. From what they could tell, Nathan had slept in the master bedroom and showered in the master bath, and believe it or not, he had washed all the linens and towels and made the bed before he left.

When Jamie described the pile of bloody clothes in the downstairs bath, a huge flurry of enthusiastic questions followed, which only served to confirm that the family didn't have any real details to share.

Then Kendra read the note:

Dear Mr. & Mrs. Nicholson and Kids,

I hope I got your name right. It was the one on your Time *magazine. I'm sorry I broke into your house. I tried to be careful, but I broke a window out of your back door. I cleaned up the glass, and when I get the chance, I'll be happy to pay you back.*

You have a really nice house. You have the best TVs I've ever seen. Please tell your boy that I had to take some of his clothes. Please tell him thank you and I'm sorry. I found some laundry and I did it along with the sheets I slept in last night. I didn't use any bleach because I'm not very good with it and sometimes people don't like it.

I also had to take your other car. I've drove before and I promise I'll be really really careful. So don't worry. I'll figure out a way to tell you where it is when I'm done.

You probably figured out by now that I'm in pretty bad trouble with the police. I did some bad things but it's not like they think, honest. If it's okay with you, please don't call them for a day or so or maybe even a week after you find this. I really will take care of your stuff.

> *Your friend,*
> *Nathan Bailey*

P.S., sorry about the mess in the bathroom. It's pretty grose.

As soon as Kendra raised her head from the page to signal that she was finished reading, the media mob erupted with new questions. She answered them as best she could, with Jamie's perpetual help. The note had been left on the kitchen table. It was written with a ballpoint pen on plain notebook paper. No, the paper in her hand was not the original, and she didn't know if the press could get a copy; they'd have to talk to the police. On and on it went, simple answers to inane questions, until a single inquiry from the local paper rendered her silent.

"In the note, Nathan asked you not to call the police for a couple of days, yet you called them right away. How does that make you feel?"

Kendra blushed and looked to Steve for help with the answer, but he was preoccupied with the detailed study of a fingernail. Even Jamie fell silent.

Pointer laughed out loud. "Ha! Shut you up, didn't she, bitch?" He was still smiling as he turned his gaze down to his work and slid six Hydra-shock Magnum rounds into his weapon and squeezed the cylinder home.

He knew he'd get the break he needed soon. Now he was ready for it.

Michaels left the Nicholsons' house in a rush to get back to the station in time to pass along to Patrolman Thompkins the County Executive's best wishes, and to excavate a new asshole in the young officer's butt. Whether or not Thompkins had any kind of a career left would depend largely on how he took his ass-kicking. If he copped an attitude, he was done.

As Warren pulled out of the driveway, reporters flocked to his car, shouting questions that he pretended not to hear. They tried to block his progress by pressing against the vehicle, a tactic they often used, on the assumption that their prey would stop to avoid the risk of running someone over. Obviously, they didn't know Warren well enough. At this stage of this investigation, he'd have welcomed the opportunity to flatten a reporter, though it proved unnecessary. He just kept rolling along at a snail's pace, with the windows rolled up, until they finally chose to save their feet and stepped out of the way.

Once on the road, Warren tuned his car radio to NewsTalk 990 for The Bitch. He wondered if Nathan would be brazen enough to call a second time. As soon as the digital display on the radio locked onto 990, he heard the boy's voice. He noted with vicarious pleasure that a day of freedom had greatly lifted Nathan's spirits. The boy was gleefully telling the story of how he had evaded a roadblock the night before, though he was careful not to give the location. *Smart kid,* Warren thought, *but if you keep talking, you're going to tell me something that I can use.*

And when that moment came, Warren admitted, he was going to have to push himself hard to put the information to use. Among the many feelings he had dissected and analyzed last night on the front porch was one that he had not yet had to confront in a meaningful way. Deep in his heart, Warren hoped that Nathan would get away. Whatever doubts he had harbored on the issue were washed away by his conversation with Aces. That talk in the empty classroom of the JDC reinforced in Warren's mind two undeniable truths: First, the juvenile court system created criminals, it did not reform them, and second, Nathan was not a danger to society.

Without a doubt, he was a killer—he had said so himself. But he was no murderer.

* * *

"If you get away, what are you going to do?" asked Nadine from Pleasantville, New Jersey.

Nathan used his thumb to pick the dirt from under a toenail as he considered the question. "I don't know," he answered at length, as honestly as he could. "I guess I'll just start over."

"But how can you do that?" Nadine pushed. "You're a celebrity now. Everyone knows what you look like. Everyone's going to be watching for you."

It was a very good point, Nathan thought, but another one on which he couldn't afford to dwell. "If I'm such a celebrity, and if people want to help, maybe they'll just look the other way for a while." *And not shoot their mouths off like the Nicholsons,* he didn't say.

"Thank you, Nadine," The Bitch said, moving on. "Frank from Coronado, California, you're on the air with The Bitch and Nathan the Kid."

"Hi, Bitch. Hi, Nathan," Frank said. "Great show today."

"Thank you," Denise said.

"Nathan, yesterday you told us that your mom died when you were a baby and that you were raised by your dad, but then you wouldn't talk about him. What happened to him?"

Nathan took a deep breath before he answered. Thinking about these things was so much harder yesterday. Today, he felt calm, collected, like he could talk without breaking down in tears. "He was killed in a car wreck when I was ten," he answered clearly.

"What happened?"

"You mean in the car wreck?"

"Yeah. I mean, did he hit a tree, another car or what?"

"Frank, I'm ashamed of you," Denise scolded. "Don't you think the kid has enough on his mind without dredging up more bad memories?" She said it because it was the appropriate thing to say. In her heart, she hoped he'd answer.

"That's okay," Nathan said agreeably, fulfilling Denise's wish. "I don't mind. Not today, anyway. He was crossing some railroad tracks—not the kind with lights and gates and stuff, but the unmarked kind—when he got hit by the train. The doctor told me he was killed right away."

"So how did you find out?" Frank persisted. "Did the police come to your door or what?" This line of questioning made Denise nervous. Her hand remained poised over the dump button in case she had to get rid of Frank in a hurry.

"No," Nathan explained, "I was staying over at my best friend Jacob Protsky's house that night. They're our next-door neighbors. I guess the police told them, and then Jacob's dad told me. It was pretty sad." Like so many of the images that played on the movie screen of his mind, this one was as vivid as it could be. They waited until he awoke that morning to break the news, and he remembered how Mr. Protsky cried harder than he did. He remembered that he stayed with the Protskys through the funeral, until Uncle Mark finally sobered up enough to come pick him up and take him to his hive.

You remember to give us a call if you need anything, Nathan remembered Mrs. Protsky telling him as she gave him a hug, big tears balanced on her lids.

Then the memories turned bitter as he remembered

calling her from a pay phone after the first belt-licking, begging her to take him back as blood trickled down the back of his legs under his jeans. He remembered how cold and flat her voice was as she ordered him to stop calling them. *You have a new life now, Nathan,* she had said. *We can't be a part of it anymore.*

"You also implied yesterday that you were abused . . ."

"I don't want to talk about this anymore," Nathan said abruptly.

"Good," Denise said, stabbing the dump button. "Neither do I. Sometimes people just don't know when to quit."

"My dad was the nicest guy in the world," Nathan announced.

"I'm sure he was, honey," Denise said soothingly. "And the reason I'm sure is because I think he raised a pretty nice son."

"Thanks," Nathan said warmly, "but there's lots of folks who don't think much of me at all."

"Well, what do they know?"

Nathan smiled and stretched his back. "Um, ma'am? I mean B-Bitch?"

Denise laughed heartily at Nathan's continued discomfort with her name. "Tell you what, Nathan," she said. "Because we're such buddies now, and I want to make you as comfortable as I can, I'm gonna let you call me Denise, okay?"

Nathan sighed audibly, genuinely relieved. "Okay. Thanks."

"Sure. But to my other listeners, I warn you. Unless you're a runaway with as cute a voice as Nathan's, don't you go trying to call me by my real name. Now, sweetie, what can I do for you?"

"If I ask you a question, will you promise to give me an honest answer?"

Denise shot a look to Enrique, who just shrugged, as usual. "Sure," she said.

"Even if you think your honest answer would make me feel bad?"

"Okay."

Nathan took another deep breath. The answer to the question he was about to ask was important to him, but he didn't know why. He was far from certain that he even wanted to hear it. Pushing his doubts aside, he asked, "I know that if I was just some kid, you'd never put me on the radio. But if I did get through, would you still like me, even if I didn't make your ratings go up?"

Denise thought for a moment before answering, then went to commercials so she could think some more. When they came back, she still wasn't ready, but she owed him an answer.

"Nathan, I can't deny that your calls have been good to my show. For example, I know that I'd have never been invited on *Good Morning America* if it weren't for your phone call. You remember yourself that I didn't believe a word you said at the beginning of yesterday's call. But I've gotta tell you, there is something about your voice and your personality that is really very charming, and your situation is truly heart-wrenching. As a mother, I want to help you, just as most of our listeners would come to your aid however possible. So, yes, Nathan, I think I can honestly say that I would like you even if you made our ratings go *down*. And if you knew me better, you'd know that that's a whole lot of liking."

Her answer made Nathan smile; made him feel warm in a way he hadn't felt in a very long time. It had been two years since anyone had been kind to him, two years since anyone had clapped him on the back or given him a hug. For the first ten years of his life, he'd never had to worry about being tough or being brave, and the thought of fighting other people for the very essentials of life—food and rest or even a place to sit unmolested—had never entered his mind for even an instant. Ever since that train had sheared away everything that was good and kind, Nathan's life had been one continuous fight, first with Uncle Mark, then with the assholes at the JDC, and now with hundreds of cops. The stakes were always the same, always his very survival. He longed for the times when his biggest worries centered on where he'd be assigned on the soccer field or whether or not he'd get an A on his spelling test.

Nathan refused to believe that those times were gone forever. If he worked hard, told the truth, and stayed lucky, he'd get another chance. To hear someone as hardassed as The Bitch say something nice bolstered his faith in himself, but more importantly, renewed his faith in other people. They weren't all cops and lawyers and judges and supervisors. There were still people out there who were willing to listen. Not everyone made their living by calling you a liar, or gaveling you out of order when you tried to tell the truth. And if The Bitch could think nice things about him, and believe him, then maybe other people could do that, too. Even if he got caught, at least maybe now people would pay attention to what he had to say.

"Are you still there?" Denise prodded.

"Huh? Oh, yeah, I'm sorry." Nathan paused again, gathering his strength to execute the plan that had flashed through his mind just an instant before. "I was just thinking about something. Do you think it would be all right if I asked the people listening to tell their friends that I'm really not a bad kid? And that I might need help? Maybe the newspeople could stop showing my picture all the time, so that I might be able to start over without everyone recognizing me?"

As Denise replied, her tone was all mother. "Honestly, Nathan, I think it's too late for that. You're already a news item, and I think you're destined to remain that way until this thing is resolved. As far as people are concerned, they've already made up their minds about you, good or bad, but what they think really doesn't matter. What matters to everyone, Nathan, is your safety. Whether they think you're a good guy or a bad guy, I don't think anyone wants harm to come to you.

"What *worries* me," Denise continued, leaning on the words, "is the thought of you driving cars and running roadblocks, and just being out alone at night. You're in very real danger every minute you're on the run. Sometimes I think the safest thing for you to do would be to turn yourself back in, and let the justice system work for you."

"The justice system got me into this," Nathan snorted.

"It works for an awful lot of people."

"Not for kids. Not for me."

"Listen, Nathan . . ."

"I can't go back, Denise," Nathan said with finality. "I won't go back. Not if they don't catch me first. You don't know what it's like to be in a concrete box. You don't know how it feels to be bent over a chair and held down by five people bigger than you while somebody pulls down your pants in front of everybody and rams a broom handle up your butt . . ."

"Oh, my God," Denise gasped.

" . . . or how it makes you feel when the supervisor laughs at you when you report it, or how the other residents beat the crap out of you for squealing on them." Nathan was shouting now. "I killed Ricky Harris because he was trying to kill me! If I go back, somebody else is going to try again, and if I fight back and win, they'll call *me* the murderer. That's the way the system works, Denise. The grown-ups are always right, and the kids are always wrong, and no matter what you say, you lose. Don't tell me I've got to go back there, because I won't do it!"

Nathan slammed the phone down on its cradle, then picked it up and slammed it again. And again, knocking the lamp off the end table and onto the floor. He stood there in the middle of a strange living room breathing heavily, his hands trembling. Suddenly he was alone. And it was quiet, so terribly quiet that he could hear his heart beating. In the silence, he could taste his anger and his shame and his sorrow. He was ready for a new dealer, because whoever was in charge of this game kept handing him piss-poor cards. But most of all, he felt terribly, terribly lonely.

Nathan desperately needed to do violence to something. He needed something to punch or to throw or to kick, but he was barehanded, barefooted, and in the home of a stranger whom he had no cause to harm. Like a caged animal, he paced around the living room twice, finally stopping dead-center in the middle.

Clenching his fists at his side, he raised his face to the ceiling and shouted loudly enough to crack the plaster.
"SHIT!!"

Police Officer Greg Preminger thanked Sister Elizabeth for her assistance and walked back up the stairs toward the sanctuary. Greg's daughter would be starting first grade in the fall, and he wanted to make sure that she was registered for the proper CCD classes— the Catholic version of Sunday school. A native of Jenkins Township, Greg had been going to Saint Sebastian's his entire life. It was hard to believe that ten years had passed since Sister Elizabeth had taught him English during his senior year at Paul VI High School.

Because this mission was technically a personal one and he was still on duty, Greg was in a hurry to get back to his squad car before he missed a call. The dispatcher was carrying him 10–7, which usually implied a bathroom stop, but he'd been out of the vehicle for nearly fifteen minutes. It wouldn't be long before they started to check up on him. He took the stairs two at a time.

As he got to his car, he noticed a fire-engine-red BMW convertible parked way off in the back of the parking lot. Interesting that he hadn't seen it on his way in. Once back in the driver's seat, he picked up the microphone and marked 10–8, back in service, then drove across the lot to check out the vehicle. Nobody had said anything at roll call that morning about a stolen BMW, and normally cars of that value got specific mention by the sergeant. There was nothing on his hot sheet, either.

He decided to let it go, but when he got back to the main road, he had a change of heart. It was just a damned suspicious way to park a good car. He returned to the Beemer and called in the license number, just in case.

Patrolman Thompkins was waiting in Michaels's office when Warren Michaels arrived, and jumped to his feet at the sound of the opening door.

"Sit," commanded Warren, in exactly the same tone he would have used for a dog.

Harry sat, his back perfectly straight, his butt barely on the seat. The man looked scared to death, and Warren had to bite his tongue to keep from smiling. From the outside, there was no trace of a smile, only the glare that so many police officers had witnessed at one point or another in their careers. It was a look of disgust, of disapproval. No first offender ever knew if there was an undercurrent of anger, because so few had ever seen Lieutenant Michaels angry. He was one of the good ones. And if he was disappointed in you, then by God the entire department was disappointed in you.

In Warren's mind, the ass-chewings for which he had become so well known were never ass-chewings at all. He never raised his voice—well, rarely—and it was always his intent to end sessions such as this on a positive note. When he took the time to pencil these meetings onto his calendar, he always used the term "attitude adjustment session."

Warren leaned way back in his squeaky vinyl chair and folded his hands across his chest, his elbows perched on the armrests. As he glared at Thompkins, the young officer made a valiant attempt for about five seconds to hold his own, but quickly looked down to a spot on the lieutenant's desk. Warren let him stew in the silence for a full minute before he said anything.

"So, you're our radio star, eh, Thompkins?" he asked evenly.

Harry's head snapped up, and his eyes locked on to Warren. He was ready to take what was coming to him like a man. "Yes, sir," he said firmly.

Warren leaned forward and made a show of opening the other man's personnel file. "Your career's important to you, isn't it, Thompkins?"

"Yes, sir, it is."

"I notice from your file here that you seem to finish first in everything that you do. That's quite an accomplishment. You should be proud."

Harry shifted in his seat. The course of the conversation made him uneasy. He was expecting to get yelled at, not complimented. "I try, sir," he said.

"Sergeant Hackner told me a few weeks ago that you have your heart set on a gold shield," Warren went on. "Is that important to you as well?"

Uh-oh, here it comes, Harry thought. "Yes, sir, that's very important. You might say that's my career ambition."

Michaels pondered the response for a long moment, gauging sincerity. "Did you cheat on your entrance exam into the Academy?"

"No, sir!" Harry's response was instant and unequivocal.

"How about all the other tests and programs you've been involved with since you got your badge. How many of them have you cheated on?"

Harry's control of his anger was slipping. "None at all, Lieutenant Michaels. And, frankly, sir, I resent . . ."

"Shut up, Patrolman Thompkins, before you say something you'll regret. Resent things on your own time. On mine, I'll thank you to answer my questions. Do we understand each other?"

Harry's jaw locked tightly. "Yes, sir," he hissed.

"So you expect me to believe that you've performed the way you have thus far in your career by working hard and following the rules?" Michaels continued. "No cheating, no shortcuts?"

Harry's eyes now bored directly through the lieutenant's forehead. "I can't dictate what you'll believe, sir, but I have in fact done it all by the book."

Warren grew quiet again and drew in a deep breath through his nose. "I gather, then, from your responses that you think cheating is wrong?"

"Yes, sir, I do."

"Even when the rewards are great? Even when it makes the difference between getting into the Academy and washing out?"

"I was raised right, Lieutenant Michaels. I was always taught that if you can't get what you want by working for it, then you shouldn't have it at all." He seemed to grow taller with pride as he made his response.

"Why, then, do you have a lesser standard for the collection of evidence?" As he spoke, Warren's eyes narrowed and he leaned all the way forward until his chest was pressed against his desk.

Harry looked puzzled for a moment, then he got it. His shoulders sagged visibly, as though deflated.

Warren didn't need a verbal response; the body language said what he wanted to hear. "You probably thought I was going to yell at you this afternoon for making a fool of yourself on the radio yesterday, didn't you?"

Harry nodded. His demeanor was suddenly that of a schoolboy in the principal's office.

"Well, take heart, Thompkins," Warren went on. "This is America, and it's your absolute, unalienable right to make a fool of yourself anytime you want, though next time I'd appreciate it if you'd go it alone, and leave the department out of it.

"The reason we're having this little chat, Patrolman, is because you cheated yesterday, and you got caught. There is a right way and a wrong way to obtain evidence, and your actions tell me that you're well aware that the right way almost always takes longer. You see this?" He held up the personnel folder.

"Yes, sir," Harry mumbled. "That's my jacket."

"That's right. And it's your career. It's the reason you're not out on the street looking for a job. You've had a long string of successes, Harry, and one huge screwup."

Harry was startled to hear the lieutenant use his first name.

"I'll cut to the chase. This department has a skewed memory. Fact is, one 'oh shit' wipes out a lifetime of 'atta boys.' You've had your oh shit, Harry. One more and I won't be able to run interference for you, do you understand?" Warren's phone rang.

"Yes, sir," Harry responded, wondering what had happened to the shouting, and how he could be made to feel this badly about himself without it.

As the phone rang a second time, Warren put his

hand on it. "Next time I see your name in writing, I want it to be on a commendation or on the committee's recommendation for the next detective's slot, you hear?"

"Yes, sir." Harry braved a smile, which Warren returned.

The phone rang a fourth time. "Now get out of here and go to work. And don't ask Petrelli or the County Executive for any favors for a while."

Harry exited and closed the door. The others were right, he concluded. Michaels was one of the good guys. He couldn't help but wonder, though, what kind of chewing out the big man himself had received after shooting his reflection in that mirror.

Michaels took the steps down to the parking lot two at a time, cradling his flip-phone on his shoulder as he fitted his weapon into its holster. He could hear his heart racing. A few seconds passed, then Jed answered on the third ring.

"Nicholson residence, Detective Sergeant Hackner."

"Jed, Warren. They've found the car in Pennsylvania, just north of Harrisburg. I'm on my way up there now."

CHAPTER TWENTY-TWO

STEPHANIE BUCKMAN WAS RUNNING OUT of important-looking tasks to consume time. The big clock in the main corridor of the courthouse read 3:40, nearly two hours past the scheduled time for the hearing. Petrelli never showed up, and Stephanie knew from experience that his absence meant that she was stuck with a loser. Fuming as she paced the corridor, she mentally inventoried her bloated caseload. With thirty-three felonies and God only knew how many miscellaneous other matters pending, she had zero tolerance for tilting at Petrelli's windmills. To make matters worse, her high-priced opponents from Omega Broadcasting sat smugly on the other side of the corridor, engrossed in quiet conversation, showing no signs at all of stress. But then, she guessed she'd be calm, too, if she were hauling down $250 an hour just for the wait. Finally, at ten minutes to four, word came that Judge Verone was ready to begin.

First appointed to the bench in 1955, Judge Clarence O. Verone appeared old enough to be an original signer of the Constitution. He was notorious for running hours behind schedule and forever refusing to explain the reasons for the delays. Theories abounded, but the simple truth was that his was an appointment for life, and he could be as punctual as he liked. That his whims destroyed the carefully balanced schedules of countless attorneys was irrelevant. *"When you get your own courtroom,"* he would tell his critics, *"you have my permission to start on time."*

Now approaching his eightieth birthday, Judge Verone looked cadaverous, his dark eyes and sunken cheeks creating a visage of evil that had served well over the years to intimidate the crap out of many courtroom guests. As he climbed onto the dais, he had to pause for a moment to allow his arthritic knees to absorb the strain. The courtroom remained silent, all parties on their feet, secretly wondering how much longer the old codger could continue.

For all of his physical frailties, Judge Verone's knowledge of the law was formidable. A fierce victim's advocate, he had sent more than his share of capital felons to await their turn in Greensville's electric chair. A staunch proponent of individual responsibility, he had watched countless plaintiffs and their attorneys limp from his courtroom with their wallets empty and their tails between their legs. The assignment of Judge Verone to the People's petition to access Omega Broadcasting's telephone records no doubt accounted for Petrelli's conspicuous absence.

When the introductions were taken care of and the opening formalities completed, Judge Verone turned to Stephanie Buckman.

"Miss Buckman, I see you're here alone," he rasped, intentionally avoiding the term 'Ms.,' which in his view represented a concession to overly sensitive activists. "I was expecting to see Mr. Petrelli here with you."

Stephanie smiled uncomfortably. "Frankly, Your Honor, so was I. But I'm prepared to proceed without him."

Verone returned the smile briefly, then made it disappear. "I'm not so sure you are, Miss Buckman," he said. "I've read your petition, and I am prepared to rule it out of order unless you can cough up a compelling reason to violate the privacy of hundreds of innocent people so you can go on a fishing trip for one caller."

Stephanie remained standing while the attorneys on the other side of the aisle lowered themselves into their chairs. She could feel their mocking smiles as she gathered her thoughts. She opened her portfolio, glanced at her notes, and began.

"Your Honor, a convicted felon and a confessed killer is running free today, following a daring and bloody escape from the Brookfield Juvenile Detention Center. We have within our reach the mechanism to bring him back into custody. By allowing access to Omega Broadcasting's telephone records, you allow us to track this young man down and put him back where he belongs. The People don't want to violate anyone's privacy, Your Honor, but sometimes, the common good must prevail."

"Is that all?" Verone asked.

"Well, no, Your Honor," Stephanie said, pulling the lengthy petition out of her briefcase. "In our petition, we cite several precedents which I'd be happy to review with you."

Verone held up a skeletal hand to cut her off. "No,

Miss Buckman, that won't be necessary. Appearances notwithstanding, I'm still young enough to read what is submitted to this court." He pivoted his head to the defense table. "Mr. Morin," he said to a gleaming attorney in a Brooks Brothers suit, "I presume that you have a slightly different take on this matter?"

Morin buttoned his suit jacket as he stood. "Yes, Your Honor, we do indeed," he said. In flawless and flowery prose, he recounted the incalculable harm that would be inflicted on the First Amendment rights of all citizens were the plaintiff's requests to be granted. After enduring three minutes of breathless oratory, Verone yawned widely and loudly, causing Morin to stop in mid-sentence.

"Do you have any information to present to me here that is not already played out in your written response?" Verone asked, taking advantage of the brief silence.

Morin smiled coyly, as though he had been waiting for this opportunity. "Yes, sir, Your Honor. In addition to all of the arguments thus far presented, the defendant feels that the entire issue is moot, due to events of this morning, in which the information sought by the People's petition was already provided by alternative means."

Stephanie's mouth dropped. She hadn't been back to the office since nine o'clock that morning, and no one had told her anything about alternative means. What the hell kind of game was Petrelli trying to play, anyway?

"I have no idea what counsel is talking about," she said in reply to the judge's inquisitive look.

Verone's gaze returned to Morin. "Enlighten us all, Mr. Morin, please," he said.

Morin told of the Nicholsons' return from vacation, and of their discoveries upon their arrival home. "Several points are proven here, Your Honor," Morin concluded. "First, that good police work does not have to involve civil rights violations, and second, that the Commonwealth's Attorney's office is wasting a lot of people's valuable time—and my client's valuable money—just to win a few votes."

"That last comment was uncalled for, Your Honor," Stephanie objected.

"On the contrary, Miss Buckman, I believe that it is overdue," Verone shot back. "I think we all know what's going on here. Your boss is taking a bath on this case, and he'll try anything to win, including leaving you out to dry all alone with this turkey of a petition. Miss Buckman, I want you to go back to your office and tell Mr. Petrelli that there is no provision in the Constitution whereby it can be suspended to support the political aspirations of prosecutors. Tell him if he tries a stunt like this again, I'll throw his butt in jail for contempt. Is that clear?"

"Yes, sir," Stephanie said with a smile. She could just see herself saying those things to Petrelli. God, what she would give to do it and still have a job.

"Petition denied." The gavel sounded like a pistol shot.

The gun made Nathan feel safer. The heft of it in his hands, the press of it against the small of his back, gave him the sense that the odds were more even. Like The Bitch had said, it was dangerous for a kid his age to be wandering around alone at night. If some bad guy chose him as his prey, Nathan would be ready.

He saw in a Western once how this cowboy had developed a reputation as a killer, and even though he tried to hang up his guns and get on with his life, the bad guys wouldn't let him. People felt compelled to prove themselves against his reputation. Well, Nathan was a famous killer now. He had told everybody that it was an accident, but maybe they wouldn't believe him. Maybe somebody would want to prove themselves against him.

Yeah, he'd be ready, all right. He'd made up his mind to take the gun with him. Like the clothes he'd borrowed from the Nicholsons, this gun would somehow be returned once he was across the border in Canada.

The Honda in the garage posed a bit of a problem. It had a standard transmission, and he remembered from the fun farm how tricky they could be. In fact, the hardest he'd ever seen his grandfather laugh was the first day Nathan had gotten the old Ford to move, jerking and jolting across the field, spewing gravel everywhere. He just prayed that he still remembered how to do it.

The laundry was finished now, and he'd already cleaned the place up. He had another note to write, but that wouldn't take long. With three hours to go till dark, he had nothing left to do but wait. The waiting drove him nuts. For two days now, he'd been stuck inside, unable to do anything but wait and worry.

After a while, boredom began to wear on you, making your mind play tricks. Boredom made you hear things that weren't there, and think things that weren't right. Sleeping was about the only activity that made real sense, but he was way too keyed up for that. Besides, he'd slept like a log that morning.

The digital clock on the VCR switched to 6:00 and he thumbed the POWER button on the wimpy little six-button remote. You couldn't even punch in the channel you wanted; you had to go through the numbers one at a time. He flopped backwards onto the couch but bounced back to his feet when the pistol in his waistband objected. He drew it out and lay back down, resting the gun on his chest.

Nathan was the lead story on the news again. They were again showing the grainy picture of him in his bloody coveralls. They cut to a picture of the BMW before Nathan could pick up on what the announcer was saying.

" . . . believe they have located the vehicle used in day two of Nathan Bailey's daring escape attempt from the Juvenile Detention Center in Brookfield, Virginia. According to police sources, a BMW sports car matching the description of the vehicle taken from the residence where the young man spent the night last night was recovered in a church parking lot in Jenkins Township, Pennsylvania, about thirty miles north of Harrisburg. For the details, we go to . . ."

He turned it off. This wasn't possible. In just a few hours, the cops had undone a two-day head start, and Nathan still had hundreds of miles to go. His mind raced for a solution, for a way to get ahead of them again.

Think, he told himself. *There's a way. There's got to be a way.*

He rolled back up to a sitting position, his bare feet flat on the floor. He needed to take a look at where he was. What could they know? They knew he was somewhere around the town, but they couldn't know where. They'd look for him in the woods, and they'd talk to people, showing his picture around. Could that hurt him?

Oh, shit! The guy in the car! Damn! Damndamndamndamn! Sure as hell, they'd made eye contact. When the guy heard the news, he'd remember. Nathan suddenly hated himself for taking stupid chances. He'd traded everything for a couple of extra minutes of rest. He was an idiot! A fool! He was thinking like a goddamn kid, and now they had caught up with him! They were going to take him back there, and they were going to try him for murder and they were going to convict him, and they were going to send him away for the rest of his life, and it was all his own doing! *Goddammit!*

A wave of despair overcame Nathan with such force that it took his breath away. Despite his thinking and his planning, despite his prayers and all the work he'd put into laying out his routes, it had all come down to stupidity and luck. He realized now that he'd been stupid even to entertain the notion of getting away.

And luck. Hell, he'd been leaning on luck for years. He clearly saw for the first time that the hope he'd been foolish enough to hold on to since the day his father was killed had only been fueled by luck. Real life had nothing to do with it. Everyone and everything had abandoned him. God let him have a few good years just so he could know how awful the future would be. That was God's little joke. Ha, ha, let's all get a good laugh at Nathan! Look at that poor son of a bitch! He actually thinks there's such thing as good fortune! He actually believes that nothing bad can happen to people who are good! Ha, ha, ha! Great joke!

No matter how dark the days, there had always been a few scattered rays of sunlight in his soul. Now, suddenly, even that comfort was gone. He had the sensation that he was in a dark room without any doors. He was so alone.

All of the monsters he'd been led to believe never existed were alive now and raging inside him. As a toddler, they'd had the decency to stay in his closet or under his bed, but now, as his future closed on him like a door, they all came out to torture his mind. Soon the cops would be on him, and they would send him back to *that place*—suddenly the words were too awful to think—and he'd have nowhere left to hide. The monsters would come and consume him. He would become one of those animals who had terrorized him for nine months in the JDC, alive on the outside, but dead in his heart.

His darkened soul guided his eyes down to the gun in his hands. A terror like he'd never known gripped his heart as he realized that he in fact had ultimate control over his destiny. He lifted the pistol up to eye level and stared down the barrel. Close up, it was like staring down a manhole. The bullets were huge.

Death was a kind of freedom, wasn't it? And it's what everyone wanted. Why waste all that electricity in some prison when he could take care of it right here, in less time than it took to blink an eye? No more chases, no more loneliness, no more beatings.

He could be with his dad again and live with the angels. He could meet his mother. He smiled at the thought of seeing in person the face he'd learned to love from a picture. He could almost feel the warmth of her hug, smell her heavenly perfume. His dad would smile at him again, and then they would all walk off among the clouds to be a family again.

Nathan's lip trembled, and a single tear dripped from his chin as he pulled the hammer all the way back and brought the muzzle of the big gun up to his head, just in front of his right ear. A little pressure, and it would all be over. He'd be free. He'd be happy. *One . . . two . . .*

Greg Preminger was nearly bursting with pride. His discovery of the BMW had been a feat of pure police work that had already awarded him a spot on the evening news—even the networks were mentioning him by name. This was the kind of thing that led to recognition and promotions. As he traveled from door to door searching for witnesses, he allowed himself to fantasize about finding the boy as well.

Problem was, it was still early; a lot of people weren't home from work yet. His current beat was Little Rocky Trail, where only three of the last twenty-two houses had been occupied by anyone, and none of those had seen a thing, though every single person had heard of the Bailey case. One woman shocked him by telling him he should be ashamed of himself for making things more difficult for "that poor little boy."

Emotions always ran strong on highly publicized cases such as this, but Greg was personally offended that the death of a law enforcement officer was so easily swept under the carpet in people's minds. People had an idealized picture of what childhood was supposed to be like, and they found it difficult to accept the reality of today's kids. In his years as a cop, Greg had seen countless hoodlums in kids' bodies, and as far as he was concerned, the size of the package didn't affect the seriousness of the crime. When this Bailey kid was caught, he hoped they'd throw him in a cage forever.

If Greg had anything to say about it, he was going to be part of that process. While most of his cop buddies thought Nathan would have fled farther away from the Beemer, Greg had a feeling that the boy was close by. According to the reports he'd read, Bailey had spent the first night less than a half mile from the prison. If Greg were in the kid's position, he'd want to get under cover just as fast as he could after ditching the car, and that would mean Little Rocky Creek.

Greg refused to be discouraged. These things often took time. At those houses where no one was home, he left his card and a hastily authored information sheet on the boy. If someone knew something, he was confident that they'd speak up.

As he approached the house at 4120, he was already folding his card into the next flier in the stack. He knocked on the door as a formality, really. He had come to recognize the look of an empty house.

*   *   *

Nathan jumped a foot and fell to the floor at the sound of the door knocker. His first thought was that the gun had fired. Then, in the next instant, he knew exactly what was happening. Through the sheer curtains over the front window, he could see the unmistakable outline of a police officer waiting at the front door. He became perfectly still, not even daring to breathe.

The cop had a bunch of papers in his arm, and the papers looked for all the world like a picture of Nathan.

"They found me," Nathan whispered.

But the cop wasn't acting like he'd found anything at all. He was acting like he was looking for something. He rapped on the door a second time, then peered through a cupped hand into the darkened living room, after checking over both shoulders to see if anyone was watching. Nathan would swear that they looked right at each other. Still, there was no reaction. For the second time in as many days, he'd come eye to eye with his enemy, and nothing had happened. After perhaps fifteen seconds more, the cop slid one of the papers behind the screen door, then turned and walked away.

For a long time, Nathan stayed frozen to the floor. He couldn't have moved if he had wanted to. As the adrenaline drained from his system, he felt lightheaded and sick to his stomach. He rose to his knees, then swung himself back onto the sofa, where he allowed himself the slightest smile. They'd been fifteen feet away from him, and they still missed. Someday he hoped he'd have the opportunity to tell them about it.

Someday.

Into his darkness crept a tiny ray of light. Where just moments before there had been only bleakness and the future had seemed unbearable, there now was reason for hope. His dad had once told him that hope was the most valuable possession a man could own. When he'd first said it, Nathan hadn't known what he'd meant. Now it was clear. Hope was where tomorrow resided.

His eyes fell once again to the gun in his hands. With its hammer drawn back and poised to fire, it looked evil, like a single-toothed serpent, offering such simple, permanent solutions to life's difficult problems. In the diminishing light of the evening, he realized the shame of what he had nearly done. A shiver wracked his body as he remembered his finger tightening on the trigger he could barely reach.

If it weren't for the cop at the door, he'd be dead now; yet it was the specter of encountering the police that had driven him to peer down that huge muzzle in the first place. He'd visited a place in his soul where he hoped he'd never return. What frightened him the most was how easy and effortless the trip had been.

Nathan let the gun slip from his hand onto the carpet, and, pressing the heels of his hands to his eyes, he started to cry.

Over a hundred miles away, Lyle Pointer swung his Porsche onto the Beltway heading north. In the uniform he wore, he looked just like a police officer.

CHAPTER TWENTY-THREE

JED HAD ASSUMED that Ricky lived alone. There was no record of a wife, and none of the JDC staff had mentioned anything about a significant other. He was certain the question had been asked; it was standard procedure. When he requested the key to look around the apartment, though, the manager told him that Ricky's girlfriend was still there and could let him in. Her name was Misty.

The Brookfield Garden Apartments were built in the early sixties to meet the county's growing need for affordable housing, mostly for young military families. Somewhere along the line, the owners of the complex had landed subsidized housing contracts from both the state and federal governments, and now it was on the police dispatcher's Trouble List: two cops minimum for any disturbance call.

Physically, there wasn't much difference between these garden-style apartments and the garden-style apartments in Fairfield that continued to attract the young professional crowd. Except, of course, that these grounds were littered with trash, the chains on the swing sets were rusted, and the in-ground swimming pool hadn't seen water in a decade.

Misty. Now there's a name, Jed thought as he ambled up the stairs to the second floor. In his mind, he'd pegged Ricky's girlfriend as a big-boobed bimbette, with frosted hair and a Texas accent. Probably worked as an exotic dancer. As he rapped on the hollow door, he held his badge up next to his chin, where it would be visible through the peephole. He kept his right hand free, just in case, pressing his elbow against his side to double-check on the Glock. In this complex, you could never be too careful.

He was about to knock a second time when he heard the knob turn and the door was pulled open, releasing a pulse of refrigerated air into the thick heat of the day.

Jed's assumptions couldn't have been further off the mark. The woman he faced looked no more exotic than a grieving housewife. She was young, maybe twenty-five, neatly dressed in a cheap shorts set. She wore her shoulder-length brown hair tied back in a tight pony-tail, which she had clipped up to the back of her head. From a distance, she would have been attractive, but up close, her only visible feature was a deep red scar that traversed the bridge of her nose and continued under her left eye, nearly to her ear. The lines of the wound were too deliberate to be anything but an intentional act of violence. Jed fought the urge to look away, concentrating intently on her eyes. She had been crying.

"Are you Misty?" Jed asked.

"Mitsy," the woman corrected, shifting her eyes from Jed's face to his badge and then back again. "About time you got here."

"Beg pardon?"

"I said it's about time you got here. I had to hear about Ricky on television. Y'all could've at least shown the courtesy of telling me in person." Her voice sounded strained. She stepped back and to the side, inviting Jed to enter.

As he crossed the threshold, Jed broke eye contact and fumbled for his notebook. "Well, fact is, ma'am, we didn't know that Mr. Harris had a . . . well, significant other."

Mitsy kind of snorted and shook her head as she retreated deeper into the apartment. "Jesus. You guys are something else. Significant other. You make it sound so romantic." She disappeared around the corner into the kitchen.

"I need you to stay out here, please," Jed called. He fought the urge to draw down.

Mitsy came back around the corner with a half-empty Budweiser longneck. "Relax, officer, I don't own a gun." She slumped heavily into the sofa, sending a puff of cushion stuffing into the air, and gestured to a sagging La-Z-Boy. "Take a load off," she said.

"No thanks, I'd rather stand," Jed replied. The apartment was decorated in early yard sale, but it was clean enough, and Jed saw none of the accumulated dust and food trash he had come to associate with Brookfield Gardens. "Are you here alone?"

Mitsy nodded pensively. "I am now," she said, all but finishing her beer in one extended guzzle. A scattered pile of empties lay on the floor near the shipping crate that served as an end table. "So, are you gonna catch that son of a bitch or not?"

"And who would that be, ma'am?"

Mitsy looked at Jed, then shook her head in disgust. *"Who would that be, ma'am,"* she mocked. "Who the hell do you think? How many son of a bitches are you looking for?"

"Look, Ms., uh . . ."

"Cahill. Mitsy Cahill."

"Ms. Cahill, look. I know this isn't pleasant, but do you think . . ."

"Sit down, dammit!" Mitsy shouted, her eyes wet. "Just sit down and talk to me, will you?" Tears splashed down her cheeks as she blinked, and she wiped them with her fingertips in a futile effort to preserve her makeup. She took a deep breath and composed herself, then softened her expression as she again motioned to the chair. "Please," she said, much more quietly. "It's been a very lonely, very difficult day. I'm thrilled to have the company. Please."

Jed shifted his stance uncomfortably, checked his watch, then sat down in the worn-out La-Z-Boy. It was like sitting on the edge of a well.

"So," Mitsy declared, using the word as a sentence, an icebreaker. She forced a smile. "Nobody knows about Ricky and me, huh? I guess that means he didn't talk about me very much to his friends." The thought seemed to sadden her.

Jed shook his head. "No, ma'am, I guess not. At least not to the people we spoke with."

She sighed and dabbed her eyes again. "He thought I was too ugly to show off to his friends. He never said it in so many words, but I always knew he was thinking it."

Jed suddenly felt obligated to contradict her, to say she wasn't ugly at all, but he sensed that Mitsy would know better. He just let the words hang in the air for a while as she seemed to travel in her mind to a faraway place. After ten seconds or so, he couldn't take it anymore.

"Were you and Mr. Harris married?" he asked.

The question seemed to bring her back into the world. She shook her head and looked down. "No," she said softly. "We talked about it a few times, but the time was never right. First we were waiting for him to have a better job, then after I got laid off, we were waiting for me just to have a job. When I finally found work, we needed to save some money. Recently, it's been Ricky's drinking. I was waiting for him to stop. All in all, we've been talking for nearly three years now. Never meant to be, I guess."

Mitsy paused for a moment, looking like she might crumble. Then she smiled again—a tired, humorless smile that seemed to be an extension of her tears. "Like my sister told me, Ricky's a man, and he was willing to take me in. With my face . . ." Her voice trailed off. "All things considered, he was a good man."

Of the two of them there in the room, Jed wasn't at all sure who was less convinced by her conclusion. "Did Ricky have anything to do with . . ." He aborted the question. There was no way to phrase it that would not seem brutish.

Mitsy let him off the hook. "My face? Oh, heavens, no. This was a gift from a boyfriend I dumped back in high school. Said he'd make me so ugly nobody else would ever want me." She shrugged, as though she had told the story enough that it didn't bother her anymore. "It worked, too. Until Ricky. And now I find out that he thought . . . Well, it's been a very, *very* long day."

Jed cleared his throat. "Well, Ms. Cahill . . ."

"Please," she interrupted. "Call me Mitsy."

Jed smiled. "Okay, Mitsy. I don't mean to pry at such a difficult time, but I do need to ask you a few questions."

"About Ricky?"

"Yes, ma'am."

"He's not just an innocent victim, is he?"

The directness of the question caught Jed off guard, yanking his eyes from his notebook. "Actually, that's what we're trying to find out."

The room fell silent as Mitsy struggled with her thoughts. "He hated that place," she said finally. "He hated everything about it."

"The JDC?"

"Ricky called it the jungle. He always talked about quitting, but he never did. Just when he'd reach the breaking point, they'd come through with another cost-of-living increase, and he'd decide to stay. It was awful." She stopped talking, as though she had run out of steam.

"Did Ricky ever mention Nathan Bailey to you?" Jed asked.

Tears flooded Mitsy's eyes again as she leaned forward in her seat. "You know, I've asked myself that question a thousand times today. I heard about what that boy said on the radio, and I've driven myself crazy trying to remember the name, but it's just not there. I'm sorry."

"You know, then, that Nathan said some uncomplimentary things about Mr. Harris. What do you think about that?"

Mitsy stewed for a long time before answering. She clearly had something to say, but she seemed unwilling to say it out loud. Jed just sat patiently, giving her all the time she needed.

When she finally spoke, she addressed Jed's shoes. "I wish I could tell you that killing one of those little bastards would be totally out of character for Ricky, but I can't. He hated them all so much. They'd never show him the respect he deserved. If somebody pushed him hard enough, well, anything could happen." She faded away again, then stood up abruptly, startling Jed. "I need another beer. Do you want one?"

"No, thanks," he lied. Actually, he'd have sold his arm for anything cold to drink.

Mitsy wasn't gone thirty seconds before she returned to her seat on the sofa. She stripped the cap from the bottle with an effortless twist and tossed it into the pile at her feet. She stared at the bottle for a moment as though reading the label, but she never took a sip. Her mind had traveled off again. As Jed watched silently, her mouth took an angry set, and she squeezed the bottle with both hands. It trembled in her grasp.

When she made eye contact again, she was angry. "I think he was planning something for a long time," she said. Her tone was one of discovery, her words carefully measured. "I never put it together until right now."

"I don't understand."

"Of course you don't. You couldn't possibly. Beginning a couple of weeks ago, I noticed things missing from the house—Ricky's things. When I'd do laundry, there'd be a few less underwear to fold. He'd take clothes out of the house, saying he was taking them to the laundry, but then he'd never bring them back. When I'd offer to pick them up at the cleaners, he'd say no. It was kind of like he was moving out of the apartment a little at a time. At first, I figured it was another woman, but then he always came home at night and he was always at the JDC when I called him. Finally, I just stopped worrying about it."

"Didn't you ever say anything?"

Mitsy smiled. "Over the years, I've come to realize that sometimes the mystery is less painful than the answer. No, I never said anything. And neither did he, but he started drinking again. Over the past few weeks, it got really bad. He was coming home drunk. I'd like to think he was doing his boozing after work with some of his supervisor buddies, but I'm not sure. I think he was getting drunk on the job. That's what worried me most. I just didn't want to go down that road again."

Jed was confused. As he scowled, his eyebrows nearly touched. "So you think that his drinking had something to do with a plan to kill Nathan Bailey?"

Mitsy scowled back at him. "No. Well, maybe. I don't know. He stopped talking to me is the thing. No conversation at all. Nothing. Looking back, putting it all together with the disappearing clothes and the plane ticket, I guess now I think he was trying to deal with something . . ."

"Whoa, whoa," Jed cut her off, making a waving motion with his hand. "What plane ticket?"

"Well, that's the biggest mystery of all. About a week ago, I found a plane ticket hidden in one of his shoes in the closet. One-way to Argentina, paid for in cash. Nine hundred dollars! I can't imagine where he came up with that kind of money. He must have been saving up, the son of a bitch. Here we go, month-to-month, barely able to pay the light bill, and he's saving for a trip! I never said anything about that either, because I kept telling myself that maybe he was planning some kind of surprise getaway for the two of us."

"Was there a second ticket for you, as well?"

Mitsy answered by looking away again.

"Where's the ticket now?" Jed pressed.

"No clue. The shoes and the ticket both joined the list of missing stuff."

Jed leaned back in the hollow chair and crossed his legs. His knees were nearly level with his shoulders. "Argentina," he thought aloud. "When was he supposed to leave?"

Mitsy shrugged. Her day was getting longer by the minute. "Best I could tell, it was an open ticket, no date on it. I didn't even know he had a passport."

"Do you remember the airline?"

She shook her head. "Not really," she said, her voice thickening. She finally took a pull on the beer. "It was an airline I've never heard of—something Spanish, I think."

Jed took a full minute to jot notes into his little book. The whole time, Mitsy faded further and further away. When he finally looked up, it was as though she had left completely. She just stared out the sliding glass doors into the blistering afternoon sky. Her eyes were so intense that Jed found himself looking to see what was so interesting.

A feeling of desperate frustration gripped his belly.

Here he had all this new information, yet he didn't know what to do with it. Clearly, Ricky Harris was not the model employee that Johnstone had portrayed him to be, but so what? What did the Bailey kid have to do with any of this?

"So, Mitsy?" Jed spoke softly as he interrupted her thoughts.

Her gaze returned to him and she smiled her humorless grin. "I'm sorry, were you talking to me?"

"I just need to clarify one last point, and then I'm done. You said you realize now that Ricky had been planning something for a long time. What, exactly, do you think he was planning?"

She shook her head and shifted her eyes back to the sky. "Honestly, I don't know. Maybe it was to kill that boy. Maybe it was to do something else. Whatever it was, I guess it was bad enough to make him leave the country. And me." In the end, her voice was only a whisper.

The Reischmann proposal had been flawless. Todd Briscow was 99 percent certain that they'd be awarded the contract within the month. He and his sales manager had spent the afternoon at the golf course, celebrating their impending victory. After the eighth hole, though, the heat had become too much, and they took their celebration into the clubhouse, where his boss was buying. As he navigated the winding turns approaching his home, Todd wondered if maybe he hadn't had a few too many. It wasn't that he felt drunk; he just had to work harder than usual to keep the Chevy between the lines on the pavement.

Todd hadn't so much as thought about the boy he'd seen until he heard the news on the radio on his way home from the party. Could it be that the kid they were looking for was the same one he had seen? The age was about right, and that would explain what he was doing wandering around so early in the morning, but Todd had trouble believing that the kid he had seen was a murderer. When he spoke to his wife from his car phone about his suspicions, she told him that the police had left a picture of the boy at the house. Once he saw the picture, he'd know for sure.

After pulling the car into the garage, he took a few minutes to set up the sprinkler in the front yard before going inside. It was getting dark, and he was convinced that the secret to their green lawn was nightly waterings. Patty handed him the flier with Nathan's picture on it before he had a chance to put down his briefcase.

"Is this him?" she asked anxiously. "I can't believe you haven't seen his picture on the news. It's all they talk about."

Like I have the time to watch the news, Todd didn't say. The flier displayed two pictures of Nathan Bailey. One looked like a school picture, a smile and combed hair. The other one looked like it had been lifted off a videotape. Feature for feature, there was little resemblance between the boys in the pictures, and nothing in either reminded him of the kid from this morning. Until he noticed the eyes in the grainy picture. Those eyes bore the same deer-in-the-headlights look as the kid he had seen. And the hair was the same.

"This is him," Todd said. "We've got to call the police."

"Are you sure?" Patty pressed. Todd couldn't tell from her tone what she wanted the answer to be.

"No, I'm not positive," he answered honestly. "But I think we ought to call."

CHAPTER TWENTY-FOUR

AT LAST IT WAS DARK, and time for Nathan to continue his journey. Finding the keys this time had been a much more difficult task. It took him nearly an hour of frantic hunting before he finally found a single Honda key among a clutter of loose change in an ashtray stashed in the back of a dresser drawer.

In a flash of inspiration, Nathan had killed the last thirty minutes in the steamy garage, using electrical tape to change the ones on the Honda's license plates to fours.

The Honda started up on the first turn of the key. He took care to make sure that the transmission was in neutral, but kicked out the clutch nonetheless. If there was one thing he'd learned in the past two days, it was that you couldn't be too careful. With the engine running, he searched for the button to the garage door opener, but found none.

"Oh, man," he grumped, turning the engine off. "Something's got to go right tonight." He groped under the seats and searched in the glove compartment for the opener, but found nothing. He'd have to use the button on the wall, an option he feared because it would bathe him in light while he was completely unshielded. His decision made, he walked to the door between the garage and the kitchen, but again found no button.

Could it be?

Sure enough, for the first time in his twelve years, Nathan Bailey had to manually lift a garage door. He was surprised by how little effort it took.

Once out of the garage, he set the parking brake, shifted back into neutral, and manually closed the overhead door again. Back in the driver's seat, he fastened his seat belt, coasted down the slightly inclined driveway, shifted into first, and gently engaged the transmission. His acceleration wasn't exactly smooth, but it wasn't anything like he'd feared.

His heart jumped as he approached the end of Little Rocky Trail. Three police cruisers, traveling bumper-to-bumper with their blue lights flashing, slid the turn into the neighborhood, speeding off down the street he'd just traveled.

Nathan figured that the guy from that morning had finally made his phone call.

"Are you sure it's him?" Greg pressed. His tone was urgent and abrupt, making Todd wonder if he had done something wrong.

"How sure do you want me to be?" Todd retorted, exasperation showing through in his own voice. "You left a picture of the kid at our door, and I'm telling you that the kid I saw for about five seconds fifteen hours ago looked like the picture." Patty, Peter, and the dog had all joined him at the kitchen table to witness the inquisition.

Greg took a deep breath and let it out. Clearly, his anxiety was showing, and he was telegraphing the wrong message to his witness. As the investigating officer for this portion of the Bailey case, he faced a difficult dilemma. If he reported to the state police that the Bailey kid had been sighted in Jenkins Township, the whole law enforcement world would descend upon them, perhaps to the exclusion of where the kid actually was. Just as surely as his discovery this afternoon could be a career-maker, a mistake could sentence him to life as a beat cop.

There had been hundreds of Nathan sightings over the past twenty-four hours, some as far away as California. None of them had panned out. Greg needed some additional proof before he cried wolf. There had to be a way to verify Mr. Briscow's story.

"Tell me again what he was wearing when you saw him," Greg said, straining inside to sound patient.

Patience, however—real or pretended—was not Todd's long suit. "I already told you, Officer, that I don't remember. He had shorts, I know that, and some kind of sports team shirt. I don't recall which team."

According to the reports from Virginia, Nathan Bailey had taken a Chicago Bulls shirt from the Nicholson house.

"And where was he headed when you last saw him?"

"When I first caught sight of him, he was coming toward our house, crossing the street."

"From where?"

"Like he was coming from the Perlmans' house."

Not knowing who the Perlmans were or where they lived, that information was less than helpful. "Could he have been coming from St. Sebastian's Church?" Greg asked.

Todd considered the question for a moment, calculating the map directions in his mind. At length, he nodded. "Yes. If he'd cut through the woods, that's the general way he would have come from."

Greg clapped his hands together. "I think that's enough to call it an official Nathan sighting," he said with a smile. Turning to the other police officers who had gathered in the front hallway, he said, "Sounds like the real thing, guys. Let's go door-to-door and find him."

It was frequently this way in police work. What you're looking for showed up in the place you'd already searched. Greg thanked the Briscows for their assistance and rose from the kitchen table to assist the others in the search. As he approached the front door, he realized that he hadn't asked the most important question of all.

"Mr. Briscow?" he said, turning around to face the family again.

"Yes?"

"Do you know if any of your neighbors are on vacation this week?"

Todd winced as though he had a sudden toothache. "Jeeze, Officer, I don't know," he said. "I really don't know that many people in the neighborhood yet. We haven't lived here long enough."

Greg nodded through his disappointment. He supposed there'd be no shortcuts on this one. "That's all right, sir. Just thought I'd ask. Thanks for your help."

"Sorry."

"No problem." He turned again for the door.

"Wait a minute!" Todd exclaimed before Greg could take a step. Todd had the look of a man who had just discovered something important. "The Grimeses up the street are on vacation," he said. "I just remembered that the kid next door's been picking up their newspapers all week."

At Greg's request, Todd walked the police officer up the street to the Grimes residence at 4120 Little Rocky Trail. To Greg, the house looked no different from the others in the neighborhood, except he remembered this as the one at which he had been compelled to look through the front window, having seen—no, sensed, really—motion through the sheer curtains.

In the daylight, it had looked just like all the other empty houses on the street, but now, at night, its darkened windows stood out like an ink stain on a white tablecloth. As he drew his weapon from his holster, Greg told Todd to wait by the curb. Todd did him one better and volunteered to go back home.

At this point, procedure mandated that Greg call for backup. A lone-officer search of a structure for a confessed killer was insanity, and even to consider doing it violated every procedure he could think of. Crazier still was the prospect of bringing every cop in the free world to bear on a property that was merely empty. In the world of the police officer, it was far better to be dead than embarrassed. With no serious thought at all, he decided to perform this search on his own. In his worst moments of self-doubt, it had never even occurred to him that he couldn't outshoot a kid. Now he was surprised that the thought gave him such comfort.

He started where he'd left off last time, shining his flashlight through the front window. In the dim, deflected glow of the light, nothing seemed out of place. Just a darkened living room, not entirely unlike his own. He walked down off the front porch into the side yard. Not sure what he was looking for, exactly, he noted that there were no footprints in the grass, and no broken glass. The air-conditioning compressor was running, but that didn't necessarily mean anything, did it?

The backyard was more of the same. He'd read in the report from the Nicholsons' house that Nathan had gained entry through the back door, but this house had no back door on ground level. Rather, it was a half-level up, where a deck might have been built, but wasn't. A wooden railing in front of the door blocked any direct access anyway.

The only conceivable means of entry would be through the kitchen windows, which seemed intact, or through one of the tiny grass-level basement windows. As a random thought, he admired the housekeeping skills of the homeowner. At his own home, the basement panes were perpetually mud-spattered, but here, the Grimeses' windows were spotless. One was so clean that it appeared not to be there at all.

The significance of the thought made Greg's skin crawl. No matter how clean the glass, there should always be a reflection of a flashlight.

"Well, I'll be damned," Greg mumbled aloud. He assumed a shooter's position on his belly, playing his light around the inside of the basement, backed up by his service revolver, with his finger a half-pull on the trigger. Once he verified that nothing was either moving or alive, he lowered himself through the window and inside the house.

The voice of his field training officer from long ago boomed in his mind to call for backup, but he ignored it. He could sense the nearness of his prey, and he was going to finish this one himself. It would be the perfect day: discovering the car, and capturing the kid. He just hoped to God there'd be no shooting. The paperwork on shooting an adult was ridiculous. Greg didn't even want to think about what would be involved with shooting a kid.

Greg's movements inside the house were spiderlike. His weapon was an extension of his right arm, held stiffly out at ninety degrees, with the base of the grip cradled in his left hand, which also held the mini Maglite, whose powerful light beam was aligned with the muzzle of his pistol, brightly illuminating his field of view. His back was rigidly straight, his knees were bent, and he advanced through the basement and up the stairs like a fencer, his feet never crossing. He was perfectly balanced for a fight.

The door at the top of the basement stairs was closed but not locked, posing only a moment's delay in his search. If the kid were there, and if he were smart, he'd be waiting on the blind side of the door, and he'd take his shot at the first sign of movement. Aware of this, and being smarter than the average bad guy, Greg paused before proceeding, playing his flashlight around to provide the boy who wasn't there with a false target. Then he charged forward and shoulder-rolled into the kitchen, recovering expertly to jerk his gun and light in a horizontal arc, covering all compass points. There were no visible targets to be shot.

It was only after a thorough search of the second floor of the house that Greg found a note on the kitchen table signed by Nathan Bailey. The good news was that this was the right house. The bad news was that they had missed the kid. The note apologized for breaking in, and assured the homeowners that he'd done the laundry for them. It went on to say how badly he felt that he had to steal their car, and that, oh, by the way, he now had a gun.

Greg lifted his portable radio and keyed the mike.

CHAPTER TWENTY-FIVE

IN THE DARK, NEW YORK LOOKED a whole lot like Pennsylvania. For the last five miles, a car had parked itself on Nathan's back bumper and refused to back off. He'd tried slowing down to get the guy to pass him, and he'd tried speeding up in an effort to lose him, but nothing worked; the guy just stayed there, about three feet behind, his bright lights in the rear- and sideview mirrors burning circles into Nathan's retinas. The other driver was playing some sort of game, racing up close, then falling back a ways. The game frightened him.

After seeing the parade of police cars entering the neighborhood, Nathan had made the decision to avoid the main highways and to stick instead to the smaller roads. On the map, they looked like they all headed in the same direction. And once he had gotten the hang of the gearshift, he was as comfortable piloting the little Honda around the curves as he was the Beemer.

Like so many other decisions he'd made these past couple of days, this one seemed to have started out well, and then turned sour. He hadn't realized how much of a sense of security there was in passing gas stations and other occupied places periodically. At 1:30 in the morning, there were no lights anywhere, and no other cars around, which to Nathan meant that there were no sources for assistance when this asshole in his mirror finally did whatever he was planning. One thing was certain, though. He had been smart to take the pistol with him.

Sheriff's Deputy Chad Steadman's orders were clear. He wasn't to make the stop until backup units were in place. According to the last report from the Pennsylvania boys, Nathan Bailey was armed and dangerous, and driving the Honda that Chad had been following for the last twelve miles. In the wash of his high beams, the driver certainly looked short enough to be a kid. And the job the driver had done on the license plates wouldn't fool anybody.

To kill the time as he waited for the other two on-duty Pitcairn County patrolmen to form up on him, he decided to play a little cat-and-mouse, falling back a few car lengths, and then roaring ahead till he nearly hit the Honda's rear bumper. If the kid bolted, he'd have probable cause to pursue on his own. The games seemed to unnerve the kid a little, but other than some erratic swerving, he kept his cool. Steadman wasn't sure how he felt about a kid keeping his cool under pressure. Wouldn't that make him all the more difficult to manage after he was captured?

Steadman saw headlights cresting the hill behind him at the same instant his radio crackled to life. "Charlie Seven's on location with Baker Fifteen," the speaker barked.

"Charlie Seven," acknowledged the dispatcher.

Steadman pulled the microphone out of its dash-mounted clamp and thumbed the transmit button. "Baker Fifteen, Charlie Seven," he said, hailing Jerry Schmidtt, his newly arrived backup.

"Charlie Seven, bye."

"Reliability is high that this is our kid," Steadman explained in the practiced monotone of one who had logged many hours of radio time. "He's been driving erratically. May have made me as a cop."

"You wanna make the stop now?"

"Negative. Command Six is en route; not sure of his ten-twenty," Steadman cautioned, noting for the tape that recorded all radio traffic that he was ready to do his job even when his boss was nowhere to be found.

"Command Six, Baker Fifteen." The speaker rattled with the gravelly tones of Sergeant Watts, the watch commander.

Steadman smiled. *Gotcha,* he didn't say. "Baker Fifteen."

"I'm at Halsey Road and Route One Sixty-Eight," his boss explained. "What's your ten-twenty from that location?"

Steadman's smile turned into a disappointed frown. Old fart was a lot closer than he'd given credit. "That'd be about a mile and a half, Command Six."

"All right," Watts decided, "we'll make our stand here. I'll set up a roadblock. Treat this as a felony stop."

"Baker Fifteen's okay," Steadman acknowledged.

"Charlie Seven's affirm."

Steadman lived for felony stops. It was the closest they ever came in Pitcairn County to being like the police officers on *Cops*. As they approached the site of the roadblock, Steadman and Schmidtt would hit their lights and sirens and wedge the Honda into a triangle of vehicles from which there would be no escape. From behind the cover of their doors, and armed with shotguns, the three officers would demand that their prisoner get out of his car and sprawl on the ground, from which position he would be taken into custody. If things went well, no one would get hurt. But if the little bastard did anything funny especially with his hands—he'd be no shit forever dead.

Nathan's heart dropped when he saw the second set of headlights in his mirror. That was no child molester in the car behind him. That was a cop. As the second car approached from behind, its lights highlighted the red and blue lightbar on the roof.

Keep cool, boy, Nathan coached himself silently. *They haven't stopped you yet. Maybe they don't know. Maybe they're on their way someplace else.* He knew the thought was ridiculous, but his brush with suicide had shaken him into a forced optimism. As long as there was hope . . .

His mind raced for a way out. As long as they were all just driving along together and he was in the front, then everything was okay. But soon they would make a move, and he wanted to be prepared. They had to catch him before they could put him back in a cage. *Just be ready for anything.*

He wasn't.

Up ahead, the woods on either side of him started to give way to darkened homes and businesses. A yellow reflective sign warned him of an approaching intersection with a school crossing, and instructed him to slow down to twenty-five. Under the circumstances, Nathan didn't think that would be a very good idea. His foot got heavier. Whatever they were going to do, he sensed it would happen soon.

There it was. A roadblock. About a hundred yards ahead, a cop car was crossways in the street, its blue and red lights sweeping the buildings around it. In his rearview mirror, two more sets of lights jumped to life, and he was startled by the electronic yelp of a siren.

"Oh, shit!" he spat, not even hearing the words as they escaped. For just the slightest instant, he took his foot off the gas, but then he realized that to keep hope alive, he had to keep moving. "Just you and me, God," he said.

Jamming the gas pedal to the floor, the rubber pad became just a tiny wedge between his sneaker and the thin-napped carpet.

Steadman couldn't believe what he was seeing. After having to hit his brakes when the kid slowed down, the distance between them grew dramatically. Over the wail of his siren, he could hear the whiny roar of the Honda's engine as it dopplered away from him.

"He's running!" he shouted into his mike.

But there was no place to go. Watts's cruiser had completely blocked the roadway, leaving only a foot between his back bumper and the four-inch curb. Nothing could get through that space.

Steadman thumbed his mike again. "Sarge, he's gonna ram you!"

* * *

Even as he approached the cop car blocking his path, Nathan didn't know where he was going to go, except that somehow he was going to get past it. The distance closed with frightening speed as the Honda's speedometer passed fifty.

More by instinct than by conscious thought, with less than a dozen yards to go before impact with the police cruiser, Nathan gallumphed the Honda over the curb, the transmission making a horrendous crashing sound as it dragged along the concrete. The car went airborne for just an instant, and then crashed back down onto the grass on all four wheels. He struggled to control the vehicle as it spun on the dew-soaked sod.

He didn't even see the shotgun before it fired.

"Dammit!" Steadman shouted aloud as he saw Watts discharge his riot gun at point-blank range into the Honda. The muzzle flash was three feet long in the darkness. "Kid's dead now," he declared, surprised by the satisfaction in his voice.

The explosion to his left deafened Nathan instantly, though he shrieked aloud as nine thirty-two-caliber pellets mauled the rear window and post, shredded the passenger seat and headrest, and then went on to blast out the windshield, leaving him a near-opaque spider-web of shattered glass to see through. It had to be a shotgun, he knew. The dickheads were still trying to kill him!

He had no time to regain his bearings before he was

back out on the flat street, with the roadblock getting smaller behind him. As he watched in the rearview mirror, he saw a muzzle flash like a yellow camera strobe, and just an instant later, the mirror, along with the rest of the windshield, was gone in a white puff of erupting glass. He yelled again and pressed the gas pedal even harder.

The car did not respond.

"Oh, God, no! Not now! Please, God, not now!" For the first time since he had seen the cars in the mirror, he was gripped with terror. The Honda was slowing! He tried to downshift, but the gears responded only with a teeth-rattling groan. The gearbox had been destroyed by the impact with the curb.

As Nathan pleaded for help from the Almighty, the speedometer crossed twenty-five on its way down to zero.

"FUCK!" he shouted. It was the worst word he knew.

He jammed the brake and the Honda jolted to a stop in the middle of the road. *I'll do it on foot if I have to,* he declared silently.

But Steadman was on him before he could reach for the door handle.

"Let me see your hands!" an adult voice shrieked from behind him. "Show me your hands or I'll blow your head off!"

Nathan sat still for a moment, coming to grips with the end of his journey. Somewhere in this mess there was hope, he supposed, but it was awfully well camouflaged. He slowly raised his hands into the air, surrendering not only to the police, but to his own fate.

His ears still rang from the gunshot, but he could

hear the sound of running feet as they approached from behind. Out of nowhere, a gun barrel propelled itself through what was left of his side window and bored painfully into his ear.

"Get out of the car!" someone yelled. "Now! Get out of the car!"

"I can't!" Nathan protested. The gun barrel was pushing him in exactly the opposite direction, making it impossible for him to obey.

"I said get out!"

"Gun!" a second voice shouted. "There's a gun on the seat! Watch his hands!"

Two sets of hands descended on him, grabbing fistfuls of his T-shirt and his hair. Using these as handles, they dragged him out of the car through the shattered side window. "Ow!" Nathan yelled. "You're hurting me! I'll do whatever you want!" He felt the rounded shards of glass embedding themselves into the flesh of his arms and his legs and his belly.

When he was free of the window, they slammed him to the pavement, driving the breath from his lungs and making purple spots explode behind his eyes. They continued to shout conflicting orders to him, but he could no longer hear what they were saying. A booted foot on his jaw pressed his face into the pavement, while a knee drove deeply into the small of his back. Nathan pleaded for mercy while the police officers bent his arms back at impossible angles to handcuff him. Another inch, and he swore that his shoulder would come completely free of the socket.

"Who do you think you are, running from me?" one of the cops hissed in his ear, just before the bracelets went from tight to excruciating.

"Please don't hurt me anymore," Nathan begged. "I promise I'll do what you say."

"You already blew that chance, asshole," the cop replied.

Using the chain between the handcuffs as their handle, the cops lifted Nathan first to his knees, then used his throbbing shoulders to bring him to his feet. His nose was bleeding freely from both nostrils, like a steadily dripping faucet. With no hands to divert the flow, the two streams converged just below his lower lip, and then fell in heavy drops onto his shirt and his Reeboks.

Nathan blinked rapidly to clear his vision, and got a good look at his captors. They looked just like every other cop in the world, clean-cut and mean as hell. A third officer approached them as Nathan was steadied on his feet against one of the cruisers. The new officer looked more than mean; he was mad and mean, and he wore a gold badge over his breast pocket, different from the silver badges of the other two. Over the other pocket, the gold cop wore a gold name tag that read WATTS.

Watts walked up to within three feet of the boy. "You Nathan Bailey?" he asked.

Nathan nodded. "Yes, sir," he said, drooling blood.

Watts was older than the others, and despite a considerable paunch, looked enormously strong. His biceps strained his shirtsleeves, and no collar could possibly contain his neck. He had the eyes of a wolf, piercing and threatening. It was the same look Nathan had seen from Ricky Harris.

"Is it true you killed a prison guard?" Watts asked.

Nathan nodded again. "Yes, sir, but . . ."

Before he could answer, Watts drove an unseen nightstick into the boy's testicles. Nathan cried out in agony and collapsed like a marionette onto the street. Unable to cradle his balls, he brought his knees up protectively, and fought for breath.

"Some judge is probably gonna let you off," Watts said, his face forming a satisfied grin, "but I wanted you to know there's a price for killing a cop." Turning to his subordinates, he added, "Get this dog turd out of here."

Steadman gave a mock salute and yanked Nathan up by his arms, dumping him in the backseat of his cruiser like a bag of dog food.

During the twelve-mile trip to the police station, Nathan never moved. He just lay on his side, knees up, waiting for hope to return.

CHAPTER TWENTY-SIX

LADY LUCK WAS A STRANGE OLD BROAD. Pointer had planned to mingle with the cops around Jenkins Township, masquerading as a police officer from Braddock County, assigned to follow the case as it progressed in Pennsylvania. Sooner or later, he'd hear something, and he'd make his plans from there. It would have worked, too. The uniform and ID card were authentic, obtained as partial payment for a debt owed by a mid-level civilian bureaucrat attached to the Braddock County PD. Even his badge number was legit, assigned to a fictitious character named Terry Robertson, who supposedly worked out of the Bankston substation. In the unlikely event that anyone might have checked, they would have found that Terry had been temporarily attached to the Drug Enforcement Administration in Houston. The hoax would be discovered, probably during the October budget cycle, but the prank would be untraceable, and no doubt written off as a computer hacker getting his jollies.

That was the plan, anyway. The reality proved to be much simpler. As he was checking into the Spear and

Musket Motor Lodge—the only hotel in Jenkins Township with an available room that rented for an entire night—Pointer's attention was drawn to the Special Report graphic on the desk clerk's ten-inch TV. He wondered what could possibly be so important as to interrupt the all-night movie channel at 3:00 A.M. The enormously fat fingers of the enormously fat clerk stopped in midword as she, too, zeroed in on the report.

The woman—her name tag read ABIGAIL—swiveled in her chair to turn up the volume on the set. Pointer suppressed a smile as he likened the clerk to a living snowman, gelatinous inner tubes stacked one on top of another.

All traces of amusement disappeared, however, when the screen filled with Nathan Bailey's picture, overlaid with the words, "IN CUSTODY." A delighted announcer reported that those residents of Pennsylvania who were still awake (both of them) could sleep peacefully for the balance of the night, comfortable in the knowledge that the nation's most famous fugitive had been apprehended by police in Pitcairn County, New York.

"I'll be damned," Pointer said softly—to himself, really, but Abigail heard him and shook her head pitifully, the skin of her second and third chins swinging in counterpoint to her head.

"That poor little boy," she clucked. "I think they should just leave him alone."

Under normal conditions, Pointer would have said nothing, but in tribute to his disguise, he offered a protest. "That poor boy killed a cop," he said.

Clearly, the badge and the uniform meant little to

Abigail. "Only after the cop was trying to kill him. What else could he have done? I mean, *look* at him. That boy's no murderer."

Pointer's head had already left their little conversation. He remembered from his *Rand McNally Road Atlas* that Pitcairn County was in the southernmost part of New York, well off the interstate routes that had seemed attractive to the kid the day before. If he hustled, he could be there in a couple of hours.

Without a word, Pointer turned on his heel and left, just as Abigail was spinning the registration card around on the counter for his signature.

"I meant no offense!" she called after him as the glass door swung shut.

By the time they arrived at the station, the agony in Nathan's groin had dulled to a throb, and his nose had stopped bleeding, though the coppery taste remained in his mouth. The various cuts and bruises had somehow melded together into a single body ache. The handcuffs had long since made his fingers numb.

During the endless ride in the cruiser, Nathan eavesdropped on the radio conversations between the cops involved in his arrest and capture. The way they talked, you'd think he was Butch Cassidy. He nearly reminded his driver—a cop named Steadman—that he was only twelve, and that it had taken three of them to beat him up. He wanted to tell them how his dad had told him that bigger guys who gang up on little guys are called bullies. He wanted to say a lot of things, but decided that silence would reap greater and longer-lasting rewards.

Steadman climbed out of the car as soon as it yanked to a stop. An instant later, Nathan felt the rush of humid night air as the back door came open, and hands were on his shirt collar and the waistband of his shorts, bringing him to his feet. The rough treatment was intentional, he knew—more lessons for killing a dickhead. They wanted him to beg some more, probably so they could think about it when they went home and jerked off. But Nathan was done begging. He was back in the system now, and silence was the only thing that really worked. Silence allowed the dickheads to think that they had won, while at the same time allowing you to preserve your self-respect.

They could hurt him all they wanted, but he wouldn't beg, and he wouldn't cry. He'd fight them silently, he decided. His will against theirs. During his ride in the cruiser, stretched out on the Naugahyde seat where the odor still clung of countless drunks and real criminals, Nathan decided that he would never again suffer the humiliations he had endured the first time around. He was going to go down for murder, the worst crime there was. What difference did it make, then, if he ultimately committed the crime for which he would pay anyway? The next time somebody tried to pull down his pants or steal his stuff, there would be a fight, and the fight wouldn't end until Nathan had won. If that meant that one of them would have to die, what difference would it make?

With the cops and the guards, you had to put up with a certain amount of bullshit and humiliation; it was built into the process. But there was a line where the institutional bullshit stopped and cruelty began. These assholes who'd just busted him had crossed the line, but there wasn't much he could do when his hands were tied behind him. There was dignity, even, in getting the crap beaten out of you, so long as you took it. Nathan had begged, and he hated himself for it. It was a mistake he'd never make again.

"Come with me, tough guy," Steadman commanded, apparently noting a change in his prisoner's demeanor.

Steadman had to unlock the front door to the station before they could enter. With Watts's participation in the chase, the shift had been stripped clean of personnel, leaving no one behind to watch the store. The Pitcairn County Police Station was tiny by most standards, consisting of a lobby with a watch desk from which extended two hallways. At the end of one hallway was a small locker room for use by the officers on duty and a cafeteria/roll call room where all meetings were held. Down the other hallway were the two detention cells, which normally remained empty during the week, and were packed with drunks on the weekend. New York state troopers, who frequented the station primarily for its bathrooms and coffee, called the place Mayberry.

The original foundation and walls of the detention cells had been erected in 1827, when the community's concern for a prisoner's well-being was very much less than what it was today. Window glass and wooden floors were considered outlandish luxuries, and in combination with a flushing toilet and cold-water sink, those luxuries defined the substance of the latest renovation effort to the facility, completed in 1938 as a WPA project.

Unlike his original arrest, in which Nathan spent the first three hours of his incarceration handcuffed to a wooden chair as he was in-processed, Steadman led him directly to a detention cell. The hallway sloped noticeably downward, toward two heavy wooden doors. As they approached, the temperature dropped an easy fifteen degrees, and the humidity seemed to top the scale.

"Not sure what kind of country club you're used to, boy, but not many of our overnight guests want to come back," Steadman explained with a smile. "Had a drunk in here one night who was so passed out the rats ate out his eyeballs before he had a chance to wake up."

Nathan tried to look impassive, but something in his expression made Steadman laugh. The cop inserted an old-fashioned iron key into the keyhole and turned the lock with a solid *klunk*. The three-inch-thick oak door swung open noiselessly, and Steadman stepped aside.

The interior of the cell was three times the size of his room at the JDC and lit only by a single lightbulb dangling near the ten-foot-high ceiling. Besides the rough red sandstone walls and concrete floor, the only objects in the cell were an ancient canvas-on-wood Army cot and a kind of toilet that Nathan had never seen before. The bowl looked like all toilets, but there was a box of some sort over top of it.

"Here's your suite for the night, Mr. Bailey," Steadman said with a grin.

Nathan tried to straighten his shoulders and enter his cell with dignity, but couldn't quite pull it off. Behind the brave mask lurked terrified eyes.

"Lean against the wall," Steadman ordered.

Still without a word, Nathan complied, pressing the side of his face against the cold red bricks. Steadman kicked the boy's feet back and to the side to form a human tripod. From there, he released Nathan's handcuffs.

"Pleasant dreams," Steadman said as he closed the door behind him. "Don't let the bedbugs bite!" He laughed loud and long on that one. As the heavy dead bolt slid into its keeper, the *klunk* reverberated through the dank cell.

So this is it, Nathan thought. *Ended just like it began, in a cage for trying to protect yourself.* A wave of tears approached from behind his eyes, but he willed them away. *You'll have fifty or sixty years to cry. No sense wasting any now.*

Jesus, it was cold in there. He carefully grabbed a corner of the wool Army blanket from the cot and shook it open, checking for bugs. There were none. Wrapping the blanket around his shoulders, he sat on the edge of the cot, which promptly collapsed under his eighty-three pounds. One of the wooden legs had been booby-trapped to look whole. The impact with the concrete floor shook his various injuries to life.

This time, he couldn't stop the tears. *Dickheads.*

CHAPTER TWENTY-SEVEN

SERGEANT WATTS FINISHED HIS REPORT on Nathan's capture at 4:30 and slid the papers into an interoffice envelope addressed to Sheriff Murphy, who had leveraged his political connections to talk himself into a fancy corner office with a fireplace up in the County Administration Building.

The more Watts thought about the irony of his luck, the more he grumped about the day ahead. He and his boys had made the collar that the big-city guys couldn't make, but by the time the press arrived to give him credit, he'd be off duty, and the sheriff would hog it all. Shift change was only ninety minutes away. He wondered if there wasn't some way he'd be able to pull double duty and give himself an opportunity to witness the bedlam that would be descending on their little community very soon.

The sound of the lobby door opening startled him. Visitors were rare at this hour. In this case, it was another cop, wearing a uniform Watts didn't recognize.

"Good morning," Pointer said cheerily. "I understand there was some excitement here last night."

Watts smiled proudly, despite the inexplicable bad feeling he had about this guy. "Yessir, we got the bad guy. How can I help you?"

"My name's Robertson," Pointer lied. "I'm with the Braddock County PD. The Bailey kid's from my beat. Just here to help out, maybe take him back to Virginia after extradition." He glanced around the lobby. "Looks like a pretty slow night."

Something in the way Robertson made the comment made Watts feel defensive. "Oh, I don't know," he said. "It's always exciting to fix a job that somebody else botched up." *Why the hell would somebody wear gloves on a night like this?* he thought, noticing the visitor's leather-clad hands.

Pointer laughed. "Well, you got me there, pal. Meant no harm, actually. Place just seems empty."

Watts shrugged and looked down at his papers. "Except for me and the kid, it *is* empty." Even as he said the words, he sensed that he had done a bad thing. Problem was, Watts had worked behind a desk for too long to react quickly enough to his senses.

By the time he saw the stranger's arm swing up to shoulder height, the bullet was already on its way.

What was that!

Nathan was startled from near-sleep by a strange noise—*phut*—like the sound of a distant air rifle, followed by the loud clatter of falling furniture, and then silence. No one was picking up anything that had fallen. Wasn't that strange?

He couldn't put it all together, yet he knew that anything out of the ordinary in a jail was bad news. Shedding his blanket, Nathan moved to the small window high in the door to see what he could observe. Even straining on tiptoes to get any view at all, his field of vision was limited to the empty cell across the hall.

Something definitely was going on. He could hear odd movement out front, a moaning sound.

Phut.

There it was again! Only this time, it didn't sound so much like an air rifle; it was more resonant than that. Nathan swore he'd heard that sound before, or something like it, in a movie or on TV.

When it came to him, his blood turned to ice. He had to breathe deeply and rapidly to keep from passing out. This couldn't be happening to him. The nightmare just wouldn't end.

Pointer had snapped the first shot off a little too quickly, sending the round an inch high and a half-inch to the left, squarely into the cop's breastbone. It was a kill-shot, sure enough, but it was a messy one. If he'd taken just an instant more, the Hydra-shock round would have blasted the man's heart into a hundred shreds, bringing instant death and very little mess. As it was, the bullet flattened to the size of a quarter on impact, then tumbled randomly through the cop's chest cavity, turning his thoracic organs to Jell-O. As the cop lay on the floor with his legs intertwined with the swivels of his chair, blood pumped like a garden hose from his chest wound, and pink sputum foamed from his nose and mouth.

Considering himself an artist in his craft, Pointer detested messy work. He cursed himself under his breath as he strode casually to the sputtering man's side. As long as the heart continued to pump, the gore would continue to spread. Pointer's task was to pull the plug.

The look in the dying man's eyes showed more resignation than fear as Pointer's second shot, this one carefully placed at point-blank range, reduced Watts's front teeth to dust and continued on to bore through his soft palate into his brain stem, where every command to every body system ceased instantly.

The giant keys to the detention cells sat heaped on the desk, in clear view, in front of three security camera monitors. Pointer smiled and shook his head.

These hayseeds have no idea what security means, he thought. Glancing around to make sure no one was near, he watched himself on the TV monitor as he leaned over Watts's body and hoisted the keys with a finger, taking care to leave no footprints in the blood.

Another two minutes, and he'd be done.

The sound of approaching footsteps confirmed Nathan's worst fears. His breathing came in quick gulps, like a panting dog's, and he was feeling lightheaded. *Why are they doing this to me?* His mind raced frantically, but there were no answers.

This wasn't Ricky, and it wasn't Uncle Mark. Whoever this guy was, he was no drunk; he was a killer with a silencer on his gun, and he wanted Nathan dead badly enough that he was willing to kill a cop to do it.

What did I do?

There was no time for thought, only for action. He had to be ready for a fight, no matter how unlikely it was that he'd win. He needed a weapon. If only one of the bricks would come free . . .

"Naaathan," a voice sang from the hallway.

It was the most frightening sound Nathan had ever heard. A weapon. There had to be a weapon . . .

"Nathan Baileeeey! Olly olly oxenfree!" Pointer laughed.

Shit! SHIT! Maybe I can lift the bed . . . The bed! The wonderful, broken bed! Nathan darted two quick steps to the cot and snapped free the broken leg. It wasn't very big, but it was heavy. It just might . . .

A key slipped into the lock in the heavy door. *Klunk. Oh, God!*

Nathan dashed silently back to the hinges, using the door's huge wooden panels as a shield. He saw the gun first. It came in quickly and made the turn, as though the intruder knew exactly where he was hiding. Nathan brought the cot leg down with both hands in a giant overhead arc onto the gun. It was the hardest he had ever swung at anything in his life, and it felt every bit as though he had impacted concrete, a shock wave reverberating through his arms and into his shoulders.

The pistol clattered to the concrete, but didn't go off. His first strike having been perfect, he recoiled for a second blow, but checked his swing and gasped audibly when he saw that his attacker was a cop!

What . . .

Pointer sensed the hesitation and saw his opportunity. He lunged at the boy.

Nathan got in a second shot, but it was all arms—no power—glancing off the man's shoulders just enough to unbalance him a bit. Nathan used the momentum for another home run swing to the side of his attacker's knee. Pointer went down with a snort, but never broke eye contact.

"Who are you?!" Nathan shouted.

Pointer didn't answer, but instead reached for the pistol on the floor.

Nathan screamed, "Don't!"

Pointer didn't hesitate for an instant. With the speed of a striking rattlesnake, he snatched the gun into his hand and brought it around, preparing to shoot through the A-frame of his armpit.

Nathan saw it coming and changed from home run hitter to woodsman, coming off his feet as he two-handed the makeshift baton down onto the back of Pointer's head. The "cop" collapsed so thoroughly and quickly that Nathan thought for sure he'd killed him.

He panicked. "Oh, God, I'm sorry!" he cried. "Why'd you do that? You made me do it! Oh, Jesus, I'm sorry!" It was like the JDC all over again. "Goddamn you!" he screamed, his shrill voice echoing through the empty hallway. "Why'd you do that?!"

When Pointer stirred, Nathan nearly cried with delight. He hadn't killed another cop after all! A bigger, infinitely more important question remained, however: Why were so many cops trying to kill him? And why were they killing each other?

He had to get out. Again. He had to run. Again.

What the hell is happening?

The hallway was clear, the doors all open. He considered that it might be a trap, but dismissed the fear as irrelevant. He couldn't stay, so he had to leave. If it was a trap, then they had him. That was that; end of story.

His Reeboks squeaked as they tried to dig into the linoleum floor to propel him up the incline. To his right, he glanced at the bloody heap on the floor and hoped silently that it was the asshole who had racked his balls. Nathan didn't even slow his stride as he plowed into the crash bar and threw open the front door of the police station and dashed out into the waiting night.

His flight from the JDC had been filled with fear and hesitation. Tonight, there was only the need to run, fast and hard.

Somewhere in all that darkness lay his future.

CHAPTER TWENTY-EIGHT

"OH GOD!"

The exclamation startled Pointer back to consciousness. His head felt like someone had lit a fire behind his eyes. *I hate that kid . . .*

"Sarge! Oh my God!" Schmidtt's voice was nearly a sob. He drew his weapon and chambered a round. "Steadman!" he called. "Steadman, are you here?"

Pointer reoriented himself in an instant, and formulated a plan. He couldn't believe that it all had become this complicated.

"Steadman!"

The new addition to the evening's cast was an unwelcome intrusion, but Pointer could handle it. Just another bullet, that's all. He needed to draw the new cop into the cell somehow. Easily enough done. Pointer groaned loudly. It took no effort to sound convincing.

Kid could have a career ahead of him in the big leagues, he observed, trying to blink away the lingering fuzziness in his vision.

Schmidtt ran the distance to the open cell in seconds, his footsteps stopping just out of sight beside the opening. After what Pointer thought a ridiculously long hesitation, Schmidtt swung into the doorway, crouched into a two-handed shooting stance.

His expression said it all. *Who the hell are you?*

Pointer sat propped up against the far wall, his head lolling against his chest. He moaned again for effect, even as he noted the bulge of the cop's chest protector through his uniform shirt. *Head shot it is,* Pointer thought.

Schmidtt nervously scanned the room for the perpetrator who had done this to his fellow police officers. If he had even the slightest suspicion of the stranger on the floor, his eyes showed none of it. In fact, he looked entirely relieved to find that whatever danger there had been had passed him by. The tension drained visibly from his shoulders as he straightened and approached his fellow police officer.

The moment Schmidtt holstered his weapon, Pointer brought his to bear and squeezed off a single round.

The bullet entered Schmidtt's head squarely at the crease of his lips and sent him sprawling backwards into the hallway.

"Brilliant police work," Pointer chided, holding his aim for just a few seconds to make sure there was no movement before holstering his own weapon.

Such a simple damn job, and from what anyone would be able to tell, he was no better at it than the slob Bailey had hired to make the hit. The Bailey kid was slippery. And fast. Pointer was surprised by the effort it took to rise to his feet. He never did get a good look at what the kid used for a bat, but he admired the skill and guts it took to use it so well.

Mr. Slater was not going to be happy. Dead cops always brought more scrutiny than they were worth, and now there were two more of them. Questions were going to be asked. Pressure was going to be brought to bear, and Pointer knew enough about his boss's business to know that people sometimes had to be sacrificed to keep the heat off. The more loyal and hardworking the sacrificial lamb, the more the right people were satisfied. That meant Pointer, unless he could turn this all around somehow.

Everyone deserves a second chance, but no one deserves a third.

As he stared at the uniformed body in the corridor, the outline of a plan began to form in his mind. Most people thought that Nathan was a cop killer already. Looking at the physical evidence in the jail, they might just draw the same conclusion again, especially if Pointer stacked the deck some.

Stepping over Schmidtt's legs to gain access to his holster, Pointer noted with satisfaction the near-total absence of blood. It was a perfect shot. He removed the cop's pistol and stuck it into the waistband of his own trousers.

"You've been a bad boy, Nathan," he mocked as he strolled back toward the watch desk. "Didn't your mama ever tell you that you shouldn't shoot policemen?" His joke pleased him.

Back at the watch desk, he leaned awkwardly over Watts's body to reach the tape decks they used to record the security cameras. Three eject buttons produced three videotapes, which he tucked under his arm. When he looked at the clock, he was startled to see that it was nearly five. Hurrying his pace, he left through the front door.

CHAPTER TWENTY-NINE

FULLY AN HOUR PASSED before Nathan heard the first siren; but when they came, they came by the dozens. Though he didn't dare peek out to take a look, his mind pictured scores of police cars zooming down the street, their tires screeching as they slipped around sharp turns. Occasionally, from his hiding place in the stairwell of an apartment building, he could see red and blue lights painting the walls above him with their rotating beacons.

He realized, looking back, that he'd made a huge mistake in his latest escape strategy, and he cursed himself for it now. As he left the police station, it never occurred to him that he would have this much time to get away. Had he realized that, he would have run much farther before stopping to hide. As it was, he figured he'd put maybe a mile at most between himself and the jail. From what the television news had taught him about police practices over the past couple of days, he knew that his position placed him squarely inside the initial search perimeter.

Unlike the JDC, which was located out of sight and

out of mind in the country, this burg's jail was an annex to the courthouse, such as it was, the most prominent structure in a downtown area dominated by storefronts and alleyways. He'd passed the silhouette of a tall pencil-like monument in what had to be the town square, but the trees and shrubs that surrounded it were only three rows thick, offering no cover for him. As he dashed through the town, every window was dark, and not a single person or vehicle moved, making him feel all the more conspicuous and exposed as the only person stirring the thick silence of the humid night.

His fear of being noticed drove him to seek cover in the graffiti-stained stairwell. Below the sidewalk, and hidden behind five galvanized trash cans, he was invisible from the street, but the sun would rise soon, leaving him unprotected and out in the open.

Nathan didn't know what to do. The sun was already painting brilliant orange brushstrokes on the horizon, so his options for running on foot or even boosting a car were no longer viable. And he certainly couldn't stay where he was. *Damn those cops,* he thought. If only they'd minded their own business, he'd be at the border by now, worrying about evading Mounties.

The old feeling of hopelessness began to wash over him again, but he pushed it aside. No doubt about it, his plan was all shot to hell; but he had more immediate concerns to address.

Funny how the obvious is often the last thing you see. As his mind sought for a new plan, the solution first appeared in the form of a question: *Where do these steps go, anyway?*

In the darkness of the night, the stairwell had been

only a black hole against the white concrete; but as the darkness turned to shades of gray, he became aware of a door to his left, obviously leading to a basement.

The instant he saw the door, he realized he'd discovered his only option, yet he hesitated before moving. Basements were places where rats and roaches lived; where it was always dark and always damp, hot in the summer and cold in the winter. Even in the nice homes of his childhood, basements had scared the bejeebers out of him. The specter of what horrible creatures might dwell in a place like this—both real and imagined—made him shiver.

Might as well be in jail as be in this basement, he thought critically.

But that was ridiculous, wasn't it? There was a big difference—a *huge* difference—between a basement and a jail. He could leave a basement any time he wanted to.

As yet another siren approached in the near-light of dawn, Nathan gathered his courage and entered the black basement through the door to his left, which, happily enough, was unlocked.

The phone rang six times before Warren even heard it through his sleep. It was like crawling out of a deep hole in his mind; the noise was at first processed as a part of a dream, making him wonder why the beautiful stranger fondling him would make such a piercing noise. By the third ring, he knew it was part of the real world; but it took two more for him to realize that the current real world was rooted in the darkness of the Spear and Musket Motor Lodge.

Pulling the handset down to his face, he grumbled, "Michaels."

"Hi, Warren, it's Jed," a familiar and wide-awake voice greeted him.

"Jesus, Jed, what time is it?"

"It's about five-twenty. Listen, some important stuff went down last night. You awake enough to listen?"

The urgency in Jed's voice brought Warren to full consciousness. He pulled himself to a sitting position in bed and turned on the light on the nightstand. "Yeah, I'm fine," he said. "Shoot."

"Nathan Bailey was caught last night in Pitcairn County, New York by some local sheriff's deputies."

"Really. How'd they get him?"

Jed explained all he knew about the chase and the arrest, and finished with the shootings. "The locals say that the Bailey kid grabbed one of the deputies' guns and just blasted his way out of the jail."

"Oh my God," Warren groaned. "Are both deputies dead?"

"They never had a chance."

Warren was quiet for a long time, allowing his tired brain to process what it all meant.

"Are you there?" Jed prompted.

"What? Oh, yeah, sure. I just really wanted this one to turn out differently." Warren sighed. "I really bought into the kid's story."

Jed understood. It had been a tough year. "You know, Warren, you weren't alone on that score. I think we were all pulling for the kid. Boys his age are supposed to be innocent."

Warren swung his feet around and planted them on

the floor, checking his watch. "I've come this far, Jed. I'm gonna head on up to Pitcairn County, wherever the hell that is, and see what we can do to assist in the kid's arrest. Pass the word to anyone who's interested."

"You got it, boss. Sorry to wake you."

"No you're not," Warren replied, careful to put a smile in his voice.

After hanging up, Warren sat still for a while, attempting to manage an odd assortment of emotions. He knew that he'd lost his objectivity on this case. Somehow or other, he'd bundled the Bailey kid's problems with Brian's death. He'd allowed himself to believe in the innocence of this boy whom he'd never met, to empathize with his fears and his desperation. Emotionally, it was a big step for him to accept that the kid could kill again. Brian could never have killed a man.

How, then, could Nathan Bailey?

The answer, he knew, was simple enough: They were different people. Each child had been raised with his own set of values, and Warren would never know which values were important to Bailey or his kin. It was just so damned hard to believe that the kid on the radio—the same kid who cleaned laundry and inventoried "borrowed" items—was capable of killing three police officers in cold blood. Perhaps Ricky *had* posed a threat to the boy, just like he claimed; but what possible justification could there be for killing two more people in an entirely different jurisdiction?

Again, the answer was simple: Nathan Bailey was a murderer and a dangerous fugitive. And it was Warren's job to help apprehend the kid before he harmed anyone else. The courts would then decide his fate.

And however the chips fell, Warren would live at peace with the result.

After all, he wasn't the kid's father. And Nathan wasn't his son.

Bertrand Murphy was beside himself with anger and grief. Never before in his four consecutive terms as sheriff—indeed, in the history of the department—had there been such a tragic day. He had fielded the phone call in the wee hours from a hysterical deputy who had discovered the bodies as he arrived for shift change. Less than ten minutes after the call, Sheriff Murphy was on the scene to personally oversee the investigation and to make sure that the bodies were treated with the proper respect.

He was not prepared for what he found. Deputy Watts was a personal friend; they and their wives had played bridge together every other Thursday night since 1985. Their kids had grown up together, attending the same schools and playing on the same playgrounds. In another year, Adam, the oldest of the Watts brood, would be off to college with dreams of someday running a sporting goods store.

Schmidtt had been a new man on the force, having just finished rookie school the previous spring, and as such, Murphy hadn't really known him. Rumors told him that his wife was pregnant with their first baby, due in December.

"What kind of animal shoots two fine deputies?" Murphy asked Deputy Steadman, whose grief was written in deep wrinkles and pallid flesh. "Shot them in the *mouth,* for Christ's sake."

Under Murphy's watchful glare, a team of young deputies worked quickly to mark the outlines of the bodies on the floor with white adhesive tape, the last step before placing them in body bags and driving them off to the morgue, where the final insult of an autopsy awaited them. Murphy was sickened by the thought of a giant "Y" being carved into the torso of his friend while a team of pathologists with tape recorders and cameras piled his guts onto a plate.

He checked his watch. It was going on six o'clock. Word of the killings was spreading, and they had yet to announce the names of the dead, pending notification of their next of kin. That notification was his job, and it was time to get on with it. He turned to the grim-faced deputy at his side.

"You knew these men, didn't you, son?"

Steadman nodded, his eyes wet. "Yes, sir. Worked with them every day."

"You want to get even with the son of a bitch who did this to them, don't you?"

Steadman turned to face Murphy. His eyes gleamed with his thirst for retribution. "Yes, sir, I do."

Murphy nodded. "Good. I think you'll get your chance. But first, I have a job for you to do."

"Tell me what it is, and I'll do it."

"I have to go and break the news to the wives of these brave men. I'll return in an hour or so. In that time, I want you to oversee things here. Make sure your friends are handled gently, respectfully. And make sure that nothing except the bodies—and I mean nothing—is moved from this scene until I get back."

Steadman nodded attentively. "Okay, sir, I'll see to

it," he said. "Do you want me to order roadblocks, too?"

"No, son, we've already got deputies out on the street doing that even as we speak."

Taking a moment longer to look down on his mangled friend, Murphy said a brief, silent prayer for his soul before leaving to break the news to Judith Watts.

Denise rocketed upright in bed the instant the newscaster's words gelled in her sleep-deadened mind. She gasped, "No!"

But the deep baritone voice from her clock radio was unequivocal.

"Police sources will not release the names of the murdered officers, but they have officially confirmed reports that America's so-called favorite criminal escaped from custody in this quiet New York town, following the brutal, execution-style killing of his two captors. It is still not clear if there are any witnesses . . ."

Denise felt as though she'd been punched. How could he do such a thing? She knew he was desperate, but who would have thought? Words from her first conversation with Nathan rang in her memory.

"I'm not going back to that place . . ."

Could he possibly have meant that he would kill to stay out? Could it be that he was giving everyone a warning, but that they had missed it in their zeal to believe in the innocence of a child?

She remembered the vividness of his account of Ricky Harris's death, in which Nathan was the real victim. Could that all have been a lie? Maybe he was one of those children you read about in a Stephen King book, who's so psychotic that he doesn't know what his other half is doing.

Denise shook her head. None of this made sense. Call it woman's intuition, call it a feeling, call it whatever you wanted, but something about all of this didn't add up. Nathan wasn't a street kid, devoid of moral underpinnings. Sure, he'd had some rough times—so rough, in fact, that he refused to discuss them on the air—but could that push a boy to murder? *Three times? Execution-style.*

Those were the words the newscaster had used. Execution-style. What did that mean, anyway? That wasn't the kind of term ad-libbed by a good reporter. Terms like that come from police sources, sometimes before they've had a chance to develop the "approved" line on their statements to the press.

Denise tried to picture Nathan—whom she featured in her mind's eye as much smaller than any real-life twelve-year-old—ordering two burly police officers up against some wall, their hands in the air, as he calmly and methodically shot them down like dogs. The image was so absurd as to be funny.

Even if he successfully shot one, how could he control the other? Handcuffs? Okay, so how does a kid get two grown men to sit still long enough to put cuffs on their wrists? For that matter, how could he get a gun away from a cop in the first place?

Something was terribly wrong with this picture. She picked up the phone and speed-dialed Enrique, who answered on the first ring.

"I just heard," he said.

* * *

J. Daniel Petrelli heard the news before most, delivered by a *Washington Post* reporter looking for a juicy quote from a sleep-dumb prosecutor. Now, as he sped north in a state police helicopter, he couldn't remember his exact reply, but he knew from the reporter's voice that it had been disappointing, properly sprinkled with the right words and expressions. Politician that he was, Petrelli wielded words like "tragic" and "untimely" with consummate skill.

In the air, Petrelli made no effort to conceal his joy at this recent turn of events. After making him look like an idiot for the past two days, the media would finally see the wisdom of what he had been saying all along. In one swift act of amazing violence, the boy who had single-handedly threatened to scuttle his senatorial campaign now stood to make him look like the truly sage philosopher that he was.

Whoever this hayseed Murphy was, he jumped at Petrelli's offer to provide assistance for the investigation. "I'll take whatever help you can give me to put that demon back in his cage," Murphy had said. Country lawmen, with their colorful language, always amused Petrelli. They said what was on their minds in the most direct and efficient language they could muster, no matter whose feelings were trampled. It was exactly the kind of venue he needed to rebuild his senatorial image.

CHAPTER THIRTY

SAMMY BELL TURNED THE KNOB so there'd be no noise as he closed the door to Mr. Slater's office. He stood quietly, waiting to be recognized. In time, the old man looked up from his papers, but Sammy knew that he hadn't been reading at all, just collecting his thoughts. They both knew what had to be said. For Mr. Slater, it would be a difficult thing, but for Sammy, it was a moment for which he'd been waiting a long time.

For too many years to count, the old man had leaned on Sammy for everything, depended on him to enforce the rules on the street. If someone stepped out of line, Sammy would set them straight. Loyal lieutenant that he was, Sammy had even buried a few bodies along the way.

Mr. Slater had run the drug, protection, banking, and prostitution trades in his chunk of D.C. for over four decades. Back in the fifties, the Schillaci family tried to muscle him out, but Mr. Slater had been able to negotiate an amicable treaty with the Italians by taking temporary custody of Schillaci's daughter. The deal was finalized twenty minutes before Sammy was to have removed one of the girl's ears and have it delivered to the don's headquarters.

Personally, Sammy had little patience for the Italians. Damn wops were a greasy, sleazy lot. But at least they had honor, and he admired that. So did Mr. Slater. In the years since their initial confrontation, Schillaci and Mr. Slater had run into each other quite a few times—inaugural balls, that sort of thing—and they'd become so civil over time that some observers thought they might actually have become friends.

Separated in age by more than twenty years, Sammy had always shown a filial deference to Mr. Slater, who in turn doled out praise and criticism in the manner of a caring father. As the business grew and competitors came and went, only Sammy had chosen to stick exclusively with the old man, never once even dreaming about selling out. There was no such thing as loyalty anymore. Not even when the penalty was death.

They'd both hoped that Pointer would work out. He'd certainly shown the right signs, sticking in there and getting the job done despite his size and his girlish looks—the traits that led Sammy to turn the youngster away at first. But Pointer had begged and he made promises; looked like he might cry if Sammy didn't give him a chance. In the end, Sammy caved in, and right away, things started to go to hell.

Pointer wasn't content making deliveries and shuttling money. He wanted to be a hit man. That was the term he used—hit man. Like some dago thumb-breaker. When Sammy told him to quit watching movies and just do his job, Pointer went to Mr. Slater and delivered the same "please just give me a chance" speech. Like Sammy had done before, Mr. Slater bought it.

The day Lyle Pointer began collecting debts, he became the Hit Man, calling himself that on the street, and Mr. Slater loved it.

But Sammy saw through it right away. He couldn't stand the son of a bitch. Pointer dressed like a pimp; like a damn wop, all leather and gold. And his shoes. Half the time, Sammy swore the punk wore women's shoes, barely as thick as a sheet of paper, and always made from the hide of some exotic reptile.

Think what he might, though, Sammy was more loyal than a seeing-eye dog, and if Mr. Slater wanted that sleazy punk representing him on the street—*Lyle,* for Chrissakes; who the hell would name their child *Lyle*—well, then that's what Mr. Slater would have.

Sammy hated the mean streak worst of all. Pointer's love of plain cruelty—the pleasure he took from it—had gotten entirely out of hand the last couple of years, starting with that Donny Jackson fiasco. The kid was just another punk; didn't know the rules yet. You don't slice off a kid's face and burn his balls off for a stupid mistake. That shit was just sick. Scary sick shit.

But Mr. Slater liked it. He said it made him feel like the old days, when the city was *afraid* of him. The respect had always been there, but it made him feel good to be feared again. Made him feel young.

To Sammy, respect was just fine. After all, *he* was the one who'd earned that respect for the old man. But Sammy was getting too old to be looking over his shoulder every day. Plus he had grandkids now, and it was about time for him to start enjoying what was left of his life.

Too old. That really summed it all up. His business had always been about violence, but there used to be rules. Killing was a part of the business, but in the old days it was always a last resort, used to deliver a particular message to a particular person. These days, killing was just sport. The gangbangers on the street—hell, even the kids in the high schools—were just popping each other for grins. It never used to be like that.

And this business of killing kids for money, that was just plain wrong. Made them look like animals; bumbling, incompetent animals at that. Sooner or later, the word would leak out that Mr. Slater was tied to this Nathan Bailey mess. When that happened, even the respect would be gone. They had to put a stop to this nonsense. They had to put a stop to Pointer.

Presently, as Mr. Slater looked up from his papers, he motioned Sammy into one of the well-padded guest chairs in front of the desk. As he accepted the offer and settled into the cushions, Sammy wondered just how many hours—no, how many *years*—of his life had been spent in one of these chairs.

They sat quietly for a while until Mr. Slater spoke. "Well?" he rasped.

"Well, what, Mr. Slater?" Though he had earned the right, Sammy felt awkward launching right into an I-told-you-so.

"You called this meeting, Sammy. I presume you want to discuss Lyle again."

Sammy cleared his throat. Even after as long as they'd known each other, it was still difficult to tell the old man that he'd screwed up. "Yes, as a matter of fact, I do. We've got to stop him, Mr. Slater."

Mr. Slater nodded. "You mean rein him in?"

Was it possible he didn't see the obvious? "No, sir. I mean . . . more than that. He's killed two cops now.

The prison guard was bad enough, but *cops*. Jesus. When word leaks out, everything we've built will come down around our ears. It's not worth it, sir. Pointer has to be sacrificed."

Mr. Slater formed a steeple with his fingers and pressed them against his lips. "Suppose word doesn't leak out? We have many secrets, Sammy. Not all of them leak out."

"We've never had a secret like this, Mr. Slater. In all the years, we've only had to whack one cop, and that was because he was playing both ends. We did the cops a favor, and even they knew it. But this shit's out of control. Son of a bitch is killing everybody. It's nuts."

The old man considered Sammy's words. "And what about the money? Do we just forget about the money?"

Sammy's mouth struggled for better words for a while, but then he gave up and shrugged. "Yeah," he said. "Yeah, we forget about the money, just like you told Pointer the other day. We make that Mark Bailey go away, and we write off the five hundred grand to bad business."

Mr. Slater inhaled noisily and let it go with considerable effort. The air made a growling sound as it rumbled through his emphysemic lungs. "Five hundred thousand dollars is a lot of money, Sammy."

"Yes, it is. And let's not forget who pitched this crazy plan in the first place."

"Ah, yes. Lyle again."

"And this business of killing a kid for money . . ."

Mr. Slater silenced him with a wave. "You've made your point, Sammy."

"Yes, sir." Sammy broke eye contact and stared at his own foot, where it rested leisurely atop the opposite knee. As Mr. Slater worked his way through the problem, only the rattling of his breathing pierced the silence.

At length, Mr. Slater spoke. "We must do what must be done. But I want some dignity for Lyle. He's served well."

"Yes, sir," Sammy agreed.

"He'll call this morning. I want to speak with him when he does."

"Yes, sir."

Sammy read his boss's body language and rose to leave, glancing at the old man one last time to check his mood. How ancient Slater looked, every year and every decision having carved a crease into his yellow-gray flesh. His boss would be gone soon, and there'd be no one to take his place. The punks would inherit the streets. That would be a tragic day, Sammy thought.

CHAPTER THIRTY-ONE

BILLY ALEXANDER WAS THE ONLY KID in Mrs. Lippincott's fourth-grade class who hated summer vacation. For all he knew, he was the only kid in the world who preferred school to time off. He talked about his feelings one time to an older kid who lived down the hall, a white dude, but the reaction he got convinced him that it was best to keep such thoughts to himself.

At school, there was always something good to eat, and there were friends to play with and air-conditioning to dry up the sweat. Billy's apartment, on the other hand, was a sweatbox, stuck on the side of the building where breezes rarely stirred. When his mom was home—she worked *all* the time—she'd pick up some groceries and maybe even cook a real dinner. Most of the time, though, he'd be stuck picking through whatever was left in the cupboards. This morning, he'd boiled himself some macaroni for breakfast. It would have tasted better with some tomato sauce or some butter, but hey, you had to make do with what you had.

The very worst part, though, was the loneliness. At ten, Billy was the youngest kid in his building by about six years, and the only one who wasn't a doper or a crackhead. The people who lived in his neighborhood scared the hell out of him. Fights and shootings were the routine. Billy couldn't remember a weekend when there weren't cop cars or ambulances out front.

In the two years that they'd been living in the Vista Plains Apartments, he'd been nearly shot twice, beaten up five times, robbed of every dime he'd ever put into his pocket, and was even tossed down the fire escape stairs once. That one required a trip to the hospital in an ambulance, and got him six stitches in his forehead. Eight months later, his mom had yet to notice the scar.

Billy knew that his life sucked, and he figured that sooner or later he was going to become a loser just like all the others, but for the time being, he liked to pretend that maybe it would be different for him. If he actually *learned* all that crap they were teaching him in school, and if he just stayed away from the other kids from his neighborhood, maybe, just maybe, he could be different. Black folks had done it before. Colin Powell had done it, and Colin Powell was his hero.

So summertime was something he had to endure. He had his books and he had his television, and it wasn't like he was starving to death or anything. Most important, he had his best friend Barney, a golden retriever-and-god-knows-what-else mix that Billy had found in an alley, trying to make a meal out of a tipped-over trash can. For both boy and dog, it had been love at first sight, and they'd been inseparable for nearly three months now. Billy noticed with some interest that even people who had no respect for a kid showed respect to a kid with a big dog.

At the moment, Billy was doing the one chore that he hated above all others: taking the trash downstairs. The basement of his apartment building was a dark, damp, stinky place where people who had no homes would go to camp out, or shoot up, or sometimes die. He'd never seen anything particularly scary down there himself, but he'd heard stories.

As always, he let Barney go down first, to flush out whatever bad guys might be lurking. Dutifully, the beast trotted on down, then paused at the bottom, staring back up at his master. The stupid, expectant look on the dog's face made Billy laugh.

"You haven't figured out that you're the bait, have you boy?" Billy said as he negotiated the stairs. Barney's wagging tail was unbalancing the dog's back end, causing him to do a silly little dance with his hind legs just to keep from falling over.

Billy wasted no time doing his duty. Lifting the lid of the galvanized trash can with his left hand, he slung the three plastic trash bags—they'd been grocery bags in their past lives—into the opening.

He'd just turned to go back up the stairs when he heard it. Some boxes in the corner moved. Barney heard it, too. The dog braced his legs and lowered his head, the fur along his spine rising like porcupine quills. The ferocious noise that issued from the dog's throat was unlike anything Billy had ever heard.

"W-who's there?" Billy called out to the shadows near the furnace. Barney seemed confused, not knowing whether to attack or to stay back and defend his master.

"W-whoever you are, you better come out before

my dog kills you." Despite the fear in his belly, Billy's voice carried the firm conviction of one who was stating the obvious.

First one, and then two, and then three at a time, boxes and trash bags fell away from the stack in the corner and tumbled to the floor. Like peeling away a banana, the falling boxes revealed a terrified white boy, who slowly rose to his feet, his hands outstretched in front of him to ward off Barney's threatening moves.

Billy had watched the news that morning. It took him five seconds to put it all together.

"You're Nathan, aren't you?" Billy said.

Nathan nodded and swallowed hard, his eyes never leaving the angry beast. "I-I w-won't hurt anybody," Nathan declared.

"What are you doing—"

"The dog . . ."

"You killed those guys."

Nathan shook his head frantically, never moving his eyes from the snarling mutt. "No. No, I didn't, honest. I don't know what's happening, but I'm not the one."

"Then what are you doing here?"

Nathan swallowed again and jumped when Barney moved his head. "Cops. Th-they're looking for me."

Billy studied the other boy for a long moment. "So I hear," he said.

"Could you . . . The dog . . ."

Billy hesitated for a few seconds, then stooped down to rub Barney's ears. "Be cool, Barney. Let's hear what the dude has to say for himself."

"How come you know who I am?" asked Nathan.

Billy snorted out a chuckle. "You're in deep trouble,

man. Everybody knows who you are. You were on *Nightline* last night."

Nathan's eyebrows shot up as he felt a rush of pride. You had to *be* somebody to get on *Nightline*. Hell, the *president* had been on *Nightline*! Then again, so had Charles Manson.

"What'd they say about me?"

Billy shrugged. "Half the world thinks you're a murderer and the other half thinks you're some kind of hero."

"I'm no hero," Nathan said, shaking his head. "But I'm no murderer, either."

For the first time, Billy made long eye contact. Billy had adult's eyes, Nathan saw. They were the eyes of someone who'd seen his own share of adversity; hard and warm at the same time.

"Until this morning I might have agreed with you, bro. But those dead cops they found last night didn't keel over from heart attacks. How do you explain that?"

"*I* didn't kill anyone!" Nathan declared, missing Billy's use of the plural. "A cop killed that cop. Then he tried to kill me." It took a few minutes to tell the story. Billy seemed to accept it as fact.

"So, who killed the second cop?" Billy asked at the end.

Nathan scowled. "What second cop?"

Billy explained.

Nathan gasped and sank slowly to the floor. He ran a hand through his greasy hair. "Oh, shit, they think I did all that?"

Billy nodded. "Yep. And they're talking hardcore

about not letting you get away with it." Then he laughed. "Like they were just gonna let you get away with killing the guy in Virginia. You *did* kill that one, right?"

"Yeah . . . well, not until he tried to kill me."

Billy's attitude turned suddenly skeptical. "So how come everybody's trying to kill you?"

Nathan tossed his hands in the air. "I don't know. It's worse than that. Not everybody is trying to kill me, only cops."

"Who'd you piss off?"

"I don't know! But I sure did a good job of it."

Another long silence followed. "What are you gonna do next?" Billy finally asked.

Nathan studied the other boy before answering. "I don't know. What are *you* gonna do?"

"Well, I ain't gonna call the cops, if that's what you mean. Too many of them suckers around here as it is."

Nathan considered his next question for a long time before asking it. "Can I hide in your place for the day?"

Billy's answer came easily, as though he'd been anticipating the request. "Sure, why not?" he said. "Don't got much to eat, but we got a TV and I got some games and stuff."

Nathan winced. "Watching TV's gotten pretty depressing for me recently."

Billy laughed again. "I bet."

"What time is it?" asked Nathan.

Billy shrugged. "I don't know exactly. It was about eight-fifteen when I came downstairs. Why? You got an appointment?"

Nathan smiled and shook his head. "No, but come ten o'clock I got a phone call to make."

CHAPTER THIRTY-TWO

BY THE TIME WARREN ARRIVED at the Pitcairn County Sheriff's Office, the place was a media circus, with satellite trucks parked nose-to-tail down the last quarter-mile of Main Street. Approaching the front entrance, he saw two network reporters whom he recognized from the evening news broadcasts. *Good Lord,* he thought. *They're bringing their New York staffs into this thing.*

His gold badge granted him unimpeded access into the building, through the crowds of reporters and citizens. Just as he opened the glass doors to enter, one of the reporters recognized him and called his name. Warren didn't even break stride.

The first face he saw belonged to Petrelli, who was already holding court in the hallway, issuing instructions to people over whom he had no authority, but who nevertheless seemed to be listening. Warren could tell from the body language alone that he was in the middle of one of his "let's-go-out-and-get-'em" Knute Rockne pep talks.

With too little sleep to his credit and way too much

caffeine in his system, Warren knew he was ill-prepared to encounter Petrelli just then, and he tried to become invisible as he passed the crowd. It didn't work.

"Lieutenant Michaels!" Petrelli called in his most pompous tone. "Can you come here a minute, please?"

Warren stopped, sighed, and then worked his way through the knot of police officers to stand next to Petrelli.

"This is Detective Lieutenant Warren Michaels," Petrelli announced to the group. "Notwithstanding a bit of trouble getting a handle on this particular case, the lieutenant is one of Braddock County's finest police officers. I've asked him to travel here to New York to assist in our efforts to catch Nathan Bailey."

Warren shot a withering look at Petrelli. Nobody had asked Warren to do anything. He was in Pitcairn County of his own volition, and he was none too certain how the chief was going to respond when he heard.

"Sorry about fumbling the ball, there, J.," Michaels mumbled, just loud enough for Petrelli to hear. "We can't all be as successful as you've been these last few days." This was Petrelli at his finest: center stage, big case, hungry audience, and manufacturing facts at will.

A pro at selective hearing, Petrelli ignored the comment. "We all know what's at stake here," he concluded. "Now let's work together to stop this animal before he can hurt anyone else."

"Have we got the green light to take him out if we have to?" asked one of the deputies. He looked maybe twenty years old. "I mean, he's just a kid. I don't want to have to spend the rest of my career in a courtroom if it comes down to him and me and I win."

The rumbling murmur through the crowd indicated that it was a shared sentiment.

Petrelli was ready. "I've said all along that I think we should treat this monster as an adult. Clearly, he's capable of unspeakable violence. But that's really not my call, Deputy. Sheriff Murphy's got to make that decision."

All eyes turned toward a bald, heavyset man standing on the other side of Petrelli from Michaels. Till now, the man had looked distracted, as though his mind were elsewhere, like a platoon leader who'd just lost his troops in combat. With attention now focused on him, Murphy set his jaw and faced his men.

"Two wonderful families lost fine husbands and fathers this morning," he said softly. Though barely audible, his voice was the very essence of strength. The hallway grew silent as he spoke. "Those men were friends of mine, colleagues of yours. A murderer took these peace officers from us in cold blood, and I have no intention of seeing him take any more. To answer your question, Deputy, yes, you have the green light. If you feel threatened, you take him out."

It was what they wanted to hear. "Kid's history," Deputy Steadman said at the front of the crowd.

"There you go, men," Petrelli concluded, careful to rob Murphy of the last word. "You have your orders. Go out and bring the bastard in."

Warren was horrified. As the group of police officers broke up and headed out to fulfill their orders, he turned to face Murphy and Petrelli, his mouth agape. "My God, Petrelli, you just issued a death warrant on that kid."

"Oh, for heaven's sake, Warren, don't be such a woman." He turned his back on Michaels.

Warren leveraged a shoulder to spin him back around. "What gives you the right to form a lynch mob? You're an officer of the court, counselor! You can't authorize an execution!"

Petrelli's eyes burned with self-righteous anger. "Get your hands off of me, Lieutenant, or I'll have you arrested for battery. Save your theatrics for that incompetent staff of yours. All we're trying to do is finish the job that you couldn't. If the kid gets killed, it's because he deserves it. When his arrest comes down, he'll just have to be very careful, that's all."

Warren knew that Petrelli was an asshole; there was no use trying to talk to him. He turned his attention to Murphy. "Sheriff?" he said. "You've got to tone down the rhetoric, sir. Those men think you just authorized them to kill a twelve-year-old boy."

Warren wasn't sure what to make of the look he got from Murphy. It wasn't angry; it wasn't sad. Tired. That was it, he looked tired.

"Look, Lieutenant," he said patiently. "My boys know how to do their jobs. If the kid can be taken alive, that's how it will go down. If he poses a threat, he's toast. It's that simple."

"It's not that simple!"

"It's exactly that simple!" There was the anger. Suddenly Murphy seethed with it. "Don't you tell me how to run my department, Michaels. That animal killed two of my deputies. Here are the pictures." He thrust a fistful of Polaroids at Warren. "The way I look at it, if you hadn't screwed up on your end, I wouldn't have had to console two widows this morning. This is my case now, and I'll run it my way—which is to capture the bad guy and eliminate the threat to the community. That's what I'm elected to do. If that means that a young killer doesn't get a chance to grow up to be an old killer, then I can live with that."

A long moment passed with Michaels and Murphy staring angrily at each other. Then the anger disappeared from Murphy's countenance and he just looked tired again. Without another word, the sheriff turned and walked toward his office. Petrelli followed.

I hate politicians, thought Warren.

The very last thing in the world that Pointer wanted to do was call Mr. Slater. Nonetheless, the call had to be made. Pointer was a professional, and one of the duties of a professional was to own up to his mistakes. Sammy Bell answered the phone and passed him right through to Mr. Slater. Said he'd been expecting the call.

"Is it true what they say on the news, Lyle?" the old man asked, his raspy voice giving testimony to fifty years of unfiltered Chesterfields. "Is it true that you let this Bailey boy get away again?"

"I'm sorry, Mr. Slater," Pointer explained, surprised by the shakiness of his own voice, "but it's like this . . ."

"Be quiet, Lyle," commanded Mr. Slater. "I don't want to hear any more of your excuses. Do you comprehend how much embarrassment you've brought down on us with your incompetent screwups? Do you know what the others will say about us? Even the bangers will laugh at us. Punk kids, Lyle, and they'll be laughing at us."

"It's not like you think, Mr. Slater," Pointer offered.

"Shut up," the old man commanded a second time. "You don't know what I think, Lyle, and I don't care what you think. I care about performance, and you've let me down. Now, here's what I want you to do. Leave the boy alone. It appears that the police are intent on keeping him from our grasp. I want you to come home. We have some things we need to discuss."

Pointer felt himself hyperventilating, but he could not control his breathing. "What about that asshole Mark Bailey? Don't you want me to . . ."

"We'll take care of him."

"Please, Mr. Slater, at least let me . . ."

"I said we'll take care of him, Lyle. I want you to come home. I want to see you in my office this afternoon at five."

Pointer closed his eyes and concentrated on his breathing. For a moment, he thought he might cry.

"Do you understand me, Lyle?"

"Yes, sir." Pointer's tone was flat, as though he were dead already.

"Lyle?"

"Yes, Mr. Slater?"

"Make it easy on yourself, son," the old man instructed, an unexpected touch of kindness in his voice. "Don't make us come after you."

Unable to make his voice work, Pointer placed the phone gently on the cradle. He cocked his head oddly as he stared at his hands. He had never seen them shake before.

* * *

Warren set up camp in an empty office, where he leafed through the Polaroids for the sixth time. Not knowing the officers involved personally, the pictures were no more or less shocking than dozens of others he'd seen, but the sheer violence of the act was baffling. The marksmanship was amazing. Three shots were fired, each one a kill shot. *Where does a kid learn to shoot like that?* He jotted the thought down on a yellow legal pad. One shot like this might be luck. To score three meant skill.

The circumstantial, physical evidence was undeniable, but Warren still couldn't put it together in his head. How did a kid who had spent most of his formative years in upper-crust suburbia learn to kill with such skill? How did a twelve-year-old who was known by his peers as a wimp muster the courage and physical strength to overcome three adults and kill them? Okay, so the first one was drunk and unlucky—or so said Nathan—but what about the ones last night? How does a boy wrestle a gun from a man and still have enough composure to snap off perfect kill-shots?

For that matter, what were the cops doing wearing firearms in the cellblock? That violated the most basic security procedures followed by every jail in America.

He tried to reduce it to a time line on his legal pad. Assuming that Nathan got as far as his cell, and according to Deputy Steadman, that was where the boy was the last time he saw him, Schmidtt had to be the first one killed. Otherwise, where would Nathan have gotten the gun? Warren wrote on his pad, *Smuggled in gun?*

No, the gun he took from the Grimeses' house was found in the Honda, unused. There could always have been a second piece, but where would he hide it? Steadman's report said that Nathan was thoroughly frisked before he was put away.

So, one way or another, Nathan whacked Schmidtt. With the door open, he had free access to the hallway. So why didn't Watts react? He was shot in his chair, once close up, and once from farther away. The Polaroids clearly showed powder burns around the mouth shot, but none on the chest. When you hear shooting down the hall, you don't just stay in your seat. You react. At the very least, then, there should have been a shoot-out in the hallway, but that wasn't the way it happened. Watts was shot dead where he sat. Shot twice.

Michaels strolled out to the watch desk and ran some quick mental calculations. The young deputy assigned to maintain security stepped aside to let him past. Standing at the side of the watch desk, at the doorway to the cellblock, Warren pantomimed a shot. His extended arm came within three feet of the taped outline on the floor. This had to be where the head shot was fired. The circled hole in the linoleum even showed where the bullet exited Watts's brain and lodged in the floor.

That meant Watts was already on the ground when Nathan allegedly fired point-blank into his mouth. In all his years on the force, Warren could only point to a handful of sociopaths with the *cojones* to shoot a man in the face at close range.

Why would he do that? Warren asked himself.

Taking care not to step in the blood slick, Warren

stepped in behind the watch desk to pantomime the events. "Okay," he said aloud, talking himself through the timeline. "I'm sitting here doing paperwork, and I hear a shot from down the hall. What do I do?"

"You'd go and check it out," the young deputy answered, apparently thinking the question was addressed to him.

"Huh?" The comment briefly broke Warren's concentration. "Right. Yes. That's exactly what you'd do." He again stepped over the mess to enter the hallway. "So, reacting to the noise, you run out into the hall like this, with your weapon drawn, right? I mean, you'd be ready for a fight, right?"

"Hell, yes," the deputy declared.

Warren nodded. It was coming together. "Yes. Hell, yes. Like you said." He fumbled through the Polaroids again. "But Watts's weapon remained in its holster. Why wouldn't he draw his weapon?"

The deputy shrugged. "Beats me."

"Yeah, me too."

"Maybe he holstered it after he was hit."

Warren considered that. "So, you hear gunfire. You react. You come out into the hall, and you're bushwhacked with an incredibly good shot. You're hit in the chest. Surely you know you're dying, or at least you know you're in a hell of a lot of pain. Are you going to take the time to reholster your weapon?"

The deputy shrugged again. "Don't know. Never been shot."

Warren chuckled. The logic amused him. "Fortunately, neither have I. But I just can't imagine that. The last thing I'd do is take away my last chance for fighting back."

"What else could have happened?" asked the deputy.

"Suppose he never drew his weapon in the first place?"

The deputy snorted, "That don't make no sense, either."

Warren nodded pensively. "No. No, it doesn't. A cop hears shots, he's gonna pull his gun. It's instinct. Unless . . ."

Suppose somebody shot Watts first? Chest shot first, then, as he lay on the ground, the head shot. That would work. And Schmidtt? He had to be shot second. Well, maybe he didn't *have* to be, but it sure made sense.

The accomplice!

So, somebody comes in the front door, pops Watts, and then goes into the cellblock to break out his buddy, Nathan.

Okay, so where was this accomplice now? Helps the kid break out of the JDC and then disappears, only to reappear in New York in time to kill two cops. That was some accomplice!

Then he saw it.

The mind is a funny thing. You program it with a certain set of assumptions, and it will dutifully draw dozens of conclusions, all of which are plainly obvious—common sense, even—so long as you never question the validity of the assumptions. The most oft-forgotten job of a police detective is not only to seek evidence, but to continually question the most basic assumptions on which the case was based.

In a single moment of inspiration, Warren realized that they'd been looking at all of the evidence surrounding Nathan's escape from the wrong angle. Even when he had allowed himself to accept the kid's version of what happened at the JDC, he hadn't seen it. Those two deputies were never the target of whoever shot them. They were just in the way.

Warren's body jumped visibly when it all crystallized for him. Nathan was in far deeper trouble than any of them had realized.

"Deputy, get me Sheriff Murphy right now," he commanded.

The young man seemed startled by Michaels's suddenly harsh tone. "I'm sorry, sir, but I don't know where he is . . ."

"I didn't ask you if you knew where he is. I told you to go get him. And point me to a phone."

Jed Hackner nearly dropped the phone when he heard Michaels's theory. "A *hit*? Are you sure?"

"Think about it, Jed," Michaels said urgently. "If we assume somebody's got a contract out on Nathan, everything else falls into place. This kid's not a killer. He's just defending himself."

Jed admitted that the theory had merit, but making sense didn't make it so. Perhaps Brian's death last fall was making the boss lose perspective. "With all due respect, Warren, don't you think maybe you're taking benefit of the doubt too far?"

"I know what you're thinking," Warren acknowledged, his voice getting more anxious. "I know it sounds like I've lost it, but *think*. It's more than just the killings. How do you explain the breakdown of the video security at the JDC—not the whole system, mind you, but just the parts that would show Ricky coming and going."

"And the plane ticket." Jed saw it, too.

"What plane ticket?"

Jed told him about his visit to Ricky's apartment and his talk with Mitsy.

Warren's excitement showed in his voice. "I think that pushes it over the top," he said. "Why else would Harris go to so much trouble just to kill a kid? You don't trash your whole life just because you don't like a resident at the JDC. Hell, he didn't like *any* of the residents of the JDC. Somebody had to be paying him."

"So who's gonna put a contract out on a kid?" Jed asked.

"Beats the hell out of me," conceded Warren. "That's what I want you to find out. I've got to call off the dogs up here. You said you were gonna do some digging into Ricky Harris. Try his financial records. See if you can ID who's funding him."

Jed frowned. "We've already started, but we haven't turned up much. Wait." A manila envelope had materialized in Jed's in-basket since the last time he had visited his office. It bore the logo of Braddock Bank and Trust. "Cancel that. We have his bank records. Must have just gotten here."

"All right, good. Start there. Get me a good solid case that Nathan's a good guy and that Ricky's the bad guy."

"You got it, boss."

"And Jed?"

"Yeah?"

"Get that kid Thompkins involved in the investigation. After the week he's had, he could use a few 'atta boys.'"

Jed smiled. "Nobody was ever that nice to us, you know."

Warren laughed. "Yeah, I know. Well, if I'm wrong on this one, there'll be plenty of career mobility for all of you."

CHAPTER THIRTY-THREE

NATHAN DIALED CONTINUOUSLY for over an hour before the phone line finally rang. Billy caught the change in the rhythm of dial-hang-up, dial-hang-up, and instantly shifted his attention from *The Price Is Right*.

After thirty rings, a familiar voice answered.

"You've reached The Bitch line," Enrique said. "What do you want to talk about?"

"Hi, it's me," Nathan said simply. "I need to talk to Denise."

Enrique recognized the voice right away. "Hold on, Nathan, I'm sure she'll put you right on. Callers have been pretty tough on you today."

"I bet," Nathan said dejectedly. "Been a tough day all around."

"Did you do any of what they're now saying?" Enrique probed gently. It wasn't his place to ask such a question, but he couldn't help it. He had to know.

"I didn't kill those cops, if that's what you mean."

"Glad to hear it," Enrique said, meaning every word. No doubt about it, he was a believer. "I'll put you through now."

While on hold, Nathan could hear the end of the last conversation. Some lady was calling him a "bad seed," whatever that meant. Denise hung up on her abruptly, and his line went live.

"Nathan Bailey, are you there?"

"I didn't do it!" Nathan blurted out.

Denise read the panic in his voice and fought away tears. "Okay, honey, I believe you," she soothed. "Tell us what happened."

He did. When he was done, The Bitch was fifteen commercials behind. The list would grow considerably longer before it began to shrink.

Harry Thompkins couldn't believe what he'd just heard. "You mean he named me specifically? I thought he was pissed."

Jed laughed. "I've known Lieutenant Michaels a long time, kid. Trust me, if you leave the meeting able to stand, he's not pissed."

Thompkins was overcome with a sense of respect and warmth that he had never before felt on the job. Michaels could have had his ass fired, and no one would have said a thing. Instead, he ordered him by name to be put on the most visible case of the year— hell, of the decade.

Jed laughed again. "Don't look so stunned. He was a rookie once. A pretty stupid one, at that."

Harry smiled. "The mirror?"

"Yep, the mirror."

"So that actually happened?"

"Sure did. Took him years to recover the ground he lost that day."

Harry couldn't shake his feeling of incredulity. "I guess I owe him one."

Jed clapped the younger man on the shoulder. "Yes, you do," he said jovially. His mood turned suddenly serious. "Now to the business at hand," he said. "The lieutenant wants us to swim upstream on this case. Wants us to prove that somebody has a contract out on the Bailey kid; that that's the reason Harris tried to kill him. We've got bank records on Ricky that show a twenty-thousand-dollar deposit three weeks ago and then a total withdrawal of all funds the morning he was killed. When we're done there, he wants us to show that the cops in New York were killed by a hit man, not by Nathan. We're both convinced that Nathan was the intended target."

"A hit man?"

Jed nodded. "Makes sense, really, if . . ."

"Holy shit, that's it!" Harry proclaimed, cutting Jed off in mid sentence.

"What's what?"

Harry didn't answer. Instead, he picked up Jed's phone and dialed information.

"Braddock Hospital, please," he said after a short pause. "Emergency Department."

Tad Baker hadn't given the Bailey matter much thought since he had last spoken with Harry Thompkins. When he heard that the police officer was holding for him, it took Tad a minute to piece together their last conversation.

"Hi, Harry," he said cheerfully as he snatched up the hand set.

Harry was all business. "Tad, you remember our little talk the other day?"

Tad shrugged. "Uh-huh."

"You remember our rules of engagement? Say nothing if you agree and . . ."

"Yeah, I remember," he interrupted, none too comfortable about walking the ethical tightrope on an open phone line.

"Okay, I've got one more theory for you. You ready?"

Tad looked around casually. No one was within earshot. "I suppose."

Harry took a deep breath. "Okay, here goes. I think that Mark Bailey's fingers were broken intentionally, by someone *intending* to do him harm."

There was a pause. Tad said nothing.

"And I think that to do that, the perpetrator would have to be one sick individual."

Another pause. More silence.

"Like maybe a hit man."

Tad didn't say a word.

"Are you there, Doc?" Harry asked at last.

"Yeah, I'm here, but I've really got to go," Tad said hurriedly.

"Thanks a million, Tad," Harry said, genuine affection in his voice.

"Yeah, right. We're not doing this ever again."

The line went dead, and Harry placed the receiver on the cradle.

Jed was getting tired of feeling like he had entered this show in the middle of the third act. "What was that all about?"

"Come on," Harry said, heading for the door. "I'll explain it in the car."

Jed followed without thinking. "You think the kid's uncle did all this?"

"No. But I'll bet you a hundred bucks he knows who did."

CHAPTER THIRTY-FOUR

LYLE POINTER HAD ENDURED just about as much of Nathan Bailey as he could stand. His face was everywhere: front page of the newspaper, the morning news, the evening news, every damn place. Now the son of a whore was on the damn radio again.

As he replayed the screwups from the night before in his mind, Pointer absently rotated his wrist, trying to work some of the soreness out. What he needed was some aspirin for his throbbing head and arm, but he refused to give in. The dull pain helped him focus on what he had to do.

One way or another, Lyle knew that he himself was a dead man. Even if Mr. Slater didn't have him whacked outright for bungling such a simple job, without the old man's tacit protection, Pointer's countless enemies would stand all night in long lines just for a chance to take him out. It was the curse of being good at your profession.

Faced with his own mortality, he found himself surprisingly at peace with it all. Mr. Slater had a business to run, and the kind of sins Pointer had committed made it very difficult to conduct that business. But if the old man thought that Lyle was just going to saunter on into a trap—if he thought that he was just going to write off this Bailey kid and then make a suicide trip into the paws of Slater's attack dogs—well, he had another think coming. Lyle had a job to do, and that job was right here in Pitcairn County.

Lyle had thought a lot about death over the years. It was his business. It was his future. Hell, it was everybody's future.

He'd always had a premonition of how his own end would come. In his fantasies, it was always a gallant thing, perhaps taking the bullet meant for his boss, propelling himself into the special company of heroes among villains.

Now there'd be no heroics, only shame. He could hear the mocking laughter now as his rivals pissed on his grave. Lyle Pointer—the Hit Man—beaten by a little boy.

Nathan Bailey had robbed him of his honor. A punk kid had made him a laughingstock. Who'd have ever thought it was possible?

One thing was for sure. The little bastard wasn't going to be around to share in the laughter.

Until now, killing had always been business. Suddenly it was personal. And Lyle was going to enjoy every minute of it.

Where does a kid go when he gets driven underground by the cops? he thought. His first two nights, the punk had time to scope out his hiding places. But this morning was different, wasn't it? He had to work fast. He'd get out of the business district quickly; head for the boonies. Would he take a car? Maybe, but he always had keys before. Hot-wiring was a lot harder than television led people to believe. Pointer was willing to bet that the kid didn't know how to do it.

That meant he had stayed on foot. How far could he go on foot? Depends on how long he ran, doesn't it? Young kid like that, in good shape, could probably run forever. He didn't run forever, though, did he? Hell, no, he's on the radio right now!

Pointer prided himself on his sense for things like this, and he knew that the kid was close. If only he could pinpoint where.

The telephone. The radio. The link was there somewhere. What was it that he'd read in the paper? Not the part where the idiot prosecutor couldn't get his way, but something else. Something about that witness in Pennsylvania. He worked for the phone company, didn't he? Yes, by God he did! Bastard said he felt "terrible" that he hadn't put the pieces together sooner. Poor fool seemed to be really beating himself up over dropping the ball on identifying the kid when he saw him.

A plan started to form in Pointer's mind. The witness—Todd Briscow, there it was, right in the paper—probably would do just about anything to assuage his guilt, wouldn't he? Given an opportunity to redeem himself—say, to cooperate with the prosecutor's investigation—Pointer was by God certain that old Todd would just jump at the chance. If not, well, Lyle had made a very good living at being persuasive.

Pointer figured it would take five phone calls to get the number he needed. It only took three.

* * *

To his considerable relief, Todd had discovered that his friends and coworkers were much easier on him than he was on himself. Rather than chastising him for his failure to act, he was widely praised for being so responsive. "Heads-up thinking," and "community watchdog" were two of the terms used by his supervisor to describe his actions.

In fact, from such a low starting point, Todd had begun to feel right proud. A lesser man might have done nothing, he told himself. It took a certain community spirit to get involved at all. And if he hadn't done at least that much, God only knew where that pint-sized murderer might have gone.

By noon, Todd Briscow had come to recognize his role for what it really was: the critical element that solved the Nathan Bailey case. And who would have thought that the boy could have traveled so far so quickly?

When his secretary told him that the prosecutor's office from Braddock County, Virginia was on the line, he donned his most self-important expression and nearly strutted into his office. He closed the door and lifted the receiver.

"This is Todd Briscow, how can I help you?" he said smoothly.

To Pointer, the other man sounded like a panting dog. "Mr. Briscow, this is Larry Vincent from Mr. Petrelli's office here in Braddock County," Pointer lied. "How are you today, sir?"

"Very well, thank you."

"I wanted to say on behalf of Mr. Petrelli just how appreciative we are of all your assistance in helping us solve our problem with Nathan Bailey."

Todd giggled like a schoolgirl. "Oh, it really wasn't much at all," he gushed.

"Like heck it wasn't," Pointer gushed back. "If it weren't for the efforts of people such as yourself, we'd never be able to get a handle on crime in our communities." For a full two minutes, Pointer lauded Briscow's sense of community and his dedication to his fellow man. The thicker he laid it on, the more willing Todd seemed to hear it.

It began to get a little embarrassing. "Well, I certainly appreciate your call," Todd said at last, trying to end the conversation. "And tell Mr. Petrelli thank you for being so thoughtful."

"I'll certainly do that," Pointer acknowledged. "You know, before I lose you, I was wondering if you could do me a favor."

"Certainly," Todd said. "I like to do my part."

Pointer chuckled at Todd's magnanimous understatement. "As well you have proven. We need your help just one more time."

"Tell me what it is and it's yours."

Pointer told him.

Todd didn't know what to say. "Mr. Vincent, I'm sorry, but that's not possible. You know yourself . . ."

"Oh, now, Mr. Briscow, I don't think you're seeing the complete picture," Pointer said smoothly. The smile remained in his voice, but with a decidedly sharp edge. "We have to bring Nathan Bailey back into custody, and you hold the key to finding him."

Todd earnestly wanted to help, but this was just out of the question. "Mr. Vincent, look at this from my point of view. I could get fired. Besides, the court already decided . . ."

"I'll be honest with you, Mr. Briscow," Pointer interrupted again. "Your point of view really isn't important to me right now. The greater good of society is at stake here."

"But you're asking me to break the law!"

Pointer donned his most condescending tone and took a deep breath. "Think about how many laws you break every day, Mr. Briscow. There's the speed limit, maybe one drink too many before you drive. I'll bet even one or two of your tax returns aren't all that they might be."

Todd was angry now. These analogies were absurd. "Perhaps you're right, Mr. Vincent, but what you're suggesting is orders of magnitude beyond . . ."

Pointer broke him off again. "Mr. Briscow, think what life would be like if every time you drove your car, someone was there waiting to write you a ticket for doing one mile an hour over the limit. Think what it would be like to have every one of your tax returns audited, starting from seven years ago. You know, even a few dollars adds up over seven years, what with interest and penalties . . ."

Suddenly, Todd realized that he had no options. He was furious. "How dare you blackmail me!"

Pointer winced at the term. "Mr. Briscow, you have nothing to fear unless you have broken the law. And if you've already broken the law, what's one more time?"

The full spectrum of emotions flooded Todd's mind all at once: anger, fear, loathing. This pompous jerk—a lawyer, no less—was forcing him to violate the law by leveraging his fear of having violated the law! It was ridiculous, but what choice did he have but to go along? What an incredible twist this hero business had taken!

Pointer correctly interpreted the silence as Todd's acquiescence. "Very well, then," he said. "I'll give you thirty minutes to gather the information I need, and then I'll give you a call back. Is that all right?"

"No, it's not all right!"

"Do it anyway." Pointer's tone was flat, leaving no room for negotiation. "I'll call you in exactly a half hour. And Mr. Briscow?"

"What?"

"Time is of the essence in this matter. You don't want to get on my bad side."

Todd stared at the dial tone for a long time. Deep in the pit of his stomach, he had the feeling that he'd just been threatened with more than legal action.

Mark Bailey just wanted the agony to be gone—both mental and physical. Hearing Nathan's voice again on the radio had him balanced on the very edge of his sanity. He had to hand it to the little guy. He had the luck his Irish ancestors had intended for him.

As soon as Mark saw the news on television, he knew what had happened. And though he allowed himself a brief moment to feel vindicated by the failure of a "professional" killer to finish the job he'd paid Ricky to do so long before—could it possibly be just three weeks?—Mark knew the bottom line of what had happened last night. Pointer was not the kind to shoulder the blame himself. No, he'd want to share the glory with a friend. Even through the haze brought on by the recent death of yet another bottle of cheap bourbon, the swollen mass at the end of his arm reminded him of just how giving Pointer could be when he was in the mood to share.

Upon draining the last of the bottle, Mark made a pact with himself to sober up enough to make a plan. If history was any judge, he knew he'd be coherent again in a few hours. Meanwhile, he thought he'd engage in some serious introspection.

My God, he thought, *what have I become?*

Street-smart survivor that he was, it was not a question he often allowed himself. For thirty-three years, Mark had had to live off his own wits, thoroughly lost in the shadow of his perfect brother Steve. A year ago, when he was pressing charges against Steve's progeny, it brought a smile to Mark's face just to think of what Mr. Perfect Lawyer/Businessman/Class President would have been thinking as he watched the fruit of his loins treated with exactly the same respect that Mark had become accustomed to.

The look on the runt's face as he was escorted from the courtroom to the jail had said it all. *Why me?* Nathan's eyes had pleaded. *Because I said so,* Mark's smile had replied. The look on the judge's face had been a different matter entirely. The look of pure contempt had made Mark feel oddly recharged, contented. Brother Steve had been a star among the sanctimonious assholes who called the courthouse their office. And there they all stood, powerless, while Mark the Survivor sent Perfect Steve's kid to the hoosegow. Revenge felt sweet and thorough.

It had all seemed so simple then. Who could have guessed how complicated it would all become?

None of it was his fault, of course. If he'd gotten the

same respect from dear old Dad that Steve had, then Mark would never have had to seek quick cash. When his old man told him that his inheritance was contingent upon finishing college, Mark never thought for a moment that he was serious. As much of a cantankerous old fart as he was, Mark never dreamed that he would disinherit his own blood for something as trivial as a piece of paper from some snotty ivy-covered building. But he'd been serious, indeed. Serious as a heart attack.

When the old man died, his will became cast in iron, unchangeable. Steve had everything. Mark had nothing. Even Nathan got a big chunk, but not Mark. Nope, he was just a doormat, and who ever heard of leaving money to a doormat?

But then, Steve had always been the talented one. No one could suck up to the old man quite like old Steve-o. Butt-buddies to the end.

Yes sir, Dad sir, I'd be happy to shit all over Mark sir.

What, sir? Mark got a "C," sir? Why, that's terrible, sir. Have you seen my straight A's, sir?

So Steve and his seed got all the money and Mark got screwed. What else was new?

Once, when times got tough, Mark actually tried a little sucking up to the master himself, but all he got from his dear rich brother was a lecture on how he should get some "focus" in his life. Shithead.

Instead of sharing, Steve invested everything in real estate and in his practice. Then, two months after the real estate market collapsed, Steve-o became Jell-O at a railroad crossing.

When you're a survivor, you become adept at finding the opportunity hidden in the disguise of adversity. Now that there was a new orphan in the world, Mark had naturally figured that there would be money to support him. Dear old Dad's money at that. The irony was delicious.

Except there was no money. Steve-o's fortune had evaporated when real estate collapsed, and Nathan's funds were tied up in a trust managed by some hotshot lawyer in New York. Even Nathan couldn't touch the money until he was in his twenties. The kid whined constantly, grew like a weed, and ate nonstop. That all cost money. Lots of money. Old Steve-o would have done well to concentrate more on the present than the future. An insurance policy would have been nice. Sure, there was that one policy for a quarter-mil, but that went pretty fast. That was when Mark was in his pimping era. Nasty little business, managing whores. Bad crowd, too. For the life of him, he had no idea where all the money went.

The real cash, he found, was in the import business. Through some friends, he came to meet people who knew people. If he could cough up $500,000 and make a trip to Colombia, he could be set for life. That five hundred thousand could become five million, and with $5,000,000 in the bank, Mark could be anything he wanted to be. Poor alcoholics were bums; rich alcoholics were eccentric. All he wanted was respect.

That's where Pointer and Mr. Slater entered the picture. Mark had heard about their "bank" through street sources. It took all the salesmanship he had to leverage the cash—a thirty-day loan at 20 percent interest. But what was a hundred grand when you were looking down the pipeline at five million?

On May 27th, his hired pilot took off in a hired airplane to make the buy that would make Mark a rich man. When the pilot failed to return, Mark's troubles began in earnest. Some speculated that the pilot was killed in a sudden storm over the Gulf, but Mark knew better. He knew that somewhere someone was spending his five million dollars, having never had to invest a penny of his own money.

Thirty days to the hour after he had borrowed the money, Pointer showed up at his door demanding payment. In retrospect, Mark knew that he should have told the truth in the beginning, but it just was not his nature. He stalled for time. There were some problems getting the stuff cut, he explained, smooth as silk, and Pointer gave him an extra day. Even Mark thought it sounded like the truth.

But the clock kept spinning. His plan was to withdraw the last of his insurance money—twenty thousand dollars—and offer it up the next day as a down payment.

By the thirty-first day, though, Pointer had discovered the lie, and when Mark offered the twenty grand, Pointer laughed like it was the funniest joke he had ever heard. No, it wouldn't do, he said. Suddenly the Hit Man had lost all interest in why Mark couldn't repay his debt, replaced instead with a well-developed plan to introduce Mark to whole new worlds of pain. Kidneys seemed to be an especially favored target, though Pointer was equally talented with gut punches. And when he drove that bony knee of his into your balls, well, that was a really special adventure, too.

The beating lasted off and on for the better part of a

half-hour before the Hit Man said anything of substance.

"You know, Mark," he had said, lounging back on
Mark's sofa as he methodically unwrapped a stick of
gum, "I did a little research on you, buddy. You come
from money. It pisses me off that you've got millions in
the family, yet you expect Mr. Slater to believe you
can't pay back a mere six hundred thou. Oops, this is
Thursday, isn't it? Make that six twenty-five. Now, before I rip out your windpipe, you want to tell me why
you're holding out on us?"

Though a month had passed, Mark still felt the pain
of that afternoon; how new jolts of agony would self-
generate from various bruised organs without Pointer
laying another hand on him. He could still remember the
Hit Man's exaggerated patience as he waited through
the whole story of Mark's banishment from the family.
When Mark was done, Pointer had seemed genuinely
disappointed that there really was no choice but to cut
his throat.

It was the sight of the straight razor that made Mark
think the unthinkable.

There was a way, he'd gasped hurriedly as Pointer
prepared for surgery. Mark had remembered a clause
in his father's will—a paragraph that had caught his
eye years before, during the first reading. Dear old Dad
had established a trust for his grandkids, of which
Nathan was the only one.

Valued at just over three million dollars, the trust
was supposed to send the grandkids to college and then
to give them a jump-start on their lives. But there was
a back door. As he lay there on the floor, sucking in car-

pet dust, he'd been able to remember the clause with perfect clarity. Looking back, he felt ashamed.

"In the event that any grandchild dies prior to his thirtieth birthday and prior to having completed an accredited course of study as defined in Paragraph 8(A)(c)(ii) above, the bequeathed amount shall be distributed to the child's father, or, if such distribution is not possible for whatever reason, said share shall be distributed among my surviving progeny, *per stirpes.*"

When the unthinkable had first occurred to him in the lawyer's office, Mark had seen the potential, but, he'd have had to kill the whole family. Nobody needed money *that* bad.

Not until you'd spent some time with a pain expert, anyway. Lord, that razor looked sharp.

It turned out that Lyle was a survivor, too, with a keen eye for his own pocketbook. Within a minute of hearing about the backdoor clause, Pointer had developed a plan. Mark would be allowed to live a while longer, for the sole purpose of killing his nephew and taking delivery of the inheritance money. Pointer, meanwhile, would shelter Mark from the wrath of Mr. Slater in return for a $200,000 fee.

The details were left up to Mark, but Pointer made it clear that he expected a clean job. Recognizing that details can be expensive, he had even returned the twenty grand down payment.

The rest had been shockingly simple. Mark found Ricky by following the guards as they left the JDC at shift change and gathered at the Woodbine Inn for drinks. They were not a happy lot, bitching constantly about every aspect of their jobs. Of all the guards, a young skinny one named Ricky Harris, was the most vocal.

"I'd do anything to get out of that hellhole," he'd said.

Mark bought Ricky a drink. Over the course of the evening, Mark bought him a lot of drinks. It was nearly midnight when Mark made his pitch. All Ricky had to do, he explained, was kill the kid and skip out of the country. Twenty thousand dollars went a long way in some parts of the world. As luck would have it, twenty grand was more money than Ricky Harris had ever seen in one place, and with that much cash up front, he didn't seem especially bothered by the prospect of killing one of the worthless pukes under his care. When he found out that the target was that pussy Bailey, he seemed thrilled.

And so it had started.

As Mark now sat alone in the sweltering heat of his soon-to-be-repossessed house, he marveled at just how wrong everything had gone. The stack of legal sheets strewn on the table served as yet another monument to his crappy life. And in the sureness of his own approaching death, he grew terrified of his appointment with hell. Somewhere deep within his self-pity, there was even a growing tumor of remorse for what he'd forced Nathan to endure.

He was pulled from the past by a knock at his front door. He was frightened at first, until he realized that it was impossible for Pointer to have gotten back so soon. He considered for a moment that it might be a cop. In his stupor, he was unable to decide if that would be good news or bad.

By the time Mark staggered to the door, the visitor had grown impatient, pounding with his fist.

As he swung the door open, a large man, maybe six-three, stood silhouetted against the brilliant white background. Mark winced in the wash of sunlight.

"What do you want?" Mark demanded.

The man stepped in without being asked. "I came to talk to you, Mark," the man said. "Mr. Slater sends his regards."

CHAPTER THIRTY-FIVE

IN THE CAR, JED AND HARRY LISTENED to The Bitch on the radio, and her ongoing interview with Nathan. Warren was right, Jed realized. If you listened to Nathan's side of the story and accepted it at face value, Warren's hit man theory explained it all.

Jed suddenly felt terribly guilty. He'd allowed himself to get so wrapped up in the boy's escape and the events surrounding it that he hadn't taken the time to look at the obvious. In his heart, he'd always believed that Ricky Harris probably deserved to die; that he was caught in the act of something despicable, perhaps even sexual. But until his conversation with Mitsy, he'd never considered that his sole purpose was to kill the boy. And even then, it hadn't made any sense.

In an effort to manage the frustration, Jed had written off such details as irrelevant in the short term. The whole department had. All that mattered was the boy's capture. They'd all rationalized that whatever motivation Nathan might have had for killing the supervisor was between him, the prosecutor, and the jury.

Jed silently berated himself and his colleagues as he

realized that this collective myopia had nearly cost a young boy his life. The very police force that was supposed to protect him had in fact eased the burden on his killer. That thought—and the thought of those poor cops in New York—sickened him. Soon, though, they'd set it all straight.

The first thing Jed noticed about Mark Bailey's untidy little house was the drawn curtains. They gave the structure a haunting, abandoned look.

"I wonder if anybody's home," he thought aloud.

Things didn't look right. A Ford Bronco sat in the driveway, its image shimmering in the heat rising from the driveway. Nothing moved this day but the thermometer. It was barely noon, and the temperature had already topped ninety-eight degrees. The weatherman on the radio said to expect a new record at 104. Jed longed for the fall.

"That's his car," Harry offered. "In the same spot as yesterday."

"Does the place look odd to you?" Jed asked.

Harry studied the front of the house for a moment. "No," he said. "Looks like a house. What are you thinking?"

"I don't know," Jed mused. "Looks odd to me for some reason. Like nobody's home. All the blinds are shut."

"Well, his car's still in the driveway," Harry reminded him. "My guess is he's just trying to keep the place cool."

Jed said nothing else. He opened the car door and walked silently up the sloping front yard toward the porch. Harry followed, three steps behind. The younger man was startled when Jed withdrew his big nine-millimeter Glock from the high-hip holster under his sportcoat.

"What's up?" Harry asked as he drew his own weapon.

"Don't know," Jed replied, whispering now. "Just doesn't feel right."

Standing off to the hinge side of the door, out of harm's way in case someone blasted bullets through the door, Jed knocked loudly enough to draw a look from the neighbor across the street. There was no response. Harry took a mirror position to Jed, on the knob side. Seeing the guns, the neighbor moved quickly inside, gathering her five-year-old daughter in her arms.

Jed knocked louder. "Mark Bailey!" he shouted. "This is the police. Open the door!" In the humid air of the still neighborhood, his voice echoed off the houses. Despite the noise, nothing moved from within Mark Bailey's house.

Jed eyed the doorknob, then nodded to Harry, who reached down and tried to turn it. When it didn't budge, he returned his eyes to Jed and shook his head.

Jed swung away from his defensive position and took a shooter's stance, two-handing his aim at the door, while Harry swung around to jam the sole of his boot into the door just adjacent to and a little above the knob. As though blasted open with dynamite, the steel door exploded inward with a crash and rebounded closed, just as Harry dove sideways to catch the door with his shoulder. From his awkward position on his left side, Harry could cover the front hallway to the right. In three quick steps, Jed darted into position to cover the left.

"Mark Bailey!" Jed yelled again. "Police officers!"

Harry scrambled to his feet, staying crouched down low, ready for action. Still, nothing moved.

"Check out this level," Jed instructed. "I'll go upstairs."

They split up, and even as they parted, Jed knew what they would find. There is a smell to death, a thick sweet odor. Over the years, he'd learned to detect even the faintest traces of the stench. Mark Bailey's house reeked of it. Jed had just reached the top of the stairs when Harry called out from the living room.

"Oh, shit!" shouted Harry, clearly unnerved. "Oh, Christ, Sergeant, I found him! He's in the living room! He's dead."

I knew it, Jed thought as he headed back downstairs.

Harry was finishing a frantic primary search of the first floor while Jed entered the living room, holstering his weapon. "Bad guy gone?" he asked, inwardly amused by the fear on the young cop's face.

Harry nodded. "Yeah," he said, "the place is clean. Look at him, though. That's disgusting."

"Yeah," Jed agreed as he surveyed the body, instinctively reaching for his little notebook. "He sure as hell pissed somebody off."

Mark Bailey's body was tied rigidly into a dining room chair, his head cast backwards over the chair back. His mouth was open wide, a yawning cavern rimmed with crimson smears. His graying blond hair dangled heavily, matted and violet. In the middle of it all, a long finger of extruded brain tissue extended like a ponytail from a ragged hole in the crown of his skull. Both arms dangled limply at his sides. Harry was the first to notice that the cast had been removed from

Mark's right arm, and that his purple, swollen fingers were twisted at horrifying angles.

Using a handkerchief to hold the receiver and a pencil eraser to push the buttons, Jed used the phone on the end table next to the sofa to call for the criminal investigative unit and the coroner. While he waited on the line to pass along the critical information, he surveyed the interior of the tiny house, taking particular interest in the broken television set with the empty booze bottle resting where the picture tube should have been. Three days' worth of newspapers had been stacked next to the sofa, each issue opened to a story about Nathan. Jed remembered his briefing on the details that had sent Nathan to the Juvenile Detention Center, and he wondered what the boy's Uncle Mark had thought about the events of the past three days. Was he remorseful? Titillated? Amused?

"C'mon," Jed urged impatiently, waiting for somebody in the coroner's office to pick up the phone. He shifted the receiver from his hand to his shoulder, where he held it in place with a sustained shrug. His eyes wandered to a sheaf of papers; legal documents, he recognized from the numbered lines and exaggerated indentations. There it was, on the front: The Last Will and Testament of somebody named William Steven Bailey. Having nothing better to do, he casually thumbed through the stapled pages.

Something underlined on page fourteen of the will caught his attention, and his mind shifted from scanning mode to reading mode. Halfway through the second paragraph, his backbone straightened and he sat down on the edge of the sofa cushion.

"I'll be damned," he said aloud.

"What have you got?" Harry asked, taking advantage of the opportunity to examine something other than the body.

"Our motive," Jed said sharply.

"Medical Examiner's office, this is Julie," a voice said in his ear.

Jed told her to hold on for a minute.

CHAPTER THIRTY-SIX

"SO LET ME GET THIS STRAIGHT," Sheriff Murphy summarized after listening to Warren's presentation. "You want me to go before the voters of this county and tell them that on the advice of a police detective from Virginia, I should ignore all the physical evidence gathered thus far—not the least of which is an admission of guilt from the kid himself—and shift our efforts to find a phantom hit man. Is that what you're telling me, Lieutenant Michaels?"

Warren scanned the faces of the sheriff and Petrelli, who sat perched like a parrot next to his fellow politician. A deep, abiding belief in the criminal justice system was the only thing that kept Warren from popping them both. This was a useless exercise, he realized. To these two, police work was about votes. Nothing more.

When Warren didn't answer, Petrelli filled the silence. "Warren, I'm worried about you," he said, shaking his head, his voice dripping with condescension. "We all know how hard the loss of your son was on you last year. I think maybe you've lost perspective on this case. Perhaps you should volunteer to step down from it. That way, I don't have to ask Chief Sherwood to remove you from it."

Petrelli's words hit him in the chest like a hammer. Bang! Warren had known going into this meeting that his arguments were not yet well formed, and that they directly contradicted much of the physical evidence. He knew that he would have to change their entire approach to the facts, and he had, in fact, done the sales job of his life.

To anyone else, the arguments would have been persuasive, but he had underestimated the depth of political ambition jammed into this tiny little office. By refusing to be persuaded, they had made Warren look like a fool. It had been an opportunity for which Petrelli had been waiting for years, and there it was. Find the most vulnerable weakness in your opponent, and concentrate all your forces on that spot. It was every bit as reliable a rule in politics as it was on the battleground.

Worst of all, Petrelli was right. He had no business remaining a part of this case. Warren had known it ever since he'd seen the still picture from the JDC video. His heart was every bit as involved in this case as his mind, but he believed nonetheless that he could keep them separate; he believed he could be professional and objective when he had to be.

But objectivity was not the issue here. Fact was, he was right! And these assholes knew it! For Petrelli, though, the opportunity to make his historical adversary squirm was a far more important prize than justice. By discrediting Warren—the flatfoot in charge of the investigation—Petrelli would be able to recover a portion of the political damage done by Nathan's celebrity.

"So, what do you say, Warren?" Petrelli pressed. "Why don't you step down?"

Warren smiled politely. "Why don't you kiss my ass, J.?" He knew when he'd lost. He also knew that Chief Sherwood was the only human being on earth who hated Petrelli more than Warren did. Petrelli's threats were as hollow as his spine.

"That'll be enough!" Sheriff Murphy intervened. "Lieutenant Michaels, I think this meeting is over."

Warren turned away from Petrelli and faced Murphy. "Look, Sheriff, all I ask is for you to tell your men to take it easy. They're looking for a murderer named Nathan, not a victim named Nathan. That makes a huge difference in how they take him down. You authorized a green shooter's light, for Chrissake!"

"Do I need to arrange an escort for you to leave, Lieutenant?" Murphy offered. The phone rang. "I can arrange that, if you want."

Warren stood still for a moment longer. There was nothing left for him to do. As he turned to leave, he heard Murphy answer his phone and pass it to Petrelli.

"What the hell are you talking about?" Petrelli exploded. "I did no such thing!"

Warren stopped short of the door to eavesdrop. Seeing Petrelli blow his cool always lightened his day. Now the prosecutor-cum-senator seemed as confused as he did angry.

"Look, Stephanie," he said after a long spate of listening, "I'm telling you I didn't call. Do you think I have a death wish? Judge Verone would have my butt in jail before nightfall."

The pieces fell together for Warren. "Stephanie" would be Stephanie Buckman, who had represented

Petrelli's ridiculous petition before Judge Verone the day before. When it all focused in his mind, Warren's heart started racing. Somebody was trying to trace Nathan's call.

As much as he wanted to suspect Petrelli of foul play, he knew that the slimebag would let his mother be lynched before he'd violate a court order. After all, the lynching would earn him tons of voter sympathy; the bad press from violating the court order would kill him. He realized in an instant that Nathan's would-be killer was making his next move.

Warren moved quickly back across the office and snatched the telephone away from Petrelli, pushing him aside with a forearm. J. Daniel looked shocked at the lieutenant's strength.

"Stephanie, this is Warren Michaels," he said hurriedly. "I understand that somebody was trying to trace Nathan Bailey's telephone call?"

Stephanie's voice showed surprise at the sudden change in characters. "Well, y-yes," she stammered.

"Did he get it?"

"Y-yes. But why . . ."

"How long ago?" Warren interrupted. His voice was abrupt and insistent.

"Look, Lieutenant . . ."

"How long ago, Stephanie?" Warren was shouting now.

"I-I don't know for sure. Twenty minutes, maybe." Stephanie seemed hesitant to speak to him about the details.

Warren checked his watch without seeing the time. "Shit. What's the number?" he asked.

"Lieutenant, what happened to Mr. Petrelli?" she stalled.

"No one knows for sure," Warren said without missing a beat. "We think he was born an asshole." He looked directly at Petrelli as he spoke, lest there be any doubt. "Look, Stephanie, I need that number. The guy who was asking for it is our killer. Please. Tell me what it is."

Petrelli made a move to wrestle the phone back, but retreated immediately from Warren's threatening glare.

"You know if you use this, any evidence will be tainted," Stephanie warned, a broad smile in her voice from Warren's comments about her boss.

"I don't care," Warren promised. "I just need that number."

With more than a little hesitation, she gave him the number. As soon as the seventh digit passed Stephanie's lips, Warren dropped the phone onto its cradle.

Without a word, Warren left Murphy's office, dialing his cell phone as he walked.

Denise marveled at the margin by which the afternoon callers were favoring Nathan's side. Having been so terribly unnerved at first, Nathan seemed to have calmed down a lot, though he was a mere shadow of the jovial personality she'd had on the air yesterday. For the most part, he was sparing of the details surrounding his capture and escape. All she really knew for sure after nearly two hours on the phone with him was that he was convinced that he was the target of a police conspiracy to kill him, and that he had had nothing to do with those police officers' deaths the night before.

When Denise pointed out that law enforcement people had an uncanny way of turning up dead in Nathan's presence, he had no rehearsed response. He only reiterated that he was victim just like all the others—or a potential victim, anyway. And if cops were trying to kill you, what better place to do it than at a prison?

Much as she hated to admit it, today's phone call with Nathan was getting repetitive and boring. Pretty soon she was going to have to cut him off and move on to other things. The thought tugged at her heart, though. It seemed as if he *needed* to talk on the radio today.

Carter from Tuscaloosa was on the phone asking Nathan about life with his Uncle Mark when a stranger joined them on the line.

"Excuse me," the voice said, "this is the telephone operator, with an emergency break-in call from Lieutenant Michaels from the police department. Go ahead, sir."

There was a click, and then Warren's voice joined the conversation. "Nathan, this is Lieutenant Michaels from the Braddock County Police Department," he said.

"Wait a minute, Lieutenant," Denise protested. "How did you break in? In case you hadn't heard, we won our case yesterday . . ."

"Yes, ma'am, you did," Warren confirmed. "I'll be happy to explain all the details to you later, but right now Nathan is in grave danger. Son, you need to run away from where you are. Now. The man who tried to kill you last night is on his way to do it again."

* * *

Nathan turned pale, causing Billy to move closer to the receiver where he could hear. Barney followed. It didn't even occur to him to turn on the radio.

The police had traced his call! They couldn't do that! He'd heard this morning on the news that a judge had told them they couldn't do that. Now a cop was telling him to run away, but it was cops who had tried to kill him in the first place.

"H-how do I know you're not trying to trick me?" Nathan asked, his voice taking on a dazed quality.

"You don't," Warren answered simply. "You'll just have to trust me."

Denise blurted, "Trust! You break into a private conversation—against court orders, I hasten to add—and you talk about trust? It seems to me . . ."

Warren cut her off. "Shut up, Bitch!" *Boy, that didn't sound right.* "Nathan has no choice but to trust me, because if he doesn't, he'll get killed, and there's nothing I can do about it. Believe it or not, son, I'm one of the good guys. Now, run!"

"Where to?" the boy asked, desperation building in the pit of his stomach.

Oh, shit! thought Warren. He hadn't planned that far ahead. There was only one landmark he could think of, and it was out in the middle of everything: the obelisk in the town square.

"Can you take us off the air for just a minute, Bitch?" Warren asked, his tone pleading and polite.

Denise heard the sincerity in the police officer's voice, the fear. She didn't have to do anything he asked, but she decided that she could ill afford not to.

"All right," she agreed, "but I'll be able to listen in."

"Must you?" Warren asked.

"Unless you want an earful of dial tone," Denise replied.

"Suppose you were to take your earphones off?"

Denise sighed loudly into the microphone. "Okay," she conceded. "You've got thirty seconds of dead air."

Enrique looked at her as if she'd gone completely over the edge, but followed suit anyway, removing his own earphones. In all his years in radio, this would be his first half-minute without his ears covered. They felt strangely cold.

"Go ahead, guys," Denise instructed. "Your clock is running. Let's go to commercials, Rick."

As Nathan listened, he felt his world becoming very small, just himself and this cop named Michaels. He started to object twice, but Michaels wouldn't let him. During the first ten seconds of the monologue, Nathan learned that there was a plot to kill him, and that it didn't involve the police. In the next ten, he heard that most of the police who were on the street thought that Nathan had killed the cops in the jail last night, and that they were cleared to shoot him if he resisted arrest. Finally, he learned that this Lieutenant Michaels was the only person in the universe that he truly could trust, and that the most important thing that Nathan could do was let Michaels bring him in.

"The running's over, Nathan," Michaels concluded. "You have to trust somebody now, and I'm all you've got. Do you know where the Lewis and Clark Memorial is in the square?"

"You mean the tall pointy tower?" Nathan said. "Yeah."

"Make your way over there and we'll find each other. I'm wearing a brown suit with a blue shirt and a striped tie. You'll see me. I look like a cop."

In spite of the danger, Nathan smiled. "I guess you know what I look like," he offered.

"The whole world knows what you look like, pal. Now, move! You've got no time left."

Nathan hung up the phone and looked at Billy.

"Well, do you trust him?" Billy asked.

Nathan thought for a moment before answering. "Yes." The answer surprised both of them.

The commercials had run a full five minutes, giving them an extra 270 seconds of privacy, not because Denise had been conned into it by the cop, but because she really feared for Nathan's safety. When the spots were done, she and Enrique reentered the world of electronic noise, only to hear the screeching tone of a telephone that had been left off the hook.

"Well, folks," she announced to her audience. "It seems we're all alone here . . ."

Billy's directions to the obelisk were brief and complete, matching Nathan's dimming memories of his flight the night before. The young fugitive was impressed by the distance he'd actually run: over two miles, according to Billy.

Nathan hurriedly tied his shoes and went to the

front door, where Billy was waiting with Barney to say good-bye.

Nathan smiled sadly and nodded. "Thanks, Billy," he said. "You didn't have to help me. I appreciate it."

Billy looked down at the floor. "Sure I did," he joked halfheartedly. "You're a murderer. You might have killed me." He reached into his pants pocket and handed the older boy a three-inch-tall X-Men figure, Cyclops. "Here," he said. "He brings me good luck."

Nathan felt moved. He took the toy gratefully and stuffed it into the front pocket of his ragged denim shorts. "Thanks," he said. At once, they both became aware of the sounds of sirens growing in the distance. "I gotta go," Nathan said, and he disappeared out the apartment door.

Nathan's plan was to use the back stairs; to get out the way he'd gotten in, through the basement. Somehow that made more sense to him than going out the front door. When he'd taken only three steps down the hall, he heard the pounding of running feet behind him.

"Hey, Nathan!" a voice called.

Nathan's body reacted to the sound of the voice even before his brain could process its source. He sprawled face-first onto the stained carpet of the hallway, like a baseball player sliding into third, just as he heard the familiar *phut,* and a tiny geyser of plaster fountained from the wall. He shoulder-rolled to his left as a second bullet slammed into the spot he'd just occupied on the carpet.

Nathan scrambled on all fours to a sharp turn in the hallway to his right and dove the last four feet for cover behind the wall. Plaster dust stung his eyes as a shot aimed for his head blasted through the outside corner of the wall instead. Just before the last shot was fired, Nathan caught a glimpse of his attacker through his peripheral vision. He was dressed in a cop's uniform.

Nathan never stopped. He shoulder-rolled again to his feet and charged down the second hallway, ignoring the bitter profanity that exploded from the cop. Only fifty feet more, and he'd be at the stairwell door, over which only a bare lightbulb remained in the sign that had once read EXIT. Twenty feet now, and the pounding of his own footsteps was joined by the heavier stride of the cop, beating a bass counterpoint to the quick staccato of his borrowed sneakers. He knew better than to look behind him.

When he heard Pointer's footsteps stop abruptly, Nathan knew he was in trouble. Without a conscious thought, he zigzagged the last ten feet to the exit. He heard the suppressed gunshot at the same instant as an invisible fist slammed into the right side of his rib cage and a neat round hole appeared in the metal door three inches in front of him. The impact of the blow forced an *oof* sound from his lungs, and he staggered as he propelled himself through the fire door.

Nathan didn't run down the stairs; he flew down them, using the steel railings to vault from one landing to the next, barely touching a single concrete step on the way.

When he reached the bottom, he risked a quick look back up the stairwell. Pointer was two levels behind, but gaining quickly.

Nathan whirled away from the interior stairwell and tore through the basement on his way to sunlight. The clutter of boxes and equipment all seemed so harmless now. A drunk arose from a corner near the exit door, perhaps intending to relieve Nathan of a few dollars, but he shrank away from whatever he saw burning in the boy's eyes.

Propelled by fear, Nathan plowed through the exterior door as if it weren't there, slamming it against the wall hard enough to break the doorknob. Thirteen steps later, he was at ground level, sprinting across the street toward a schoolyard. The sirens were extremely close now.

The drunk startled Pointer as he pursued his prey through the basement, earning him a bullet through the heart.

By the time the Hit Man had cleared the exterior stairs and reached ground level, the first of the arriving police cars was already visible down the street, and Nathan had started to blend in with the schoolyard scenery across the street. Just before disappearing around the far corner of the school building, the boy paused and gave him the finger.

Pointer found that amusing. In a smooth and well-practiced motion, Pointer unthreaded the silencer from his weapon and surreptitiously slipped the Magnum back into its holster. He nodded politely to the first string of arriving cop cars and strolled casually across the street toward the school.

CHAPTER THIRTY-SEVEN

PETRELLI CALLED STEPHANIE BACK, and within minutes, they'd matched the telephone number to its address. And because the number originated with a third party, Petrelli remained compliant with Judge Verone's order. The arrest would stick.

So screw you right back, Michaels, Petrelli thought with a smile.

Sheriff Murphy had dispatched all available units—some thirteen police vehicles—to the Vista Plains Apartments to take Nathan Bailey into custody. Just as moths are drawn to lights, television news crews were drawn to the sounds of the sirens. Those who'd been monitoring the police scanner knew that they were making their move on the Bailey boy. Those who'd been monitoring The Bitch knew that he'd be gone when they arrived. What no one knew for sure was where he was going to go.

The first police units to arrive at the apartment building sealed off all the exits, posing ominously with their weapons supported by the hoods of the vehicles, using the steel fenders and engine blocks as cover. Later, neighbors would joke about the fear in the eyes of these officers as they faced down a little boy who'd already left.

With the exits controlled, they could buy the time they needed to await the Pitcairn County SWAT team, which arrived one at a time, each in his own vehicle. Deputy Steadman was one of the last team members on the scene, having started his response from way out on the Hartford Road side of town. The instant his vehicle came to a stop, Steadman's door swung open and he dashed around to the trunk. Trained as the team's lead sniper, he assessed the current situation and decided that his M16 carbine was more appropriate to the task at hand than his Remington sniper rifle. He snatched the weapon with one hand and his utility vest with the other, slammed the trunk lid closed, and trotted off to the command post.

The SWAT leader made the decision to go in fast and strong, crashing the door and taking the kid without negotiation. The leader reminded his troops that their prey had a proven history of killing cops and that he was an accomplished marksman with a pistol. He told them to take no unreasonable chances. If the kid showed aggression, they were to take him out.

The seven-member team charged straight up the front stairs, one man covering the rest as they leapfrogged from one landing to the next. Once on the sixth floor, they moved swiftly and silently to Apartment 612. Tommy Coyle kicked the door and went in low to the left while Gale Purvis went in high to the right to neutralize any traps that might have been laid for them. After a two-count, the rest of the team poured into the apartment, weapons to their shoulders and ready to shoot.

"Police Department! Don't move!"

Straight ahead in the living room, a young black boy, maybe ten years old, lay stretched out on a sofa. As the cops streamed into the room, the boy sat up and smiled at them, surprisingly unfazed by all the guns.

"Hi, guys!" Billy said cheerily. "You're on TV."

When there was no one around, Nathan ran full tilt, as fast as his legs could pump; but when he thought he could be seen, he slowed to a fast walk, hoping to blend in. Twice that he knew of, he'd been recognized. You could see it in their eyes.

In the first case, an older woman looked confused after she made eye contact, like she was trying to place him with a family she might know. The second time, though, there was definite recognition. A young mother with two little children first showed curiosity and then fear as she placed his face, and she hurried into a store. Crowds be damned, Nathan decided to run after that; to get to another block, at least.

Each time he checked over his shoulder, there was no sign of his pursuer. Nathan told himself that he'd lost the guy, but he knew better.

Everything had changed. He wasn't avoiding capture anymore. He no longer cared why Ricky had done what he had. That was all irrelevant now. All that mattered was that the police were trying to kill him. They knew he had killed Ricky, they thought that he'd killed those other cops, and now they were going to kill him.

Even Nathan's purpose for running had changed. Staying free had taken a backseat to staying alive. Here he was, seeking out a cop who said he was trustworthy, so the cop could take him back to where it all started in the first place. And once he was back at the JDC—if that's where they were sending him—that Petrelli asshole and others like him would go right to work getting the state to take care of what the crazy cop with the gun thus far hadn't been able to do! It was a ridiculous world people had built. Just to keep going, Nathan forced himself to believe that one day he'd be able to change it somehow.

As he ran on, dodging people and ducking in and out of corners and alleyways, sweat poured off his body, soaking his tattered T-shirt and lighting afire the pain in his ribs. When he thought it was safe to take a break, he ducked behind a Dumpster and sat down on an old milk crate.

Breathing hard through his mouth, he dared his first look at his side, where blood had begun to soak through his shirt in spots. The bullet hole in his T-shirt was through-and-through, a kill shot for sure if the shirt had fit him properly. Nathan gently eased the shirt over his head and laid it across his lap. By slinging his right arm over his head, he could get a good look at his injury.

It looked awful, a swollen purple mass about three inches below his armpit surrounding a gash in his flesh the width of a Magic Marker and the length of a birthday candle.

"Oh, my God, I've been shot," he said aloud, leaning against the Dumpster. The metal was hot against the bare flesh of his back.

The flow of blood had slowed to a trickle now, but a wide, crimson road map down his side and into the waistband of his shorts was testament to a respectable wound. The tear in his flesh hurt no more than a bad scrape, but he still couldn't bring himself to touch it. The real pain came from the area around the gash, which felt every bit as bruised as if he'd been kicked by something big.

He thought vaguely that he should feel more than he did, that being shot should be a more frightening experience. Maybe on a different day or at a different time. Today, though, it was just one more jolt of pain resulting from one more attack by one more grown-up who didn't understand anything.

Knowing it was time to move on, Nathan stood and slipped the Bulls T-shirt back over his head. It was filthy, smeared with blood and snot and road grime, and torn in a dozen places, not even counting the bullet holes.

Sorry, Tubbo, Nathan thought, remembering the huge closets and thick carpets of the Nicholsons' house, *you probably won't want this back after all.* The thought made him smile as he shoved his arms through the sleeves.

"Hey, you!" a man yelled from the back door of a restaurant. Nathan reacted instantly, dashing out of the alley without even turning to see who was shouting.

"Hey! You're that kid! You're Nathan Bailey! You get back here, boy!" The man, who was about fifty and had consumed way too much beer and pizza to entertain any serious notions about catching his quarry, nonetheless chased him as far as the sidewalk.

"Stop him!" the man yelled to no one in particular. "Stop that boy! That's Nathan Bailey, the kid that killed those cops!"

Half a block away, Pointer heard the shouting and was drawn to it like a beetle drawn to a sex lure. He was close and he knew it, but until he saw the old cook pointing frantically down the street, he had no idea just how close he was.

At about the same time that Sheriff Murphy received word from the SWAT team leader that the kid had left the Vista Plains Apartments, Nathan sightings began pouring into the Pitcairn County Emergency Operations Center faster than the call takers could keep up with them. Each sighting was sent out over the police net as an update, providing a reliable route of travel for the boy. Sheriff Murphy's job was to plot the sightings on a map in the command van and try and figure out how to get ahead of him. Initially, he assumed that he was getting the sightings in the wrong order, figuring that the last place a kid would go would be back toward the center of the town where his crimes had been committed. Sure enough, though, that's where he was headed.

"What's he trying to do?" Murphy wondered aloud, and finally the answer came to him. "Michaels, you son of a bitch!"

All of the news agencies monitored police frequencies, and reporters all over town plotted the same map that Murphy made. News vans joined the fleet of cop cars as they tried to close in on the fleeing boy. Overhead, news choppers from Buffalo and Syracuse TV stations followed the action from the air, the reporters and cameramen concentrating on the ground while the pilots concentrated on avoiding a midair collision.

The network affiliates had all been notified to stand by for a special report at any moment when the action got interesting. CNN was already showing live footage, even though there was nothing more to show than a lot of marauding police vehicles.

In Washington, D.C., a tiny television had been brought into The Bitch's studio at NewsTalk 990 so that Denise could track the events as they unraveled. She was prepared to give a play-by-play rundown to her audience regarding what was going down in Pitcairn County. During a commercial break, she told Enrique to air only those callers who were on the boy's side.

"We don't need any more fuel on this fire," she told him.

Enrique assured her that the calls were running three-to-one in that direction anyway.

Once he'd reacquired his prey, Pointer moved through the crowd like a torpedo racing toward its target. He walked swiftly without running, steadily closing the distance between Nathan and himself. They were about fifty yards apart now, separated by just enough people that he couldn't take a clean shot.

The kid moved smoothly, clearly wanting to avoid being recognized and clearly unaware that Pointer was so close. The Hit Man had decided to play the takedown as an arrest rather than just popping him on the

street. He'd cuff the kid and haul him into "custody."
When they were alone, he'd do him where there were
no witnesses.

The kid was fast, though. He'd have to wait until he
was nearly on top of him to make his move. Pointer
figured about three minutes more.

Then events took yet another unexpected turn.

CHAPTER THIRTY-EIGHT

NATHAN WAS GETTING CLOSE. He could see the obelisk in the distance now, rising above the heads of his fellow pedestrians. He walked among them as though he belonged, avoiding eye contact, and receiving none in return.

That guy behind the restaurant had unnerved him, shouting so loud. If the killer cop had been within a hundred yards, he would have heard that buttinsky shouting his name. Why couldn't people just mind their own business?

Someone grabbed Nathan from behind in a crushing bear hug, pinning his arms to his sides and lifting him off his feet. "It's all over now, kid! I gotcha!" All Nathan could see was a pair of beefy forearms across his chest. The pressure of the man's grip drove Nathan's elbow squarely into his bullet wound. The pressure and the pain made it impossible to take a whole breath.

"Let go of me!" Nathan yelled. "Help! Get this guy off of me!" He kicked wildly and wriggled in every direction. As the man's grip weakened, Nathan started to slip through his grasp. The man grunted and staggered back as a flailing heel found his kneecap. When Nathan drove the back of his head into the man's nose, he let go completely and staggered backwards. Nathan landed on his feet and coiled into a half-crouch, preparing to defend himself against the next attacker.

For a long moment, no one in the crowd moved as the realization hit them. Nathan heard his whispered name work its way through the crowd like The Wave at a baseball game.

"I didn't kill those people," he declared in a voice so soft that only the four or five people closest to him could hear it. "People are trying to kill me. Please let me be."

The big man on the ground groaned loudly and cursed the boy. "Somebody grab him!" the man yelled.

"No!" Nathan yelled. "Please, no. I didn't start this. He—"

"Just hold it right there, Mr. Bailey," a voice said from behind.

The sound of Pointer's voice made Nathan jump as though zapped with electricity. He whirled around, and there the killer was, still in his police uniform, his gun drawn and pointing directly at Nathan's chest. Both of them knew that he couldn't miss at this range.

The cameraman in the *Action News* helicopter was the first to notice the activity on the ground, about a block and a half from the square. It looked as if there were a fight in progress. When he zoomed in with his big telephoto lens for a better look, he saw that an arrest was being made.

"They've got him, Paul!" the cameraman shouted

into the intercom. "They've got the kid! I'm getting
the arrest on tape!"

Paul Petersen, the on-air reporter, darted to the monitor to confirm his cameraman's report, then radioed
the station.

"It's going down right now!" Petersen exclaimed to
the news desk. "Tell the network we've got a live feed
of the arrest!"

A patrol car spotted Michaels at the base of the
memorial.

Sheriff Murphy's plan was simple enough. Find
Warren Michaels, keep an eye on him, and sooner or
later, they'd have Nathan Bailey in custody. From the
way the lieutenant had been acting, it only made sense
that he'd arrange a meeting. And after Petrelli had explained the business about Michaels's son, the intense
protective streak made sense as well. Clearly, the man
had lost perspective.

Or such was the message delivered to Deputy Steadman. Now code-named Sniper One, he'd been dispatched to commandeer a corner office belonging to an
accountant on the third floor of the professional building
across from the Lewis and Clark Memorial. From
there, he would have a clear view of the area around
the obelisk. For the last ten minutes, while Steadman
had been on station, Michaels had done nothing but
pace and check his watch. As Sniper One watched him
through his ten-power scope, the detective seemed dis-
traught. Steadman read that as proof that his party was
running late.

Steadman had rehearsed this scene and dozens like

it in his mind hundreds of times. After three years as a SWAT sniper, he'd been called out only once to prepare a shot, and that time the bad guy gave up without a struggle. Nonetheless, he knew he was ready, physically, psychologically, and technically. He'd read everything he could find, talked to many successful snipers, and shot thousands of rounds into all manner of targets— moving, stationary and partially concealed. He knew he'd be able to handle whatever came his way.

The thought of avenging his friends' deaths made it all that much easier. Steadman had seen firsthand how the kid reacted when he was cornered. He'd seen the gun on the seat of the car and he'd seen the gaping holes blasted through his buddies' heads.

Steadman wasn't fooled by Nathan's age. He knew what a criminal mind like that was capable of. The arrest was going down soon, and if the cop-killing bastard even thought about violence, Steadman was going to blast him straight into next month.

The sniper's nest sat back about six feet from the open window. Two phone books and an accounting manual stacked on top of the expensive wooden desk served as the rest for his beanbag rifle support. Steadman sat comfortably on the edge of a high-backed leather chair that he'd wheeled around to the front of the desk. He double-checked to make sure the safety was on and took care to ensure that his finger stayed out of the trigger guard before bringing the crosshairs to bear on Michaels's head.

The range was seventy-five to eighty yards, close enough that Steadman could put a round through the center of a dime. Though Michaels's head filled the sight picture, Sniper One concentrated on the single spot over his eyebrow where the crosshairs intersected: the no-reflex zone. He inhaled deeply, let out half the air and held it. He tightened his finger on the trigger guard.

"Pow!" he whispered, simulating the rifle's recoil. Piece of cake.

"He's the one, not me!" Nathan cried as he backed toward the circle of bystanders. "He's the one who killed those policemen!"

Pointer felt his face flush red. He wasn't used to performing his craft in front of an audience. He fought the urge to scan the crowd for its reaction, fearing that it would appear out of character.

"Get down on the ground, boy," Pointer commanded, gesturing with the muzzle of his gun.

Nathan shook his head frantically and tried to worm backwards through the line of people. They wouldn't let him through.

"I didn't do anything!" he yelled, his eyes pleading for someone to help. "Don't let him take me! He's the guy I talked about on the radio! He's the guy who killed the cops!" Still, no one made a move to assist. "You've got to believe me!"

A tall man dressed in a business suit stepped forward out of the crowd and positioned himself an arm's length from both the police officer and the boy, taking care to stay out of the line of fire. He wore his thick mane of gray hair slicked back in a pompadour and sported a neatly trimmed white beard. Nathan saw kindness in the man's eyes.

"My name's Albert Kassabian," the man said. "I'm an attorney. I think I have a solution to this problem."

"So do I," Pointer hissed. "Mine is for you to stay out of the way and let me do my job." His eyes never left the boy.

"I don't recognize your uniform, Officer," Kassabian said smoothly. "Where are you from?"

Pointer felt his control slipping. These assholes were going to screw it up for him again. He should just take his shot now and make a quick getaway, but that would be stupid. If the crowd pounced, he wouldn't be able to fight them all. He decided to play the charade one step further.

"I'm from Braddock County, Virginia," Pointer explained, "where this young man is wanted on a murder charge."

Kassabian nodded pensively, as though he'd been sold on Pointer's answer. "Tell you what," the attorney offered amicably, "let's just hold what we've got here until one of our own sheriff's deputies can come and make the arrest. That way, we won't have any jurisdictional improprieties."

Nathan knew that Pointer was going to have his way in the end, and he knew that right now was the best chance he'd have to make a break. He bent low at the waist, pivoted to his left, and squirted into the crowd.

Pointer saw the boy disappear before his eyes and snapped off a quick shot, splintering the kneecap of the lady standing behind where Nathan had been. The Hit Man cursed bitterly and turned to Kassabian, firing a round into his intestines. The intent was not to kill, but to inflict maximum pain. The old lawyer doubled over and fell to the sidewalk, spewing blood and vomit onto the white concrete.

Pointer brought the gun around again, and the crowd parted, dropping to the ground as though they, too, had been shot. In less than ten seconds, Nathan had gained a good fifty yards. Pointer took off after him.

The race was on.

"Oh, my God," Denise gasped into her microphone. "The police officer has just shot two people! Nathan's running down the street trying to get away! The poor thing *has* been telling the truth." She was crying, something she'd never before done on the radio.

"Run, sweetie!" she begged. "Where are the *real* police, dammit!?"

The 911 lines exploded at the Emergency Operations Center, giving frantic reports of people shot outside Fisher's Hardware Store. More than half of the callers took the time to explain that Nathan Bailey had been there, but that he hadn't done the shooting.

In the command van, Petrelli hovered over Murphy's shoulder as they watched the drama unfold live on television. At first, the sheriff was pleased with news of the arrest. Then he saw the strange uniform and watched two voters fall to the ground, and he knew right away that Michaels had been right all along. He also knew that all of his deputies were out of position, setting up a trap for the Bailey boy at the Lewis and Clark Memorial.

He issued orders for the dispatcher to move all units in the direction of the shooting, then countermanded them a minute later when he realized that Nathan was leading the chase toward the square.

Michaels considered the possibility that the first shot was a backfire. At the sound of the second report, he knew better. He drew his S&W snub-nose and took off in that direction.

It wasn't until he saw the commotion on the street that he noticed two helicopters hovering low about a block ahead. He took a few seconds to hang his gold shield in his suit coat pocket, then sprinted toward the action.

Lord, it was hot!

Steadman was pissed. No one seemed to know what was going on. First he was told to set up the sniper's post, then he was told to break it down, then he was told to set it up again. Shots had been fired, yet no one was authorized to leave their posts. Murphy insisted on commanding things himself, but he couldn't make a damned decision.

From his position, Steadman couldn't tell where the shots had been fired, so he followed Michaels with his scope, having to move from the front window to the side window to track his progress. The range had changed, though, and he couldn't keep focus in the scope, so he looked away to get oriented to the full range of vision.

Steadman's heart skipped a beat when he saw a

filthy, tattered boy fitting Nathan Bailey's description dart into his field of view. A uniformed cop he didn't recognize was only a few steps behind.

He brought the rifle up into position and hurriedly adjusted the scope to the new range.

Nathan tried to speed up, but there was nothing left in his legs. He willed them to pump faster, and they would for a few steps, but they had gotten clumsy. He felt himself start to trip three times, and was able to recover, but he knew he'd lost valuable distance. The same heavy stride he'd heard in the apartment building was drawing steadily closer, and there was nothing he could do about it.

People all recognized him now as they jumped out of his way to avoid a collision. He didn't have enough wind in his lungs to ask anyone for help, not that they would have given it anyway.

"That boy is a fugitive!" Pointer bellowed from behind him. "Stop him!"

A huge high school kid wearing a football jersey emblazoned with a big "78" did just that, stepping in front of the boy and catching all of his momentum with his left arm.

Nathan didn't have the strength left to fight the football player. When he felt Pointer yank him back by his shirt collar, he knew that he was dead. He swung wildly with his fists as he was spun around, but stopped when a powerful backhand caught him square in the face. He heard a snap as his nose broke, and his vision disappeared in a blur of tears and blood.

* * *

Action News caught it all, in extreme close-up. Alone in his apartment, Billy Alexander covered his eyes and cried.

Denise Carpenter wished she didn't have to be on the radio anymore. "Oh, Jesus, no," she pleaded. "It can't end this way. Someone has to help that poor boy."

Warren slowed his stride when he saw Nathan plunging through the crowd toward him, relieved that he was still alive, though the terror in the boy's eyes told him that danger was right on his heels. He remembered Nathan telling him that the killer was a cop, and so he was. In a Braddock County uniform, no less!

The kid in the football jersey came out of nowhere and really screwed things up. Before Warren could react, Pointer had wrapped a forearm around the front of Nathan's throat and had begun to drag him off.

Warren dashed another thirty feet to get a better angle, then shouted out to the police imposter.

"Police officer! Don't move!" Warren yelled, his voice breaking from the effort.

Pointer reacted instantly, lifting Nathan off the ground by his chin and using his wriggling body as a shield. The boy brought his hands up to his attacker's arm, doing a chin-up to keep from strangling.

"Back off, pig, or I'll pop him here!" Pointer yelled, bringing the Magnum up to the boy's temple. His threat was barely audible above the din of the hovering choppers.

"I'm not going anywhere!" Michaels declared.

"You let the boy go, and you live. That's the only deal you get. Anything else happens and you die!" Warren tried to look menacing in his two-handed shooter's stance, but in his heart he knew he could never make the shot without hitting Nathan.

The situation had been played to a standoff. No one would shoot as long as Pointer had the boy as his shield, and Nathan was the only bargaining chip that Pointer had left. As he played out his bluff, Warren was vaguely aware of the arrival of a swarm of other police officers.

In the command van, Murphy slammed his fist on the console. "I don't believe it," he declared to the room. "I've got a murderer being held hostage by a kidnapper impersonating a police officer! Where the hell are the good guys?"

He snatched the microphone away from the dispatcher. "Command to SWAT Leader. Give me a report."

"It's bad, Sheriff," said a metallic voice from the speaker. "We're stuck until something breaks. I think it's a bad idea to move in any closer."

Shit. "Command to Sniper One, what kind of shot do you have?"

The range had increased to a hundred yards, and Steadman's sight picture was half-cop and half-boy, and moving around crazily.

"Bad," he replied. "Who's my target, anyway? The police officer or the kid?" It seemed obvious enough, he supposed, but one doesn't blast another cop without being very damned sure.

After a pause, Murphy answered, "It appears that the cop is your primary target, unless the kid poses a threat to somebody. Remember, he's still a killer."

Nathan couldn't breathe. With his feet dangling in the air, his arms didn't have the strength to continue supporting him. As he lost his grip, Pointer's arm crushed his windpipe. He felt like his head was going to explode, the increased pressure causing blood to stream faster from his damaged nose. As the muzzle of the gun bored into his ear, Nathan wet his pants.

Out in front, through the blur and the pain, he saw a man with a gun, dressed in a brown suit with a blue shirt and a striped tie. He was shouting something that he couldn't hear. He had soft eyes that looked sad. He looked like a good guy.

"Sniper One to Command, do I have a green light if I've got a shot?"

Typical of a politician, Steadman thought. Murphy wouldn't make that decision on his own. Rather, he bumped it to the real leader on the street.

"SWAT Team Leader?"

"The situation is critical here, Sheriff. I say take what he can get."

"That's affirmative, Sniper One, you have the green light if you have a shot."

Steadman smiled. Finally his moment had arrived, but the best shot he had was a terrible shot. At this range, a slight breeze, a sudden movement by the target could turn a sure kill into a tragedy. He worked the bolt to chamber a .30-caliber round and rested the stock on the windowsill. He'd have given a lot for the comfort of his first station at the front window, but he had to settle for what he had.

He thumbed the safety off and settled in to await his opportunity.

Then it happened. Pointer looked straight at him.

Nathan felt like he hadn't breathed in an hour. He knew death was coming to him, but he wasn't prepared for this much fear and pain. Noise and activity swirled all around him. None of it had form or meaning until Pointer hiked him up a little higher and growled in his ear, close enough that he could feel his hot breath on his cheek.

"Say good-bye, you little shit."

Nathan closed his eyes.

Steadman knew it was over as soon as they made eye contact. The target hoisted his hostage higher, reducing the sight picture even more, then said something in his ear. A sick, crazy smile appeared on the target's lips, and Steadman saw movement in the muscles of his forearms. The cylinder of the Magnum began to turn.

Sniper One had exactly no time to plan his shot. He brought the crosshairs to bear just above the target's right eyebrow—the no-reflex zone—and he pulled the trigger.

The shot was perfect. As millions of people watched live on television throughout the world, Lyle Pointer's head erupted in a gruesome pink cloud, and he crumpled instantly to the ground, as if all his bones had suddenly disappeared.

A bone-jarring impact reverberated through Nathan's body as he heard a heavy, wet *thwop,* followed by a sharp explosion. He screamed and dropped to the ground, certain that he had been hit. Blood was everywhere, but the pain hadn't found him yet.

As though someone had flipped a switch in his brain, he suddenly became aware of an army of armed men, all in police uniforms, charging toward him.

Not again, he thought. *I'm not going through this again.*

He snatched Pointer's Magnum from the sidewalk where it had landed and brandished it with both hands. "Stay away from me!" he screamed. "Stay away from me or I'll shoot!"

The blue line stopped its advance instantly, and there was a clatter of weapons as fifteen police officers dropped to shooting positions.

Across the street, Steadman worked the bolt on the Remington and settled the crosshairs on Nathan. "Sniper One to Command, second target is acquired. Requesting instructions," he said into his radio.

"Stand by," crackled his reply.

Warren darted out in front of the others, ostentatiously holstering his weapon and holding his hands out where Nathan could see them.

"It's me, Nathan," he said softly. "It's Lieutenant

Michaels. We talked on the phone. We're friends, Nathan."

Nathan's eyes were wild. He cocked his head slightly at the sound of Warren's voice, like a puppy who's trying to make sense out of something unfamiliar.

"Nathan, this is over now. I know what happened. I know you never meant to do anybody harm. You're not in trouble anymore, son, so just put the gun down and let's sort this all out."

Nathan had been here before. He'd listened to their promises and their guarantees. He'd believed in good guys and in trust and in hope, but every time, it was just another lie. All people wanted was to hurt him, and all Nathan wanted was to be left alone.

"No, it's a trick," he declared. "You're going to kill me. Everybody's trying to kill me."

He thumbed back the hammer on the Magnum.

"Sniper One to Command, I read this situation as critical. The target is acquired. I have a perfect shot. Do I have the green light?"

Even as he asked the question, Steadman ran some calculations through his head on the damage this much bullet would do to so little a boy. The results were horrifying.

"Nathan, listen to me," Michaels said gently, looking past the gaping muzzle of the pistol into the eyes of the boy holding it. "Look at me. I wouldn't hurt you for the world, son." He took a step forward. "This is over, Nathan. You've seen too much killing. Let's let it end here." Three more steps, and he was only ten feet away.

"You've got to trust somebody, Nathan. Start with me."

Trust me. How many times had he heard that? Trust Uncle Mark. Trust the social worker. Trust the judge. Trust the supervisor. Now trust the cop.

But this cop had friendly eyes. And a smile. Nathan remembered his face from television, the one in the tennis shirt.

Staring past the heavy pistol, Nathan wanted desperately to shoot; to be shot; to end it all. But even as his finger tightened on the trigger, he knew he wouldn't do it. Maybe if Michaels had been one of the assholes from the night before, but not this guy. Not the cop with the friendly eyes.

"Let's be friends," Warren said, moving a step closer.

And that was it. Nathan's lip started to quiver as he lowered the gun and let it drop to the pavement.

"I don't have any friends," Nathan said pitifully, and he sank to his knees. His shoulders slumped and his eyes filled with tears. "I can't do this anymore," he said, and his features dissolved into those of a sad little boy who needed to be held. As he sobbed there on the sidewalk, trying to hide behind hands pressed to his eyes, his whole body heaved at the effort of it all. There was movement among the line of cops, but no one seemed to know what to do next.

Warren watched awkwardly for just a moment; then, smoothly and slowly, with the grace of one who had done it many times before, he moved to the boy and sat down next to him on the sidewalk. Self-consciously at first, but then with the warmth and tenderness of a grieving father, he drew Nathan close, his hand disappearing into the grimy tangle of the boy's hair.

Amid the blood and filth, Nathan caught the faintest aroma of sweaty aftershave, the smell of strength. He closed his eyes and allowed himself to be transported back to sunnier times.

"It's over now, son," Warren said, his voice catching in his throat. "No one can hurt you now." As he pulled Nathan closer still, he rocked him gently back and forth. "It's okay," he whispered.

For the longest time, they just sat there together on the sidewalk and cried like babies on national television.

Beyond the line of cops, applause started softly at first, and then raised to a cheer as it caught on. Somewhere in the noise, someone started chanting "Nathan, Na-than!" It spread through the crowd and grew in both volume and tempo until it was clearly audible above the roar of the helicopters.

"Na-than! Na-than!"

The boy looked confused. "Are they cheering for me?" he asked, wiping his face with the front of his shirt.

Warren smiled and nodded. "Everybody wants the good guys to win," he said.

As they rose together from the sidewalk and headed off toward the command post to get it all straightened out, Nathan smiled and gave a shy wave.

The crowd went wild.

CHAPTER THIRTY-NINE

Five months later

DENISE CARPENTER WAITED for her cue, seated at the edge of her seat, her back straight and her hands folded properly on her lap. The set was decorated for the holidays, and she was wearing her favorite Christmas outfit. When the applause light over their heads instructed them to do so, the studio audience thundered their applause, and the red light on camera one jumped to life.

"Thank you very much," she said into the camera. "Welcome back to *The Denise Carpenter Show*. Our next guests are very special to me, though I have never met them. During the July Fourth holiday this year, the world was captivated by the tragic and triumphant events surrounding a young man's escape from a juvenile detention facility in Virginia . . ."

Backstage, Nathan fidgeted with his tie as he listened to Denise say nice things about him. This would be his first interview.

"How do I look?" he asked.

"You look great," Warren replied. "How about me?"

"Fine."

". . . Nathan Bailey and Lieutenant Warren Michaels."

As the studio audience erupted in applause, Enrique ushered them onto the stage.

Ever the composed on-air personality, Denise started to cry when she saw Nathan in person. He looked so different. He was thirteen now, the boyish looks edged out by encroaching manhood. They hugged for a long time. During the embrace, Nathan told her that she was the reason he was still alive.

The applause rolled on and on, embarrassing them all. When it finally died down, Denise started with the question everyone wanted to hear. "So, Nathan, are you completely out of trouble now?"

Nathan smiled and shrugged. "I'm in a lot less trouble now than I was last time we talked." He smiled when he drew a laugh from the audience. Denise noted that his voice was starting to change. "I was lucky that nobody I borrowed from pressed charges."

Warren added, "No, but you'll be paying back damages till you're fifty."

Denise shifted her attention to Warren. "It's a big step from arresting officer to foster parent," she said, coaxing a warm smile from both of them.

Warren shrugged. "Not as big as you might expect," he said.

"Could this be a permanent arrangement?"

Her guests smiled at each other, as though they had expected the question. Warren earned an angry glare by rumpling Nathan's hair.

"Anything's possible," Warren said with a wink. "But that's kind of a grown-up concern. For the time being, I think we're going to concentrate on giving this remarkable young man a chance to be a kid."

That was the biggest applause line of the program.

Dear Reader,

Gilstrap here. I hope you enjoyed *Nathan's Run*. It's a special book for me.

Nathan Bailey changed my life in every way one can imagine. I now define the arc of my life in two parts: "before Nathan" and "after Nathan." Before Nathan, I was a safety and environmental engineer who wrote part time on the side. After Nathan, I became a bestselling author.

No one can anticipate the kind of success that Nathan brought into our lives. March 1, 1995, dawned like every other morning, my wife and I working hard in our professions to eke out enough of a living to keep the bills paid. By dinnertime, we'd learned that the book had sold for hundreds of thousands of dollars. By March 3rd, publishing rights had sold in ten foreign countries and we'd inked a movie deal. By April 1st, rights had sold in one form or another in a total of twenty-three foreign countries. It was beyond stunning. It felt as if I'd saddled a rocket.

Here it is twenty-five years and nineteen books later, and I'm thrilled to see *Nathan's Run* back in print. Consider this: if Nathan were real, he'd be thirty-seven years old now. Even after so many years, people ask how he turned out as an adult. Those of you who read *all* my books know the answer to that, of course. He's made cameo appearances in both *Nick of Time* and *Friendly Fire*. Suffice to say that despite his inheritance, he's living a very ordinary life in service to his community.

My original title for *Nathan's Run* was simply *Nathan!*—complete with the exclamation point. The story came to me during a long ride across Montana in a rental car whose radio did not work. Over the course of a six-hour trek through God's Country, the parts came together. Beginning on the flight home, I went to work on the story. From outline to final draft took only four months. I knew I had something special on my hands when I found myself crying as I wrote the final pages.

There's an X-factor about Nathan's story that resonates with people. Even as the author, I don't really know what the factor is, but I often hear from fans that of the countless characters I've written, Nathan Bailey is their favorite, and his story their favorite of my books. It's humbling.

There's an interesting story behind Nathan's name. As I wrote the book, my son, Chris, was about the same age as Nathan, and given what lay ahead for the boy, I couldn't bring that kind of suffering onto his namesake. So Chris was out. Because I wasn't using his name, though, I also couldn't use a name shared by any of his friends. Elementary school is hard enough without inviting accusations that "your dad likes my name better than yours."

I wanted the title character's name to project noble innocence. Or maybe it was innocent nobility. Nathan Hale came to mind. His only regret was that he had but one life to give for his country. You don't get more noble than that. Plus, there were no Nathans among Chris's galaxy of friends. Done and done. I chose Bailey as his last name because there is no more noble a character in American culture than George Bailey from the Christmas classic *It's A Wonderful Life.*

While *Nathan's Run* is not categorized by the publishing industry as a young adult novel, I hope it appeals to young people. In fact, when it was first released, the book won the Alex Award, which is bestowed by the American Library Association on the best adult-market fiction that appeals to young readers. I was stunned yet gratified when that news broke. I never imagined that the novel would be selected by middle school librarians from coast to coast.

Then the world discovered that many middle school librarians don't read the books they order. That first iteration of *Nathan's Run* had a *lot* of bad language, causing it to become one of the hundred books most banned from school libraries. According to one industrious critic, that first iteration had 409 bad words in it. Out of 107,000 words, 409 doesn't seem like that big a number, but banned is banned.

I didn't get it at the time. At one level, I still don't— I mean, words are just words, right? They're inanimate. I don't understand how a word, taken by itself, can be offensive.

Then a fan sent me an email that changed everything. She told me that as much as she loved my stories, she couldn't share them with her friends because of the language. The F-bomb was particularly offensive to her, and she thought I should show more respect for my readers.

That hit me hard. My readers are everything to me. Without you, this is a really tough business. I would never show my readers anything but the deepest respect.

I looked through my file of fan letters and online reviews and I was shocked by the number of readers who shared an aversion to top-tier profanity. We're talking dozens of letters here. When I went back to the story and read it as a reader instead of as an author, I saw their point.

So, when the rights to *Nathan's Run* reverted to me and I resold them to Kensington, I scrubbed it of the F-word and other high-end profanity. Okay, you've read the book, so you know that one F-bomb survived, but surely you'll agree that no other word would have worked at that point in the story.

Though I had the opportunity to rewrite the entire story, I decided to leave it otherwise untouched. If I wrote it today, much about the novel would be different, but I thought I should leave it as it was when I sold it back in 1995.

Note the above wording. I left the book as I *sold* it, not as it ultimately appeared in print. The ending of this edition of *Nathan's Run* is substantively different than that of the previous print version. I have changed it back because I always liked this version better. I only changed it in 1995 because in those days I didn't have the clout to push back.

I hope you enjoyed your time with my buddy Nathan, and if you did, I hope you tell your friends about it. If you have kids, I hope the story inspired you to give them a hug. If you're a young person reading this, I hope Nathan inspired you to be strong—to never give up.

I'd love to hear from you. If you've got comments or questions, please feel free to reach out to me at john@johngilstrap.com. I read and answer my own email, and I love to interact with readers. I also encourage you to rummage around my website, www.johngilstrap.com. I try to keep it interesting.

Until next time, please take care. And please keep reading.

John Gilstrap
Fairfax, Virginia
April 6, 2019

Don't miss the next gripping Jonathan Grave thriller
by JOHN GILSTRAP

HELLFIRE

Coming soon from Kensington Publishing Corp.
Keep reading to enjoy a sample excerpt . . .

CHAPTER ONE

RYDER SIMS HAD HEARD every word spoken from the front seat. They thought he was asleep, and like every other adult, they believed that just because a kid's eyes were closed, he'd been struck deaf. He should be so lucky. He hadn't slept more than a few minutes in the past three days. Since the FBI crashed their house and tore his world apart.

Now, everything was ruined. He and his brother Jeff were being driven to some kind of orphanage by a lady driver, who he figured had to be a cop, and a priest named Father Dom. Both were nice enough to their faces, but it was the quiet conversations that revealed their true thoughts. They pitied him and his brother. They felt *sorry* for him.

When the lady driver wondered how *the boys* would ever get past *this kind of trauma,* Father Dom shushed her, said that such things ought not be discussed within ear shot. As if Ryder hadn't already wondered a thousand times how much his life was going to suck from now on. He'd never let it show to these people, but he was freaking *terrified* of all that had gone down.

Mom and Dad had warned him that that trouble was coming. Ryder didn't understand all the details but he wasn't completely surprised when the cops kicked in their door. Okay, he was *terrified* when the SWAT team pulled him out of bed and onto the floor at three in the morning. And the handcuffs hurt. But only for ten or fifteen minutes, until they figured that a thirteen-year-old and his eleven-year-old brother didn't pose any real hazard. After that, the cops were pretty nice. They let him get dressed, but not without a cop with a rifle watching the whole time. He felt better that the lady who watched him seemed as uncomfortable with it all as he did. After that, they walked him and Jeff straight out to a car where they whisked off to a stranger's house.

He never got a chance to say good-bye to his parents. Hell, he didn't even get a chance to *see* them.

Dad wasn't specific about why they'd done the things that got them sideways with the FBI—those were the words he used, *got sideways*—but Ryder was smart enough to know that pissing off the FBI was a big deal. That meant that Mom and Dad had committed a federal crime, not a state crime. Ryder wasn't sure why one was worse than the other, but everybody knew that federal crimes were the worst.

And man, oh man were there a lot of FBI windbreakers among the cops that invaded his house.

"You're going to hear a lot of bad things about me and your mom," Dad told him just hours before the invasion. "I wish I could tell you that they'll be false, but they're not."

"We've done bad things," Mom added. "We've killed people, but you have to know that it was never because we were angry. It was never an emotional thing."

"Sometimes business requires difficult decisions," Dad said, as if that made anything less head-spinning. "You don't need to know the details."

"You don't *want* to know the details," Mom said.

Ryder remained silent during that talk. It was a time to listen and pay attention. Questions never changed bad news, they only slowed it down.

Dad continued, "Of course, when this happens, it will have a huge effect on you and your brother." He said it as if they were planning a family trip. "We've taken steps for you to avoid foster homes. There's a very good school for people like you—"

"Children of people like us," Mom corrected. Again, as if making an important point.

"Yes, exactly," Dad said. "You've done nothing wrong. This is all on us. But there's a school—it's called Resurrection House and it's in Virginia—and it has a wonderful reputation."

"It's an orphanage," Ryder said, cutting to the chase.

"No," his parents said together. Dad expounded, "You're not an orphan."

"But you are going to jail, right?"

"Maybe," Mom said. Then her shoulders sagged. "Probably."

"We're still going to be alive is the point," Dad said. "Orphans don't have parents."

Ryder had no idea what this Resurrection House thing was all about, but that's where they were headed.

If it wasn't an orphanage, then maybe it was a workhouse. He'd seen *Oliver!* so he knew what to expect. For now, he figured that the Resurrection place had to be better than the house of douchebags they'd been staying with the last couple of days. Their whole house smelled like hot dogs and old socks, and the family stared at them all the time. It was weird. *They* were weird.

He was ready to take a gamble on the workhouse.

Ryder had always possessed an uncanny ability to read people. Not their minds—not like one of the Legimens from the Harry Potter stories—but he was great at reading their intentions, their state of ease or the lack thereof. It was like what they called *stranger danger* in school and what Dad called *situational awareness* at home, but not always. Like right now, he knew that the grown-ups in the car were upset about something. They leaned in close to each other and talked quietly. The driver lady kept glancing up into the rearview mirror.

Ryder quietly clicked his seatbelt open and rose from his captain's chair to turn around and look out the back window. He could see only one other car on the road behind them and it was driving way too close, the way Dad would when he was getting ready to pass.

"Please get back in your seat," Father Dom said.

"Are they trying to pass us?" Ryder asked.

The lady driver—her name was Pam—said, "If they were, they've had plenty of time to do it."

The priest repeated, "Ryder, I really want you to be in your seat."

Ryder opened his mouth to argue, but he decided to comply instead. This didn't feel right to him.

He'd just turned back to face front when the follow

car's high beams lit up the back window and blue strobe lights painted wild shadows all over the van's interior.

Jeff jumped awake in the chair to his right. "What's happening?"

"Shut up," Ryder snapped. He didn't want to be mean, but if little dickhead was talking, he wouldn't be able to hear what was being said up front.

"I don't like this," Pam said. "I'm not doing anything wrong. There's no legit reason for us to be pulled over."

"Well, we can't just ignore them," Father Dom said.

The cop behind them popped his siren, as if to cast his vote on what they should do.

The driver pushed the button on the dash to turn on the hazard flashers. "I'm slowing down to thirty-five," she said. "Call nine-one-one to see—"

"Tell me what's happening!" Jeff insisted, blocking out the rest of the driver's command.

Ryder would be happy to call 911, but the FBI had taken their phones. And their computers. Hell, they'd taken everything. He and Jeff weren't allowed to take anything with them but underwear, clothes and a jacket.

As the van navigated a curve, another wall of blue lights erupted out front.

"I guess that decides that," the priest said.

The driver had to lean hard on the brakes, making Ryder feel better about his decision to sit back down and belt himself in.

"I'm scared," Jeff whined.

"Shut up," Ryder said. "We're all scared. Saying it doesn't help."

* * *

Very little about this pickup and delivery had felt right to Dom, and now this traffic stop was icing on the cake. He fumbled with his phone as he extracted it from his pocket.

"What do we do now?" he asked.

"We sit," Pam replied. A retired cop, she'd chosen social work as her second career. The same customer base, she'd explained, but nobody wants to shoot the lady with the clipboard and a smile. "Put the phone back in your pocket. You don't want to have anything in your hands. They'll tell us everything we need to know."

Out front, the cop's door opened and a uniformed officer took a position behind his engine block, his hands full of pistol. "Holy shit!" Dom exclaimed out of reflex. It came out much louder than he wanted.

Pam seemed less unnerved. "What the hell?"

Behind them, Ryder and Jeff almost collided heads as they leaned into the center space to see out the front windshield.

"Oh, my God," Jeff blurted. "Are they going to shoot us?"

"Stay in your seats, boys," Dom said. He thought it was a damned good question, though. He waited for Pam to explain, but she continued to scowl at the man with the gun.

An electronic loudspeaker popped from behind. "Driver, turn off your engine and drop the keys out the window."

"Remember," Pam said in a clipped tone as she keyed the engine off. "You want your hands to be empty."

"What the hell is going on?" Dom asked.

"Ask me again in five minutes," Pam replied. "They

think we're people we're not, and this is a felony stop. Do everything they say. Move slowly and keep your hands visible at all times." She made a show of dangling her keys out the window before dropping them to the pavement.

The cop on the loudspeaker said, "Driver, open your door and step out of the car. Keep your hands visible at all times."

"I told you," she said. Pam moved carefully. With her left hand extended out her window, she reached across her body with her right hand to pull the handle that opened the door. When it was unlatched, she used her foot to push it all the way open.

"Driver, step out, hands at your sides, fingers splayed, and side-step two steps to your left. Leave the door open."

Pam gave Dom a look he wasn't sure how to interpret and went about the business of following directions. She slid off her seat, her feet found the ground, and then she stepped off to the side. She stood with her arms out to her sides, cruciform, in a posture that impressed Dom as one that would quickly become exhausting.

"I'm really scared," said the younger brother. Jeff. Dom owed it to them to remember their names.

"This will all be over in a few minutes," Dom assured.

"Front seat passenger," the guy on the loudspeaker said. "Same drill. Open your door, keep your hands visible . . ." The instructions were pretty much the same as before.

Dom turned so he could see both faces. Adolescents

looked so much younger when they were frightened. "Ryder and Jeff, listen to me," he said. "There's been some kind of misunderstanding. I'm sure everything will be fine. After I get out, I want you both to listen carefully and do exactly what the officer tells you to do."

"Are we in trouble, Father?" Ryder asked. His voice trembled.

"I don't know," Dom said. "But if you do what they say, everything will be fine."

Father Dom slid out of the passenger side door and then moved away from the van.

"Hands farther out to the side," the cop commanded. Dom raised his hands higher, splayed his fingers further out. Could they not see his white collar?

"Stay cool, officers," Dom said. "I'm a priest and my driver is a retired police officer."

For a second or two, nothing happened. Maybe longer. This was wrong. All of it seemed unreal. Unearned.

The kids.

Dom turned to look back at the boys, and that's when he heard the gunshot. Pam fell, and then something kicked Dom hard in the chest. As he fell to the street, he wondered how anything could feel so hot and not set him on fire.

He thought, *Please, God, forgive me.* Everything went dark.

The spatter from Pam's exploding head painted the window just inches from Ryder's face. He jumped and screamed something even he didn't understand. Another shot followed an instant later, and Father Dom dropped from view.

"No!" Jeff yelled. "Oh, my God they killed them!"

Ryder didn't say anything. His mouth wouldn't work. Through the smear of gore, he watched the cop from the front racing toward the van. His flashlight beam bounced as he ran. Ryder's stomach churned. He thought he might puke.

Except he didn't have time.

The cop pulled his sliding door open at the same time the other cop opened the slider on Jeff's side. They opened them hard, causing the panels to rebound halfway closed again.

"Get out," the closest cop said.

"What did you do?" Ryder shouted. "You killed them!"

The cop pressed his pistol against Ryder's forehead. "Open that mouth of yours again if you want to join them."

To Ryder's right, Jeff started to yell. "Leave me alone! Ryder! Help!"

The other cop slapped Jeff across the forehead with the barrel of his pistol, and the boy collapsed.

"Jesus!" Ryder yelled. "Jeff! Goddammit, leave him alone!"

The last part of his words sounded clipped and garbled as a rough sack was shoved over his head and tied tight across his neck. Out of reflex, Ryder brought his hands to his throat and pulled at the cinch.

"No!" he yelled, and he punched blindly at his attacker. "Get this thing off—"

A light flashed behind his eyes and there was nothing.

* * *

Dom hurt. His chest felt hot, hollow and numb all at the same time. He thought his eyes were open, but the world was very dark. He thought he could see the outline of trees across the black sky, but he couldn't be sure.

"I'm alive," he said aloud. It was a test of his voice. It didn't sound right, as if coming from someone else and far away. "But I'm dead soon." The words didn't frighten him, though maybe they should. What they did was *focus* him.

He needed help, but out here at this hour, he could go undiscovered for longer than it would take for him to bleed out.

Ancient first aid training from back in his Army days tried to form in his mind. Should he raise his legs to counter the onset of shock, or should he try to raise his torso to slow down the bleeding?

Dom winced against anticipated pain as he finger-walked his left hand to his pants pocket where he could find his phone. Moving an arm meant flexing a chest muscle, though, and that brought the fiery agony back in Technicolor.

"Awww, *dammit!*" he grunted as he brought the phone up to his face. He shut his eyes against the brightness of the screen. He pressed the voice command button and said, "Dial Digger on cell."

The phone replied, "Dialing Digger Grave on cell." The electronic lady's voice sounded even bitchier than usual.

As the call connected and he heard the ring tone, he prayed not to hear the voice mailbox message. Dom didn't know if he had that much consciousness left in him.

After the third ring (or was it the thirtieth?) he heard a click, and then the raspy, sleep-addled voice of his old friend. "Jesus, Dom, it's late. What the hell?"

"Dig, I've been shot."

"Are you serious?" Jonathan Grave seemed one hundred percent awake now.

"I'm somewhere on the Cove Road," Dom said. He spoke quickly because he knew he didn't have time. "Trace the cell signal and get me some help. It's bad."

"Oh, holy crap," Jonathan said. "Shit."

"Dig, listen to me," Dom continued. "It was cops. They shot me and the driver."

"The kids, too?"

"I don't know. I think they took them. I need help, brother."

"It's on the way," Jonathan said. "Keep your phone on."

Dom nodded his answer as he lost his grip.